Dreamthorp

Esther was humming when she entered the grove of trees, but she stopped when she saw Sam lying on the ground, his back to her. At first she thought he'd had a heart attack. Then she noticed that the trunk of the tree beside him was coated with something strange.

No, not coated, but wrapped, wound around like a thick, wet grayish pink ribbon. A ribbon. Attached to Sam.

Numb, she walked closer. She had never seen anything like it before. Even when she stepped around Sam's body and saw the red, gaping crater of his abdomen, even when she started to scream, she didn't know what it was.

Even when they found her and took her away, still screaming, she didn't know what it was.

She had never before seen her husband's, or anyone's, viscera.

Dreamthorp

CHET WILLIAMSON

AVON BOOKS ◬ NEW YORK

All quotations from Alexander Smith's *Dreamthorp: Essays written in the Country* (1863) are from the L.C. Page & Co. edition of 1903.

This novel is a work of fiction. Names, characters, places and incidents either are the product of the author's imagination or are used fictitiously. Any resemblance to actual events or locales, or persons, living or dead, is entirely coincidental.

AVON BOOKS
A division of
The Hearst Corporation
105 Madison Avenue
New York, New York 10016

Copyright © 1989 by Chet Williamson
Front cover illustration by James Warren
Published by arrangement with the author
Library of Congress Catalog Card Number: 88-92956
ISBN: 0-380-75669-2

First Avon Books Printing: July 1989

AVON TRADEMARK REG. U.S. PAT. OFF. AND IN OTHER COUNTRIES, MARCA REGISTRADA, HECHO EN U.S.A.

Printed in the U.S.A.

K-R 10 9 8 7 6 5 4 3 2 1

For my son, Colin McCandless Williamson, with love, and with the hope that he will find his Dreamthorp.

The author wishes to thank Jack Bitner, chronicler and historian of Mount Gretna, another Pennsylvania Chautauqua community even more beautiful—and far safer—than Dreamthorp.

Love!—does it yet walk the world,
or is it imprisoned in songs and romance?
—Alexander Smith, *Dreamthorp*

Beginnings and Awakenings

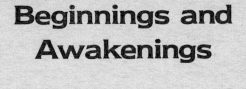

It matters not to relate how or when I became a denizen of Dreamthorp; it will be sufficient to say that I am not a born native, but that I came to reside in it a good while ago now. The several towns and villages in which, in my time, I have pitched a tent did not please, for one obscure reason or another: this one was too large, t'other too small; but when, on a summer evening about the hour of eight, I first beheld Dreamthorp . . . I felt instinctively that my knapsack might be taken off my shoulders, that my tired feet might wander no more, that at last, on the planet, I had found a home. From that evening I have dwelt here, and the only journey I am like now to make, is the very inconsiderable one, so far at least as distance is concerned, from the house in which I live to the graveyard. . . .

—Alexander Smith, *Dreamthorp*

Soon, in the great theatre, the lights will
be put out, and the empty stage will be
left to ghosts.
                    —Alexander Smith, *Dreamthorp*

It happened at the beginning of the second act. The intermission was a long one, since *The Pirates of Penzance* was
in two acts, and everyone had time to fill up with instant
coffee or Coke in Styrofoam cups, munch on party mix from
plastic bags, and have a cigarette out in the cool night air.

The Dreamthorp Playhouse was ideal for such casual treats.
Its circumference was bound by canvas walls suspended by
cords, while its roof was a giant, squatting cone whose edges
came down to less than five feet from the ground, with in-
termittent breaks for entrances and exits. This cone was sup-
ported by forty-eight stout pillars of chestnut, their bases set
in concrete. Since the storm of 1920, in which heavy snows
had driven the pillars partially into the ground, causing the
addition of the concrete the following spring, the Dreamthorp
Playhouse had never suffered from any structural deficiency.
On this particular Sunday evening, it stood just as solidly as
when it had been built in 1899.

The lights dimmed, then brightened again, signaling the
end of the intermission. Charlie Lewis tossed his cigarette
down onto the gray asphalt, stamped it out, exchanged a few
more words with Sam Coffey about the comparative merits
of Duke Ellington and Art Tatum, then wandered back into
the playhouse and sat on the spot on the padded benches
where he had left his program. Dorothy Newhouse was sit-

ting next to him, slurping a Diet Coke through a straw. He noticed the nearly full bag of party mix in her lap, and ran a hand through his short, gray hair, praying silently that she wouldn't crunch through most of the second act.

"What do you think?" he asked her.

She looked at him dully. Was that, Charlie wondered, still a *third* chin she was working on? "About what?"

"Take your choice—the show or the current world hunger situation."

"Oh. Oh yes, the show." Dorothy came to every show, always without her husband. Her husband liked baseball, and after teaching high school biology for thirty-eight years, felt that retirement should be spent watching what he wanted to watch. He did not want to watch Gilbert and Sullivan. "It's fine," Dorothy said, her chubby fingers burrowing into the party mix bag so that some of the Wheat Chex bubbled out the top onto her wide lap. "I think it's very good."

"Well," Charlie replied, "I suppose everyone is entitled to their own opinion."

Dorothy eyed him shrewdly. "You don't like it?"

"Let me put it this way, if the Dreamthorp Gilbert and Sullivan Society's annual show was not part and parcel of the season ticket for the *professional* company, which I await with bated breath, I would not be here now. Nor, I daresay, would Gilbert and Sullivan."

"Well," said Dorothy through a mouthful of party mix and Diet Coke, "I guess the professional actors are a little better. . . ."

"That, my dear lady, is why they call them professionals."

Whatever reply Dorothy might have made was prevented by the extinguishing of the house lights and the raising of the lights on stage, revealing cardboard gothic ruins, which were immediately invaded by a young fat man with an obviously false moustache and an assortment of middle-aged women in gowns who were supposed to be his daughters. Charlie sat back, eased his bony posterior forward until he was sitting on the base of his spine, and wondered whether the off-key singing from the stage or the rhythmic crunching at his side made the less mellifluous noise.

By the end of Mabel's solo about happy daylight being dead, Charlie began to look around in boredom. The play-house was only half filled now, and Charlie could have sworn there had been more people there at the start of the first act. Cowards, he thought, and turned his gaze directly upward to the apex of the roof.

The joists soared up from the edges as if in some primitive cathedral or high-tech tepee, meeting at the center tip of the cone, and Charlie marveled at it anew, as he did every time he attended a show or concert there. The design was sound and simple, but unique. In Charlie's thirty-five years as a structural engineer for Bentson Industries, he had never seen its like, neither in older nor contemporary building designs. He always wished there would have been some way he could have reproduced it in one of his own projects, but there had never been an opportunity, and now, since he was retired, there never would be.

So he dozed and dreamed in seat number H-9, at the exact center of the auditorium, the seat he always chose for the season, as the dialogue droned on from the stage and the munching droned on beside him, until the company began singing about what happens "When the foeman bares his steel," and the first choral "Tarantara!" awoke Charlie with a start that jostled Dorothy's party mix arm, earning him a sharp, reprimanding glare. He pushed himself erect, reminding himself to bring a pillow to the next performance, took a deep breath, and wished they had a smoking section in the playhouse. After all, there was no real danger of fire—everyone could just push the canvas walls down and hie themselves to the great outdoors.

And it was just as Charlie Lewis was thinking how safe the playhouse was, and as the chorus was singing, "Go, ye heroes, go and die!" while marching about the stage in a sundry array of penny loafers and perforated oxfords disguised as riding boots, that the roof fell down.

Although Charlie didn't see it happen, he had the unmistakable sense that all the pillars had broken at once, as though a giant hand had grasped the cone and twisted, like a jock tearing a beer can in two. With the pillars gone, the roof fell straight down.

The people on the perimeter were crushed, and those between the edge and the center were hit by the falling debris of wood, cables, and lighting instruments. Charlie Lewis and most of the people sitting around him in the direct center of the structure were unharmed but greatly surprised. Only Dorothy Newhouse died. A wooden shaft three feet long and an inch wide had been driven into her lap, perforating her abdomen. In the gleam of a fallen Fresnel, Charlie could see her staring at it. She dropped her party mix and Diet Coke and clutched the dark and dusty wood with both hands, looking, Charlie thought, like a flag bearer in the Dreamthorp Memorial Day parade. Then she coughed blood and slumped onto Charlie's shoulder. He held her, and when, after a moment, he realized she was dead, he also realized that he might be in shock. He swallowed hard, pushed Dorothy away, thinking how hard it was going to be to tell her husband about this, and looked around.

The playhouse was an asylum. People were screaming, the fallen lighting instruments were sending up sparks that threatened to ignite the dry and ancient wood, the crash of toppling benches was deafening as the still mobile survivors tried to make their way toward the edges, where Charlie could see the dull glow of open spaces where the roof had split and broken, leaving escape routes.

Yet it was a claustrophobic and terrifying escape, as Charlie found when he started to move toward the nearest aperture. At the center, the roof was three feet above his head, and that distance shrank the closer he drew to the edge. By the time he was halfway there, he found himself crawling over the dead and the dying, with the sharp and broken framework of the ceiling tearing and cutting him, almost, he thought, as if the splinters and boards had a will of their own.

Over the screaming and the rending of wood, he could hear sirens now and knew that help was on the way. He turned and looked behind him and saw sparks and stage lights still shining, but no flames; and he thought that maybe if he just lay there and waited, they would get him out eventually, move all these *people* in his way—these people who weren't moving anymore or who were moving feebly, just a little, as if there was something very wrong with them, and there *was* something wrong with them, Charlie could see that from the way their faces were so pale even in the gleam of those lights that were blue and pink and yellow. He could see it from the way they waggled their jaws and from the way the blood was oozing from their mouths and ears and noses, from the way their heads were turned so that they were looking behind them, and their arms and legs were twisted in ways that weren't, goddamit, *normal*. And if he just lay there, if there wasn't any fire, maybe then they'd come and *move* these damned people so he could crawl the hell out and go home and listen to Miles Davis; and God, he wished he could hear Miles now, but all he could hear were these moans and the siren and the sparks chattering away, and he wondered why the hell somebody didn't cut the goddam power.

And somebody did.

It was as dark as a tomb, and as soon as the lights went out Charlie wished they'd go back on again, sparks or not, and he panicked and tried to crawl over the people who were in his way, but stopped when his hand went into something warm and wet and slippery. He pulled back his hand and wiped it on his shirt. It was then that he began to cry, very softly, and decided to wait, to just wait for someone to come and help.

They came. Charlie heard voices, strong and commanding, and saw lights, from the outside now. It wasn't very long before the person who was lying in his way, wedged between the concrete floor and the splintered ceiling, slid away from him, and then someone's hand gripped his, and a ripping sound took part of the ceiling away from above him, and a light shone in his face.

"Jesus, Charlie," he heard a voice say.

"Hello, Tom," he said huskily, and made himself smile as Tom Brewer's burly arms pulled him out of the rubble and set him shakily on his feet. "Damned if they didn't bring down the house tonight." He laughed, and felt it grow suddenly dark again.

Five centuries effect a great change on
manners.

—Alexander Smith, *Dreamthorp*

Scarcely five hundred yards away from the Dreamthorp Playhouse, but many hundreds of years before, a group of men
stopped beside a spring. One-Who-Runs-With-Deer fell onto
the cushion of leaves that covered the floor of the forest and
unwound the strips of leather from around the wound on his
leg, while Many-Arrows brought him water in cupped hands.
One-Who-Runs-With-Deer drank it and then examined the
hatchet gash.

"It is bad," Many-Arrows said.

One-Who-Runs-With-Deer nodded. "But the one who
struck the blow is dead."

"You need rest. You cannot go on."

"I know. I shall stay here. I shall fight them and give you
time to run."

"You are Chief of the Alligewi," Many-Arrows said. "We
will not leave you."

They had been running for many weeks, ever eastward, to
escape the arrows and hatchets of the tribe they had allowed
to cross their land. It had all begun so innocently. There had
been a party of three families who had asked to establish
homes in the lands of the Alligewi, tallest and strongest of
people. One-Who-Runs-With-Deer refused, but gave them
leave to pass their mighty river, the Namaesi Sipu, and the
forests of the Alligewi beyond in order to seek a land farther
east.

Then more of these small men, who called themselves Lenape, came and requested permission for their tribe to pass the river, which One-Who-Runs-With-Deer granted. But when the Alligewi saw their many thousands as they crossed over the water, they grew alarmed, fearing that the Lenape had a force strong enough to attack the Alligewi. One-Who-Runs-With-Deer called his tribe to arms, and they attacked the unarmed Lenape who had crossed the river. Young and old, braves, women, and children were killed, and the Namaesi Sipu turned red with Lenape blood. Those on the western side were told that any Lenape who tried to cross the river or who came into the land of the Alligewi would meet the same fate.

But the Lenape, as One-Who-Runs-With-Deer was quick to learn, were not children in the art of war. Made furious by the slaughter at the river, they enlisted the aid of the Mengwe, a tribe which had always coveted the rich forests of the Alligewi, and a great war came to the land, a war which lasted many years and killed many braves.

Slowly the Alligewi were beaten back, reduced by the greater forces of their enemies, and the large, flat mounds that covered the Alligewi dead marched like giant footprints toward the east, where the tribe was constantly being pushed. At last the only recourse for the Alligewi lay in abandoning their lands completely and fleeing down the great river to the south to unknown lands. A party of one hundred of the fiercest Alligewi braves, led by One-Who-Runs-With-Deer, would lead the vengeful and pursuing enemy eastward, away from the handfuls of survivors who would move south. The plan was for the hundred, made swifter by the absence of the old and weak, to elude their pursuers and eventually join the others in the south.

But the Alligewi had not reckoned on the speed and energy of the pursuing Lenape, who were determined to wipe from the earth all who belonged to the hated tribe of Alligewi. Skirmishes had diminished the band of a hundred to a mere twenty, the swiftest and strongest of the braves, many of whom were wounded but none so badly as One-Who-Runs-With-Deer.

The chief drank again from Many-Arrow's hands, and knew that he could run no more. He would fight and die where he lay, in this stand of tall pines and oaks, near this quiet spring, with water that tasted cooler and sweeter than the precious water of the Namaesi Sipu. It seemed a fine place to die, and he hoped to take many Lenape with him, if they had the courage to close with him and not simply shoot him with arrows from afar.

"We will not leave," Many-Arrows repeated, his mouth grim.

"If you do not join the others in the south, who will plow the women and make new sons? Who will keep the Alligewi alive?" asked One-Who-Runs-With-Deer.

"We will not leave our chief. We run no more. We fight."

"They come!" shouted Eye-Black-As-Crow, who had clambered to the top of an oak, and now dropped to the carpet of dead leaves. "Many hundreds of them." Eye-Black-As-Crow was young, scarcely a man, but he had proven himself in as many battles as One-Who-Runs-With-Deer had fought when he was made chief. There was no fear in the young man's dark eyes, and One-Who-Runs-With-Deer felt pride as Eye-Black-As-Crow drew his hatchet from his belt. "I will kill many," the boy told the chief of the Alligewi.

The braves formed a circle facing outward, and One-Who-Runs-With-Deer harangued them, saying, "Fight bravely! Take their lives! Remember how they killed our women and children, our fathers and mothers! We are the last warriors of the Alligewi! Let our hate drag them into death with us!"

One-Who-Runs-With-Deer kept shouting, and his cries grew more shrill with the agony of staying erect, as the wound in his leg opened anew, sending warm blood over his moccasined foot, turning the dead leaves black beneath him. He looked down, saw the dark blood pooled in cups of leaves, and heard the screams of the Lenape as they ran out of the brush. The last thing he yelled to his braves was "Darken the ground with their blood!"

The battle lasted less than ten minutes. At the end of it all twenty of the Alligewi lay dead. But their deaths did not stop the hundreds of Lenape from pursuing their vengeance. They hacked with their stone hatchets over and over at the unmoving Alligewi, hewing off arms, legs, and heads until not one Alligewi body lay whole, and their own brown limbs and faces were coated with blood.

Then the Lenape danced and laughed and fell down on the ground, and finally tended to their own wounds. Miraculously, not a single Lenape had been killed that day, though some would later die of the wounds they had suffered.

The Lenape chief asked the shaman what should be done with the bodies of the Alligewi, and the shaman, who had been called Old-With-Wisdom ever since his twentieth winter, told the chief that they should be buried in a large grave, but with no mound to mark the place.

"Let them and their name be forgotten," said Old-With-Wisdom.

In the middle of the stand of trees the Lenape dug a pit wide and deep enough to hold the twenty Alligewi, and dropped the pieces of the bodies into it, with no regard for the direction in which the heads faced. When the pit was filled in, the shaman took a piece of stone from a leather bag that hung from his belt. Its sharp edges had been smoothed, and the pointed end rounded and chipped until it roughly resembled a squat human figure. The old man held it aloft.

"Here their bones will lie," intoned Old-With-Wisdom, "until the stars fall into the rivers. And their spirits will lie with them, torn and divided as their bones. One-Who-Makes-Spirits-Lie-Still will keep them in the earth."

He knelt and set the piece of quartz in the center of the turned earth, and muttered several words none of the braves could hear. Then he rose, turned, and walked toward the west. The others followed, leaving only the grave behind in the stand of trees, the first human habitation in what would later come to be known as Dreamthorp.

Soon the fresh earth was enriched by what lay buried below and as the days and months passed, seedlings grew from the blood-rich soil, and trees grew from the seedlings. Oaks and pines were the descendants of the Alligewi. The roots drank deeply of their flesh, and what had become of the strong muscles of the braves, the iron will of their chief, passed upward through the trunks, into the branches, the trees reproducing, growing more of their own kind.

Through the centuries the trunks broadened, the branches reached the sky, the pines and oaks multiplied until the stand was now a mighty grove filled with life, life which the Alligewi and their frustrated hatred had sustained. And through those centuries One-Who-Makes-Spirits-Lie-Still remained faithfully over the grave, the rains and the soft earth eventually covering it, drawing it ever deeper into the ground, until at last it was submerged, buried above the braves whose vengeful spirits it was intended to subdue forever.

And many years later the trees fell to the saws of white men. They were cut down, and the pine was planed into planks and made into cottages, the oak into chairs and beds and tables, and the people who lived in the little houses, who ate off the tables, sat on the chairs, and slept in the beds never knew what had fed the wood, never knew what they harbored, or what they lived in.

> The resemblance to a human figure was, of course, remote, but the intention was evident.
>
> —Alexander Smith, *Dreamthorp*

The trees had been cut from the grove in the first few years of the twentieth century, when most of the summer cottages were built. That was the time when the Eastern Pennsylvania Chautauqua, which had its home in Dreamthorp, was at its most influential, and new dwellings seemed to go up daily. The appetite for wood was enormous, and the grove was filled from dawn to sunset with men felling trees, lopping off limbs, and planing planks at the ramshackle sawmill that had been erected nearby. As a place of constant activity, it was an ideal location for Sam and Esther Hershey, over eighty years later, to canvas with their metal detectors.

The Hersheys were retired—Sam from a welding line, Esther from a life of housewifery and child rearing—and they had taken up metal detecting as a hobby, never expecting it to become the focus of their lives. But it did. In good weather and bad, year round, they were out with their matched set of Coin-Finder IIIs and their bags full of digging implements. Each had several jars full of coins and trays full of tokens and memorabilia to prove their expertise. They had milked dry the obvious sites around Dreamthorp—the old park now gone back to brush, the place where the railroad station used to be, the sparsely wooded area where the annual Dreamthorp Art Show was held every June—and they were in desperate need of some undiscovered burial ground of old coins and buttons.

Charlie Lewis, on whom the Dreamthorp Playhouse would fall the day after Sam and Esther mined the grove, had told the Hersheys about the former lumbering site, which, not having been used as a source of lumber for fifty years, was now overgrown and forgotten. Forgotten, that is, by everyone except Charlie Lewis, who prided himself on his encyclopedic knowledge of Dreamthorp.

Whenever Charlie wasn't listening to his collection of jazz, he was tracking down some bit of information that would add to his overall trove of facts about the community. All his life he had lived twenty miles away in Harrisburg, the closest major city to Dreamthorp. Although he always liked the tiny community, and attended a number of concerts and shows there every year, he had not become truly infatuated with it until his wife died the year before he was due to retire.

Following the first concert he went to after her death—the Blackbird Jazz Band in the playhouse—he had walked up and down the narrow streets in the darkness, the candles and Japanese lanterns from the cottages giving him enough light to guide his steps. He had felt more at peace with himself than he had at any time in the weeks before, answering the greetings of the people who sat on their porches and said hello to the aging stranger walking their streets, not at all suspicious, but warm, welcoming even, and he decided that Dreamthorp would be the place to which he'd retire.

As he took on the role of resident, he also took on that of historian as well, going through county records, newspaper morgues, and more obscure private sources to recreate the reality of what Dreamthorp had been. His sincerity and zeal earned him a reputation even among those who had lived in the town their whole lives, and he became one of them, totally accepted into the fabric of the village.

He also became the logical one for Sam and Esther Hershey to see when they wanted to find a new digging spot. They had met Charlie Lewis when they were hunting coins on the beach of the lake, had chatted briefly, and Charlie had offered to tell them about some possible places to hunt. Now the three of them sat on Charlie's porch at ten o'clock on a Saturday morning, cool there among the trees, and he told the Hersheys how to find the lumber site.

"Go down Emerson to Pine Road," he told them. "Turn to your left, and between Thoreau and Whittier there's a foot-path. Follow it for three or four hundred yards, and you'll find a dried up spring and a lot of fairly young white oak mixed in with some white pine. North of the spring is where most of the felling took place. There's a large spot that's still pretty bare where they had the sawmill equipment."

"Anybody ever hunt there before?" asked Sam Hershey suspiciously.

"I assume not since Daniel Boone. A year or two ago I personally went down there and found pieces of machinery lying on the ground, so I knew that was where the sawmill was. But I don't think anyone ever did any digging for bottles or anything. Hell, hardly anyone knows about it. And you are sworn to secrecy, of course," Charlie finished dryly.

Esther Hershey giggled.

"I do not jest, my dear woman. And it goes without saying that a third of all gold bars you find will be donated to the Charles Lewis Dreamthorp Preservation Foundation and Chowder Society. But I think it more likely that you'll turn up a lot of nails and gears."

"Oh, we'll probably find coins, if that many people worked there," said Esther.

"For many summers," Charlie said, "that grove echoed to the sounds of numerous workmen. None of whom had any money to speak of."

Esther giggled again. "I'd be happy with a few Indian heads."

Charlie shook his head. "I know of no definite Indian intrusion into the area, and even if there was their heads would long since be decayed."

"Well, we'll see what we can find anyway," Sam said, chuckling. "And if we find any buried treasure, we'll cut you in, Charlie."

"Oh, forget it. I wouldn't mind seeing what you turn up, but anyone could've located the site who had three hundred hours and a ton of elbow grease to spare. The nails are all yours. Now if you'll excuse me, Bix Beiderbecke awaits."

The Hersheys were as excited as children as they made their way to the grove. They walked in shade, occasional sunlight coming through the roof of leaves to dapple the narrow street down which they scurried. But for all their excitement, Dreamthorp was somnolent in the June warmth. Saturday mornings in summer were a time of peace. People slept late, lolled in bed when they did awake, and lingered long over their breakfast coffee and magazines. A few people began to stir outside by eleven, and at noon activity began in earnest—painting latticework, repairing shingles, sweeping leaf dust from porches, trimming back limbs that encroached too closely upon the second-floor window screens—all the jobs that living in the uniquely sylvan community made necessary.

But now, only a few people saw the Hersheys walking to the forest, and of those only Cyrus and Nancy Haldeman acknowledged them by waving to them from their porch swing where they were having coffee. The Hersheys waved back and grinned out of self-consciousness at not being residents of Dreamthorp, as though only certified cottage owners could have digging privileges in the woods.

A few minutes after passing the Haldemans' place, Sam and Esther found the path that Charlie had told them about. It was narrow and overgrown in places, but neither had any trouble walking it. They came upon the clearing several hundred yards east.

"Here's the spring," Sam told Esther, pointing to an arch of weathered stone that now covered only a patch of dried ground. "And all this new growth—this has got to be the place."

They turned on their machines, awkward metal devices that looked like a broomstick with a pie plate at one end and a recipe box covered with switches and dials at the other. They put on their earphones and went to work, holding the machines like scythes, walking in closely articulated patterns, sweeping the ground before them as they went. Back and forth the white, round discs of the metal detectors moved, like spaceships cruising over strange terrain searching for lost crewmen.

Now and then Sam or Esther would hear a rising beep in their earphones and stop, then move the disc in slower swathes until its center was directly over the place where the noise was loudest. The machine would be set aside, and a metal spike plunged into the ground and rotated. Then the digging began.

They used small garden trowels which were able to remove

a maximum of earth with a minimum of effort. Usually they were careful about taking up plugs of turf, putting the excavated earth on a small sheet of canvas, and then carefully replacing it again. But in this untenanted grove in the middle of nowhere, they felt no need to be so fastidious and merely shoveled out the dirt and roughly dumped it back in again when each individual search was over.

By one o'clock an ecstatic Esther had found fourteen coins. There were eight Indian head and three flying eagle pennies, an 1887 nickel, two 1900 dimes, and a 1901 quarter. Sam, on the other hand, had only turned up four Indian heads, a flying eagle and a vast assortment of nails, screws, and twisted bits of iron.

"Why don't you turn on your discriminator?" Esther asked him. "It's no wonder you haven't found more coins, you spend so much time digging up all that *junk.*"

Sam's face soured at the rebuke. "Hey, a place like this, you've got no idea what you might turn up. Besides, at least the junk is from the period—there aren't any pull tabs or beer cans, are there? There might be some tools or who knows what else. You go for the coins, and I'll keep trying potluck. Speaking of which, are you hungry?"

They ate some sandwiches then, and, after a trip into the bushes to relieve themselves of their morning coffee, continued to hunt.

At three o'clock, after finding two more coins and a large assortment of mangled ironmongery, Sam received a very strong signal in his earphones. "Got a big one," he said to Esther.

"What?" she asked, taking off her earphones.

"I said I got a big one. There's something under here all right."

"Probably a rusty steam engine," Esther said. Her rapidly filling coin bag jingled gaily as she replaced her earphones.

Sam ignored her teasing, fell to his knees, and started to dig. Six inches down he struck, if not what Esther had predicted, than at least something that could have been *part* of a steam engine. It was iron, and rusty, and as he uncovered it he saw that it was a small piece of a wheel rim, the wooden wheel it had guarded having long since rotted away. He sighed, but figured that he would excavate it completely, just in case something might be beneath it and so that it would not fool him again.

When most of it was uncovered, he dug his fingers beneath it to lift it out. But as his fingertips plunged into the soft earth beneath, they came into contact with something else, something smooth and cool, something that inexplicably made him freeze where he knelt.

"Sam!" The sound of Esther's voice made him realize that he had been kneeling there far longer than he had thought, and he looked up at her stupidly. "What's wrong?"

Sam simply shrugged and brought his hand up, taking the piece of wheel rim with it. Esther laughed when she saw it and turned her attention back to her machine. "There's something else," Sam said. "Something else down there."

He pressed into the dirt carefully with the trowel, and was at first disappointed when what he found seemed to be nothing but a piece of white quartz. But when he drew it wholly from the earth and saw that it was a crude but definite piece of carving, he ran over to Esther, clutching it like a trophy.

"Look!" he said.

She took off her earphones and examined it. "What is it, like a little statue?"

"Yeah. It's quartz. But it's a statue, see? It looks like a man, doesn't it?"

"A little," Esther said, piqued at having her own cache of coins overshadowed by this chunk of dirty rock. "You sure it's not just a natural thing? You know, shaped by water or something?"

"Are you kidding? Look at that, you can see the little marks there. Probably a stone tool, maybe even *prehistoric.*"

"It could just be something one of the lumbermen made."

But it was impossible to puncture Sam's balloon. "No, no, this is a *sculpture,* Esther! Primitive art! I can't wait to show this to Charlie Lewis. Maybe it's Indian—do you think it looks Indian? Sort of like those Eskimo carvings, you know?"

Sam brushed the quartz tenderly, wrapped it in a piece of canvas, and put it in his knapsack, then picked up his digging tools and shoved them into his utility belt. "You're quitting?" Esther said.

"Yeah, sure." He unplugged his earphones.

"But the coins—I mean, I've found *dozens* of coins. . . ."

"Coins, shmoins, this thing could be worth *hundreds* of coins. Come on, I want to show Charlie." And he picked up his machine and headed for the path. Esther, annoyed beyond endurance, gathered up her things and followed her husband.

In this way was the vigil of One-Who-Makes-Spirits-Lie-Still broken, so that nothing kept watch over the grave of the Alligewi, who were now, if they could, free to awaken.

There was, the next day, a true awakening. It occurred in a room at the Wyoming State Hospital in Casper.

Gilbert Rodman was suspected of a great many things. He had, however, never stood trial for any of them, since from the time of his capture, he had been in a coma from which doctors were unable to extricate him. His wounds had healed, and, although he had been fed intravenously for the past nine months, his physical condition was surprisingly good, something that amazed his doctors. When he was arrested, Gilbert Rodman weighed 185 pounds, most of it muscle, and stood 6 feet 1 inch. In the nine months of lying supine in bed, needles stuck in his arm, his wastes being drawn away by plastic tubing, Gilbert had lost only twenty pounds.

Although he was under suspicion of raping, killing, and mutilating over a dozen women—with one positive eyewitness to his final crime—he had no permanent guard after the first month. There was no indication that Gilbert would come out of his coma, and, if he did, he would be so weak that a guard could be summoned before the man was able to rise from his bed. This, at least, was the consensus of opinion among the staff. The staff, however, had not reckoned on the strength, nor the mental talents, of Gilbert Rodman.

Gilbert awoke at nine o'clock on Sunday morning. His

20

eyes opened. His fists clenched. There was little dopiness about him when he woke. Instead, he felt rested, lean, ready. He also felt empty, as if something had been taken away from him, something that could never be replaced. He knew what it was before he put his left hand underneath the sheet. The knowledge had been with him for nine months.

For Gilbert Rodman had not been merely in a coma. He had been in a self-induced trance, a state of meditation which nothing had prepared him for and that he had not previously known he was capable of attaining. When the bullet had struck home, he had to escape, and he did, diving deep into himself, like the shamans dived into the heart of the Great Spirit in the books he had read, and refusing to come out, not even after the pain was dead. If he had come to the surface too soon, he would have gone mad.

So his body closed down its circuits so that only his mind lived, and for all those months Gilbert played out his life on some inner screen, his body dead, but his thoughts functioning, churning inside him, coping, coming to terms with the new reality of what he had become and would remain forever.

Even with all that time to consider it, when he woke to that understood reality and touched the place, he could not bear to let his fingers feel the flesh, not yet. Instead he pressed gently on himself through the thin hospital gown. First he felt the tube, and then let his hand follow it up until it met flesh.

It was a remnant of what it had been. It felt like nothing more than a strip of tattered skin, and what bulk it had was due to the catheter that pierced his urethra. He forced himself to reach deeper into his body, and found only a empty pouch where his testicles had been. He could feel the ragged scar through the rough cotton of the gown. Empty. It was empty. The woman's bullet had crushed them, and the doctors had taken them away.

Gilbert did not weep. He had already wept within himself. But he trembled and brought his hand back above the sheet. Then he waited for his shaking to subside, and touched himself again, beneath the gown, flesh to flesh this time. He familiarized himself with the feel of his sundered body, touched and touched again until he felt no revulsion. Then he lifted the sheet with his pierced right arm, drew back the gown, and looked.

It was as ugly as his soul, and he decided that before he left he would kill a doctor for making him look like that. This, he thought, is not a surgeon's work but a butcher's. He knew about butchers.

He put back the gown, rearranged the sheet, and laid his arms on top of it as they had been before he awoke. Then he worked his muscles, contracting them, stretching them until he grew tired and rested, after which he worked them again.

At noon a nurse came in to change his IV bottle, and he feigned coma. She noticed nothing, performed her work quickly and methodically, and left. No one came into his room for the rest of the day.

By eight in the evening it was nearly dark, and Gilbert Rodman withdrew the needle from his arm and let it dangle from the hanging jar. He took the tube from his anus, and painfully slid the catheter from his urethra. A mixture of blood and urine trickled out of what was left of his penis, and he looked at the blood and thought that there would be more blood to come. There would be payments people would have to make, bills he would have to collect. He was as empty as his scrotum, and only blood would fill him up again.

Gilbert lowered his legs over the side of the bed, and slowly began to put his full weight on them. It felt strange, but his muscles responded, weakly at first, then stronger, until he stood, tottering but upright, beside the bed in which he had slept and dreamed and come to life a different Gilbert Rodman, just as insane but now with a more sharply focused insanity.

For a half hour he stretched and squatted, expanded, reached, and closed, until every muscle was tense and alive again. Then he took the IV bottle from its hanger, listened at the door until everything was silent, and broke the bottle against the aluminum sink. One of the shards of glass was perfect for his purposes, and he picked it up, the smooth part against his palm, the thin, razor edge away from him. He thought about what he would do to the woman who had shot him and wished for a moment that it had been a man so that Gilbert could do to him what had been done to Gilbert, maybe with something as simple as the piece of glass he now held.

But it was a woman. And he would find other ways, worse ways than that. After all, he had already found them, already performed them. It would be nothing new. But it would be very, very special.

First, though, it was time for the doctor. Oh, it wasn't the doctor's fault, of course. The doctor hadn't shot him. But a doctor was still going to have to pay. Any doctor would do, really. They were, after all, symbols. So what if he couldn't kill the doctor who had sewn him like some Salvation Army turkey? He would kill another one, and that would be almost as good.

Symbols. It seemed he was always dealing with symbols. He could never kill the Great Bitch herself, could he? So he had killed all those symbols of the Great Bitch. The Great Bitch herself was dead and rotten, but that didn't stop him. It would *never* stop him. Not even that other bitch who had shot him had been able to stop him, had she? Because here he was, weak but alive, with the sharpness in his hand.

He would find her. He would not accept a symbol for her. He would find *her*. He remembered her name, where she was from, what she looked like; and he would find her and have her and hurt her, and since she took away what he would have had her with, then he would find something else.

Something cold. Something sharp.

Gilbert Rodman stepped quietly into the hall. Five minutes later he found a doctor, sitting alone, smoking a cigarette in the lounge. He crept up behind him, slit his throat with the edge of glass, and castrated the man while he bled to death.

As he sliced at the flesh, Gilbert felt a wave of hate roll through him far more intense than any orgasm he had ever known, and he saw the face of the woman who had shot him, saw her mouth open in an ''O'' of surprise, and, for an ecstatic instant, he believed that it was she he was working on and not this poor scapegoat of a doctor, whining through bubbles of blood; and Gilbert whispered harshly into the dying man's face, *''Laura!''*

But now he was finished, and the vision passed. He washed his hands in the bathroom, then found some clothes in the closet, dressed in them, although they were a size too small, took the keys and wallet from the doctor's pocket, and went out to the parking lot.

It took him no time to match the Volkswagen key to the new Jetta in the Reserved—Physicians space; and he unlocked the door, got in, and drove to Route 25 South. He figured he could reach Orin before the news of his recovery, escape, and crime caught up with him. He would ditch the car there, roll it back into some trees, take the money from the wallet, and get something to fill his furiously empty stomach. Then, since they would be watching the highways, he would work his way on foot down the Platte River. The weather was warm, and he could sleep on the ground, as he'd done so many times before. He planned to surface at Lyman, just over the Nebraska border, then hitch east, toward Pennsylvania. Lancaster, he remembered she had said. He had never been to Pennsylvania, but he would find her.

It would take several days to walk down the river to Lyman, but he had the time, and it would be good for his body to move again, to get back in shape for what lay ahead. It would be all right if it took weeks, even months, to reach her. She would still be there, and he would be all the stronger for the passage of time. And of course he could always practice on the way.

He switched on the car radio and turned the dial until he found a station that played jazz. He recognized the tune, Ornette Coleman's "Tomorrow Is the Question," and he smiled as he listened to the familiar riffs.

"Tomorrow is the *answer*, Laura," he said aloud, then laughed, and continued to drive east. It felt good, like going home.

June

Here I can live as I please, here I can throw the reins on the neck of my whim. Here I play with my own thoughts; here I ripen for the grave.
—Alexander Smith, *Dreamthorp*

> Having discoursed so long about Dream-
> thorp, it is but fair that I should now in-
> troduce you to her lions.
> —Alexander Smith, *Dreamthorp*

Nothing in Dreamthorp's history had prepared it for the slowly developing reign of terror whose advent was the collapse of the Dreamthorp Playhouse the day after Sam Hershey found his artifact. On the contrary, the town of Dreamthorp had a history of tranquility, gentility, and cultural development that made nearby communities look like hotbeds of ignorance and animal passions.

Dreamthorp's roots went back only as far as the 1880s, when Richard Weston, a young man whose family owned a local and highly profitable iron works for over a century, built a railroad line to connect the works with the Pennsylvania Railroad's main line near Harrisburg. When Weston was investigating the best locations at which to put stations along the way, he was favorably impressed by a hilly, wooded area at the halfway point of his new line, and felt that it would be an ideal place for a picnic ground.

So, along with the station stop, Weston built pavilions and stone walks, installed tables and toilet facilities, and walled some of the many natural springs. By the summer of 1885, thousands of people flocked to the grounds, paying their fare to Robert Weston's conductors, and buying cold drinks and food from Robert Weston's concessions.

The park expanded, and the following year picnickers were able to indulge in lawn bowling, billiards, and shooting at clay ducks. Boats could be rented at the nearby lake, and by that summer's end there was a "Flying Menagerie" whose organ played fifteen different tunes, while children and their parents whirled around it on hand-carved horses.

More land was cleared every spring, until by 1895 the park's estate, now known quite logically as Weston Park, comprised five thousand acres, most of which was woodland. Despite the genteel commercialization, there were still sequestered paths and lovers' walks in abundance; and the primitive character of the park, scrupulously maintained by Richard Weston, far outweighed its proto-Disneyland qualities.

Eighteen ninety-five was also the year in which the true and lasting personality of Dreamthorp was set, for that was the year in which the first Eastern Pennsylvania Chautauqua was held, established for "the advancement of scientific and literary achievement among the populace, and the promotion of culture in the name of Christianity," as it was proclaimed in the charter. The resultant hamlet, Dreamthorp, was named by Dr. Hiram Marcus, the first president of the chautauqua, after an idealized village created by a Scottish author, Alexander Smith, whose book, *Dreamthorp: Essays written in the Country,* appeared in 1863. At the time Dr. Marcus named the village, its derivation was already obscure, even to the well-read attendees of the chautauqua.

The grounds were laid out, with north–south streets named for writers (New England transcendentalists had the edge) and west–east for trees indigenous to the area, and cabins and meeting houses were built. Much of the wood came from the forests around Dreamthorp, and most of the structures were still standing a hundred years later.

And a hundred years later the town retained its chautauqua-like respectability as well. Dreamthorp was as crime-free, drug-free, adultery-free, in short, as *vice*-free as any community in America. It was also, as many young people or older bohemians living there could attest to, as Victorian as the wooden gingerbread that graced its gables. Any variation from the norm or infraction of the unspoken rules met with swift disapproval. It was not so much the disapproval of the rich as that of a priestly class whose frontier temples had crumbled, and who now, prisoners within their own home tabernacle, guarded a dying way of life from the sensual encroachments of a new and pagan religion. This disapproval most often took the form of being ignored at the tiny and ancient post office, or the general store that served the function of a 7-11. It was a subtle disapproval that Tom Brewer most definitely thought he felt, as he handed Mrs. Purviance the card he had found in his mailbox.

It was Mrs. Purviance's habit, when given a card that indicated a package was behind the counter, to say to the lucky recipient, "Package, well, that's nice," and place it on the counter with a benign grin, as though delivering smallpox vaccine to a dying village. But today she only took the card, nodded, and set Tom's package on the counter without a word.

He thanked her, received no acknowledgment of his good manners, and walked out the door. The package was the set of German tools for which he had been waiting six weeks, and he unwrapped them as he walked up Elm Road, taking care not to drop them and so ruin their beautifully tooled edges.

He had needed new tools desperately. His grandfather's had been sharpened and resharpened so many times that he felt as though he was carving wood with scalpels rather than chisels. It was time to retire the old set while they still had some bite left. At first he didn't look forward to using new tools after working for so many years with the old ones, knowing that his grandfather's hands had held them as well, his sweat polishing and smoothing the wooden handles to that deep burnished tone only years and hands can give to wood. But now, as he gazed down at the German tools nestled in their case, he thought it fitting that he should have new tools for the new direction he wanted to take.

The old tools had never seemed to want to bend to his will when he strayed too far from the work they had done for so many years. They responded wonderfully when he carved four-foot eagles and four-inch chickadees, when he did panels for boxes in which people could keep old photographs, when he took commissions to carve golfers or bowlers or doctors, and, oh Christ, he did a lot of doctors. But when it came to the larger pieces, Tom's attempt to bring wood, a living thing, to represent life more fluidly than the predetermined, commercial work he did, the tools failed.

Or at least he told himself it was the tools. Inside, he knew what it really was. But maybe these tools would work for him. Maybe they would.

He wrapped the new tools up again, and turned right on Emerson, wondering now about Mrs. Purviance and why she had treated him, if not rudely, then with none of her usual warmth. How many people knew about him and Karen anyway? And was that what had gotten Mrs. Purviance's bowels in an uproar?

No. He was being paranoid. The last week had been hell for everyone in Dreamthorp. There was not a resident who had not lost a friend or an acquaintance in the collapse of the playhouse. It was a miracle that only fourteen people had been killed, but that was enough of a tragedy to bring in all three major networks for coverage. They were gone now, but the insurance investigators had taken their place, and were going over what was left of the playhouse with cameras and calipers and fine tooth combs. And the lawsuits were starting to trickle in. If Vernon Wolgemuth, the owner of the playhouse, had any sense, Tom thought, he'd declare bankruptcy or get the hell out of the country.

There were a few of Tom's friends among the dead and more among the injured, and as he neared Charlie Lewis's cottage, he was pleased to see Charlie sitting on the front porch. "Charlie!" he called, and the older man waved.

"Back, and meaner than ever. Come up and sit a spell."

Tom walked up the steps to the porch of Charlie's cottage. Although all the dwellings in Dreamthorp were called cottages, Charlie's strongly belied that appellation. It was a gothic minimansion, complete with a widow's walk that looked out on nothing but treetops, ten rooms, three of which were rimmed with shelves containing both $33\frac{1}{3}$ and 78 RPM recordings as well as a vast collection of reel-to-reel tapes, and a roofed porch that went around the entire house. It had been built in 1907 by a nephew of Richard Weston, and Charlie had lived in it since 1981. The wicker porch furniture dated from the time of the first tenant, and Tom Brewer slid onto one of the padded armchairs. "How's the ribs?" he asked.

"Hurt like a bitch. But when I consider the alternative, the pain lessens amazingly. You want a beer?"

Tom began to look at his watch, then stopped himself. "Sure."

"Mind getting it yourself? I'm sore." Tom stood up and walked toward the door. "Clever boy like you probably knows it, but they're in the fridge. Bring me one too."

Tom brought the beers and handed one to Charlie. "Shitful thing, that playhouse," he said, opening the bottle.

"It was indeed." Charlie took a long, cold swallow. "And it doesn't make a goddam bit of sense."

"The way it happened?"

Charlie nodded. "Like the hand of de Lawd. Just one twist and boom, straight down like in a Bugs Bunny cartoon. I've never been so scared in my life. Afterward was bad—getting out, or having *you* get me out, for which I shall remember you in my will—but seeing that happen . . ." He took another swallow. "It was not possible. That's all there is to it. It was not possible, so it did not happen, and none of those people are dead, and my ribs don't feel like I've been used as the Giants' tackling dummy."

"They've got investigators down there now, Charlie."

"I don't care if they get Sherlock Holmes. I saw four dozen chestnut posts a foot thick all snap at the same place and do a side step. And that was impossible. I saw the impossible, Thomas."

"Maybe you thought you saw it."

"Meaning what?"

"Maybe you were in shock, and what you remembered—"

"Wasn't what I really saw—yeah, sure. Sorry, kid, I saw what I saw, and I don't care what the hell they turn up down at ye old ruins. That place was built to last till the last trump."

"So what do you think happened then?"

"There's the rub, bub. I haven't an idea in my head short of some terrorist organization that planted forty-eight separate plastique charges and set them off at the same time. Either that or divine intervention, take your pick. Hell, this beer gets warm fast." Charlie set the bottle on the smooth boards of the porch. "So what's it been like around here?"

"Sad. At least all the funerals are over."

"Good. I hate funerals. I plan to skip mine."

Tom remembered then. "Except one. Harold Thatcher's is tomorrow."

"Fell down the stairs. I read about that in the paper Wednesday."

"Thursday."

"Whatever." Charlie shook his head. "Thatcher had to be ninety. I'm amazed he could still climb stairs, let alone fall down them. Loose board or something, wasn't it?"

"Yeah."

"Well," Charlie said, "on to more important matters. They still going to have the season of shows?"

"In the Hall of Culture. It's a lot smaller than the playhouse, but they're going to have extra performances."

"Ah, the tenacity of Dreamthorpians. Whate'er may befall, we endure. Faulkner would've been proud. I just hope to hell that that building doesn't fall down too." Charlie made the atypical gesture of shaking his head sharply, as if flinging water from his hair. "So how's your love life?"

Tom smiled glumly. "Word gets around."

"It doesn't take a genius to see what's in front of your eyes, especially if you live next door. She's a pretty girl."

"Yeah, well . . ."

"It's okay if you don't want to tell your nosy neighbor about her, I understand. Just because I've been like a father to you— "

"You've *never* been like a father to me. My father is next door right now, along with my mother, so don't tell me you've been like a mother to me either."

"All right, maybe an uncle then. Who is she? I've seen her at your place every weekend for a few weeks and have had the good grace not to ask about her till now."

Tom sighed. "Her name is Karen. She's a student at the college."

"Graduate student?"

"Undergrad." Charlie's eyebrows raised. "She's a *senior,* Charlie."

"Oh, well, that's okay then. In one of your classes?"

"No."

"That's reassuring."

"She's very mature for her age."

"Sure, all college girls are. And you have a lot in common."

"We *do.* "

"She an artist?"

"No, but she likes art. She's a music major."

"Ah. Baton twirling?"

"God*dam*, Charlie, you can be a pain in the ass."

Charlie Lewis laughed. "I'll remember that next time you ask me to help put in your air conditioners."

The laughter relaxed Tom, and he slipped further down in the chair. "She's a nice girl, Charlie, she really is. She's been good for me."

"How's Josh taking it?" Josh was Tom's fourteen-year-old son.

"He's taking it."

Charlie lit a cigarette and dropped the match into his beer bottle. "He took his mother's death hard, didn't he?" It wasn't so much a question as a statement.

"So did I, Charlie," Tom said quietly. "She was my wife."

Charlie looked at him keenly. "I didn't mean anything by that, Tom."

"I know you didn't. I'm sorry. I guess I just feel a little guilty, like I should plant a memory garden and wear black for the rest of my life."

"Nobody expects that. Not even the traditional citizens of Dreamthorp."

"Josh does."

A long moment went by. "It's like that, is it?" Charlie finally said.

"He was . . . very close to his mother. It's funny, but there were times when I actually felt jealous of what was between them. Oh, I don't mean she loved me any less after Josh was born—just . . . *differently.*" Tom shook his head. "He's been like a different kid since she died, Charlie. Never talks anymore, never touches his guitar, doesn't go out with his friends, won't even talk to them on the phone."

"I've noticed. He doesn't laugh when I kid him anymore. How about his schoolwork?"

Tom shrugged. "His grades were better the second half of the year. Seems like all he does is study—I should complain about that? But school always came easy for him." He took another sip of beer. "He hates Karen."

"Well, that's . . . to be expected. The Hamlet syndrome in reverse, I guess. I'm sorry I don't have any suggestions, but I haven't watched *My Three Sons* in years."

Tom's laugh was loose and easy, something he'd been waiting to release for a long time. "Goddamit, Charlie, you'd joke during the holocaust."

"I did. That's why the guards let me go."

"And *I* gotta go," Tom said, standing up. "Thanks for the beer, but I've got a carving that's due next week."

"Speaking of carving, that reminds me—you know the Hersheys, that couple with the metal detectors?"

"I've seen them around."

"They found something pretty interesting last weekend. A quartz carving. Pulled it out of the old lumber site."

"A carving in *quartz?*"

"Yeah. Pretty rough stuff, but Sam Hershey said it was about eight inches down, so I suspect it's fairly old."

"Indian, you think?"

"I don't know what else it could be, but I went over to Pete Zerphey's place, and he couldn't identify it. Said it didn't look like anything the Susquehannocks or the Shenk's Ferry People would've carved. I made a sketch, thought I'd hit the Archive Building at the William Penn Museum as soon as I can move without feeling agony in every joint. The Hersheys said they might take it over there themselves and see if somebody can identify it."

"Well, let me know. Quartz, huh? Jesus, I'd hate to try and carve that stuff. It'd chip like crazy. Don't know how you'd get any shape out of it."

"Like I said, it didn't look like much. Take care."

The heat of inspiration may be subtracted
from the household fire.
　　　　　—Alexander Smith, *Dreamthorp*

Once Tom was on the street, it was only a few yards from
Charlie's cottage to his own. The place was built into the side
of the steep hill, as were most homes in Dreamthorp. The
streets in the old chautauqua grounds ascended the side of
the hill in tiers, so that the second floor of one cottage was
on the same level as the first floor of the cottage on the street
above it. Since the basements were on street level, diagonal
latticework covered those that were not enclosed by solid
walls, and even some of the enclosed cellars had a false front
of lattice, most of which had been constructed at the turn of
the century.

Tom's basement workshop, though fully enclosed, had such
latticework surrounding it, except for a door on the side that
faced Charlie's house, and it was that door that he unlocked
and opened now. He did it quietly, not wanting his mother
and father to know that he had come back to the house. He
wanted to lay out his new tools in peace.

He still could not quite figure out how it was that his parents were spending most of the summer with him. In the past
he had suggested it might be nice for them to come up from
Florida for a month or so during the summer, but that was
when Susan was still alive and could act as a buffer between
the three volatile personalities.

Tom had never gotten along well with his father, a retired
high school history teacher, bookish and scholarly, who had

shown only the required minimal interest in Tom's art. To him, art was something done with oils, charcoal, or pen and ink. Sculpture, and especially woodcarving, with its crude and forceful use of chisels and knives gouging forms and making chips and splinters in the process, was too physical for him to feel totally comfortable with.

Part of his father's discomfort, Tom thought, stemmed from disappointment that Tom had chosen to follow in his grandfather's footsteps rather than his own. Tom's grandfather had been a jack-of-all-trades. He had painted houses, done carpentry, and, though he never called them art, made numerous carvings of birds and animals as well as high relief panels for boxes that were as fine as anything Tom had ever seen. His grandfather was the one who had taught him the joy of working in wood, and Tom had taken to it immediately. By his senior year of high school, when his grandfather died, his carving had won him a number of awards and a partial scholarship to Penn State, where, at his father's insistence, he entered the art education department. A teaching degree would be "something to fall back on," as his father claimed. If Tom would not become a scholar, at least he would follow in his father's footsteps closely enough to teach.

It was odd, Tom thought, how talents and dispositions skipped generations. Ed, his father, could not so much as whittle a stick, and Josh, his son, seemed lately to be a mirror image of the old man, a similarity that was greeted with delight by Tom's mother, who was a different fish from his father entirely.

While Ed was content to express disapproval by sullen silences or subtly guarded remarks, Frances would lay everything right out on the table like one of her one-pot dishes. Everyone always knew what Frances thought about something for the simple reason that she would tell them. Tact was alien to her, and diplomacy unknown. On visits when Susan was still alive, Frances would constantly wipe the nearest smooth surface with her fingertip and rub it on her thumb. The resultant dustball (for there always was one) clung to her flesh like sin, and she examined it with disgust before flinging it from her into a waste can. "You should have a cleaning lady" was her mantra, with "Why don't you let me clean this place up?" a close second.

Because Frances was his mother, Tom would curse and

explain that he worked and Susan worked and who the hell cared if there was a little dust around or not; and then wonderful, patient Susan would still the waters and draw Mom into the kitchen to ask her what she put in her stuffing to make it taste so good, and everything would be fine until the next time.

But Susan was no longer around to still the waters, and Tom's mother was driving him absolutely, certifiably insane after having been in his house only four days. He had wanted to use the collapse of the playhouse as an excuse to have them stay in Florida, but arguing with his mother proved to be impossible.

"I'm sure you're all upset," Frances told him over the phone, "and Josh too, and that's why we should be there. I can take care of the house and Josh if you have things to do, and after all, we already paid for the tickets so we might as well come, and you *did* invite us. . . ."

Although Tom was unable to remember the exact phrasing of his purported invitation, they came, and they were planning on staying through the end of July, a total of six weeks.

If Susan had been alive it would have been bearable, but with her gone, Tom had acquired a live-in cook and housecleaner, who inspired guilt with every tidy act, and a scholar-in-residence, who positioned himself in the living room with a book for twelve hours a day. When boredom struck, both of them thought nothing of descending into Tom's sanctum sanctorum and talking to him while he worked. When Susan was alive, she had gently but firmly stopped them from disturbing him, knowing that he worked best alone. He had never realized just how much she had done for him until she died.

The previous winter, Susan had been working late at the Merrill Lynch office in Lebanon, when it had begun to snow. The country roads, already wet, had iced over quickly, and she lost control on the curve right before the bridge across Little Conewingo Creek. The car hit the bridge abutment. Although Susan was wearing her seat belt, it had not saved her. The steering wheel was driven into her chest, and she was dead by the time the next car came along and found her.

A state policeman came to Tom's house with the news, and he knew what had happened as soon as he saw the man standing there in his ruff-collared coat and trooper's hat. The policeman had looked cautiously at Josh, who was standing right behind his father, but Tom nodded, and the trooper gave them the news. Tom went numb, but Josh reacted violently, vomiting immediately and explosively over the rough planks of the foyer, then falling onto the sodden floor in a paroxysm of weeping.

Caring for his son over the next few days sheltered Tom from his own grief, and it was not until after the funeral that he realized the abyss that Susan's death had cut into his life. It was like the absence of a limb that one is unaware of until he tries to use it, then finds that life has changed irrevocably, and for the worse. Tom felt betrayed, both by Susan and by life itself. She should not have driven so fast on the icy roads; she should have spent the night at some motel in Lebanon, she should not have gotten herself killed, stupid, stupid woman. . . .

But his outrage at her for dying was nothing compared to his fury at the uncaring hand of fate, at a world in which an unexpected snowfall, a patch of ice, the position of a tire on a road, an abutment planned and built some thirty years before by some forgotten highway engineer could kill the woman he loved, the person around whom he had planned his life.

A world like that, he thought over and over again, was a world in which anything could happen, in which bombs could fall, children could be tortured, death could come as easily and simply as a knock on the door on a snowy evening. It was a conclusion and a knowledge that made him feel immeasurably old.

And that was how he felt now, despite the close presence of his parents, who, he fancied, tried everything in their power to make him feel like a child. He decided to call Karen, although talking to her caused him equal ambivalence in how he perceived his age. Being with her sometimes made him feel far younger than his thirty-six years, as if her youth and enthusiasm were contagious. She was still discovering things about the world that he had known for many years; and although he felt the joys of sharing her discoveries, there were also times when her naive and unformed tastes embraced things for which his appreciation had diminished years before, and his impatience and boredom with them made him feel like her father.

Still, he needed her now, and picked up the extension

phone next to his drafting board. Karen's roommate answered and put Karen on the line. Her voice sounded like spring. "I'm glad you called," she said. "I've been missing you."

"Me too. I've been so damn busy, what with Mom and Dad here, and a bunch of commissions to finish, and my classes."

She asked him about the playhouse, and he told her what he knew, which was little. She had called him on Sunday night after she heard about the disaster on the 11:00 news, and he had assured her that he had been neither present nor harmed. They had met for lunch on Wednesday at the college, and had not seen each other since. "Are we still on for this afternoon?"

"Sure. It should be warm enough."

"Hello?" It was another voice.

"Hello?" Tom said.

"Tommy?"

"Mom, I'm on the phone in the workshop."

"Oh," said his mother. "I'm so sorry, I didn't know you came in. I was going to call the Acme to see if they had any fresh pork, I wanted to make some pork for supper. Would you like pork?"

"Pork would be . . . fine."

"I didn't know you were talking."

"Okay, Mom, I'll be off in a minute."

"All right, well, I'm sorry." There was a click.

"Karen?"

"I'm still here."

"Sorry about that."

"Aren't we going out to dinner?"

"Yes, sure."

"Oh, because you said that, I thought . . ."

"It's easier to explain to her later that I'm going out."

"Oh, okay. Well, what about afterwards? Can I stay with you?"

"Ah, Jesus, I don't know . . ."

"You don't *know?*"

"I mean, sure. But not here . . . I don't think . . ."

"Josh never minds."

"Yeah, well, Josh isn't my parents."

"God, Tom, you're a grown man, and I'm a grown woman, I'd think that we could—"

"It doesn't matter that there's nothing wrong with it, Karen, it's just that it wouldn't be comfortable, believe me. What about a motel?"

"A motel?" The springtime had gone out of her voice.

"Sure. It might be fun. Surreptitious meetings, lovers' trysts, the whole works."

"Oh, I guess."

"Okay, fine. I'll pick you up at two?"

That Tom would not be present for the pork dinner was a minor shock compared to his news that he would not be home at all that night. "Well, where are you going to go?" his mother asked him.

"A motel, probably."

"A motel? With this girl?"

"She's not a girl, she's a woman, and I'm taking her to a motel because I don't want to offend your sensibilities."

"You bring her here when Josh is here?"

"I have. A few times."

"Do you think that's a good example to set?"

Tom sighed. "Mother, I'm sorry, but I cannot become a monk."

"Nobody's *asking* you to, but a little discretion . . ."

"Look, I bring her here so I don't have to leave Josh alone, all right?"

"Well, are you going to marry this girl?"

"We haven't discussed it, and I'm sorry, but I don't want to discuss it with you."

All this time, Tom's father had been sitting on the sofa, his eyes on the book in his lap. Now he looked up. "If we're in your way, we can always leave."

"Jesus *Christ,* you don't *have* to leave, I'm not *asking* you to leave, I'm doing this because I *want* to, all right? Josh will be *fine,* he understands, so please don't make such a goddam big deal over it!" Tom turned his back on them both and walked through the entry and up the stairs to find Josh.

Tom was lying to his parents. Josh made no pretense of understanding, none at all. He did not like Karen, and made no attempt to hide it, even after Tom had told him that he should stop acting so rude when she was around. He had tried to explain things to his son, but the boy had not even wanted to listen. Though he had never come right out and accused

Tom of betraying his mother's memory, it was apparent to Tom that was what he thought.

Still, Tom wanted to bring the two of them closer together, so he knocked on the door of the boy's room at the head of the stairs, only to hear him call, "Over here," from the den. Josh looked up from his comic book when Tom entered the room, then began reading again.

"How ya doing?"

"Okay," Josh said.

"I, uh, was wondering . . . Karen and I are going over to the beach this afternoon for a swim. You want to come along?"

"Uh-uh."

"You'd be welcome. Get some sun, a little exercise."

"I got things to do."

Bullshit, Tom thought, but didn't say it. "Yeah, well, if you change your mind we ought to be there around 2:30."

"Okay," Josh said.

"Also, tonight I won't be coming home. Karen and I are going to dinner."

The boy looked up at Tom. He didn't say a word, he didn't sneer or frown or grimace. But there was something in the eyes that made Tom want to slap his face at the same time he wanted to hold the boy. Still, after the confrontation with his parents, he didn't think he could handle another one. He would lose his temper and say something he'd be sorry for later. So he just nodded, gave a weak smile, and went back downstairs.

In summer I spend a good deal of time floating about the lake.
—Alexander Smith, *Dreamthorp*

No one said much of anything over lunch, and Tom was relieved to get out of the house and pick up Karen. She was wearing a white cotton blazer over a yellow two-piece swimsuit, and looked terrific. Her annoyance had cooled, and she gave him a long kiss after she threw her overnight bag into the backseat of his Subaru.

It was a warm day with enough of a breeze to dry the sweat that coated them as they lay on their blanket at the beach. The lake at Dreamthorp, though not large enough for powerboats, was spacious enough to support a white sand beach with diving boards and floats, as well as canoes and rowboats. Tom and Karen lay side by side, their flanks touching. From under his sunglasses, Tom admired the soft, fine hairs covering Karen's thighs. They glowed gold in the blinding light, and he felt an urge to move his head down and rest it there, to feel her smooth skin against his rough cheek.

But instead he reached over and put his hand on her shoulder, slick with tanning oil. He kidded her about the oil she used, which offered no sunscreen whatever, while he had to use fifteen or suffer one hell of a burn. Youth, he thought. She was the rich shade of white oak and as soft as velvet, and by the time her skin turned to leather in her fifties, he'd probably be dead.

The thought depressed him, and he turned to her. "Want to go in the water? I'm starting to cook."

42

"You go ahead. I'm feeling lazy. Maybe a little later."

Tom rubbed her shoulder for a moment, then stood up and stretched, looking down at his body. It wasn't bad for thirty-six, he decided. A trace of paunch, but he exercised every day to keep it at bay, and double time in the summer, when he always drank more beer than he should. He had a blocky build to start with—Karen called him a furry bear in bed—and the older he got, the harder it seemed to stay trim. The hundred sit-ups, morning and night, took forever now.

As he walked down to the water, he waved and smiled at his neighbors, many of whom knew him from when he had come to Dreamthorp as a boy to spend a week every summer with his grandparents. He'd done that right up until he'd been drafted the year he was graduated from Penn State. That summer he was in basic training, and the next he was living through the fall of Saigon. By the summer after that, his grandparents were both dead, and their cottage sold.

Still, he went back to Dreamthorp the first summer after he was discharged. He had stayed in a cheap hotel in Lebanon and walked through Dreamthorp's groves, climbed its hills, and sat on its beach for a week, until he felt that the sun and the trees and the peace had drained the army out of him and he could see Susan again. Now, as the cold water bit at his ankles, he thought back on that week, did some quick calculations, and realized that Karen had been only seven years old at the time.

He did a lot of similar calculations—she had been two when he'd lost his virginity, seven when he married Susan, eight when they'd had Josh. The numbers fascinated and appalled him. It was true that he needed someone. Even though he was an artist and liked to work alone, he had never been the type to *live* alone. He liked women and could not conceive of a life without one as a partner, as a friend, as a lover.

But he also liked a *comfortable* life, and that was something that his relationship with Karen had not brought him. There were times when she was too intense for him, *too* full of life. He knew that there was no further place to which their relationship could go, but still he clung to it like a lifeline, which, in a way, it was.

You're scared of death, he thought. *Thirty-six fucking years old and scared of death*. It seemed ludicrous, and he knew that it was because of Susan. Terrified of random death, he had turned to youth. He knew it, he could admit it easily enough. But still, he was powerless to stop himself, to tell her what he knew but what she had not yet learned.

He dove into the cool water savagely to drive away the thoughts, and stayed under for as long as he could, kicking hard toward the ropes buoyed by red markers that indicated the limits of the swimming area. He broke water and gasped for air, and was surprised to hear an echoing gasp beside him.

When he blinked his eyes free of water, he saw Laura Stark bobbing beside him, her ash blonde hair darkened by water. She lived on the other side of Charlie Lewis, in the small cottage that had once been the carriage house for Charlie's place.

"My god, you startled me," she said, breathless from her own swimming. "You just came up like the Creature from the Black Lagoon or something."

He panted for a moment before he spoke. "Sorry . . . just swam underwater . . . didn't mean to scare you."

She got a funny look on her face, Tom thought, then smiled again. "You didn't scare me, not really. How's the carving going? You're the carver, right?"

He smiled too, and nodded. "It's going fine." She had been in the cottage, Tom recalled, for only a few months. Charlie had introduced them last March when they'd all three been in the general store, and they had chatted a bit. He thought he remembered that she worked in advertising in Lancaster. "How's the advertising business?" he ventured.

"A thrill a minute."

"What company are you with again?"

"Brown Advertising. Not with it, really. *Am* it. With another woman."

"She's Brown?"

"No, we bought it from Brown. Kept the name along with the clients." Tom nodded, smiled, was unsure of what to say next. As if aware of his discomfort, she went on. "Well, maybe I'll see you at one of the concerts, huh?"

"Yeah, fine."

She gave a little wave and kicked herself away from him, stretching her arms in an impressive backstroke. A pretty girl, he thought, then corrected himself—a pretty woman.

She had to be thirty, although she looked younger. After all, kids don't own advertising agencies, even small ones.

He floated on his back for a while, thinking that Laura Stark was the kind of woman he *should* have become involved with, a career woman like Susan had been, someone older, a woman who apparently liked Dreamthorp as much as he did. He'd noticed her working on her cottage, painting, doing carpentry, even trimming the branches of her trees at the top of a ladder high enough to give him pause. She was a big woman, even a bit mannish, perhaps, but he liked her independence. No, he had the feeling that Laura Stark wasn't the traditional type. She wouldn't be easily annoyed like Karen, or easily impressed, or easily scared. . . .

And then he remembered the look on her face when he had unexpectedly surfaced next to her, and thought in retrospect that the look of shock in her eyes was greater than one might expect as a result of being gently startled on a warm and sunny day.

He shook the thought away, deciding that he was reading too much into it. That he had been drawn to her he knew, and perhaps he had projected the fear there to give her more of a feminine vulnerability and so make her more attractive to him. No, he decided at last, this was a woman who would not scare easily. He was sure of it.

> If you represent a woman bearing wrongs
> with a continuous unmurmuring meek-
> ness, presenting to blows, come from
> what quarter they may, nothing but a
> bent neck, and eyelids humbly drooped,
> you are in nine cases out of ten painting
> elaborately the portrait of a fool. . . .
> —Alexander Smith, *Dreamthorp*

Laura Stark did not have nightmares about the incident. Ever since she had been a child she had slept heavily and well. If she dreamed, she never remembered her dreams in the morning. When other people spoke of dreams, and even night-mares, Laura felt jealous, as if they had experienced something ineffably wonderful.

But that feeling died after the incident with Gilbert Rodman. Laura's waking moments were so filled with fearful memory that she no longer coveted dreams. What had seemed a withheld blessing now seemed a narrowly escaped curse, and she thanked God daily that her sleep was a quiet escape from her churning, conscious mind.

Now she found herself in a part of the lake far away from anyone else, and she slowed her strokes, gliding through the cool water, feeling the ripples run through her hair like . . .

. . . blood.

She twisted, dove, surfaced, kicked toward the shore, pull-ing herself with powerful strokes, not stopping until her cupped hands scooped sand from the lake's bottom. She stood then and walked to the huge beach towel, where she flopped down and gazed at the diamondlike surface of the lake. She thought about it. She didn't want to, but she couldn't help herself. She thought about it just as she had thought about it every day since it had happened, every day for nine long months.

It had started off so beautifully. All her life Laura had wanted to go out west and camp, but she had never had the time. Her first few years after college had been filled with being a wife to Hank and building her advertising career, twin goals which, she quickly found out, were incompatible. Hank had wanted a hausfrau, and it took Laura four years to accept that a hausfrau was not what she wanted to be. Unfortunately, Hank never accepted it, and the divorce was less than amicable. At least there were no children, and their property consisted of little more than the two cars and their personal belongings.

Laura, finally free to devote her entire time to her career, plunged into it with all her energies. By the time she was thirty, she was earning fifty-five thousand dollars a year as manager of Kleenline Industries' consumer products division, and found the Peter Principle to be in full force. The creative side was now forbidden to her, except for corrective input on promotions and campaigns that were already completed. Out of boredom she began taking on free-lance jobs for some of the smaller advertising agencies in Lancaster and Harrisburg. She met Trudy Doyle at the Brown Agency in Lancaster, where Trudy was assistant to the president, Bob Brown, a sixtyish man with high blood pressure and lethal dandruff, who had founded the agency, one of Lancaster's first, back in 1946.

When Brown died, his widow wanted to sell the agency, with its large assortment of well-established and conservative clients, to Trudy, who unfortunately did not have the money to buy it. But by that time, she and Laura were good friends, and Laura's antipathy toward Kleenline had reached a state as terminal as Brown's stroke. The best part was that Laura *had* the money. Her career was her life, and the only things she had spent her income on were clothes and memberships in her various athletic and sporting clubs. She lived inexpensively in the apartment she had moved into following her divorce, drove a '78 Chevy Nova, and packed her own lunch so that she could work at her desk.

Laura and Trudy bought the agency as partners in 1985, and it became even more successful than it had under Brown. They lost a few clients too tradition-bound to listen to women but replaced them with better and more progressive ones. Trudy handled the business end, and Laura the creative; and by 1987 they were doing well over a quarter million a year.

Laura never would have taken the vacation if Trudy hadn't insisted. "Do it, Laura," she said. "You're caught up, and the free-lancers have all worked for us before—Tim Cleveland is doing most of it, and you *never* touch his stuff. When's the last time you had a week off?"

Laura couldn't remember, and that fact as much as anything made her decide to take Trudy's advice. She had dumped her dying Nova for a Toyota Cressida that she had put barely five thousand miles on in a year, and which was ripe for a long trip. She knew precisely the route she would take, and she knew who she wanted to go with her.

Kitty Soames was young and silly and wealthy, and Laura liked her very much. Her father was on the board of the country club to which Laura belonged, and they had met when both Laura's partner and the final member of Kitty's foursome had failed to show up by their respective tee-off times. After the round, which Laura had won by three strokes, the other two women excused themselves, leaving Laura and Kitty alone in the clubhouse bar, where they drank until it was dinnertime, ate together, and went back to Laura's to continue their tipsy conversation.

That evening was the beginning of a strong friendship, one that Laura suspected, and grew to fear, might one day turn into something deeper. They played tennis and golf together nearly every weekend, went to movies, and frequently had dinner. The one thing that Laura did not like about Kitty was her self-proclaimed promiscuity.

Although only twenty-three, Kitty claimed to have made love to more men than she could count, although Laura never saw any evidence of it, aside from the flirting that she did when men tried to make a move on them in the bars they frequented. Still, she never left with any of them and never broke a date with Laura. Laura never met any of the men about whom Kitty spoke, and eventually grew to believe that the assignations, the long nights of fucking so explicitly described to her, existed only in Kitty's mind. It was at the same time that she began to wonder if Kitty might be a lesbian, a notion that was arrived at logically, since she had the same worrisome suspicion about herself.

Laura had always been tall and big boned, towering over the other girls in elementary and high school. An only child, her father, a senior vice president for a large corporation in Harrisburg, had spoiled her terribly, and she had loved him for it. Widowed early, he took her nearly everywhere, and where she loved to go most was the rod and gun club of which he was president. She was a proficient archer at the age of ten, and learned to shoot shotgun, rifle, and pistol by the time she was twelve. He also took her on fishing trips, and many of the summer weeks of her teenage years were spent happily in the trout streams of Dauphin County.

All of the boys her age, and most of the girls, thought she was strange, but she was still popular; and although she was seldom asked out on dates, and then mostly as a matter of convenience, she was happy in school.

She met Hank in college. Hank was an outdoor type and was delighted that he was able to find an attractive girl who would be a buddy as well as a lover. She lost her virginity to him, and found that making love with Hank was pleasant but not the earthshaking experience that movies and cheap fictions promised it to be. They were married the summer after graduation, the same summer her father died, and Hank quickly learned that a hunting and fishing buddy was not what he had really wanted as a marriage partner after all, and especially not a hunting buddy who had a career of her own.

"Jesus Christ, sometimes I feel like I married a guy with tits!" he had told her during a particularly vicious argument over household priorities; and nothing he had ever said, nothing *anyone* had ever said, had stung her so deeply. It was crude, it was malicious, and, she was afraid, it was just a little bit true. Though he had never explicitly called her a dyke, she knew that was what he was thinking.

They were soon divorced, and Laura threw herself into her work. She accepted a few offers of dates but drew back at any suggestion of the bedroom, and, after a while, received no more offers. She had no desire for sex with any of the men she dated. Sex with Hank had turned from pleasant but unexciting to annoying and tiresome, and by the end of the marriage he had been using it as a weapon, a prod to punish her with rather than as an instrument of love. Since the only man she had ever known physically had never been tender, it followed, illogically but irrefutably, no man ever could be.

It was only in the company of women, energetic women like Trudy and athletic women like Kitty, that Laura felt at ease and happy. And there were times, when she stood next to Kitty in the shower room of the tennis club, both of them surrendering to the steamy lassitude their exertions had caused, their bodies nearly touching, that she was curious enough to wonder what it would be like to hold her and kiss her and feel her body, hot and wet and slick, against her own. The curiosity would grow in her until she had to avert her eyes and turn away.

She had never spoken of these feelings to Kitty or to anyone, and Kitty had never indicated that she held such feelings toward Laura. They were friends, and that was how they were viewed by the world and by themselves, at least openly; and there would be no raised eyebrows if the two of them went on a cross-country jaunt for four weeks.

Kitty accepted the offer as soon as Laura made it, and then went shopping, buying enough outdoor gear to outfit a scout troop, including a large and expensive two-person tent, two sleeping bags that, Laura noticed, could be zipped together, and a trousseau of outdoor clothes from Banana Republic so complete in function and color line that Laura laughed. "Jesus, Kitty, we're going to be gone four weeks, not four years!"

"Suppose we meet Paul Bunyan? Suppose we meet Robert Redford? I mean, I wanta look at least as good as Meryl Streep did."

"That was in Africa, Kitty."

"Yeah, but Redford really *lives* in Utah."

Between the two of them, there was so much equipment to pack in the Cressida that Laura had a luggage rack put on top of the trunk to carry the tent and sleeping bags. Several days before they left, Laura decided to bring along a handgun. They were, after all, two women alone and would be going through some desolate parts of the country. So she took from her gun cabinet a .38 caliber revolver, put five cartridges into it, set the hammer on the empty chamber, holstered it, and put it deep under the front seat of the Cressida.

They started out in mid August, driving across the Plains

states as quickly as possible, stopping at a campground every night and getting up early every morning. They ate at restaurants until they reached Colorado, since they were unwilling to put up with the hassle of cooking on the Coleman stove and washing dishes until they reached a place where they could settle for a few days at a stretch and see the sights.

They spent two days at the Black Canyon of the Gunnison, then drove down into Arizona to see the Grand Canyon, up through Utah to visit Bryce and Zion National Parks, then north into Wyoming and the Grand Tetons. They loved Yellowstone and spent a few extra days there, then headed east across the state toward the Black Hills. Three weeks had gone by, and they were on the homeward trail. Not once had either of them made any approach toward the other, aside from sisterly hugs and girlish, excited squeezes on Kitty's part.

This hesitation to touch, to come too close, was conscious on Laura's part. She had decided that she would not be the one to initiate anything, although she did not know what she would do if Kitty were the instigator. They had had a fine time together. Most of the sights were new to Laura, and although Kitty had seen them on a trip with her parents when she was in the ninth grade, her memory of them was dim, so it was as if they were both seeing the wonders for the first time.

On the night before they left one site to go to the next, they made it a point to have dinner and drinks at a local watering hole and get pleasantly sloshed. These mild bacchanals had been largely fun, except for an incident in Egnar, Colorado, where a couple of cowboys—or morons *dressed* as cowboys, as Kitty later put it—put the moves on them a little too strongly for comfort. Laura had finally tossed down cash on the table, and they left without finishing their dessert. The cowboys followed them to the parking lot, where they sat on the Cressida's hood, one on each side, as Laura started the engine.

"Come on, now, honey," said the taller of the pair. "You girls don't wanta run off now without gettin' yourself some lovin' western style, do you?"

"We do it like they don't do it back there in—where'd you say—Pennsylvania?" the other added. "You ain't had nothin' till you had a Colorado dick."

"Get off the car," Laura said, trying to keep her voice

from shaking, afraid that they would mistake her anger for fear.

"What can I get *on* then?" said the tall one, not moving.

Laura reached under the seat, pulled open the snap on the holster, and drew out the .38. "You can get on this," she said, sticking her arm out the window and pointing the weapon at the man.

He tried to smile, but it was a poor attempt. "Now, listen, don't get so excited—"

"I'm not, but you damn well better be. Now get off the car. And that goes for your needle-dicked friend too." They both hopped off, looking uncomfortable. "Where's your car, cowboys?"

The two men glanced quickly at each other, and the tall one nodded toward the end of the small lot.

"Let's go. Lead the way." The men walked toward the vehicle they had indicated, a light blue Chevy pickup with an open cab. Laura turned the Cressida around and followed them, her revolver trained on the tall man. "Now unlock it," she said when they reached it.

"It's already unlocked," the tall man growled.

"Stick the key in and turn it," Laura told him. "I want to make sure it's yours. And don't go reaching for the rifle you've got on the rack either."

The man pulled a fat leather case full of keys from his pocket and inserted one into the passenger door, then flicked it back and forth.

"Okay. Now use the key to let the air out of the two tires on this side."

"What!—"

"I wouldn't put it past you bastards to follow us. Now do it. Try anything funny, and this gun goes off in self-defense. I'm sure you bozos have a reputation in this town, so you think they'd believe you or a couple of innocent women on vacation?"

The tall man hesitated for a moment and looked at his friend, who seemed to have gone into a state of mouth-breathing shock. "God*dam*," the man muttered, then knelt, pulled off the valve cap, and pressed a key against the stem. The loud hissing sounded like a hymn to Laura, and she smiled at Kitty, who, she was surprised to see, was sitting there with the biggest, most shit-eating grin that Laura had ever seen her wear.

"Okay," Laura said when both tires were flat, "now crawl under the truck."

"Crawl under the truck?" the tall man protested.

"That or lose your Colorado dick."

The tall man nodded grimly. "All right, all right. But you bitches are gonna get yours. You don't treat people like this, people who are just havin' a little fun. . . ."

"Under the truck, fun boy."

The men crawled under, and Laura gunned the engine of the Cressida, tearing down the road in the direction of the campground. "I suggest we break camp tonight," she said to a hysterically laughing Kitty.

"Oh, god," Kitty said between her sobs and hoots, *"needle dick! Oh god!"*

In the campground, they literally tore the tent pegs out of the ground and threw the tent and equipment, unfolded, uncased, and unrolled, into the backseat, and sped north on 141.

"Hell bent for leather!" Kitty cackled. "Calamity Jane and Annie Oakley fleeing from the posse—the *pussy* posse!" She roared out a laugh, then, as her giggles slowly died away, she said, "I didn't know you had a gun."

Laura shrugged. "I hoped you wouldn't have to know."

"I'm glad you did."

"It was dumb," Laura said. "They wouldn't have done anything. But now they're *really* pissed off."

"You don't know. They might have. Done something, that is." She was quiet for a moment, and they watched the Colorado night through the windshield. "You don't know what people will do," Kitty said softly, and Laura thought later, in retrospect, that Kitty had said the only logical thing that could be said about Gilbert Rodman.

They had no more problems until Saddle Junction. Most places were friendly, and, if Kitty did occasionally talk with men they ran into in the bars and restaurants, the men seemed perceptive enough to recognize that there was no seriousness in her, that she was not so much a cockteaser as a flirt, and that she was doing it as much for her friend's benefit as for any fun of her own. The only one who didn't see it was Laura. When she finally learned the truth, it was too late.

They were both tired by the time they reached Saddle Junction at seven o'clock that night. They had stayed longer at Yellowstone than they had intended, and their hopes of making the campground at Gillette were out of the question. Though Saddle Junction had no campground, they stopped at the police station, a small, blocky building at the end of the single street, and asked if there was any place they could pitch a tent for the night. The chief—and sole officer, Laura decided—said that anywhere on the grasslands just outside of town would be all right and that there was a real nice patch down near a stream that backpackers used a lot. He told them how to get there, and when they asked about a place to eat suggested Ted's Big Horn Bar and Grill. Nothing fancy, he said, but good food and full drinks.

They decided to eat first and drove down the street to Ted's, a plain, brick-fronted building with a neon-wreathed window on either side of the glass door. Inside, a bar ran down the right wall, and on the left were the rest rooms. Farther back, tables were in the center of the room, the kitchen on the right, booths to the left. Laura and Kitty sat in a booth and looked overhead at the trophy heads hung on the wall.

''Jesus,'' Kitty said, nodding at the yellow-furred mountain goat hanging directly over their table. ''I hope he doesn't drool on our sandwiches.''

The place wasn't crowded, and Laura wondered why the waitress looked so hassled as she took their order for sandwiches, fries, and light beers. There were three men at the bar, two together, and one alone at the end, drinking a beer and wearing a Walkman. An older man and woman were in the next booth, and three men in their fifties sat at one of the tables, talking quietly. Laura couldn't see a cook through the open window into the kitchen, and found out why when she saw the waitress throwing frozen fries into a deep-fryer and slapping their sandwiches together.

''Busy night here at Ted's,'' she said to Kitty, who grinned and nodded.

The waitress brought their beers and told them breathlessly that their food would soon be ready. ''Marlene din't show up tonight,'' she added, scurrying away.

''That damn Marlene,'' Kitty said.

''Life's a bitch.'' Laura raised her beer glass. ''To Wyoming.''

Kitty shook her head. "To South Dakota, babe. We've *been* to Wyoming."

The man sitting alone at the bar turned his head in their direction. Laura noticed that he had removed his headphones and they were now hanging around his neck. He looked at her quizzically, then smiled, stood, and walked toward their booth.

"Heading toward Dakota?" he said.

"That's right." Kitty gave him a big smile, and Laura could see why. He was *darling,* as Kitty would have said— about six feet, a hundred and eighty pounds, but trim in the waist. He had dark curly hair, olive skin, large wet eyes, and a smile that split his clean-shaven face into two equally handsome parts. He was wearing a denim shirt, jeans, and a pair of artfully scuffed Reeboks. He looked, Laura thought, like Hollywood's conception of an Indian detective.

"Me too. Hey, may I join you?" He looked back at the bar with dismay. "The locals aren't too friendly."

"Sure," Kitty said, and slid over so that he could sit beside her.

"Great! Let me grab my beer."

When he went back to the bar, Laura gave Kitty the eye. "Kitty . . ."

"Oh, Laura, he's *sweet.*"

The man came back and sat down across from Laura. His breath smelled of beer and mint. "My name's Gil."

"Gill like a fish?" Kitty said.

"Gil like in Gilbert," he said.

"Gil like in Gilbert what?" Laura asked. She liked to know people's names.

"Gilbert Rodman," the man answered, and grinned. "And you two are . . . ?"

"Laura Stark."

"Kitty Soames. So you're not from around here?"

"I look like a local?"

"You look . . . western," Kitty said.

"You were going to say Indian." Gilbert's face lost its smile for a moment. So Kitty had noticed too, Laura thought.

"No, no I wasn't—"

The smile returned as quickly as it had vanished. "It's okay. My mother was part Indian. But not from around here.

I'm seeing the sights, just like you. I always wanted to do it, and now I have the time. I've got a bike.''

"God," Kitty said, "how can you stand these hills?"

"Not a *bike* bike—a motorcycle. Lightweight sleeping bag and a change of socks, that's about it.''

"That big thing parked outside?" Laura asked, and Gilbert nodded. Laura had noticed it when they'd parked their car. It was massive, loaded with pannier cases and fronted with a giant console that looked like it held an entire recording studio. "That's quite a monster.''

"Nah, it just looks big because of all the stuff I've got on it—a real junk wagon. All the comforts of home.''

"And where's home?" Kitty asked him.

"Wherever I hang my earphones.''

"Come on," Laura said. "Everybody's from someplace.''

"And maybe somebody's from everyplace.'' Gilbert grinned. It was a thin grin that didn't show off much of his teeth. Kitty seemed to like it. Laura didn't. "And where are you two from?''

"Pennsylvania," Kitty said. "Lancaster.''

"Heard of it. Never been there.''

The food came then, and Gilbert remarked that he was feeling hungry too, and ordered a burger and fries, earning a withering look from the harried waitress. "Marlene didn't show up," Kitty told Gilbert when the waitress had gone into the kitchen.

"Who's Marlene? A friend of yours?''

"The cook.''

They talked about Yellowstone, where Gilbert said he had been about the same time as Kitty and Laura. "It's too bad we didn't meet there," Gilbert said. "We could've had a ball.''

Had a ball. Laura thought that sounded strange. She hadn't heard anyone say that in years, and when they had, they were over fifty. Gilbert didn't appear to be out of his twenties.

"Those bears are something, though," Gilbert was saying. "You feed any?''

Kitty shook her head. "I wanted to, but Miss Crabby here wouldn't let me.''

"They're not pets," Laura said. "A lot of people get mauled by bears every year.''

"That's because they're not careful," Kitty said.

"You can be careful and still get mauled."

"You're too cautious, Laura," Gilbert said.

"You can't be too cautious around a thing with claws and a mouthful of sharp teeth."

Gilbert cocked his head and looked at her. "You may be right," he said. "Yeah, you may just be right."

Kitty changed the subject. "What have you got on your Walkman?"

"Jazz. I really like jazz. Got a deck on my bike, bunch of tapes in my cases, play it all the time."

"You must really like it if you play it in here too," Laura said.

"Well, you know, you come in these western bars, they got this country shit on the jukeboxes all the time, the Judds, and Waylon and Willie, all that shit."

"Outlaw music," Laura said.

"Outlaw," Gilbert repeated. "Outlaw, hell. Guys wouldn't know an outlaw one bit 'em in the ass."

"And you would?" Kitty said.

He looked at Kitty, Laura thought, like a cat about to gobble down a sweet and crunchy bird. "I might," he said softly.

The waitress brought Gilbert's burger and fries and tossed the plate on the table in front of him so that it twirled for a moment like a dropped coin, settling with a final clatter. By the time it stopped, she was back in the kitchen.

"What do you do, Gil?" Laura asked as Gilbert soaked his fries with ketchup.

"What do I do? Or who am I?"

Laura smiled thinly. "Sorry. There's often a difference, isn't there?"

"Not always." He licked ketchup from his finger. "Not in my case."

Now what the hell, Laura wondered, was *that* supposed to mean? Gilbert made her uncomfortable, not only because of what he said but also because of the way he looked at Kitty. There was no doubt that Kitty was a pretty girl, and men had looked at her before when Laura had been with her, but never in the way that Gilbert Rodman was doing now. It wasn't even with lust, which would have annoyed Laura but not frightened her the way she was frightened now. There was something else there, something that Kitty seemed unaware of, for she was smiling at the man, giggling, even stealing his french fries.

"I wouldn't do that if I were you," Gilbert said with a touch of comic menace. Laura wondered how much truth was in it.

"Oh yeah?" Kitty said. "Why not?"

"Because of what I did to the last woman to steal my french fries."

"And what was that?"

"I killed her," Gilbert Rodman said quietly, holding up his fork and pressing his thumb onto the tines. "I stabbed her in the neck with a fork and buried her in the woods."

Laura felt a chill go through her, but she was unable to take her eyes off the fork. Kitty was silent for a long, uncomfortable moment, then forced a laugh. "Oh, is that all?"

"No, but I don't want to spoil your meal."

His face across the booth was dead serious. Then, slowly, it melted like wax into that razor grin again, and he laughed so loudly that most of the other customers turned to look.

"You've got a weird sense of humor, Gil," Kitty said.

"Yeah, that's what they tell me." He chuckled and bit into his hamburger, but Laura noticed that Kitty took no more french fries, and Gilbert didn't offer her any.

The two women sipped their beers and watched Gilbert eat. No one said anything until Gilbert picked up his napkin for the last time, wiped his mouth and fingers, and dropped it next to his plate. "So," he said through his final mouthful, "where you two staying tonight?"

Kitty started to answer, but Laura interrupted her. "We're not. We're driving on."

"At night?"

"I like to drive at night. There's less traffic. We spot each other. One sleeps, the other drives."

"Yeah? Well, maybe we could travel together. I mean, we're both heading toward Dakota, right? The old Badlands?"

"Oh, I don't think so, we've come this far on our own, and—"

"You don't want to travel with me."

"Well . . . no."

Gilbert stuck his tongue into his cheek and moved it

around, as though trying to dislodge a piece of food. "I said something wrong? I offended you somehow?"

"No, not really, it's just that—"

"Because if I did, I apologize. I was just joking."

"There's nothing to apologize for."

Gilbert looked at Kitty. "How about you? You're not saying much now. You don't want to travel with me either?" He was frowning now, and Laura thought that for the first time he looked angry.

"I . . . I don't think so. . . ."

"You don't like guys or what?"

"That doesn't have anything to do with it," Laura broke in.

"You don't think so, huh?" There was real menace in his voice now, but he spoke softly, as if not wanting anyone else in the bar to hear what he was saying. "Well, I'll tell you what *I* think." His eyes flicked back and forth between them as he launched into a remarkably fast tirade, barely pausing to draw breath. "I think that you're a couple of dykes who—"

"Jesus Christ!" Laura said.

"Who eat each other out and maybe use vibrators and dildos and shit. I don't think you'd know a real man if he—"

"You shut the hell up—"

"If he boned you for ten hours straight, you ball-busting cunt, you the guy, huh? You pretend to be the guy and she's the chick and you fistfuck her? Or is it the other way around or maybe both ways, it all depends on how you feel on a particular night?"

He clapped his mouth shut. Laura could feel herself sweating, could feel the pain as her nails dug into the heels of her hands. Gilbert was looking at her, not at Kitty, directly at her with eyes that caught all the cheap neon light in the place and turned it into fire. "You're a sick person," she finally said, and it took all her courage. "You really are sick. You ought to see a doctor. I feel sorry for you." She licked her dry lips. "We're going to leave now, and if you follow us, we're going to the police."

Gilbert smiled. It was just as open and seemingly honest a smile as he had shown them when he first came over to their table. "Now why would you want to do that?" The anger had completely vanished from his tone. It was calm and reasonable. "Darn," he said, and chuckled. "I really am afraid I've offended you two now."

Laura, trembling, stood up. "Come on, Kitty," she said, stepping out of the booth. Kitty didn't rise. Gilbert would have to move first. He didn't. "Let her out," Laura told him.

Gilbert turned to Kitty, his arms crossed on the table, and cocked his head, still smiling. "You want out? Or you want to stay here with me?"

Kitty swallowed hard before she answered. "I want out. Will you excuse me?"

"We could have fun if you stayed, you know, just you and me. We could have a ball."

"Kitty—"

"Hey," Gilbert said, snapping his head around. "You let *her* decide, all right?"

"I've *decided*," Kitty said, standing up. "Now let me out."

"I tell you," Gilbert said, shaking his head and looking down at the table, "I have never met two ruder women in my life. It's a shame."

"Let me *out*, dammit." Kitty raised her voice, and now the old cowboys at the table were all looking at them.

"Hey, son," said one of them, a man with a brown and leathered face, "why don't you stop bothering those ladies now."

Gilbert gave him a look of bemusement. "Just kidding around, pardner. No harm done." He slid off the bench and stood up, bowing deeply as Kitty extricated herself from the booth. "Milady," he said.

Laura stepped up to the window to the kitchen and called through to the waitress, asking her for the bill.

"I'll take it," Gilbert said from behind her. "It's the least I can do for such fine company."

Laura ignored him, and the waitress, pushing moist hair back from her forehead, handed her the check. She went to the bar to pay it, Kitty trailing behind her like a puppy, taking short steps to stay as close to her as possible. Gilbert shrugged, slipped back into the booth, his back to them, and began eating his fries. Laura heard one of the cowboys say something to him, though she couldn't make out the words. Gilbert said something in return, nodding his head toward the front where she and Kitty stood, and the cowboys laughed, then looked curiously at the two of them. Despite her rage, Laura felt herself blushing, and grabbed the change the barman offered, stuffed it in her purse, and barreled out the front door, Kitty in her wake.

"Bastard!" she spat out when they were both in the car. "That filthy son of a *bitch.*"

"What are we going to do?" Kitty asked.

"We're going to go to that place and go to sleep, and in the morning we're going to get the hell out of here."

"God," Kitty said, "I'd feel better if we got out now."

"We're both too tired to drive, Kitty. You want to have to pull over on the road and have that scum find us? Besides, he'll expect us to drive on, and if he really wanted to, he could probably catch us on that motorcycle of his. The thing he *won't* expect is that we'd camp out here."

Kitty thought for a moment. "You've got your gun, too."

"That's right," Laura said. "I've got my gun."

They found the place the sheriff had told them about, and turned off the main road onto one paved with loose stones. There was a place to park several cars, and a path that led downward through some high brush. Laura took the holstered pistol from underneath the front seat and slipped it onto her belt. Then they took their tent, sleeping bags, knapsacks, and a Coleman lantern, though there was still some light in the sky, and followed the trail until they came to the edge of a stream. There were several picnic tables, a trash barrel, and a few raised, flat spots of earth that were ideal for pitching tents. In a few minutes they had the tent raised and their sleeping bags unrolled.

"Can you sleep now?" Laura asked Kitty.

"It's almost dark. Let's just watch the stream until then."

They sat next to each other on the grass as the sun sank behind them. "He frightened me, Laura," Kitty finally said.

"He frightened me too."

"I don't know." She shook her head. "I don't know about men. You think they seem nice, and then . . . even those men at the table. They were on our side, and then he said something to them, some . . . *men* talk, and they were on his. Are they *all* shits? I mean, are they all interested in women to screw and nothing else?"

Laura didn't know. The only man except for Hank that

she'd ever known well had been her father, and as far as she knew, after her mother died, he was sexless. "I don't think so," she said. "I remember my mom and dad—she died when I was six—but they got along really well, always laughing and things. Hugging, but not like *sexual* hugging. Oh, I guess that was part of it, though I didn't realize it at the time. He was a good man."

"What about Hank?" Kitty asked.

"Hank was . . . selfish. I didn't realize he would be, but he was. I was unlucky, I guess. Just didn't find the right guy."

"I don't think there *is* a 'right guy.' "

"Well, you oughta know, honey, you sure been lookin'."

Laura intended it partly as a joke, partly as a rebuke, but Kitty took it purely as the latter. Her mouth tightened, her chin shook, and tears formed in her eyes. "Oh god, Laura," she sobbed. "I feel so dirty. . . ."

Laura put an arm around her, almost drew back, but stayed. "What is it?" she whispered. "What is it?"

"I don't . . . *go* with men anymore. I mean I used to, and we'd go out and then I'd let them take me to bed, since that was all they were interested in anyway, all of them, and I never felt a *thing* because it was just *them*, it was what *I* could do for *them*, never the other way around, oh shit, oh god, I hate them. . . ." She continued to cry.

"It's all right. . . ."

"I'm sorry, Laura. . . ."

"It's all right. I'm here."

"Just hold me, okay?"

"Yes, yes. Shh."

They sat there until the darkness came, her arm around Kitty, Kitty's head on her chest. Kitty's tears had soaked through Laura's denim shirt, and she could feel the moisture on her skin. It felt cold as the night air grew cooler. Kitty had stopped crying, and Laura could just make out the tracks the tears had made across her face.

"Let's go to bed," she said to Kitty.

Kitty didn't answer at first, then said, "I'd like to go to sleep right here. Sleep here forever."

"I know," Laura said. "I know."

She gently disengaged her arm from around Kitty and stood

up. "It's chilly," Kitty said. Laura held out her hand and helped the girl to her feet. "Laura?" she said.

"What?"

"Let's put our sleeping bags together."

Laura felt fear mingled with desire. She tried to ignore the obvious. "Is it that cold?"

"I just want to be beside you tonight. I'm upset. I need you to be with me."

It sounded rational, Laura thought. There was no suggestion of anything sexual in it, was there? Kitty needed closeness, that was all. God knew there were enough times in her own life when she had needed to have someone close and no one was there. Well, she was there for Kitty now. "All right," she said.

They crawled into the tent and zipped the two bags together. When they took off their jeans, Laura put the pistol near her pillow. They climbed into the large dual bag together wearing panties and t-shirts, as they always did at night. There was nothing special about it, Laura kept telling herself. They were just sleeping together, that was all.

Laura reached over to extinguish the lantern, but Kitty stopped her. "Just turn it down. Just so there's a little light."

Laura looked at her, a plea in her eyes. "Kitty . . ."

"Please, Laura. I want to see you."

"Oh, Kitty," Laura said, something clutching at her throat.

"Laura," Kitty whispered, reaching out for her, putting her own head on Laura's pillow, kissing her cheek as Laura turned her head away. "Laura," she said again, her voice full of need. "Please . . ."

Laura saw her hand reach up, as if with a will of its own, and turn the lantern low, and now it was as if the tent was washed in candlelight. She felt Kitty's arms go around her and pull her near, and she pressed her body against Kitty's, her own eyes filling with tears now with the relief of receiving something needed and desired far too long. Kitty's mouth tasted sweet, and her skin felt soft. Her fingers on Laura's body were so gentle and knowing that the fear left her now, the sense of wrong that she had carried ever since she had met Kitty.

She answered Kitty touch for touch, and soon their hands were where the heat and the need were greatest, and something grew within Laura that she had never felt before, grew and pressed inside her, arching her back, stiffening her legs, stopping the breath in her throat until it finally broke free, like some great bird that she was giving birth to, broke free and flew away, leaving her exhausted, happy, warm.

Time passed. She became aware of Kitty lying next to her, her t-shirt up around her neck, her face flushed and sweating, a wet smile on her face. "Laura," her friend, her lover said, and touched her cheek with a finger and then her lips. Laura, self-conscious, closed her eyes, then kissed Kitty's hand. "It's okay," Kitty said. "I don't know what to say either."

Laura opened her eyes and nodded. "We can talk in the morning," she said softly, and smiled. "Let's go to sleep."

Kitty nodded, and Laura reached up, turned off the lantern, and made the tent dark. Kitty moved against her, and they closed their eyes, feeling each other's warmth.

Laura did not sleep right away. She lay there, her arms around Kitty, thinking about what they had done. It did not seem wrong. On the contrary, it seemed as right as anything had ever been before, far more tender and loving than those fast bursts of energy and passion she had experienced with Hank.

It wasn't wrong, she thought as sleep slowly came over her. Whatever else it was, it couldn't be wrong.

> But why do death and dying obtrude
> themselves at the present moment?
> —Alexander Smith, *Dreamthorp*

When she awoke, she thought at first that the sound was that of the zipper of the sleeping bag, and dully wondered why Kitty was getting up in the darkness. Then she realized that it was a harsher sound, a sound of tearing, or . . .

Cutting.

She gasped as she recognized the sound for what it truly was. Someone was ripping their way through the canvas of the tent, and now they were through; and she felt a weight fall on her chest, driving the air from her lungs, and suddenly something struck her on the head, and she nearly lost consciousness but awoke again, and was struck again, and this time her head felt as if it was shrinking into itself, and she found that she was falling down a long, black spiral, and the pain kept growing, growing larger than her shrinking head could contain, until her head burst open, and she felt as if her blood was raining down upon her, and then she felt nothing.

When the blackness left, she heard the music. Somewhere a saxophone screamed, drums hissed a furious tempo, a bass throbbed like a heartbeat. At first she thought she was dreaming, but the pain that battered her skull told her that it was real. There was music here, and it was real.

Her eyes opened, and she pressed them shut against the fiery light that cut into them. When she opened them again, the first thing she saw was Kitty, lying naked beside her. Her eyes were bulging wide, and blood trailed out of the side of her mouth like a string that Laura could have picked up and pulled. Kitty's breasts had been savagely chewed. Both nipples were gone, leaving only two gaping wounds the size of jar lids. The girl's stomach was caked with blood, as were her spread thighs. Her groin was a sodden mass. It oozed like a sponge.

Laura's scream was neither abrupt nor loud. It was choked, born of shallow breaths and sobs of pity, mixed with retching at the cloying smell of fresh blood and other, more vile, fluids. She stopped when she heard Gilbert Rodman chuckle.

The Coleman lantern, turned to its maximum brightness, illuminated him vividly. He was naked too, crouching at Kitty's feet, his skin streaked with drying blood. His penis was stiff and red, dripping, she thought, with Kitty, with what he had taken from Kitty. He was holding a long knife.

"I waited until you woke up," he said. The words were thick and wet and rhythmic, a rough counterpoint to the cruel music that played somewhere outside. "I wanted you to be awake for this." He smiled, and the red lips pulled back to show his teeth, stained with rust.

Laura felt as if she had suddenly grown up, as if she had been only a child before, unaware of reality, of what people could really do. Now she knew, and thought about what *she* could do. She could grieve for Kitty later—and she would—but she could only grieve if she survived.

Only the gun would let her survive.

Her mind raced. If the gun was still there, if he had not found the gun and moved it, then it was under the canvas, the canvas he had cut with his knife, the canvas her hand was leaning on, and if it was still there, could she reach it, draw it from its holster, bring it up? And could she pull the trigger to kill him?

"I'm not finished yet. First this . . ." he said to her, holding up the knife so that she could see the blood on it, the lines of scarlet that rimmed his knuckles. "And then this." He reached between his legs with his left hand and gripped his erection like a club. "How does that—" His voice broke and he cleared his throat roughly, as if angry at himself for showing weakness. "How does that make you *feel?*"

His eyes glistened, and the hand holding the knife shook with excitement, and she could tell that he wanted her to be afraid, that that was an important part of it. If she could put him off his guard, the rift in the tent was behind her, and somewhere there was the gun.

"Please," she whispered. "Oh God, please don't hurt me . . ."

It was not difficult to say the words, for she felt them. Still, inside her she was as rational as a veteran soldier, her mind fixed on the gun, on finding the gun, picking up the gun, aiming the gun, firing the gun.

"You're scared . . ." he said, beginning to move his hand up and down, like a piston, on himself. "Are you scared?"

She shrank back from him, moaning, her hand on the canvas, patting it as if in panic, and god, yes, there it was, she could feel it through the material of the tent, but she could not *look* to see where she could put her hand beneath and grasp it, she could not take her eyes away from him.

Twisting her body so that it was between him and her probing fingers, she whimpered and began to cry. "Why are you doing this? Why do you want to hurt me?" She wanted him to talk, to give her time, but she wanted to *know* as well.

"I don't want to hurt you," he said, laughing so that each word was an element of the laugh. "I just want to make you feel good. I just want to give you what you want."

Her hand touched a ripped edge of canvas, and her breath caught in her throat. She reached beneath, and in another moment her fingers felt the soft leather of the holster. "What . . . what do I want?" she babbled, trying desperately not to look away from her executioner toward her salvation. Outside, a trumpet was playing now, high and fast and savage. Cymbals sizzled.

"You know what," he said, jerking roughly at his penis.

"No . . . no . . . I—"

Now she had it out of the holster and remembered that the hammer was on an empty chamber. She did not dare to cock it in case he heard the click, so the trigger pull would be greater than usual. But it wouldn't matter, not this close. If she could only bring it out and fire in time, if only she did not hesitate when the moment came . . .

"You know, you cunt . . ." he said, passing the knife back and forth in front of his face, his tongue flicking in and out, his eyes fixed on her own—impossible not to see the lie there, she thought, impossible.

"You know . . ." he said, "you know . . . you want . . . *cut!*"

And then she had the pistol out from under the canvas, just as he rose off his toes and came toward her, and she fired, twice, quickly, at his chest, but he was already moving, and the bullets caught him low. The first tore through his erect penis, passed though his bladder, and lodged in the peritoneum. The second round smashed into and through the scrotum and creased the right buttock.

The crash of the shots filled the tent, along with the smell of cordite, and Gilbert Rodman's face made a huge O of surprise and shock, and he fell onto his back like a turtle, the knife falling from his fingers. His arms and legs shot out stiffly, and then his whole body became limp and unmoving, except for the blood that ran from between his legs. It looked, Laura thought, like a red snake creeping out from inside him, like evil escaping his body to lodge in someone else.

As sharply as what happened up until then was to etch itself into her memory, what happened afterward was as dull and murky as a dream. She threw on some clothes, ran out of the tent past the motorcycle from whose speakers the music still blared, started her car, and drove back to the police station in Saddle Junction, where she found that she had been wrong about the chief being the only officer in the town. A young man named Willis listened to her story. Then he called an ambulance, bundled her into his police car, picked up the chief, and they drove back to the campsite, siren screaming. Laura stayed in the police car while Willis and the chief, their guns drawn, went into the tent.

The music had stopped. Kitty Soames and Gilbert Rodman were still there, but only Gilbert was alive.

> We never get quit of ourselves
> —Alexander Smith, *Dreamthorp*

Gilbert Rodman did not die. He did not move or open his eyes. The first medics on the scene thought that he was in a deep state of shock and did what they could to stop his bleeding, while the sheriff and Willis treated Laura with a strange ambivalence. It was as though they felt that Rodman had deserved the worst for what he had done to Kitty, but when they saw the worst, it was more than they were prepared for. Laura overheard Willis talking to someone on the radio in the police car and caught the words, ". . . shot his goddam *balls* off, man . . ."

Laura spent the night in the same hospital to which Gilbert Rodman had been taken. A matron stayed with her, for which she was grateful. She did not sleep at all.

Even after Gilbert Rodman was out of danger, he did not wake up. The doctors could find no reason for the coma, as there was no head injury except for a small bruise on the temple, hardly the type of injury, they felt, to cause such a trauma.

A brief hearing was held, at which it was ascertained that Laura had acted in self-defense, and the evidence was such that Gilbert Rodman, if and when he awoke, would be charged with Kitty's murder. Since there was no telling when Gilbert would wake up—if ever—Laura was permitted to return east with Kitty's body. She could not go to the funeral. It was as though her sense of loss was so great that she could not bear to share it, not even with Kitty's grieving parents.

Yet with that loss was a sense of responsibility. She felt as though Kitty's death had been her fault, that if they had traveled on instead of stopping for the night at the place that the sheriff probably told every camper about, including Gilbert Rodman, Kitty would still be alive. The idea, irrational though it was, haunted her, and when she got home in the evening from work, she walked into the living room of her small apartment and remembered Kitty there, remembered Kitty talking and smiling and hugging her when they met. She saw Kitty in the kitchen or sitting at the dinette. The apartment was filled with memories of Kitty, memories that she could not bear to be continually confronted with, for they brought into her mind that other memory, the memory of that night in the tent, of that night when they had gone to sleep in each other's arms.

Like a delicious sin, it tormented her, moving like a succubus into her thoughts as she lay in bed at night, unable to sleep, to descend into that dark, dreamless chasm where she could be free. She would feel Kitty in her arms and remember that embrace, that sweet moment of time before Kitty went into the cold, sharp embrace of Gilbert Rodman.

And then she would hear the ripping of the tent, the sound of that music, and far away, on the edge of her mind, Kitty's screams.

It was so hard to believe that what she had done was not responsible for what had happened to Kitty. There was, inextricably linked in her mind, the concept of her sin and Kitty's punishment. It went far deeper than responsibility for not traveling at night. In some part of her, Laura believed that Kitty had died because of what they had done together, that Kitty was punished with death, Laura with loss.

She considered seeing a psychiatrist, but decided against it. She could never, she knew, tell anyone about loving Kitty. That would remain a secret. Beside her, only one other person knew, the man who had found them together.

She was glad she had shot him. The only thing she wished was that she had killed him. Laura was not cruel. She had no desire for Gilbert Rodman to suffer. If she had killed him, he would not have suffered, and she would not have borne the fear of his waking and coming back to life. Coming for her. Coming with his knowledge and with the hate he must feel for her.

The ironic thing was that she did not even know who she had mutilated and who she feared. Gilbert Rodman was not his real name, but what it was no one had been able to find out. His wallet held no Social Security card, no credit cards, no identification at all except for an Ohio driver's license made out to one Robert J. Mendoza. When a check was run, it was found that Robert J. Mendoza had been murdered, presumably by a hitchhiker, on a barren stretch of road between Republic and West Lodi seven months before. His wallet had been stolen.

The F.B.I. did a computer search and found that there were forty-three people named Gilbert Rodman in the United States. They were, however, all accounted for. The Gilbert Rodman who had murdered Kitty Soames, and, in all likelihood, Robert J. Mendoza, was now referred to as John Doe, and his fingerprints and dental peculiarities were recorded and checked against police files nationwide but were not identified as belonging to any living person.

So it was a nameless man Laura Stark feared, a man without a true name or an identity, without even consciousness.

At least until this past week.

Laura received the call at work on Monday. It was a Sergeant Chambers of the Wyoming State Police. "Miss Stark," he said in a gruff voice, seasoned with a smoker's hack, "I have some unpleasant news for you concerning the man you knew as Gilbert Rodman."

As soon as he identified himself, she had known. She spoke before he could go on. "He's escaped."

It seemed to startle him. "You know?" he asked her.

"No. No, I didn't. I just . . . what other reason would you have for calling me?" Her heart was pounding, and Trudy was looking at her oddly. Laura forced a smile at her partner.

"Well, I'm sorry to say so, Miss Stark, but you guessed right. Yesterday he regained consciousness. Apparently he kept it a secret, and last night, before anyone realized he was conscious, he murdered a doctor and drove away. We've located the abandoned car, and we're following his trail on foot. We should apprehend him soon, but I felt that I should call and let you know about the situation."

"You think he'll be coming after me?" She tried to make it sound casual and unafraid.

"I have no idea, Miss Stark. I would consider it . . . a

possibility, however. But in his condition and all . . . Besides, we have quite a manhunt out for him. The whole state's been alerted, as well as Nebraska and Colorado. It would be very difficult for him to get through. Still, I felt you should be warned, since you did tell him where you lived.''

''Yes, yes, thank you, sergeant. Will you let me know if anything happens?''

''Sure, Miss Stark, we'll let you know right away. I really wouldn't worry, though.''

''No. I won't.''

''Laura,'' said Trudy, after Laura hung up, ''is it . . . that man? The one who . . .''

''Yes. He seems to be alive and well. And free.''

''Those *assholes!*'' Trudy said, fumbling in her desk drawer for a cigarette, as she always did when she was upset. ''How the hell could they let him get away like that?''

''I suppose they thought there was no danger . . . that they would notice him coming around. But they didn't.''

Trudy found her cigarettes and jammed one in her mouth, then started to search for matches. ''Well, are they going to catch him?''

Laura removed a small box of wooden matches from her blouse pocket and dropped them on Trudy's desk. ''You left them in my car again.''

''Thanks.'' She lit up. ''So are they?''

''Oh . . . well, of course, I'm sure they will. That policeman sounded very confident.''

Trudy thought for a moment, puffing nervously on her cigarette. ''Why don't you come home with me tonight?''

''No, Trudy, that's not necessary.''

''You'd probably feel better.''

''No, really. I mean, even if that . . . maniac caught a plane and flew out here, which is not too damned likely in the condition he must be in, he thinks I still live in Lancaster—if he even remembers hearing that.''

''There are phone books, you know. He could find you.''

''It's not in the phone book. I've only lived in Dreamthorp for a few months.''

''Laura . . .'' Trudy whined.

''No. I'll be all right. Really.''

Just the same, she was glad she'd moved. Driving home, she toyed with the idea of going away for a few days, maybe to Philadelphia, but by the time she drove through the over-hanging bowers of trees that marked the limits of Dream-thorp, she decided against it. The sad and terrifying memories that Gilbert Rodman (for she could think of him as no one else) had caused had driven her from one home already, and she would not let the fear of him drive her from another. No nameless madman was going to chase her out of Dreamthorp.

The previous winter, her apartment had become unlivable, and when she realized that she was doing everything within her power to avoid going home to it, she decided that the time had come to move. Since she loved going to summer concerts in Dreamthorp and was fascinated by the tiny and unique community, she called a realtor with whom she oc-casionally played golf and asked her to check on available properties. Most cottages in the town were kept ''in the fam-ily,'' if not in terms of blood relationships at least in terms of acquaintance, and it was difficult if not impossible for an outsider to make any inroads.

But a month later the realtor told her that a small, two-bedroom cottage would be available in March and that she had persuaded the owner, a personal friend, to give Laura first look. Laura had fallen in love with the place, and, al-though it was small, it was far larger than her apartment.

There was a covered porch that ran across the front of the house, with a low, latticework railing. Inside, the porch was paralleled by a front hall, with doors that led into the living room on the right and the dining room on the left. A kitchen was in the rear. Upstairs there were two bedrooms separated by a hall, and a roomy bath. The basement was open to the elements.

Although the lot was small, and Laura's windows looked directly into those of the cabins on either side, it felt far more private than her apartment, due in large part to the trees. White pines reached up all around the cottage, and the nee-dles of years past had made a permanent carpet on the ground. It was impossible to grow decent grass at most of the cottages in Dreamthorp because of the shade, but the needles were just as attractive in their own sylvan way, Laura thought, and they did not have to be mowed.

Laura moved in at the beginning of March, and found that most of her furniture was too contemporary for the rustic interior. The house had been built in 1908, and bare wood was nearly everywhere—on the lintels of the doors, on the rails of the bannister, as the molding where walls met ceiling. Laura sold most of her furniture and bought more from antique dealers south of Lancaster. The pieces cost considerably less than she had thought they would, for there seemed to be little demand for the kind of old but utilitarian furniture that Laura wanted. Her sole luxury item was a four-poster bed for which she had paid over two thousand dollars. Although some of the pieces were as recent as the forties, the whole bespoke the turn of the century, an impression further aided by the period prints that replaced the contemporary graphics that had hung on Laura's white apartment walls.

She did not make a museum out of her cottage, however. Her living room boasted a twenty-five-inch Sony monitor and a state-of-the-art VCR, as well as a sound system with very unthirtyish Bose speakers, and her kitchen was bright, cheery, and glistening with modern appliances that contrasted pleasantly with the framed fruit box labels that hung above them. The place had become her home, something that her apartment, with its monthly rental and its people on the other side of the walls, had never been.

Laura loved her house, and she loved Dreamthorp, and she told herself again, as she opened her door and inhaled the outdoorsy aroma of decades of wood fires, that she would not be driven from it by an as-yet groundless fear.

Still, that evening she pulled all her blinds, and when she went to bed, she locked all the windows, despite the summer heat, turned on the air conditioner in her bedroom, and put a .38 revolver on the ornate bedside stand. She felt foolish about doing it, but there was no one there to see and it made her feel secure. A gun had stopped the man once. It could do so again. Even with the gun there, however, it took her a long time to get to sleep, and when she awoke she felt scarcely rested, as if she must have had particularly violent and energetic dreams which, as usual, she could not remember.

Sergeant Chambers called three days later with the news. Gilbert Rodman, whoever he may have been, had been found.

"They found him, Miss Stark," Chambers said, "on a little side road near Long Pine, in Nebraska. He's dead. The head was crushed in the fall, but . . ."

"Fall?" Laura sat at her kitchen table. "I don't understand. How . . ."

"He took his car—not his car, really, the vehicle had been stolen—he took it up to the top of a bluff, doused the whole insides, including himself, with gasoline, let the vehicle roll, and apparently lit a match just as he hit the edge of the bluff. A little kid was walking about a half mile away saw it happen."

"But . . . are you sure it was him?"

"He left a note. They found it at the top of the bluff. Said he couldn't bear it anymore, what he'd become—I suppose he meant after the shooting and all."

"Yes, but are you sure it was him? I mean, was he identified?"

Chambers hesitated. "Well . . . we feel pretty sure it was him. The car exploded when the fire hit the gas tank, so there wasn't much left. The hands were burned, so there were no prints, and the skull was pretty well crushed, so there was no way to make a positive ID from dental records either."

The discussion of the details caused none of the nausea that Laura might have expected. On the contrary, she felt coolheaded and rational but filled with the desire to be sure. "Then you couldn't be certain it was him."

"From what the pathologist was able to piece together, Miss Stark, the man had the same size and weight as Rodman. He also had the same blood type—we did get samples from charred blood. So if you're asking me for proof beyond the shadow of a doubt, no, we don't have that. But if you're asking me for enough proof to let you sleep good at night and never have to worry about this man again, I can say that yes, we're certainly confident that we do have that."

Laura said nothing.

"It *was* Rodman, Miss Stark. Believe me."

She sighed. "All right, sergeant."

"Miss Stark . . ."

"Yes?"

"I think perhaps if you read the note . . . I think that would help you believe it."

"I . . . could you read it to me?"

"It might be better if I sent you a copy."

"That'll take time, and—"

"The language, Miss Stark, it's pretty rough."

"Oh. Well, I don't mind."

"No, ma'am, but . . . well, I do. If you don't mind. I can get it to you by tomorrow. Overnight mail."

Chambers was true to his word. Laura received the note on Friday afternoon at her office. It read:

Fuck life fuck god fuck it all. I can't do this Was going to carve that cunt who did it But never get there not so far and won't be caught again. Cant go to jail like this no goddamm DICK Burn myself up Go to HELL in a big ball of fire And the DEVIL will give me a dick again, a dick of fire, a dick thats a KNIFE and when that CUNT goes to HELL for what she did to me then ill FUCK her with my FIRE COCK fuck her for all ETERNITY for ever and ever

TELL HER! Im going first, but youll come LAURA! Ill see you in HELL so get ready for it Think about my new COCK think about a KNIFE in there where you FUCK WOMEN!

Ill see you LAURA I LOVE YOU

GILBERT RODMAN

She felt filthy after she finished reading it. The photocopy had clearly reproduced the smudges, the thick, savage pencil strokes, even the rough texture of the paper Rodman had used. It was as though even the photocopy had been imbued with the mindless rage and frustration that Gilbert Rodman had meant to convey in this sad and terrifying message. In spite of herself, she read it again, then felt something churning in her stomach, working its way into her throat, and she made it to the bathroom just in time.

"Laura?" Trudy called from outside. "Are you okay?"

"Yes . . . yes," she choked out after the final spasm had passed. "I just . . . got sick." She coughed up the last pungent, bitter traces of vomit and blew her nose into a wad of toilet paper. When she came out, Trudy was holding the letter. She looked up at Laura, her face pale.

"Oh my god, Laura. Oh my god, that madman . . ."

Laura cried and Trudy hugged her until she stopped. Then Laura wiped the dripping mascara from her eyes and shook her head. "It's all right, though. He's dead. I know it. He's dead now. He can't hurt me again."

And now, a day later as Laura Stark lay on the warm,

sandy beach of Dreamthorp Lake, she tried to make herself believe it. The whole sweet summer lay ahead, not only for her, but for Dreamthorp as well, her home, which she had come to love so much.

It had had its share of horror too, with that terrible accident at the playhouse. But the horror was over now for her and her town. Children laughed at the edge of the lake, people walked hand in hand, the sun shone warmly, and the wind caressed her face like a lover. The funerals were over, the dead were buried, and Gilbert Rodman was nothing but pieces of charred flesh. And if that were all true, then she should forget, and go on, and live her life.

If.

> What enumerator will take for us a census of the dead?
> —Alexander Smith, *Dreamthorp*

Gilbert Rodman hated Iowa. Nothing but flatness as far as you could see. Flatness and those great big fields of wheat and corn and whatever all that other crap was. At least in Nebraska he'd found enough of a hill to roll that little Chevy off. Even so, he'd felt damn lucky to find it.

But he had. Just like he'd found that guy hitching right after he'd stolen the car in Valentine. The guy had looked like him, tall and about his weight, though a few years younger. He had been just what Gilbert had been looking for, really—a New York boy, hitching across the country. Gilbert had found out what else he needed to know easily enough. He had told the hitcher that he was a medical student at the University of Nebraska, had gotten him talking about medicine and then about AIDS and how careful you had to be now about blood transfusions, and how some rare blood types were getting harder to keep in stock, and did he know what kind of blood type *he* had?

Sure. O positive.

When Gilbert had heard that he had known that there was something watching over him, maybe God, maybe the devil, but something. That had been the icing on the cake. The fingerprints had been no problem—he could saturate the hands with gasoline first—and the teeth, assuming that they had made records of his at the hospital, would be messed up by the explosion. But there could be no faking blood. They'd find some, charred, wet, or dried, and they could type it from that. So when Larry had said that he was type O positive, Gilbert had known that he was home free.

Larry had questioned Gilbert when he had pulled off onto the side road, but Gilbert had told him that it was a short cut because of construction up ahead. After seeing no cars for several miles, Gilbert had pulled off the road. "What's up?" Larry had asked.

"Gotta take a crap. How about you?"

"Naw, my tank's good for another hundred miles."

Gilbert had reached behind the front seat. "Toilet paper," he had muttered, grabbed the tire iron he'd placed there, and rapped Larry lightly on the back of the skull. The boy had slumped semiconscious in his seat, and Gilbert had taken the handful of rags he'd found in the trunk and had pressed them over Larry's mouth and nose.

Larry had taken a long time to die. When his breathing had begun to slow, he had retained consciousness for a moment but was already so weak that he had struggled only feebly against Gilbert's pinioning arms. Gilbert had felt a stirring in his groin, but there had been nothing else, no erection, none of the real excitement that he used to feel.

There had been only hate, hate for the woman who had shot him; and he had felt it sweep over him like a cloud of ice, its sharp, knifelike crystals melting into drops of poison that flew eastward through the air as if searching for her, taking her the message that this was the least he would do when he met her face-to-face, this was the best, the sweetest, the most tender embrace she could hope for.

When Larry was dead, Gilbert had removed his wallet and had found sixty-three dollars in cash and a Visa card, along with the usual ID. He had changed clothes with the boy, all except for Larry's now-soiled underwear, then had driven to a small bluff he had seen from several miles away. He had driven off the road to reach its top, moving slowly because of the approaching darkness.

At the top of the bluff, there had been a slight downgrade toward the edge. He had aimed the car toward it and pulled the brake. Then he had tossed Larry's knapsack out of the car, placed him in the driver's seat, and removed the two gallon can of gasoline from the trunk. Gilbert had splashed half its contents over Larry, pouring some in the boy's mouth

and pooling it around his hands. He had set the can on it
side on the passenger seat and rolled up the windows excep
for the one on the driver's side, which he had left open si
inches.

From his pocket he had taken a paper and pencil, leane
on the Chevy's hood, and wrote what he hoped would b
considered his suicide note. He had known that it had to b
convincing, so he had put much that was true into it, al
though it had hurt him to write it, hurt him to admit hov
deeply, how irredeemably she had wounded him. But the tru
est thing of all was what he had said at the end—that he woul
see her.

Not that he loved her. He had written that because the
thought he was mad, and that would merely make them thin
it all the more, perhaps think he was mad enough to ki
himself in this way. Also, it would strike the woman, if sh
ever read it, as perverse, as more filthy than anything else h
had written in the letter.

I LOVE YOU.

And it was filthy. He knew what love was. His mother ha
loved him, hadn't she? Oh yes, oh Jesus, she had loved hir
so much.

He had thought about his mother as he had put the not
and pencil, both smelling of gasoline, in a bare spot wher
they were sure to be found. He had thought about the Grea
Bitch as he had taken the Bic lighter from his pocket, opene
the car door, and released the brake. As the car had slowl
started to roll, Gilbert had slammed the door shut and jogge
along with it. Less than twenty yards from the edge, he ha
lit the lighter and tossed it into the car through the window
then leaped to the side.

The interior had caught fire with a terrifying rush, an
Gilbert, from where he lay on the thick grass, had seen Lar
ry's form become a giant torch. He had heard the hiss an
crackle of the burning, and had seen the hair ignite and stan
on end like a fiery halo.

A second later, just as the car teetered on the edge, th
flames had found the gas can. The explosion had blown ou
the windows, and it was no car but a ball of fire that fe
thirty feet to the plain below. Gilbert had picked himself u
and gone to the edge, where he had stood in the darkne
and watched the car burn. When the fire had reached the g

tank, which he had filled, it had exploded in earnest, as if the gas can blowing had been merely a dress rehearsal. Pieces of burning metal—and flesh, Gilbert had supposed—had gone flying through the air, many higher than the bluff on which Gilbert had stood. He would have liked to watch until the flames died away, but someone would surely notice the glow on the prairie and come soon.

He had picked up Larry's knapsack, put it on his shoulders, and had started to dogtrot across the fields. It was less than ten miles to Bassett.

After he had covered several miles, he had remembered the list. He had sat down under a tree, taken a folded paper from his shirt pocket, and found the stub of a pencil in Larry's knapsack. Then he had unfolded the paper and jotted down beneath the name of the doctor he had killed Larry's name and the date. He had decided to keep a record for Laura, to show her how many people he had practiced on, to give her an indication of how worthy she was of his ministrations. And if it made the bitch feel guilty that people had died because of her, so much the better. Every type of pain he could inflict upon her, even the most subtle psychological kind, would be precious to him.

Gilbert had put the piece of paper back into his pocket and patted it. It caused no danger, no risk. It was nothing but a piece of paper, thin and porous, easily edible if he were to be stopped by a policeman. And even if there was some slight risk, it was worth it, He did not know if he would be able to remember all the names, all the dates, and he had to know. He had to tell Laura everything, everything he had been through to get to her side.

> How he lived, what he did when he was a
> student, are unable to discover. Only
> for a moment is the curtain lifted . . .
> —Alexander Smith, *Dreamthorp*

Two days later, while Laura Stark was lying in the sun on the
beach at Dreamthorp, Gilbert was standing outside a truck
stop in Denison, Iowa, Larry's knapsack still on his back,
his thumb extended toward the east. He had fifty dollars in
his pocket, along with a Case pocketknife with a six-inch
blade. He had just shaved, washed, and brushed his teeth in
the men's room, and gotten a meal of steak and fruit salad.

A truck coming out of the truck stop slowed and drew to
a halt beside him. A blonde woman leaned out of the passenger window. "Where you headed, honey?" she asked him in
a gritty but somehow syrupy voice that had the accents of the
South in it.

"East," he said, smiling. "Just east."

"Clamber in," she said, opening the door and sliding over
nearer the driver. "I'm Cherry, and this's Hod."

Hod was a thin, wiry man who smiled at Gilbert with bad
teeth. He wore a sleeveless t-shirt with a hole at the sternum,
as though he scratched there frequently, a Royals baseball
cap, and dark blue, new-looking designer jeans. "We're goin'
east till we hit 61, then headin' south," he said.

"New Orleans," Cherry explained, looking at Gilbert appraisingly, "where we're from."

New Orleans. The name hit him like a fist. He forced a
smile and studied Cherry.

82

She was a big, blowzy woman in her late thirties. A whore, Gilbert decided. Just another bitch hot for it. She wore a sleeveless t-shirt like Hod's, but with no scratch hole. There was no brassiere either, so that her breasts drooped hazardously low, the fat nipples hanging like cow's teats, Gilbert thought in disgust. Her eye makeup looked as though it was laid on with a trowel, and the reddest of lipsticks hung like globules of paint on her mouth.

"We're married, Hod and me," Cherry went on, still watching Gilbert with fascination. "We drive around the country together, all around."

Gilbert nodded and looked out the window.

"Some people think that's strange," Cherry said.

Gilbert shrugged. "Not so strange. Women can drive trucks."

Cherry laughed. It sounded like a bear gargling. "Oh, hell, I don't *drive,* I just come along for the *ride.* " She stretched the word out to two syllables.

"Damn right," Hod responded with a chuckle. "For the *ride.* "

"Hod gets lonely on the road, don't you, baby?"

"Damn right."

"Likes a little lovin' along the way, ain't that right?"

"That's right."

"And I don't want him dippin' into any strange wells, you know what I mean, mister? Say, what's your name anyway?"

The woman's round closeness made Gilbert uncomfortable. He could feel his thigh sweating where her fleshy hip pressed against his. The seat was wide, so there was no reason for her to be so close to him, and he tried to move over but the armrest pressed against his ribs.

"You hear me, hon? I asked what's your name."

"Gil . . . Gilbert," he said.

"Gilbert. You hot, Gilbert? You're sweatin'. Hod, turn on the A/C, huh?"

Hod rolled up his window, and Cherry reached across Gilbert to roll up the one on the passenger side. Her breasts rubbed against his belly, and hair the color of old straw and the scent of dying flowers brushed across his face like a veil. He closed his eyes and saw her then, her head resting on his chest, nothing visible in the candlelight but the dark cloud of hair like some thunderhead, exploding across his field of view.

Mother . . .

"Honey?"

He opened his eyes. Cherry was sitting next to him, looking at him. A frown dug creases into her makeup.

"You okay? You gone be sick or somethin'?"

He smiled weakly. "No. No, I'm all right. It must have been the heat." The air conditioner, on now, jetted out cool streams of air. He inhaled sharply to purge the odor of Cherry's stale cologne from his nostrils. "I've been walking all day. Thanks for picking me up."

"Oh, we're always happy to give people rides," Cherry said. "Especially good lookin' boys like you, Gilbert."

Hod chuckled appreciatively but didn't say anything. He kept his eyes on the road.

And suddenly Gilbert knew. Hod was a watcher, and Cherry was a doer. Hod might like to do it too, but he got his main kick out of watching his wife screw other men. Then, after things were all juiced up, Gilbert thought, Hod just might dive in himself, whether into Cherry or into her stud was a moot point.

Gilbert started asking questions then—how long they had been married (four years), how long Hod had been a trucker (seventeen years), how he got started in that line of work (just liked cars, and trucks were one step up), where he traveled most (the South, but all over the goddang country), what Cherry used to do before she started riding along (beautician), and how long she had been riding with Hod (two years, ever since he brought home a case of crabs from fuckin' around on the road).

They asked him questions in return, which he answered as interminably as possible, expanding upon his own answers ad infinitum, so that the hours passed, the sun set, and the truck kept moving eastward.

Cherry was markedly impressed by Gilbert's skill as a raconteur, and Hod too listened raptly to Gilbert's lies. He told them about joining the army when he was eighteen, spending time in Germany and frequenting the Hamburg whorehouses. When Cherry asked him to expound, as he intended she should, he went on to describe countless perversions, from coprophagia to a drug-induced seminecrophilia. Cherry and Hod hung on every word.

At first Gilbert thought that the longer he could keep them

interested in what he said, the farther they would travel before they brought up the subject of a threesome. But the more he talked, and the more excited they became, the more they disgusted him and the more he wanted to do them both.

At midnight, they stopped for coffee and sandwiches at a diner near Ames, and when they got back in the truck Gilbert said that he was sleepy and wanted to take a nap. Cherry acted disappointed, but Hod said to go right ahead. "Hell, we slept into the afternoon today, so I'm still rarin' to go. You go ahead and snooze—you too, Cherry, if you want. Then you'll be fulla energy when you wake up." It was the most that Hod had said at one time since he'd picked up Gilbert.

"I'll just stay awake for a while," Cherry said. "Maybe cuddle up to my honey a little," and she moved away from Gilbert and against Hod, who put a skinny arm around her broad shoulders.

Gilbert, glad for the rest and wanting to be full of energy when he woke up, though not for the reason Hod intended, leaned his head against the window and closed his eyes. Although he was tired, he feigned sleep in order to hear what Hod and Cherry would say about him. It was a long time before they spoke.

"You like him?" Hod said softly.

"Mmm-hmm. You?"

"Yeah. Yeah, he's okay. He surely knows his way around, don't he? You believe that stuff about fuckin' them girls act like they're dead?"

"Oh yeah," Cherry said. "They're goddam crazy over in Germany. They're inta all sortsa weird shit."

"Yeah, but that stuff he said about shittin' on glass and all?"

"He said he *seen* it," Cherry said. "Which don't mean he *done* it."

"You think he's gonna wanta do it with us?"

"Hell, yeah."

"Yeah, once you get that t-shirt off and he gets a load of those titties of yours."

"You foul-mouthed pussy eater, you." Cherry giggled, and the seat shifted slightly under Gilbert. Bile rose into his mouth, and he swallowed it back down like a lump of bitter fire. ''Whyn't you give 'em a squeeze right now, you like 'em so much.''

''I'll rub *them* if you rub on *this* a little,'' Hod countered, and Cherry giggled.

''Do better'n that, you anxious fucker, you.''

Gilbert heard the sound of a zipper, of bodies shifting, of Hod's bony rear rising and plopping back down onto the seat again. He heard wet sounds then, licking sounds, and Hod breathing heavily. But the truck stayed on the road like a train on a track, the tires hummed on the blacktop, the motor growled softly, like a resting, restless beast that no one should annoy. Gilbert moved his hand, quietly and cautiously, down the side of his right leg, and patted the knife he had slid down his boot. Touching it made him feel safe and sleepy.

Gilbert slept. And Gilbert dreamed.

He dreamed of his mother.

He dreamed of his mother after his father had left them for the last time and not come back, after he had come into Gilbert's room and whispered to him in the night, said:

I'm leaving, Gilly. I won't be back this time. You listen to your mother, you do whatever she says. Remember, you're the man of the house now. You'll have to take my place.

Just do whatever she says.

Whatever she says . . .

He was ten. He didn't understand why she was so upset. He would be there for her. He was the man of the house now, his father had said so. But his mother got sadder every day. And stranger. She saw things that Gilbert couldn't see, that he could swear weren't there, but she still said she saw them. She said she saw that his friends were bad, evil, and she didn't want him to see them anymore, to come straight home after school, and he did because he was supposed to do whatever she said. And one night he woke up and found her sitting beside his bed naked, and now his dream remembered that—

his mother sitting naked, her legs spread, beside his bed, and her hand on that part of her where something that he had was missing, and he wakes up and looks at her in the pale glow of his night-light, and he sees, behind her, the Mod Squad poster on the wall, so he knows that he isn't dreaming, and he closes his eyes again and wakes up in the morning, and his mother has his breakfast ready and is smiling his mother coming into his bedroom and saying *come into my bed*, and he thinks that it would be fun, that it used to be fun, warm and cuddly, when he slept with his mother before, when his father was out on a road trip playing his sax, and he goes into her room and into her bed

his mother touching him where she used to touch him when she gave him his bath, but where she hasn't touched him for a long time, and it feels *better* now, funny but good, and it seems like his mother likes it too, and she takes his hand and puts it on her, and he is surprised by what he touches, by the softness and the wetness of it, and he wonders at first if she is sick and bleeding

his mother whispers in his ear, like his father the night he went away, *just do whatever I tell you, it's all right, all boys do this with their mothers, but you must never never tell, never tell anyone*

all boys do this
all mothers do this
boys love their mothers
mothers love their boys

his mother's hand on him, touching, rubbing, pulling him closer to her, opening herself like one of those coin purses that's like a mouth with teeth, but painted teeth, not hard and sharp, but soft and wet

and the part of him getting bigger than he thought it would ever be, and his thing going *into* her

all boys do it
and they'll tell you they don't, but they lie
so don't ask them about it, don't tell them, because they'll lie, they will
all boys who love their mothers
do it

and he loves his mother, and his father said do whatever she says, and this is what she wants and this is what *he* wants too, yes, because it feels so warm, so close, and something inside him feels as though it is going to break, but he *wants* it to break, even though he knows that when it does that nothing will be the same as it was before, that when it breaks it cannot be fixed again

but it doesn't matter, because if feels so hot, so good

and he falls, and it happens

It is broken forever.

Mother

"Mother . . ."

He awoke slowly, swimming up from the thick fluid of his dream, and in the darkness he could feel a hand on his knee.

"Listen to him," someone said. "Callin' for his momma . . ."

Cool air brushed over him, the hand rubbed his thigh.

"I'll be his momma, that what he wants."

The hand moved up toward his groin, and he remembered Cherry and Hod then, and remembered the Great Bitch and the bitch Laura in the tent and how everything gets broken, and he reached down into his boot and brought out the knife and slipped it gently into Cherry's round stomach.

She gasped, and Hod said, "Cherry?" and Gilbert cleared the sleep from his throat.

"Pull over," he told Hod. "She's sick, I think she's sick. . . ."

Cherry's eyes got so wide Gilbert could see their whiteness by the dim light of the instrument panel as he turned the knife round and round inside her, like a diner spooning out a melon. The truck lurched, then steadied, and drifted toward the side of the road. "Jesus," Hod muttered, "aw Jesus, Cherry baby, take it easy now. . . ." He brought the truck to a stop, pulled the brake, and leaned over. Gilbert slid the knife out of Cherry and cut Hod's throat with it.

The blood started to pour out, and he pushed the man back against the door so that he wouldn't get any on his clothes. Hod gaped for a moment, then died. Gilbert looked at Cherry, whose mouth was opening and closing, her eyes nearly popping from their sockets.

"You're not dead," Gilbert whispered. "Not yet. You won't die for some time yet." He held the point of the knife to her left eye. "And we'll have lots of time for fun before that happens, Laura."

The clock on the dash read 2:38. Only an occasional truck whizzed by on the road. Gilbert took the keys from the ignition, opened the passenger door, grasped Cherry under her armpits, and dragged her out and back to the doors of the van. They were unlocked, and when Gilbert opened them, a wave of cold air and the smell of chilled meat rushed out. He lifted Cherry up into the darkness, then went back to the cab, hauled out Hod's body, and rolled it over the shoulder of the road into some weeds below. He quickly wiped up the blood and tossed the rags under the truck. Then he climbed into the van, closed the door behind him, and turned on the interior lights.

Cherry was lying between stacks of wooden crates, her eyes still wide, her breath white puffs in the chilly air of the reefer. Her hands were pressed to her stomach, as if she was trying to hold the blood in. The first thing Gilbert did was to cut out her tongue so that she could not scream.

> . . . Just as, gazing on the surface of a
> stream, admiring the ripples and eddies,
> and the widening rings made by the but-
> terfly falling into it, you begin to be con-
> scious that there is something at the
> bottom, and gradually a dead face wa-
> vers upwards from the oozy weeds, be-
> coming every moment more clearly
> defined. . . .
> —Alexander Smith, *Dreamthorp*

Tom Brewer always felt an ache when he found himself beside Karen. Often when he woke in the middle of the night
and reached out, he thought at first that it was Susan he was
touching. But as his fingers explored further, he noticed
dreamily that there was a difference, that if this was Susan,
it was Susan as she had been years before, that time had
moved backward, that Susan's skin was as soft as it had been
when they had first slept together in college, that the extra
pounds that had come with her pregnancy and the years had
vanished, that her breasts, which had always been larger than
she liked, had decreased in size to little more than comfortable handfuls.

Usually by this time in his exploration, he knew that it was
Karen, and not Susan, who lay beside him, and the novelty
of it, of being in bed with this girl literally young enough to
be his daughter, aroused him even as it saddened him. He
would press against her, and she would wake in that immediate way that the young have, turn toward him, and kiss him,

90

regardless of the dark night taste in their mouths, ready for sex again, and he would willingly oblige.

Her readiness had surprised him at first and still frightened him a little, and he tried to remember if he and Susan had been like that, and thought he remembered that they had, that every incident of making love had seemed new and electric, every shared spasm like some exciting and alien landscape, before familiarity and the day-to-day routine of married life had leveled the peaks, slowed the rivers.

But now the freshness and the novelty had returned, and he was asked to feel the first passions of youth all over again, and was not certain if he could. It was not a question of performance, for he was sufficiently priapic in Karen's presence. But afterward, when he lay in her arms, he felt as though something more than semen had flowed out of him, as if what little youth he had was being drained away by this silly, futile, male-menopausal affair that could have no happy ending. He felt as though he was making a fool of himself but was powerless not to.

Karen held him, and he found it easy to admit to himself that he was obsessed with her. That it was ultimately self-destructive he knew. Marriage was out of the question, as was any long-term relationship. She would graduate the following May, and then what? Her degree would be in performance, not teaching, so there could be no idyllic marriage and life in Dreamthorp, him teaching art at Harris Valley College, and her teaching music at one of the local high schools. Instead she would take her flute and go to graduate school in New York or Philadelphia, trying to squeeze a career out of a decent technique, a less than inspired artistic sense, and a not altogether accurate ear.

Karen was not, in Tom's opinion, an especially good flutist. That she played only second chair in Harris Valley's orchestra made that clear enough. Yet, despite her shortcomings, she had immense self-confidence in her gifts and was convinced that she would someday play with a major orchestra.

"I just haven't had the kind of training that I need," she had told Tom on their first date together. "But I've got a kind of raw talent that a really good teacher would pick up on."

Tom didn't suggest to her that her raw talent might be greatly aided by practicing more than the token hour a day she put in. He had gone that route when Josh had taken piano lessons for a year, and it had been a big enough pain to drive his son to practice, let alone start all over again with his young lover.

Whatever the reason, any future together was impractical as long as the dream of playing under Zubin Mehta came first in Karen's mind. In a way, Tom was relieved. It would be difficult for him to make a commitment to a woman again, especially after having lived so long with as strong a woman as Susan.

But now, as he lay in the motel room bed beside her, and the first traces of daylight added a more natural tint to the yellow light that leaked in around the curtain from outside, he did not want to leave her nor have her leave him, and he thought that perhaps he did love her, that what had begun as infatuation and flattery that a girl so young and attractive would find him appealing had become something deeper. He wasn't sure. He only knew that if he could not be with her again, laugh with her, and make love to her, he would feel far more empty than he had before he had met her.

She stirred softly, and turned toward him. He could see that her eyes were open. "Hi," she said.

"Good morning," he whispered, conscious of the terrible taste in his mouth and wishing that he had sneaked into the bathroom to brush his teeth before she awoke.

"Is it morning? With that dopey light I can't tell." She rolled over on her back and stretched. "Why is it that you can never get those damn motel room curtains all the way closed? A little light always comes around the edge."

He opened his mouth to ask her how much experience she had with motel rooms but decided not to, thinking that she might not take it as a joke, and wondering if he meant it as one. The first time they slept together, it had been obvious from her behavior that she was not a virgin. Tom had expected it but did not relish the thought, even when he remembered the rather indiscriminate couplings he and his friends had engaged in while in college, one of which had led to Susan's pregnancy and their marriage, which, odds stacked against it, had hung together right up to the day of her death. Susan had had two lovers before they started dating, and that had bothered him in the first year of their marriage; but he grew used to the knowledge, and in time, assured by the years of the exclusivity of Susan's love, forgot about it.

But he could not as easily forget about Karen's previous affairs. One of her ex-lovers was a senior in his summer intro to sculpture class, a tall boy who was on the basketball team's first squad. Tom was certain the boy knew about Karen and him. There was a condescending note in his voice when he answered Tom's questions in class or when he discussed his latest piece with Tom. The boy was not very good at sculpting, wasn't even an art major, and said that he was taking the course just to pick up a few extra credits and that sculpture had always interested him. Tom thought that was bullshit, and suspected the boy had taken his class to be around Tom and try to drive him crazy with his knowledge of his and Karen's relationship.

The situation was uncomfortable, but not impossible. After all, the affair was common knowledge, and Tom felt relieved that Dr. Martin, the chairperson of the art department, had not called him in and talked to him about it. He wondered if it was because it embarrassed her. Still, as far as he knew, there were no regulations about teachers dating students as long as those teachers and students were both unmarried. It was, after all, a liberal arts college, unrelated to church or state, and had to prove its liberalism in some way.

"What time is it anyway?" Karen asked him.

He looked at his watch. "Six-fifteen. You want to sleep some more?"

She moved toward him and rubbed her hand on his chest. "I don't know. What else is there to do?"

What he really wanted to do was take a shower and brush his teeth, and have her do the same. He was as fastidious in matters of personal hygiene as Karen was enthusiastic about oralism, and the thoughts of her fellating him and his reciprocal performance upon her without washing away the dried remains of the previous night made him uneasy.

"Want to get a shower together?"

"Ohhh," she moaned in disagreement, "we ought to have a *reason* to take a shower first, huh?"

To continue to protest would have been rude and, worst of all, unromantic. He did what she wanted, and, in a few minutes, was relaxed enough to almost enjoy it. Still, it was with a sigh of relief that he moved into the traditional position and entered her. Afterward, her hand massaging his testicles, she asked him, "How come you're so uptight?" It amazed him that people her age continued to use the word. At least something that his generation had contributed would live on.

"I'm not uptight," he said. He thought that a woman with more experience with men would have let it go, but Karen had the tactlessness of youth.

"You *are*," she told him. "You're all stiff."

"Don't you want me stiff?" he joked, and she giggled. "Okay," he said. "I know what you mean, and yeah, maybe I am a little tense."

"Why?"

"I just . . ." What was he going to tell her—that he felt self-conscious as hell because he was afraid he smelled bad? What a tight-assed, old fart admission that would be. Christ, he *had* to come up with something else. "I . . . I don't know what direction things are going, that's all."

"Is it your work?"

"Partially." That much was true. And since she had suggested it, he decided to amplify it, although he had no idea how much she might understand. "Everything seems so stilted. It's like there's nothing fluid about it at all anymore. And when I started, I thought it would be." He put his hands behind his head and exhaled deeply. "It's living material, you know? So why shouldn't I be able to make it live again?"

"Wait a minute," she said, frowning and putting a finger to his mouth. "What are you talking about, your classes or what?"

Now he was confused. "My . . . my work. My carving."

"Oh." She nodded. "Oh, oh. I thought you meant your *classes.*"

"My classes?"

"You said your work, and I thought . . ." She shrugged.

"I consider my carving my work," he said, with more annoyance than he liked.

"Well, you don't make most of your *money* doing that," Karen said, and for a moment Tom imagined that he was in bed next to his mother.

"It's not money that defines what somebody does." And a damn good thing too, he thought bitterly. On last April's tax return he had declared a salary of $23,000 from his teaching, $22,000 from Susan's job, and only $2500 from selling his carvings.

"Maybe not," Karen said. "But it should be what you spend most of your time doing, and that's teaching, isn't it?" She tugged up the sheet to cover her breasts, a childishly petty gesture, Tom thought, like someone taking their toys and running home.

"For now it is."

"What's *that* supposed to mean?" She sounded younger than her twenty-one years, and Tom wondered what the hell he was doing in this bed with her, how this whole fucking thing had ever started. He was angry at her and angry with himself.

"It means that maybe I won't be teaching all my life, okay?"

"What, you're going to be a professional bird carver?"

"Why are you busting my balls?"

"Oh, am I?"

He lay there seething, trying to keep from lashing out at her with words.

"I don't know what's the matter with you," she said. "I mean, I just misunderstood, that's all." A moment later she said, "I'm sorry."

He should have said that's okay, and forgotten it, kissed her, made love to her again, but he didn't want to. What he wanted to do, although he knew he was incapable of the act, was slap her or roll her over on her stomach and spank her, not with any sexual aim in mind or even because he thought she needed it, but to make him feel better, as if hurting someone else would ease his own pain.

"I'm going to get a shower," she said. "You, uh, want to come along?"

He shook his head. "No. No thanks."

She got up and padded across the shag carpet into the bathroom. He didn't watch her as she left him. In a few seconds he heard the bathroom fan running, and then the sound of the shower. He was tempted to join her, but didn't.

Instead he lay there thinking about his life and what, to himself alone, he patronizingly referred to as his art. Both had the same flaws, stiffness and lack of fluidity. His life, perhaps, with its puzzling neuroses, he couldn't help, but his art he could.

For God's sake, his art was formed of *wood*, living and breathing wood. It could be as smooth as the finest marble, hacked and rough as steel shards, whatever he wanted it to be, whatever he was capable of drawing from it. It wasn't the wood's fault that he had not yet realized his capabilities, it was his. Wonderful things, awesome or beautiful or terrifying, lay within those chunks of tree for the man skillful enough to bring them forth, to excise them like the living tissues they had been, to make new life from what had once lived. He could do it, and he would. Someday, even though he had not yet come close to what he knew was possible, he would. He would leave behind these damned birds and ducks and doctors and make the wood come to life.

He had read somewhere that you had to be a little bit insane to be creative, and that was all right too. Maybe he would go insane, just a little bit, just enough.

"Tommy?"

Karen stood in the doorway, a towel draped around her hips, her breasts bare. Her hair was wet, and her skin, freshly scrubbed, glowed pink.

"See anything you like?"

There was a petulant, mocking smile on her face, as if in an attempt to make herself look even younger than she was, and suddenly Tom felt guilt and grief sweep through him and wished, so desperately that he would have given his soul for it to be true, that Susan were still alive.

"Well?" Karen said, a hand on her hip.

Tom dropped his head back onto the pillow. "I think want to sleep for a while. It's early."

Karen gave a little snort in which Tom read a great many things, but mostly contempt for his age, for his pretensions, for his lack of desire. Then she dropped her towel on the floor and climbed back into bed. She turned her back to him, and in a few minutes he heard the deep, regular breathing that told him she had gone back to sleep.

Though he tried, he could not sleep again. As the thought of Susan grew stronger, he felt the warmth of tears pool in his eyes, and rubbed them away with knotted fists. He drove the memories from his mind, thinking instead about wood, great blocks of it, and his hands strong as hammers, fingers long and sharp as chisels, molding the slabs like putty. But every time, just as he started to see what was within the wood, the vision vanished and instead he saw the cheap, stained tile of the motel room ceiling.

They checked out at nine-thirty and had breakfast at a metallic, forties-style diner near the turnpike entrance, then drove back toward Dreamthorp. "You want to go to the lake this afternoon?" Tom asked Karen, more from politeness than any real wish to be with her.

She seemed to have gotten over her pique, and nodded. "Why don't we go back to your place, laze around with the paper, and go . . ." She caught his change of expression. "What's the matter?"

"My . . . parents are there."

"So what? It's your house, isn't it? They don't like it, they can take a hike. Jesus, it's not like we're going to fuck right in front of them or anything."

"Karen, it's just that . . ." He didn't finish because he didn't know what to say. She was right. It *was* his house, and there was no reason why Karen and his folks shouldn't at least get along as well as his parents got along with anybody. He sighed. "All right. Let's pick up a *Times* at the store first."

Summer days are long, often wearisomely so.
—Alexander Smith, *Dreamthorp*

It was nearly eleven when Tom pulled his Subaru into the little parking spot in front of his cottage, getting as far off the street as possible. As it was, there was barely room for one car to get by on the tiny, narrow lane. He and Karen got out and climbed the steps to the porch. Charlie Lewis was sitting on his own front porch, the sound of jazz coming from inside his house. It sounded familiar to Tom. He thought it was one of Charlie Parker's groups but wasn't sure. Charlie waved to Tom and smiled an avuncular smile at Karen, who responded with her own smile and a lift of her chin.

"Come on in," said Tom. "I'll introduce you to my folks."

When they stepped into the entry, Tom heard the television in the living room. He glanced in and saw Josh lying on the sofa, his feet on the arm. "Hey, Josh," he said. "Karen's here."

Karen leaned past Tom and smiled at the boy. "Hi, Josh."

Josh looked at her but didn't smile back or say a word. In another second his eyes were back on the TV screen.

"Where're Grandma and Grandpa?"

"Kitchen," the boy mumbled.

They were there all right. Ed was sitting at the kitchen table reading the local newspaper, a cold and forgotten mug of coffee in front of him, and Frances was clad in a short apron which hid her shorts and made her appear seminude, as if in some middle-aged man's Victorian maid fantasy. Her arm was concealed behind the refrigerator, and when she removed it, Tom saw that she was holding a wet sponge. She smiled tight-lipped at Karen, and tossed the sponge into a yellow plastic bucket.

"Sunday morning and you're cleaning?" Tom asked her.

"Well, I'll bet *you* never cleaned behind there," she said defensively. "Have you? Honestly?"

"No, Mother." Tom sighed. "I have never cleaned behind there. Now if you'll take off that apron, I'd like to introduce you to Karen."

Tom tried to make the introductions as quick and painless as possible. Ed didn't change expression, but a dozen expressions flashed across Frances's face as she made brief and polite conversation. In his parents' old eyes he could see how young Karen was, and he practically pulled her away from them and back out onto the porch, where they began to go through the *Times,* Karen leisurely, Tom swiftly and systematically, as though he had an appointment to keep.

Just before noon, Ed and Frances came outside. Frances was carrying a small picnic hamper, and Ed was holding a book. "We thought we'd have a little picnic down near the tennis courts," Frances said. "We asked Josh if he wanted to come along, but he didn't."

Tom couldn't read his mother's expression. He wasn't sure if she had really wanted Josh to stay and have lunch with him and Karen as a punishment for their perceived carnality or if she had wanted to get the boy as far away from the lovers' bad influence as possible. Whatever her motive, at least Tom would be spared lunch with his parents, which would undoubtedly have consisted of his mother scurrying back and forth from kitchen to dining room as soon as someone's plate or glass or cup was less than full, and his father's dour concentration on his plate until, it being emptied, he would then scowl and follow the conversation with his eyes alone until he could get back to the unending process of filling his mind with history.

Ed and Frances muttered hasty good-byes and moved off down the street, seemingly as relieved to be going as Tom was to have them go. "You hungry?" Tom asked Karen after his parents had vanished from sight.

She glanced up from the magazine section. "No. We had a late breakfast. Maybe a little later."

He nodded, got up, and went inside. Josh had not moved from the sofa. A Tarzan movie was now on the television. "You working today?"

"At one," Josh said.

He had begun a part-time job at Ted's Mobil, the only gas station in Dreamthorp, a few days earlier. Ted Johnson, a craggy man in his sixties with permanent black oil marks rimming his fingernails, had caught his previous summer helper helping himself to the Lance cookies without paying for them and had fired him. Tom got gas just after it happened, and Ted told him about it, as Ted told everything of any consequence to anyone of any temperament. Ascertaining that Ted would need a new helper, Tom volunteered Josh, thinking that the job would get the boy out of the cottage and give him some financial independence as well. Josh had never shown any interest in cars or engines, but Ted Johnson needed someone to pump gas, wipe windshields, and add oil, not do tune-ups and change spark plugs.

Josh had been agreeable, which is to say he had not refused, and was doing an acceptable job, if what Ted Johnson told Tom was true. "A good kid," Ted had said. "Quiet, but a good worker." The boy put in twenty hours a week, got the minimum wage, and banked most of it.

"You're going to want some lunch," Tom told Josh.

"I'll get something."

"No, look, I'll whip something up for you. How about some pasta salad, a little soup?"

"I can do it."

"Really, let me. I'll call you when it's ready." Tom went back out on the porch and told Karen he was going to make Josh lunch, but that they would eat later. She nodded, not looking up. In the kitchen he heated some dried chicken soup mix and got some salad from the refrigerator, along with milk and an orange. "Come around to the dining room," he told Josh through the kitchen door, and met the boy there. Josh sat down and began to eat slowly. Tom sat across from him.

"You not hungry?" Josh finally asked him.

"I had a late breakfast. I'll eat later with Karen."

Josh stopped chewing and looked at Tom. Then he breathed

a sigh through his nostrils and looked down at his plate again. "You really like her," Josh said. He said it as though he couldn't comprehend the reasons behind it. "You going to marry her?"

Only the entry and the screen door separated them from Karen. Tom dropped his voice. "We haven't even talked about it."

"How was last night?" the boy said, still looking down at his plate.

Tom felt his ears getting red. "What's that supposed to mean?"

"You have a good time?"

"All *right*," Tom said, his voice rising.

"Tommy?" Karen called from the porch.

"Nothing," Tom called back.

" 'Tommy.' " Josh shook his head. "Mom never called you Tommy."

"I don't need to hear—"

"She never called you that." Josh's voice was trembling.

"Josh, don't make me lose my patience. . . ."

"I don't . . . why do you *like* her?"

"This *isn't* the time to discuss this—"

"It's *never* the time!" Josh looked up and Tom saw tears in his eyes.

"Josh, I've talked to you about this, I've tried to explain to—"

"Explain? What are you gonna explain? *What* are you gonna explain? How can you like her better than *Mom?*"

"Josh! . . ."

The boy pushed himself back from the table and got to his feet. "You didn't love her," he said as he ran toward the entry, toward the front door. "You *couldn't've* loved her . . ."

Tom heard the screen door slam, heard Josh's feet pounding down the porch steps. He didn't go after his son.

He sat there at the table, hugging himself as if trying to hold in all the grief that he had refused to show to anyone, that he had been ashamed of showing. *You're still young, Tom,* friends had told him over and over. *You can still find someone. The thing to do is let it pass. I know. I know how much it must hurt.*

Jesus, how they lied. They didn't know. They couldn't. But he listened to them. He played their game.

"Tom?" No *Tommy* this time. At least he was grateful for that.

"Yeah," he said to Karen, who stood in the doorway.

"What's the *matter* with that kid?"

"He's . . . upset." He unfolded his arms now, and rested them on the table.

"I don't know why you take that, Tom. If I'd ever acted that way in front of my parents, they'd have—"

"Yeah? Well, I'm not your parents. Maybe I'm old enough to be, but I'm not, so don't tell me about your parents."

She looked at him for a long time, and he could see the anger building in her face. Lines he had never known were there now stood out plainly, as if her entire youth were a lie. "I think you'd better take me home," she said coldly.

"Yeah." He nodded. "I think that would be a hell of an idea."

On the ride back to her apartment his sad rage did not subside. They said nothing to each other, not even when he took her overnight bag from the back, handed it to her, and drove away. He had been afraid to talk to her, to apologize, to try and make her understand what he and Josh had been going through. He had been afraid that she would not understand, and he had also been afraid that she would.

If she did, he might never escape her. Even now, as he drove back toward his cottage, he felt an emptiness inside him at her absence. It was juvenile, even perverse, but nonetheless there. He had tried to fill the gap that Susan's passing had left with his infatuation with Karen, and although it had worked for a time, it was doomed to failure. He tried to drive the girl from his mind now, to accept the loss of a second lover in less than a year.

But that was not right. Susan had been far more than a lover. She had been his wife, his best friend, the person to whom he confided both dreams and fears. And having her wrenched away from him was the worst thing that had ever happened to him and, he truly believed, ever could happen. His own death would be anticlimactic.

The cottage was empty when he arrived home. Still angry, he descended into the cellar, grabbed a mallet and his old number one chisel, and savagely attacked a cubic yard block of white oak he had bought the week before. These were no light, tapping strokes that he dealt the guilty wood, but harsh, bitter swings that sent chips twisting through the air. He had little idea of what it was that he was forcing from the block—the thought was dimly in his mind of a head, a massive, bestial head, but it was not the act of creation that obsessed him now. Rather it was the act of destruction. Or perhaps it was both, his aim being to bring forth art from his fury.

He stopped after several minutes, after the effort had made sweat bead on his face, and he dropped the mallet and the chisel on the cement floor, where they struck with a dull rattle. He looked at the block, at the chunks driven off its corners, and saw nothing else, no form within, only random butchery.

"Stupid," he muttered to himself. "Stupid."

Tom knelt, picked up the mallet and chisel, and set them on his workbench, then ran his hand over the wood, picking away splinters. "I'm sorry," he told the wood, he told Susan, he told Josh. "I'm sorry," he told himself.

He went upstairs, took a six-pack of Heineken from the refrigerator, and stepped outside. Charlie was sitting over on his porch, and Tom could hear, very softly, the strains of jazz coming from his house. Tom whistled, and Charlie looked up from his paper. Tom held up the six-pack, and Charlie beckoned him.

"Never one to refuse a good German beer," Charlie said as Tom came up the steps and sat on the porch swing next to him.

"It's Dutch."

"Dutch, German, whatever. They know how to brew, right?" Tom unscrewed the cap and handed a bottle to Charlie, then did the same for himself. "Now I know," Charlie went on after taking a swallow, "that I frequently indulge in the holy beverage before one o'clock on a Sunday afternoon, but I have not known you to. Might this have something to do with the fracas over at your place earlier today?"

Tom didn't smile. "Can I talk to you? Seriously?"

Charlie nodded. "Sure," he said, and Tom believed him.

"I miss Susan, Charlie," Tom said. "I miss Susan more than I've ever told anyone, more than I've ever let on. And I don't know what to do about it."

"I know that," Charlie said. "I've known that all along."

Charlie took another swig of beer. "You just have a fight with this girl, this Karen?"

"Yes."

"You think it's over between the two of you?"

"I think so. I hope so, really." Tom gave a small, wry laugh. "And yet, even now, I find myself considering calling her up again, telling her I'm sorry."

"You see any future in it?"

"Hell, no."

Charlie shrugged. "Then don't call her."

"People don't always do what's good for them," Tom said.

"Tell yourself you'll call her tomorrow. Then tomorrow tell yourself the same thing all over again. It's what I used to do when I had to call to get my trees pruned."

Tom put his bottle to his lips, then brought it down without drinking. "You get lonely," he said softly.

"You've got Josh."

"Do I? I'm not so sure." Tom paused. "He told me that he thought I never loved Susan."

"God." Charlie shook his head.

"You don't know how that hurt. I'd been—at least I *thought* I'd been—not . . . grieving for his sake as much as mine, that the sooner we were past it, the better off we'd be. Hell, that's what everybody else told me too."

"Everybody else doesn't know squat," Charlie said. "You need to grieve. Everybody needs to grieve. I did when Jane died. Like a sonofabitch. I still do. And I think it's worse when you're young like you are. You don't expect death."

"Young." Tom smiled. "I haven't thought of myself as young for a long time."

"You ought to start."

Tom sat without speaking for a while. When he finally did, it was a whisper. "You know I didn't cry? I felt gutted. Empty. But I didn't cry. I still haven't."

"It might be better if you did. Someday you will."

"I don't know, Charlie. I don't know. It's like I still don't believe it. Like I'll come home and she'll be there." He turned to look at Charlie with dry eyes. "I really don't think I believe it. I just can't believe she's dead."

When Tom's parents came back to the cottage at three o'clock, they saw Tom sitting with Charlie Lewis on Charlie's porch. The two men had finished the first six-pack and were halfway through a second, and Tom was smiling again. Frances shook her head in disgust, refused Charlie's invitation to "set a while," and went into the cottage with Ed.

By the time Josh returned at six, the bonhomie the beer had produced in Tom was gone, and he took the boy outside, away from Frances's curiosity, and told him that he would not be seeing Karen anymore.

"You two have a fight?" Josh asked.

"Yes."

"Over me?"

Tom paused, and Josh began to nod. "No," Tom said quickly. "It wasn't over you. Just . . . things in general. But I will tell you that I don't like the way you've been behaving lately."

"Yeah? Well, same here."

"Don't make me hit you, Josh. You're too old for that." Tom couldn't remember spanking Josh since he was six. "Since you don't have Karen around to be rude to anymore, don't try it on me. All right?"

Josh nodded sullenly. "All right."

"And an apology might be in order."

"For *what?*"

"For acting like a little *prick,*" Tom said.

His son stared into his eyes. "I'm sorry," he said, "for acting like a little *prick.*"

Tom nodded. "That was fine," he said with as much sarcasm as he could muster. "That was just about the most gracious apology I've heard in a long time." They looked at each other like two wolves vying for dominance. "Go get washed up," Tom finally said. "Grandma's got dinner waiting."

That night, after the others in the house were sleeping, Josh pushed back the screen in his window, stepped out onto the porch roof, and climbed down to the porch. He walked quietly down the steps and disappeared into the night.

> Death does not walk about here often,
> but when he does, he receives as much
> respect as the squire himself.
> —Alexander Smith, *Dreamthorp*

Monday was Tom Brewer's lightest class day. He had fresh-man Intro to Art at ten in the morning and office hours from eleven to noon. This particular Monday no one came to see him, so he left early, ate lunch in the snack bar, and drove home.

As he walked up his steps he heard Alice Penworth calling him. She was coming up the street, wearing her usual uni-form of faded blue jeans and sweatshirt, irregular regalia for a woman who had to be in her mid seventies. She had lived in Dreamthorp her entire life, and would occasionally join Tom and Charlie on Charlie's porch—and in a beer—and re-gale the pair of them with stories of life in Dreamthorp over the decades.

"Tom," she said now as she walked up to him, her bird-like face pinched in concern, "I wonder if you can help me."

"Sure, Alice. What's the problem?"

"Well, I have not seen Martha Sipling since Saturday, and I'm worried that something may have happened to her. Now I'm not one to pry, you know that, but I haven't seen any signs of movement in her cottage, and that's not like Mar-tha."

"You think she might have gone away for a day or two?"

Alice shook her head firmly. "Absolutely not. I mean to say we're not the closest of friends, even though we are next-door neighbors, but if she went away I think she'd let me know. And there's been a light burning upstairs. I noticed it last night after it got dark, and it's still on. And Martha wouldn't go off and leave a light burning like that, I know her. I'm just afraid something's happened to her."

"Do you want to call the police?"

"No, no. I mean, I would feel terribly silly if she *had* gone away, and she weren't there—you know, one of these hysterical old women who makes mountains out of mole-hills."

"Well, what do you want me to do?" Tom asked politely. "We really can't break in, you know."

"Oh, we don't have to break in. I've got a key. Martha gave me one in case there was ever an emergency—you know, if she was away at Bible study or something and water was pouring out of her house, or fire, or something like that." Alice's eyes narrowed. "I know, you're wondering why I don't just go in and check then. Well, to tell the truth, I'm a little scared."

Tom nodded. "Sure. I'll go with you."

Martha Sipling's cottage was two down from Laura Stark's, with Alice's on the far side. The Sipling place was one of the larger cottages, but Martha was the last of the Siplings. Her husband had died years before, and their only son had been killed in Korea.

"I remember," Alice said as they walked, "back in the fifties it must've been. Simon Beech, his name was, and he had a cottage up on Thoreau. Kept to himself, didn't make friends too easy, and one winter folks realized they hadn't seen him anywhere in about a week. He didn't get much mail, so nobody noticed right away. Didn't have a phone either. Well, they finally broke down his door, and the smell that came out of there was just atrocious. He did have a small dog, and the dog had . . . well, I guess you know. Just had a heart attack, and the furnace stayed on, kept the place real warm. It was awful. Took them months to get it to the place where they could even show it on the market. It's the cottage the Allens live in now."

"What happened to the dog?" Tom asked.

"I don't know," Alice said with some surprise, as if amazed that she had never learned that thread of the story.

But then her attention leaped to something more immediate. "There," she said. "You can see the light from here."

Tom looked up through the leaves of the trees. Sure enough, there was a pale light shining in the shadows of the second story.

"You can see it better from my side," said Alice. "It's in the hall. Come on. The key is to the back door."

They walked through the thickness of pine needles up the short grade to the back of the cottage, and Alice handed the key to Tom. When he fit it in the lock, he thought it was the wrong key, but then realized that the back door was hardly ever used, and rust had built up. He wiggled it for a few seconds, then felt it turn.

The odor hit them as he opened the door. It was not putrescence, but rather a stale, musty smell mingled with something more pungent, salty and metallic, nothing he could immediately recognize. He turned to Alice.

"That musty smell—that's her hats," Alice said quietly. "But that other . . ."

They stepped onto the clean linoleum of the kitchen and listened to a clock ticking from a room in the front. Tom looked around quickly. Everything seemed in order. There was a single plate on the checked tablecloth that covered the kitchen table, with a knife, spoon, and fork flanking it. Samplers covered the bright yellow walls, and the chrome of the appliances gleamed spotlessly.

Tom led the way into the dining room, past the massive oak pedestal table and chairs, the large china closet filled with white and blue pieces. The little light that came in through the heavily curtained windows had been diminished by the trees that arched over the cottage, and he wanted to turn on a light, but he felt that to do so would be an admission of cowardice to Alice Penworth.

As they passed through the room, Tom slowly became aware of another regular sound beside the clock's steady ticking. "Listen," he said to Alice. "You hear that? Like something . . . ticking?"

She stopped walking and listened. "It's dripping," she said. "Like a slow leak. God, I wonder if one of her pipes *did* break." She clucked and shook her head. "The room through there. The stairs are on the far side of it."

Tom stepped through the door and froze. It seemed as

though a crowd of people were sitting in the shadows of the next room, staring at him. They had no features on their faces.

Alice heard Tom gasp and quickly said, "Hats, just hats. She collected them. Turn on that light."

He pulled the metal chain of a Tiffany lamp on a table next to him, and the room was illuminated by a dark rose light. The far wall was covered by a huge, glass bookcase full of hats, and tables of varying heights stretched from wall to wall. On each was a number of mannikin heads, each topped in turn with a hat. Most were from the Victorian era, replete with feathers and ribbons, and Tom was unpleasantly reminded of stuffed birds in a museum. They looked at home in the room with its sepia-colored wallpaper patterned in deep green twisting vines that became lost in the darkness of the high ceiling. The atmosphere was redolent of age, and Tom noticed that the smell was far stronger here—not only the musty smell of the hats, but also that silvery smell he could not identify.

His attention was suddenly caught by a hat less than two yards away from him on a deal table. It was made of velvet, he thought, a dark wine color. Yet it seemed to glisten in the dim light far more than its companions. Tom took a step toward it when he heard the dripping sound again, and saw something tiny and dark land on the red velvet with an audible sound.

At first he tried to tell himself that it was only water, that, as Alice Penworth had surmised, something had gone wrong with the upstairs plumbing. But when the next drop followed a few seconds later, he reached out a hand and touched the velvet hat. It was sodden, and when he drew his hand away, his fingers were red with blood.

"My God," whispered Alice Penworth, looking upward.

Tom followed her gaze and saw directly above the sopping hat, a large, irregular, dark patch on the ceiling from which the blood was slowly dripping. He tried to talk but nothing came out, and he cleared his throat roughly. The sound made Alice jump. "Is there . . . a phone here?"

"In the kitchen."

"Okay. You call the police."

"What about an ambulance?" Alice asked, her voice shaking.

"All right, yes," Tom said, thinking that it was far too late for that now. "An ambulance." He watched the spot on the ceiling, and heard Alice turn and move across the dining room, into the kitchen.

In a way, Tom wanted to stay downstairs until the police came, but if there was the slightest chance that the old woman was still alive, then he must go up and try to help. He told himself that it was possible that whatever had happened upstairs was the result of an accident, but he did not believe it. What had happened was the result of violence, and he had the distinct and uncomfortable feeling that what had caused that violence was still here in the cottage. He was a rational man, and this was an irrational suspicion but one he could not shake.

Still, he had to see.

He walked through the room full of hats, glancing around him as he went as if to make sure that the egg-faced heads did not turn as he passed. The stairs creaked shrilly as he climbed them, and he realized that before he reached the top he would be able to look over the edge of the hall floor and see what it was that had lost so much blood. It made him pause, and in the silence he heard Alice's voice from the kitchen, muted but intense.

The knowledge that someone else was in the house and that help would soon be on the way gave him courage, and he finished his climb up the noisy stairs. The light was on, and at the far end of the wide hall he saw a blanket bin built against the wall. Nearly all of the older cottages had them. They were similar to wood bins, with heavy lids that lifted up and leaned against the wall, and were sometimes hooked so they would not fall.

This one had fallen. Martha Sipling's head and upper torso were hidden from sight, but her hips and legs were not. Streaks of dried blood ran down them, blood that had turned her fluffy slippers from white to a muddy red.

Tom looked at the blanket bin in amazement. The lid had apparently fallen down on Martha Sipling as she was leaning into it, but the lid was now nearly closed. It was impossible. There had to be some space that her stomach and back occupied, some bulk there to keep the lid partway open. But there was not.

He stepped closer, and saw that the lid *was* open, but only half an inch. Martha Sipling's buttocks and legs beneath the thin nightgown were pale where the blood did not darken them. Tom put his fingers under the lid, and slowly lifted it up.

No longer held by the lid, Martha Sipling's separated lower half slipped out of the nightgown, slid down the outside of the bin, and landed wetly on the floor next to Tom's feet. A milky strand of gray intestine trailed behind like an afterthought.

Tom retched and looked away, looked at the bottom of the bloody nightgown hanging out of the closed bin, and retched again when he thought of what was still inside it. He turned around and began to walk toward the stairs, but found that his legs had become rubbery, and he had to stop and force himself to breathe slowly. He swallowed down bile several times, and only the irrational thought of the two white legs and hips rising of their own volition and sliding after him, leaving footprints in their own blood, brought him to the stairs. He ran down them and did not look back once.

Alice Penworth was still on the telephone. "Oh, just a minute," she told someone, "here he comes now," and she looked at him with a mixture of curiosity and dread.

"She's dead," Tom said softly. "There's . . . she's dead."

"He says she's dead," Alice said into the phone. "All right. All right, we will . . . yes. Good-bye." She hung up. "What was it, Tom?" Alice asked him. "What happened?"

Tom shook his head and caught a glimpse of himself in a mirror that hung in the corner of the kitchen. It had painted angels surrounding it, and he thought his face looked as white as their wings. "She was . . . killed," he said weakly.

"You mean that she was—"

"Murdered," Tom said. "I think she was, I don't think there was any other way that . . ." He paused, felt his lunch push its way upward, saw a toilet bowl through a door that he had thought was a pantry, and ran inside. He knelt by the toilet and let it happen, thinking irrelevantly how neat Martha Sipling had been, how tidy this bathroom was, how clean the bowl.

When he was finished, he blew his nose several times into toilet paper, and went back into the kitchen. Alice was sitting at the kitchen table, looking down at the clean, empty plate

Martha Sipling had set for a meal she would never eat. Tom
sat down too.

A Chalmers police car pulled up in front of the Sipling
cottage fifteen minutes later, and Bret Walters and Stu Bottomly climbed out. Bret was the police chief in Chalmers, a
town three miles away from Dreamthorp and two thousand
people larger, and Stu was his deputy. They were hatless
and both wore gray, short-sleeved uniform shirts and match-
ing trousers. Stu's fit better because he was easier to fit—tall,
slender, and young. Bret Walters, on the other hand, had a
squat, short body that age had done nothing to improve. They
knocked on the front door just as the ambulance pulled up,
lights flashing but sirens off, behind their car.

Tom unlocked and opened the door. Bret smiled grimly at
him. "How you doing, Tom?"

"I've been better," Tom said as he stepped aside and allowed the men to enter. "Mrs. Sipling is upstairs."

"Pretty bad?" Bret asked, and Tom nodded. "Okay, well
look, we're here now, and the medical examiner'll get here
shortly. Why don't you go home—you too, Miss Penworth—
and I'll let you know what happens. Probably want to question both of you, too. Just routine stuff."

"Fine," Tom said. "You know where we live."

He knew both Bret and Stu from the annual Dreamthorp
art show. Tom was on the planning committee every year,
and the policemen, along with a few hired men, provided
crowd control for the event. They were nice, friendly men,
but Tom didn't think either one of them was ready for this.
They had been upset enough when the playhouse collapsed
and none of the victims had been in the shape that Martha
Sipling was in upstairs.

When Tom got home, Josh was at work and his parents
had gone down to the lake, so he sat on the porch, had a stiff
drink of Jack Daniel's, no ice, and thought about Martha Sipling. He had told Alice that he thought it was murder, and
although he had no concrete reason for thinking so, he was
sure he was right. If that lid, heavy as it was, had simply
fallen on the woman as she was leaning into the bin, it certainly would have harmed her, it might conceivably have
killed her if it had hit her thin, frail body in a vulnerable
place, but there was no way on God's green earth that it
would have cut her in two. It was simply not possible.

No, Tom reasoned, the only thing that could have caused what he had seen was if someone had slammed the lid down hard on Martha Sipling, and done it over and over again, with extraordinary force, until her spine, her internal organs, the muscles and flesh around her stomach and back had been compressed to a pulp. That was the only way that lid could have nearly closed, the only way that old woman could have been ripped in half.

He shuddered and felt his gorge rise again. He had not felt nauseated during the playhouse tragedy because he had things to do, people to help. But in this case he was doomed to inaction. The only thing he could do for Martha Sipling was remember.

He took another swallow of his drink and looked down the narrow street to where a dark blue car with official plates was driving up. The medical examiner, he thought. What a treat he had in store. Two men in suits—one with a camera—got out of the car and went into the cottage. Tom sat for a few minutes longer, then became aware that he smelled strongly of sweat. He went inside, took a shower, and changed his clothes. At three o'clock Ed and Frances returned from the beach, and he told them only that there had been an accident, and that Mrs. Sipling had been killed. Frances went into semihysterics, but Ed seemed calm enough about it, picking up his book and ensconcing himself upon a chair in the living room. Frances, clucking, went into the kitchen. Things were back to normal, Tom thought.

He went down to his shop, but was unable to concentrate on any work and went back out onto the street. The ambulance and the medical examiner's cars were gone, but now a state police car was parked behind Bret's. Tom walked down the street and found Bret and Stu sitting on Martha Sipling's front steps. Bret was wiping his forehead and neck with a large blue handkerchief and Stu was flapping the tails of his uniform shirt as if to dry his sweat. Stu was pale, Bret was red faced, but both looked weary and unnerved. Bret waved his handkerchief when he saw Tom.

"M.E.—that's the medical examiner, like the coroner?— he says it's definitely of suspicious origin," Bret explained after Tom sat down two steps beneath him.

"Does that mean murder?"

Bret nodded. "Appears so." He twisted his handkerchief

and drops of sweat darkened the wooden steps. "Jesus, look at that, just the thought of it makes me sweat like a pig."

"When's the last time there was a murder in Dreamthorp Bret?" Stu asked in a high, piping voice that always surprise Tom when he heard it.

"Not since I've been chief. Not even since I was a deputy Hell, I think it must've been back in the forties when tha guy killed his wife and then shot himself because he found out she was fooling around. Up on Whittier Avenue—the cot tage is still there."

"We've had some in Chalmers, though," Stu said. Tom thought it sounded as if he were bragging.

"Oh yeah," Bret nodded. "One every four or five years maybe. But, hell, that happens when you get a few thousand people together. Odds are one or two of them's gonna turn out to be a bad apple. But it sure doesn't happen much in Dreamthorp."

"Must be the mountain air," Stu said, forcing a smile.

"Any idea what happened?" Tom asked.

"Well, the state cops are in there now," Bret said. "They've got a lot more stuff than we do when it comes to murder investigations, if that's what this is."

"You saw her," Tom said. "You think there's any othe possibility?"

"No. Not really. But there was no other sign of violence no screens forced or anything. And the back door wa locked?"

"Back *and* front," Tom said, remembering turning th dead bolt to let Bret and Stu in the front.

"Somebody must've killed her," said Stu. "That was th most horrible thing I've ever seen. Must've been a maniac."

"Don't say things like that," Bret cautioned his deputy "You don't want those kind of rumors spreading. Jesus onl knows what the papers are gonna do with this."

As if on cue, a Ford Escort with WJMP-TV logos coatin it came rolling down the street and stopped right in the mid dle in front of the Sipling cottage.

"Hey!" Bret called to the driver. "You can't leave tha there. Pull on over."

The driver shook his head in disgust but did as Bret di rected, which was lucky for Laura Stark, whose Cressid now came up Emerson Avenue. She drove past the Siplin place, saw the police cars and the WJMP car, and waved uneasily to Tom, who smiled thinly and waved back, then pulled her car into the spot in front of her own cottage.

Tom listened for a moment while Diane Sherman, an evening newscaster for WJMP, questioned Bret. Then, as Tom stood up and started home, the woman called after him. "Excuse me," she said. "Sir, were you involved at all?"

"No," Tom said, neither turning his head nor slowing his pace.

Laura was standing next to her car when he reached her place. "Hi," she said, giving him a tentative smile. "What's happening?"

He smiled back. It wasn't hard. She was a pretty woman, Tom thought, tall and broad-shouldered, but she carried her size well and didn't try to hide it like so many others might have. She looked proud. He would have liked to smile more broadly at her, but the situation scarcely warranted it. "Martha Sipling—there's been an accident. She's dead."

Laura's eyes grew large. "God, that's . . . awful. How did it happen?"

"A heavy wooden lid—blanket bin—fell on her." The feeling shot through Tom that he should not lie to this woman, that she would find out the truth sooner or later. "That's the official story, anyway," he added. "The truth is that she was murdered."

"Murdered . . ." It was a whisper that Tom barely heard.

"I found her," he said. "There was no other way it could have happened."

"Do they . . . know who?" She looked scared, Tom thought, and rightfully so. He was scared too.

"No. The state police just got here."

Laura nodded. "Well . . . let me know if you hear anything else."

"I will. But I'm sure there'll be a lot on the news tonight about it. In the meantime, keep your doors locked, huh?"

She nodded grimly. "You know it. Bye."

Laura locked her doors as soon as she got into her house, and closed and locked her windows as well, turning on both the upstairs and downstairs air conditioners. She watched the local six o'clock news, but they didn't add much to what Tom Brewer had told her. "Suspicions of foul play" were as much as the police would admit, but there had been two reports of prowlers in Dreamthorp in the past two weeks, and residents were urged to be on their guard and report anything suspicious to the Chalmers police.

After her Lean Cuisine dinner, Laura worked on a project until nine, then took a bath and climbed into bed, where she read a Wodehouse paperback, hoping that the absurd and hilarious plot intricacies would get her mind off what had happened only two cottages away.

It did not work. The calamities accumulating upon the shoulders of Bingo Little and Bertie Wooster drifted from Laura's thoughts, and the volume drifted shut. There were more important plots to be untangled. She kept imagining different scenarios leading up to Mrs. Sipling's death, and in every one the face of the killer was Gilbert Rodman's, even though she *knew* he was dead, she *knew* he could not possibly have had anything to do with it, she *knew* that if, by some miracle he had not died and had come after her and found out where she lived, that he would not have vented his fury on dull, sweet, ancient Martha Sipling.

No, if Gilbert Rodman, whoever he was, had come for her, he would have been standing behind the door when she walked into her house. He would not have given the grace of a warning by killing a neighbor first.

She put her book on the bedside table and looked at her clock radio. It was only a little after ten, but she thought that if she could sleep she would at least stop thinking about what happened, both today and nine months ago. But when she flicked off the light, she kept seeing Gilbert Rodman's face etched on the inside of her closed eyelids. Her efforts to replace the image finally brought her to thoughts of Tom Brewer.

She had been attracted to him. He was not handsome, but there was a friendly, comfortable ruggedness to his features. She remembered the day she had bumped into him in the lake, and found pleasure in the thought of his grinning face, his wide shoulders, downy with fine, curly hair, dark except for a sporadic touch of gray to hint at his age. Even as he had told her about today's violent death, he had seemed calm, in control. She envied him that.

And as the full and cheerful lineaments of his face replaced the tense and strained ones of Gilbert Rodman, she slowly drifted into sleep, realizing, just for a second before unconsciousness claimed her, how much Tom Brewer reminded her of her father.

> Wherever death looks, *there* is silence and trembling. But although on every man he will one day or another look, he is coy of revealing himself till the appointed time. He makes his approaches like an Indian warrior, under covers and ambushes.
>
> —Alexander Smith, *Dreamthorp*

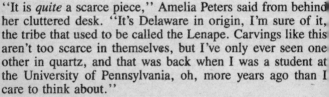

"It is *quite* a scarce piece," Amelia Peters said from behind her cluttered desk. "It's Delaware in origin, I'm sure of it, the tribe that used to be called the Lenape. Carvings like this aren't too scarce in themselves, but I've only ever seen one other in quartz, and that was back when I was a student at the University of Pennsylvania, oh, more years ago than I care to think about."

She chuckled and began to make herself a cigarette with a Laredo machine. Sam Hershey leaned across the desk and picked up the figure with a new respect. Esther sat next to him, looking amused and feeling extremely jealous. "Is it valuable?" Sam asked Amelia Peters.

The curator pushed the trigger of the machine, muttered "Damn," and withdrew something that could charitably be described as a filter cigarette, which she placed in her mouth and ignited before answering. "Oh yes, to a certain extent." She spoke slowly and distinctly but with a guttural growl, and Esther suspected that the woman had once suffered a stroke. "The museum would be willing to buy it for its Pennsylvania Indian collection, if you want to sell it."

Esther groaned inside. So she did want to buy it after all.

Sam would be insufferable for weeks after this, and the more money it brought, the more insufferable he would be. He would tell everyone at their metal detectors' club how he had found something that the William Penn Museum in Harrisburg, mind you, had been willing to pay good money for to put in their *collection!* And what had Esther found lately? Oh, just some coins . . .

"Well, yes," Sam was mumbling. "I *suppose* we'd be willing to part with it, you know, depending on the price."

"Of course." Miss Peters sucked in with such force that a good half inch of her cigarette turned to ash in an instant. "We wouldn't be able to give you much, but your name would be on the tag as the finder."

"My *name?*"

Esther winced as Sam's eyes brightened. A *tag.* A tag in the William Penn Museum. Sam wasn't just thinking money now, he was thinking *immortality.* "How much," Esther said, "are we talking about?"

"Oh," the curator said, "maybe seventy-five dollars."

Sam's eyes lost their sparkle. "Is that all?"

Miss Peters shrugged. "It's a question of demand, Mr. Hershey. There really aren't many private collectors of this sort of thing, and they build their collections mostly by trading items. Now, I'm authorized to go to a hundred, but that's the limit."

"You're authorized," Esther said, smelling the possibility of a more generous bureaucracy. "Does that mean there's a committee or something that could approve more?"

"They could," said Amelia Peters, "if I recommended it, but I would not. In fact, a hundred is pretty high, come to think of it."

"Well," Sam said quickly, "a hundred would be all right with us."

"Fine," said Miss Peters. She began rummaging around her desk top, sliding aside stacks of papers, science fiction paperbacks, and poetry journals. "I know I have some purchase orders here somewhere. . . ."

She found them, filled one out, and asked Sam to sign in the proper place.

"You should receive payment within thirty days. If you don't, don't be alarmed. Sometimes it takes longer. Now . . ." She sat back in her chair and took another drag on her cigarette that burned it down to the filter. "You say you found this near Dreamthorp. Where exactly?"

Sam licked his lips. "Why, uh . . . why do you want to know?"

"Well, it's probably a burial site," Miss Peters replied. "A valid archaeological site. And as such it should be registered and protected."

"You mean," said Esther, "that you . . . *museum* people will go in there then?"

"Of course. Our people will do a dig there. You see, this carving is a burial carving—supposed to keep the dead lying still. Now that area around Dreamthorp, quite frankly, is not known to be a site of any Lenape burials, so if we do find one—that is, if this artifact hasn't been taken from someplace else and dropped or buried where you found it, which is absurdly unlikely—then we have an interesting archaeological discovery here."

"Well, uh . . ." Sam cleared his throat. "Is there any reason that, since Esther and I found it, that we couldn't dig it up ourselves?"

"Yes, there is, Mr. Hershey, a very good reason. You're not trained archaeologists. You'd be likely to do far more harm to the site than any good you could do."

"Oh, but we're very careful, Miss Peters," Sam said, "People give us permission to hunt where they don't give other people because we're so good about the condition we leave the place in."

"There's more to sound archaeological practice than replacing divots, Mr. Hershey. This place must be recorded and protected."

"But then we can't dig there anymore," Esther said.

"That's correct." Miss Peters shuffled through the contents of her desk top until she found her cigarette machine, and slipped a paper tube over the end.

"But that's because it would be protected, right?" asked Esther, who was beginning to smile.

"Yes," said Miss Peters, loading the tobacco.

"But," Esther went on, "if you don't know where it is, then it can't be registered. And if we don't tell you, then you can go jump."

Amelia Peters pushed the trigger, ripping the paper tube open and scattering tobacco shreds like brown snow. *"Blast,"* she whispered, then looked up at Esther. "Not telling us would be a very irresponsible thing to do, Mrs. Hershey."

"Esther . . ." Sam cautioned.

"Is there a law against it? Withholding evidence or something?" Esther said, her smile sharpening into a grin.

"Of course not," Miss Peters said. "This isn't a police state, we can't *force* you to tell us—"

"That's fine then," Esther said, standing up.

"But I would think that as *good citizens,* you would feel *obligated* to," Miss Peters added.

"Well, maybe we'll *think* about it," Esther said. "Come on, Sam."

Sam stood up and looked from one woman to the other in confusion. "I, uh . . . thank you for, uh . . . buying that thing. Um, you'll still put my name on the tag?"

Miss Peters nodded sullenly.

"Oh, great. Well . . . we'll see you." And Sam followed his wife out the office door and down the hall, leaving behind a frowning Amelia Peters.

"Of all the gall," mumbled Esther as they walked past the yellow cinder block walls toward the elevator. "Thinks just like that we'll tell her where that place is, well, she's got another think coming, I'll tell you that. . . ."

"Esther, maybe we should've . . ."

"Oh, don't be silly. Do you know how many Indian burial sites there are around here? Dozens and dozens of them. That stuff she was giving us about this one being so much more important was a lot of hooey, if you ask me. She just wants to lock it up for the museum." She punched the elevator button and turned to confront her husband. "Well, why should *they* get all the glory when we're the ones who found it? And we can dig just as careful as they can. I mean, if we can sift dirt so that we don't put an extra scratch in a *coin,* we sure as heck can avoid breaking some beads or jars or bones or whatever else might be down there. Don't you think?"

The elevator doors slid open and they got on. "I guess so," Sam said. "To tell the truth, I'd really be disappointed if we couldn't dig there again. And that's right—we *are* the ones who found it."

"Sure. And it's public land too. I think. I mean, we probably pay taxes for its upkeep."

"Look," Sam said. "Let's dig, and if we find anything that we think we can't handle—like walls or buildings or something—then we'll call Miss Peters and tell her about it."

"All right, fine. But I don't think we'd find any buildings."

The elevator stopped. They got out, turned right, and walked past the gift shop and through the outside doors. "Look," Sam said. "Is that Charlie Lewis?"

It was. He was walking away from the monolithic archives building with a brown folder tucked under his arm, and waved when he saw them. "Got some information about that thing you found," he said when he was near enough to be heard over the Wednesday afternoon Harrisburg traffic. "Its provenance, so to speak. And I won't even charge you for the many hours of research spent. Next time I lose a gold bar in my backyard, however, I expect you to find it for me gratis."

Sam chuckled. "It's a deal. But you're a little late."

"Late?"

"A curator just bought it for the museum," Esther explained.

"Really?" Charlie sighed. "Well, they've gotten themselves quite a little treasure then. I hope they paid you well."

"A hundred dollars," Sam said.

Charlie nodded noncommittally. "I suppose there's not a huge market for that type of thing. Did they tell you what it was?"

"A burial statue," said Esther.

"Mmm. There's a little more to it than that. It's a totem that's supposed to be buried on top of a grave. To keep the evil spirit within."

"Evil spirit?" Sam asked.

"So the good books said. The thing was meant to be placed over the graves of enemies or murderers, someone that the Indians might not want to come back and annoy them."

"Miss Peters didn't mention that," Sam said.

"Undoubtedly thought the arcane knowledge would be wasted on laymen such as yourselves. I wouldn't take it as a personal affront." Charlie sighed. "So my research is for naught. Oh well, it's always a joy to spend a humid summer afternoon in an air-conditioned library. We old folks have to keep ourselves amused some way, don't we?"

"Speak for yourself, Charlie," Esther said, chuckling.

Then her face grew serious as she thought of something else. "Say, did they find out anything about that killing over at Dreamthorp?"

Charlie's expression of dry humor turned to sobriety. It was a subtle but unmistakable distinction. "No. Nothing yet. They seem to be certain that it was murder now. But they've got no motive and no suspects, apparently."

"Boy, there's been a lot of bad things happening over there the past few weeks," Sam observed, shaking his head in sympathy. "I heard about that fella falling down his stairs last week, too."

"We've had more than our share." Then Charlie's face brightened again. "Maybe you two are responsible."

"What?" Sam said.

"By releasing that evil spirit, of course. Shame on you."

"Oh, Charlie," said Esther Hershey, with a trace of discomfort in her laugh. "That's really nothing to kid about."

"If you can't kid about Indian bogeymen, what *can* you kid about?" Charlie asked.

"I mean . . . the deaths."

" 'Thus in the spring we jeer at Death, though he/Will see our children perish, and will bring/Asunder all that cling while love may be.' " Charlie quoted.

"What?" asked Sam.

"Just James Branch Cabell's way of saying eat, drink, and be merry, for tomorrow we die. If we laugh at death, he won't scare us so much, even though he's bound to have the last laugh."

In their car on the way home, the Hersheys argued over who this Jim Cabell was, remarked several times how strange Charlie Lewis was, but nice, and decided that they would return to the logging site the next weekend.

Summer has adorned my village as gaily, and taken as much pleasure in the task, as the people of old, when Elizabeth was queen, took in the adornment of the Maypole against a summer festival.

—Alexander Smith, *Dreamthorp*

That weekend also saw the premiere of *Arms and the Man* at the Dreamthorp Playhouse, now relocated in the Hall of Culture. The hall was built in 1903, and was still the same sickly yellow that it had first been painted. Coat after coat had gone on over the decades until some residents joked that the building's walls were twice their original thickness.

Over the years the Hall of Culture had played host to thousands of lectures, hundreds of magic lantern travelogues, uncounted chamber music concerts, and a multitude of play readings. But *Arms and the Man* was the first full-scale production ever to grace its Spartan interior, by necessity rather than design. It was not really made for theatrics. A raised platform twenty feet wide functioned as a stage, and there were no provisions for hanging curtains. The lighting instruments were placed on poles a third of the way back, and the audience had to walk around them when they came in and out of the makeshift theatre.

Another problem that created a logistical nightmare for the producers of the summer season was that the Hall of Culture seated only half the number of paying customers that the playhouse had. As proved to be fortunate, the season had not sold out, so advance sales were suspended and the number of performances increased by three a week. The playhouse would still lose money, but hoped to break even once the insurance payments were sorted out.

Still, for all its problems, the Hall of Culture was cozy and comfortable, and its intimacy highlighted the sense of community that was such a large part of life in Dreamthorp. This Saturday night, the twenty-seventh of June, the tragedy of two weeks before was, if not forgotten, at least temporarily misplaced, to be thought of again only alone, perhaps in the dark, just before sleep came.

But now, among the excited murmurs of the audience that crowded the Hall of Culture, the show was the thing on everyone's mind, the show and the new director from New York City, who had directed on *Broadway,* mind you, and the cast, of course, some of whom had been on *television* shows both here and in England.

The hubbub continued as Tom Brewer made his way down the narrow aisle and circumnavigated the stage-left light post. He arrived at his seat in the second row of folding chairs just as the lights blinked on and off to indicate that the show would begin—in another five minutes, if past Dreamthorp Playhouse history was any harbinger of the present.

Tom looked at the empty chair next to him. It was to have been Karen's. He had bought a pair of season tickets, just as he had done for the past seven years, ever since the playhouse had upgraded from local performers to professionals. This was the first year that Susan would not be sitting next to him, but he had thought Karen would. He had asked Ed and Frances if either of them wanted to go with him, but they had declined. Frances found Saturday night sitcoms more to her liking than "that Shaw. I went to one of his plays once, and it was like sitting at a three hour sermon. *My Fair Lady* was the only thing he ever wrote that I *liked.*"

The first act went remarkably well, Tom thought, under the circumstances. The primary difficulty was with exits and entrances. Since there were no wings, the actors had to exit behind five foot wide curtains on either side of the stage and stay there until their next entrance. Tom found it impossible not to wonder what the poor things were *doing* back there, especially when there were several at a time. He thought they had to be standing at attention, exhaling as much as possible in order to all fit. And he could not imagine how anyone made a costume change. It would be, he felt, impossible without rustling the curtains. *The show must go on*, he thought with grim humor. Come death, come destruction, the show must go on.

At the intermission he went outside, where the concessions were operating from tents. He bought an instant coffee, stepped away from the lights toward the trees, and saw Laura Stark standing alone, drinking a lemonade. He smiled at her. "Enjoying the show?" he said.

"What I can see of it," she told him and smiled back. She had a good smile, he thought. Nice, even teeth, very white. "I'm pretty far back. And since there's no incline, there are a lot of heads between me and the stage."

"Why don't you sit with me?" It was out of his mouth before he realized he had said it, but he was not sorry. "I'm up in the second row."

"Is there an empty seat?"

"Yeah. One I bought and paid for, so nobody's going to cruise in for the second act."

"Well . . . sure. Thank you."

Tom was careful not to read anything into her acceptance. After all, there was no reason not to accept.

They watched the rest of the play, and Tom observed Laura, impressed again with how graceful she was for her size. As they sat together he realized that they were really about the same height, but when they had stood talking he had had the impression that he was the taller. She had a wonderful laugh, which he heard many times during the remainder of the play, and occasionally she would turn as she laughed and look at him, as if sharing the joke.

After the bows, they walked out together, and he asked her if she was hungry. She said that she was, a little, and he suggested they go to the Ice Cream Shoppe.

The Ice Cream Shoppe was another institution of Dreamthorp. It served sundaes, sandwiches, and an assortment of beverages, the specialty being lime rickies. At the counter, Laura ordered a small dish of vanilla and a Diet Coke, and Tom asked for a small hot fudge sundae. "My primary vice," he told her, "next to too much beer in the summer."

When the girl handed their orders over the counter, Tom held up a hand when he saw Laura reaching into her purse. "My treat," he said.

But she shook her head. "No, really. I'll pay for mine." He

shrugged and let her. "Thanks," she said when they were sitting down out on the deck. It was a warm night, with just a hint of a breeze to blow the pine branches above them. "Most men give you a hassle when you want to buy your own."

Tom was surprised that she would even mention it. "It's not because you're a woman," he said. "I would've offered if you were a guy."

She smiled. "I'm sorry. I guess you would have at that." She delicately took a small bite of ice cream. "It's funny. Men and women."

"Funny?" he said, hoisting a spoonful of assorted goo.

"The mind games. The possessiveness. It's the same if you work together or whatever. The man always feels he's got to look out for the woman."

Tom nodded. "You're right. It's in the genes, I guess. Generations and generations of . . . what? Possessiveness? Like you said?"

"I think so."

"Well, I promise not to be possessive. After all, I've got no reason to." He chuckled. "Why don't we change the subject?"

"I'm making you uncomfortable."

"No, not at all. It's just that . . . things have been very strange for me the past few months. Relationships."

She eyed him cautiously, as if she were afraid to open wounds. Still, his manner told her that he wanted to talk about it, so she asked. "Marital problems?"

He sighed and set his spoon into his dish. "My wife was killed last winter. An auto accident."

She was sorry she had asked now, but it was too late. "Oh God. That's . . . I'm very sorry. It must be . . . very difficult."

He nodded. "It is, yes."

"I know how you feel," she said, and his expression told her that he must have heard that a hundred times.

"You do?" he said, with a touch of hardness in his tone. "Have you lost someone too?"

She had. Damn it, she had. "Yes. A close friend last year."

"A friend," he replied, as if there were little basis for comparison.

"A very *good* friend," she said emphatically. "It hurt. A lot."

He gave her a small smile but a sincere one. "I'm sorry. I'm sure it did." Then he looked down at her dish and his. "Our ice cream's melting."

She smiled too. "A little less talk and a little more action?"

"Exactly. No more words until my sundae is safely wrapped around my middle, all right?"

She held up three fingers in a scout salute, nodded, and turned her attention to the ice cream. When it was gone she felt full, satisfied, less on her guard.

"So how do you like living in Dreamthorp?" Tom asked her, putting down his spoon for the last time and patting his mouth with his napkin.

"I like it very much," she said. "Even with what's happened the past few weeks."

"A tragedy, an accident, and a murder. Pretty appalling for our little town."

Laura looked around her. People were sitting at the tables in the cool evening air, walking hand in hand down the paths that led through the old chautauqua grounds, talking, smiling, laughing in the night. "But you'd never think anything happened," Laura said. "Look at everyone. I've never been to any place more . . . sylvan, bucolic. It's like Brigadoon."

Tom laughed gently. "No, it's like Dreamthorp. The thorp . . . the village of your dreams." He sighed. "It really is a lovely place, isn't it? Unique. I don't think there's any other place like it on earth."

"You do love it, don't you?"

He looked at her oddly. "Yes. Yes, I do. I can't imagine living anywhere but here now. You stay here long enough you'll feel the same way."

"I suspect that I already do. One thing surprises me though. This place would be an ideal artists' colony, yet you're the only artist I've met who lives here. It seems most everyone else is in business—"

"Or retired," Tom interrupted. "The ideal place to live out your remaining years. At least while you're still mobile. I don't know, maybe artists thrive best under pressure. And there sure isn't much of that here in Dreamthorp."

"The lack of it doesn't seem to bother you."

"I have my own *internal* pressure. Besides," he went on dryly, "my art has not been at its peak lately. I seem to be in a creative rut."

"What do you carve?"

"Birds, beasts, shysters, and quacks, mostly. And I've been getting a lot of commissions for shysters and quacks. Sometimes I think I'd like to shoot one of each and stuff them—use them for models, you know?"

"Let me see your work."

"What?" The request seemed to surprise him.

"I'd like to see your carvings. Not especially your shysters and quacks, but the things you like doing."

"Well, that would be nothing lately," Tom said. "But I do still have a few things that I'm not too ashamed of." He cocked his head at her. "You mean now? Tonight?"

"Not if it's inconvenient," she said. She thought she might have been too blunt and hoped that he wouldn't take the request the wrong way. In fact, now that she had made the suggestion, she almost hoped he wouldn't take her up on it.

"It's not inconvenient," he said. "My parents are staying at my place now, so"—he glanced at his watch—"you'll be forced to meet them. It's only eleven, and Dad always watches the news. My son will probably be in bed. But most of my work is in the cellar anyway. I have a workshop down there. Shall we?"

He stood up, and Laura followed him across the wooden deck, out onto the path, and up Pine Road to Emerson, telling herself not to worry, that nothing could be safer, that going with Tom Brewer to see his carvings was nothing more than an act of friendly interest. It was prefatory to nothing.

As Tom had predicted, his father was watching the news when they arrived. His mother was upstairs in bed. Tom quickly but politely introduced Laura to Ed, and then they went downstairs to his workshop. "The sanctum sanctorum," Tom said, showing her around. "Pretty Spartan, but it's home."

A long workbench crossed the front of the room with a jigsaw and a band saw at one end. A lathe, a drill press, and a circular saw made small islands in the center of the room. On the side away from the stairs was the furnace, and a drafting board and carving bench completed the furnishings.

But it was not the thick platforms supporting the power

tools that attracted Laura's attention. It was rather the dozens of carvings that littered the large room, most of them unpainted. She crossed to the workbench where a figure sat, or rather squatted. It was a foot high and carved from white pine, and she ran her fingers gently over the curves of it. It was human, with oversized hands and feet and crude, brutal features. There was no decoration or elaboration on it.

"Interesting," she heard Tom say behind her, "that you should go to that one when there are all these cute little birds around."

She turned toward him, her hand still on the rough carving. "I've seen carvings of birds before," she said, "though yours are very good. What I *haven't* seen is anything like this."

He stepped next to her and touched the figure himself, with affection, she thought. "It's modeled after some Yugoslavian carvings I've seen. You try to follow the outlines of the piece of wood, rather than change the wood to suit your design. The piece is out of proportion, but it's . . ." He thought for a moment.

"Truer," she said.

"Yes. Truer. More fluid. Faithful to its source."

Laura looked around but saw no other carvings like the figure. "Do you do much of this sort of work?"

"Unfortunately, no. I did that one last fall, just before Susan—my wife—died. I wanted to do some more, but I . . . I couldn't somehow."

Laura walked to the carving bench and looked at a chunk of white oak. It looked vandalized. The corners had been roughly cleaved off, and the marks of the chisel looked more like savage gouges. "Is this something you're working on?" she asked.

"Free form," Tom said. "Just an experiment. Want to see my latest shyster?"

He showed her some of the comic figurines he was doing, along with some birds and a large eagle he was carving for over the mantel of Harris Valley College's president. "I hate to do eagles," he told her, laughing. "Everybody does eagles."

When they went upstairs he showed her a carving of a redheaded woodpecker that sat on the bookcase in the entry. "I don't usually like them painted, but this is one of the first ones I did when I moved to Dreamthorp, so he's got some nostalgic value. I didn't paint it—Bill Singer, another art prof at Harris Valley did it, does all my birds.''

"It's very lovely."

"Well, thanks. When it comes to birds, it's okay."

"There's nothing wrong with carving birds, you know," Laura said. "Even shysters. People enjoy them."

Tom nodded. "Yeah, I guess so. It's just that I'd like to carve something that would make people's hair stand on end instead of making them go, 'Ooo, how *cute.*' "

"Someday you will."

"I hope so. You want a drink or anything?"

"No thanks. It's late."

"Walk you home?"

"Just two houses away. Thanks, but I can make it."

"Are you sure? I mean, after what happened last week . . ."

"It's close. Anything happens, I'll scream."

"Well, I'll stay on the porch for a while anyway."

"All right. Fine."

"Well," Tom said, "I've enjoyed talking with you."

"Me too."

"Do you have any plans for the July Fourth picnic?"

"No, not really. I was planning to go, though."

"Would you like to go together? I'm afraid I have to include my family in the deal, just for as long as we eat."

"Oh, I don't know . . ."

"My mother makes one helluva chicken salad, I will say that for her. And I do a pretty good pasta salad myself. No mixes either. What do you say? You bring the dessert?"

She laughed in spite of herself. He seemed as fresh and ingenuous as a teenager, and it made her feel younger too. "Oh, all right, I suppose so."

"Great. I'll give you a call about the time and everything."

They said good night and she walked down the steps while he stood at the top and watched her go. In the safety of the darkness, she looked back at him standing there in the yellow glow of his porch light and thought how fine he looked, how confident and strong.

But there was something else in him. Sorrow over his wife's death, of course, but anger as well, she thought, not toward her but something else. His family? His work? Life in general? It was so easy to be angry, so hard to be appeased. She had felt that anger herself—first toward her husband, then toward the other man—say rather the monster—who had turned her life into a nightmare from which she was only now waking.

She was almost at the door of her cottage when she heard the footsteps around the side of the house. They were not the steady, firm, menacing footsteps of horror movies, but clumsy scuffling, and Laura wondered if it might be an animal.

But then she remembered what had happened to Mrs. Sipling two houses away, and quickly slipped the key into her lock, went inside, and locked the door behind her. The noise had shaken her, and she immediately took and loaded the gun that she had replaced in the bottom drawer of her gun cabinet when she had learned Gilbert Rodman was dead, and went through both floors, opening closets, looking under beds. She felt foolish as she did it, but also felt relieved when she found nothing. After checking the windows and doors, she began to unload the weapon, but stopped after she had removed the second cartridge. She thought for a moment, then reloaded the gun, and stuck it down behind the cushions of her couch. She went upstairs to bed, and fell asleep thinking of Tom Brewer.

And Tom Brewer was thinking about Laura Stark. As he turned off his porch light and went back inside the cottage, he realized that he had enjoyed being with her in a way that had been impossible with Karen. He had felt no need to impress Laura and in particular to be something—like an age—that he was not. Although her first comments at the Ice Cream Shoppe had led him to suspect that she might be a militant feminist looking for an argument, he changed his mind quickly. She had, he thought, no axe to grind. She was realistic, that was all, a human being who wanted to be treated and respected like one.

But what he had liked most about her was what she had done in his workshop, passing the tools and the birds and the inconsequentialities, and going directly to the stark, primitive figure, the piece that meant more to him than any he had ever done.

Goddamit, but the lady had taste.

He hadn't planned on asking her to go with him to the picnic. It had just come out, and he was glad of it. If he had thought about it too long, he probably would not have had the nerve to ask her. Karen had been different—Karen had come after him. But he already knew Laura Stark well enough to know that she would not be the aggressor. If he wanted a relationship with her, it would have to be his doing, not hers. Yes, he thought, she *was* a lady.

Tom looked in the living room and saw his father asleep in the chair, while the news droned on. He turned down the volume, then went upstairs.

At the top of the steps, Josh's bedroom door was closed before him. He put his ear to it and listened, but heard nothing. Then he knocked softly enough that the boy would hear it if he was awake. There was no answer. Tom turned the knob quietly, pushed the door open a few inches, and saw the familiar mound under the sheet. How much older would the boy have to be, he wondered, before he stopped pulling the sheet over his head, leaving a hole at his mouth to breathe. Tom smiled, remembering that he had done the same thing, but not, he thought, for as long as Josh had stuck to it.

He listened for his son's breathing, but the noises of the night blanketed such small sounds, so Tom turned, closed the door, and went into the bathroom to take a shower, hoping that he could make his son love him again.

The bathroom was humid and warm, and smelled of Jean Naté, the fragrance his mother had worn all her life. He was glad that at least she had been upstairs when he had brought Laura home, though Ed was sure to say something to Frances, and she would grill Tom in the morning about "this *new* girl."

He showered and climbed into his double bed, which always seemed far too large for someone sleeping alone, and thought about "this new girl," about Karen, and most of all about Susan, his wife, who had given him a son, friendship, love, joy, and endless sorrow.

An hour and a half after Tom went to sleep, and an hour after Ed woke up, turned off the television, climbed the stairs, and crawled in next to his gently snoring wife, Josh Brewer crept into his own bedroom from the porch roof, took something heavy from his belt, and placed it in his bottom drawer. Then he tiptoed to the bathroom, washed himself, and got into bed, thinking about what he had seen, and what he had done.

He cried himself gently to sleep.

> . . . Then the woods reddened, the beech
> hedges became russet, and every puff of
> wind made rustle the withered leaves. . . .
> —Alexander Smith, *Dreamthorp*

Sunday was bright and fair in Dreamthorp, too bright and
fair for most of the residents. It had been a dry spring, and
was turning out to be a drier summer. The layers of pine
needles that covered the forest floor no longer had the familiar spongy feel underfoot. Instead there was a crispness, as
though one were walking on the dried, brittle corpses of insects, hearing the thin carapaces crack by the dozen with
every step. No one had heard the rush of water in the rain
gutters for weeks, and, although the leaves of the trees were
still green, a slight yellow tint had stolen over them. The
water level of the lake was down, and layers of silt and clay-
colored mud that had not been seen for many years were
uncovered. Ends of long submerged branches finally broke
the water, a pale, unhealthy brown, like the arms of drowned
slaves.

The dryness made the air electric, heavy with static both
real and imagined. The recent deaths had set the town on a
fine edge, and the weather did nothing to dull it. The sun
baked and dried soil, leaves, and flesh, and people worried
and sweated. Martha Sipling was pieced together and put
under the ground in Grubb Church Cemetery, five miles away
from Dreamthorp, and her cottage was locked up by the police, who had learned nothing from their investigations. Even
under the trees, the temperature inside the closed-up house

rose to one hundred and ten degrees, sealing the smell of blood inside, making it seep into the rugs, the drawn curtains, the very wood of the house itself.

And while the Sipling cottage and all of Dreamthorp burned in the Sunday morning sunlight, Dubuque, Iowa, was drenched with rain, rain that the man who called himself Gilbert Rodman could hear as he sat in a supply closet in a cheap hotel and waited for a whore to wake up.

He had seen her the night before as he wandered through a section of town with a higher than average number of bars, small diners with stuttering neon signs, warehouses, and transient hotels. She had been standing in front of an arcade, wearing a pair of hot pants fifteen years out of style for everyone but working-class hookers. Her hair was long and black, her complexion dark, her cheeks mottled by acne scars. Wrinkles fanned out from her dark brown eyes. Her large breasts were jammed into a skimpy halter, and her arms and neck were covered with turquoise jewelry.

She looked so much like the Great Bitch that he wanted to gut her where she stood.

But no. That would have been foolish. It was not his way, had never been his way. He was slow, and careful, and methodical. Only by being all those things had he never been caught, never even been confronted, suspected, arrested.

And he would not be this time.

He would wait until everything was safe. Then he would do what he wanted, whatever he wanted with the Great Bitch who had used his balls and the Lesser Bitch who had destroyed them.

Destroyed them! . . .

His fingers tightened on the handle of the ghetto blaster he was carrying, and he made himself relax, made calmness flow into him. He thought about the music and glanced down at the box.

It was a cheap one, a bottom-of-the-line Sony with no Dolby or metal tape capacity, but what the hell, the price had been right. Cherry and Hod sure weren't going to use it again. Their tapes were shit though, all that country crap. But he'd found a record shop that stocked a decent selection of jazz cassettes and bought several with the money he'd taken from Hod's wallet. He had needed a place to crash for the night, asked a down-and-outer on the street where he could get a cheap room, and the rest was history. As soon as he saw the turquoise lady, he knew there would be no sleep for him that night.

It was eleven o'clock when he spotted her. He watched her for a few minutes before he decided what to do. He didn't want to take her to a hotel. He wanted someplace where he could *hear* her. He had fixed Cherry so she couldn't yell, just in case a cop stopped to check out the rig and heard her. But this time he wanted to hear it, to be in a place where the turquoise lady could scream and scream and scream her head off, and no one would ever hear a damn peep. That would be rare and rich and satisfying. He had noticed a string of warehouses a few blocks back. That would be perfect. She might think twice about turning a trick in a warehouse, but he had enough money to persuade a cheap whore. Hod's wallet had contained over four hundred dollars.

Gilbert had made up his mind to approach the woman, when a man dressed in a polyester suit, a string tie, and cowboy boots walked up to her and began to talk. Though Gilbert, from his position across the street, could not hear what was said, he quickly figured it out when the woman nodded, rubbed the man's leg with the hand not holding her voluminous straw purse, and they both turned and walked down the street.

Gilbert crossed the street then, and fell into step several yards behind them, listening over the sound of traffic, rock music, and shouts.

". . . for an all-nighter?"

"You got enough for all night?"

"You mean equipment or money?"

A car badly in need of a muffler drove by then, and Gilbert lost the cowboy's words, but the woman laughed and squeezed the arm that she was clinging to. All-nighter, Gilbert thought. That was too bad, but there was nothing he could do about it at this point. He could follow them, that was all, and wait until the man left, wait until she came out the next morning or afternoon. Or evening. But he *would* wait.

The pair went into the Hotel Excelsior at the end of the block. Gilbert waited outside, watching them through the fly-specked glass door as they went through the false ceremony of registering. An elderly, bald man took a key from one of the dozens of hooks on the wall, and handed it to the man, who gave him several bills in exchange and then led the way upstairs.

After they rounded a landing, Gilbert went in and asked the desk clerk if they had a Mr. Fenton staying there. While the desk clerk looked at the register, Gilbert examined the key board and, although he could not exactly determine which of the keys had been taken, he could see that it was on the third floor—either room 305, 307, or 309.

The desk clerk told Gilbert that there was no Mr. Fenton in residence, Gilbert thanked him and walked out. Fifteen minutes later he came back into the hotel through the rear door and climbed the steps to the third floor, where he listened at the doors of rooms 305, 307, and 309. In 309 he heard the sounds of lovemaking—sincere on the man's part, wholly false on the woman's.

Across the hall from 309 was a door with SERVICE stenciled on it in chipped and faded letters. It was unlocked. Inside was a large sink, a wet mop and bucket, and a locked cabinet. The closet reeked of urine, but the floor was clean, so Gilbert sat down with his backpack and boom box beside him, and waited for a half hour, when he once again listened at the door of 309 and heard snoring. A smile on his face, he left the Hotel Excelsior with his box and his backpack and headed toward the row of warehouses.

Two hours later, he returned empty-handed to the hotel and went back into the supply closet, where he sat on the floor, crossed his arms on his knees, and rested his head on them. He slept fitfully, waking each time there was a noise in the hall, and looking through the door to see what had caused it. At no time did the door of room 309 open.

When he was able to enter a thin sleep, his dreams were thick and dark, and he saw his mother dying in the bed, the same bed to which she had taken him over and over again, dying in the bed in her bedroom, because there was no money for the hospital, and what could the hospital do for her that had not been done? Now there was only the dying. The dying and the truth—

You did this It was you

He had learned the truth months before, had heard the word *motherfucker* in school, and laughed at it, but laughed the wrong way, and the others had looked at him and said things, and he had said things back, things that had not sounded right to them, and then they had known, somehow they had known, and accused him, and he had said more, and then they all got quiet, and the guidance counselor had called him into his office and asked him questions using words that he didn't understand, but the guidance counselor understood what *he* was saying all right, but by that time his mother was already dying, lying in her bed, her black hair like a frame around her face. She was not pale, his mother never was pale, but she was different, less ruddy, a sickly yellow-orange color that reminded him of fruit just on the verge of rotting.

You did this you put it in me and you poisoned me, my own son poisoned me, put it in his mother

gave me the cancer

He awoke just before dawn, to a gentle sound that slowly washed away his mother's dying words, words that he heard over and over again, hundreds of miles away from her, from where he had left her to die alone, while he had run away from New Orleans, gone out into the world to become Gilbert Rodman, keeping his first name, taking the second from an obscure and unfinished story by Poe about an explorer who went west.

Rodman.

He would be a Rodman.

What was that noise, he wondered, and then, as wakefulness came to him, he realized it was rain. He heard it striking the roof several floors overhead, heard the surge of it as it poured down unseen spouting in the walls. He stood up and stretched his muscles, splashed rusty water on his face from the sink. Then he sat down again and waited until the door of 309 opened.

At 7:30 the man in the cowboy boots came out and walked down the stairs. Gilbert waited another two hours until the turquoise lady left. At a safe distance, he followed her out onto the street. The rain was coming down hard, and he stepped next to her as she was standing under an awning waiting for the light to change.

"You working?" he said, with a hopeful smile.

She turned and looked at him coldly. "Not this morning, honey." Her voice was rough, abraded by vice.

"Aw, come on now," Gilbert said in his best aw-shucks, country boy manner. "That's why I hate workin' the damn night shift. You pretty ladies do the same thing, and by the time I'm ready to cut loose, you're all too tired.''

"You got that right, pal." The light changed, but she didn't cross the street.

"I could make it worth your while. Say, twenty-five bucks." Gilbert started low. He didn't want to look too anxious.

"Honey, that wouldn't get you a handjob." She started to move from under the awning, and Gilbert put a hand on her arm to stop her.

"How much then? For an hour of your time?"

She turned and looked at him closely. She was older than he had first thought. That was good. He wanted her to look older. "What did you have in mind?" She wasn't friendly, not at all. That was good too.

"Oh, you know, the usual." Gilbert grinned shyly. "Maybe some of that . . . *French* stuff."

"Blowjob," she said, making it sound like one syllable.

"Well, uh, yeah. I'd like that. And, you know, the regular stuff too. You know, the, uh . . .''

"Fucking." She sighed, and Gilbert could smell her breath. He was sure she hadn't brushed her teeth that night. "Sixty bucks," she said.

Gilbert shook his head uncertainly. "That's an awful lot."

"Overtime pay, honey." She smiled at him, showing teeth that were white at the tips and yellow at the gum. "You'll enjoy it."

"Yeah," Gilbert said, chuckling. "I guess I will at that."

"You wanta go to the Excelsior? I get a deal there."

"No, let's go over to my place," Gilbert said.

"Where's your place?"

"About four blocks over. On Lexington."

"What? That's all warehouses and shit down there."

"I got a place in one. I'm a watchman."

She looked at him oddly but shrugged. Jesus, Gilbert thought, the bitch was stupid. But that was good, that was fine, that made it all the easier. "It's raining," she said. "We have to walk?"

It was his turn to shrug. "You see any cabs?"

He didn't have an umbrella, so he got a *USA Today* from a machine and held it over their heads as they walked.

When they were half a block away from the warehouse

Gilbert had found the night before, the woman stopped walking. Gilbert, still holding the paper, took a couple of steps away from her before he stopped. "What's the matter?"

She shook her head. The rain had diminished to a fine mist, and her black hair shone. "I don't know," she said. "This don't feel right."

"Aw, come on," Gilbert said. "Look, can I help where I live? I mean, you got a penthouse yourself, you're so picky? Really, I got a nice little apartment down in the basement. That place right there." He pointed to a huge building of weathered brick. TYLER BEARINGS was dimly visible on the side, like ghost letters. "Come on. Please?" He tried to make it sound innocent, like a poor schmuck who goddamit *never* got laid, and wasn't it her *duty*, as a professional, to ease this poor, horny guy's pain?

She thought for a moment, then nodded. "Okay. Seventy bucks."

"Seventy? . . ." Gilbert didn't give a damn. He would have promised her a thousand. He knew he would get it all back. But he had to pretend to be concerned. "I thought you said sixty."

The turquoise lady shook her head. "I changed my mind. Seventy."

Gilbert gave her a sheepish grin. "Well . . . okay. Seller's market. But I hope you're good.

"I will be." She followed him.

The night before, Gilbert had gone into the warehouse through a window and had unlocked the door through which he now led the woman. The room they entered was huge, the girders of the ceiling hidden in the darkness above. What little light there was came through the dusty, translucent windows that ran down one wall of the warehouse. The place was empty except for a blanket in the exact middle of the room. Cherry and Hod's boom box sat beside it. The rain had begun to fall heavily again, and its impact on the metal roof of the warehouse sounded like pellets of lead.

Gilbert closed the door. The turquoise lady looked around uncomfortably. "I want to do it here," Gilbert said.

"Here? In this place? Kiss my ass!" The anger hid fear, Gilbert knew it.

"I was hoping you'd kiss mine." He held up a hand. "I'm

just kidding, okay? I mean, about kissing my ass. I really do want to do it here, I'm not kidding about that.''

"Christ, you mean—on that *blanket*?''

"Is your price going up again?''

"Hell, yes! Look, buddy, I don't want any part of—''

"A hundred dollars,'' Gilbert said calmly. "That's all I've got. Call it a whim, okay? I mean, I happen to like open spaces, you know?'' There was no way out for her now. He was toying with her. "No shit. A hundred bucks. Hell, it's a clean blanket, look.''

She started to walk toward the blanket. Gilbert followed.

"I've even got music. See?'' He pressed a button on the box and the sounds of Thelonious Monk's *Misterioso* came out.

The turquoise lady looked at Gilbert, mistaking the excitement in his face for sexual readiness. She shrugged. Gilbert thought she shrugged a hell of a lot. But he would break her of that. It would be hard to shrug without shoulders. "Okay,'' she said. "What the hell. But the money first, huh?''

He nodded, took five twenties from his pocket, and handed them to her. She put them in her handbag. "You, uh, want to get undressed now?''

"Sure.'' She kicked off her shoes, slid the hot pants off her hips, then pulled her blouse up over her head without unbuttoning it. She wore no bra. "How about you?'' she asked him.

"I want to watch you first,'' he said. "The panties too. Leave the jewelry on. I like that Indian jewelry. It reminds me of somebody I knew. She was part Indian. Seminole. Almost as pretty as you.''

She was smiling a little now, getting into it, Gilbert thought. They all did. It was what they all wanted, whether they sold it or gave it away. They wanted it.

"Okay,'' she said, standing naked in front of him. "Your turn.''

"Don't rush,'' Gilbert said. "I want this to take a *long* time. Now, lie down,'' he told her, and she did as he asked. He could feel the handle of the knife pressing against his ankle. The music played on, cool and sweet. He knelt on the blanket beside her, his right hand resting on his pants cuff. "You do it,'' he said. "Take them off me.''

She smiled wryly, wriggled her body so that she could reach his pants front, undid his belt, and unzipped his jeans.

"That's good," he said huskily. "Now. Put your hand in there. Touch me."

The turquoise lady licked her lips, and her heavy jewelry shifted across her breasts as she moved. She lifted a cupped hand, touched his belly, slipped beneath the waistband of his underpants. The music whined, she lost her smile, reached farther in, deeper.

Her face went the yellow-orange color, the same color the Great Bitch's face had worn when she was dying.

"Oh, no," Gilbert whispered to her. "You found out my secret."

Her mouth opened wide. Her hand froze.

"What a shame," Gilbert told her. "What a shame. You found out my secret."

Her body shook. The knife came out. The rain came down.

Death is terrible only in presence.
  —Alexander Smith, *Dreamthorp*

That afternoon, Sam and Esther Hershey's drive to Dream-thorp had been unpleasantly paranoid, with Sam repeatedly expressing the opinion that they were probably under surveillance by the state police, and wouldn't it be better to wait for a few weeks until the "cops take the heat off."

"Sam," Esther told him again as they walked across the site of the old sawmill, "the museum commission doesn't have money to hire policemen to follow people around. You're just being foolish."

"Well, I don't want to get arrested," Sam mumbled.

"We're not going to get arrested. Now where do you think we ought to dig?"

"I still think we should have brought the metal detectors."

"The Indians didn't *have* anything metal, Sam."

"I mean as *camouflage*. Anybody sees us digging here will get suspicious."

"There's nobody to see. Now why don't we dig where you found the statue. Where was that anyway?"

"Over here, I think," Sam said, trying to remember. "I covered up the hole pretty good, but I think it was near this tree." He stepped over to a thick-boled white pine that had survived the depredations of the woodcutters, and dug his shovel into the earth. "Yeah, I thought so. The ground's pretty soft here on top."

Sam began to dig in earnest then, while Esther stood and

watched. "Anything I can do?" she asked after a few minutes.

"No. Maybe you can dig a little when I get tired."

"I think you ought to dig more carefully."

"What do you mean, more carefully?" Sam panted, pushing down hard on the turned step, hearing a grinding noise as the blade struck stone.

"Well, what that Miss Peters at the museum said. About breaking things. There might be pottery or beads or who knows what down there, and you might break it."

"I'm not going to break anything. Doggone it, I can hardly get through this rock as it is."

"Rock?"

"Yeah. We've never dug down this far before. Lotsa rock under here. I guess the soft stuff on top is from all the layers of rotting trees and stuff." He grunted again as the shovel struck rock, then knelt and tugged a fist-sized rock from the bottom of the small hole he had made. He tossed it into the bushes.

Esther sat on a stump and watched him some more. "You know what you need?" she asked after seeing him struggle with increasingly larger rocks. "A digging iron."

"We don't *have* a digging iron," Sam said, pulling a red handkerchief from his hip pocket and wiping his face.

"We do at home."

"Doesn't do us much good here, does it?" said Sam, with as much sarcasm as he was ever likely to muster.

"I could go get it. Only take half an hour."

Sam exhaled strongly and leaned on the shovel. His face was red. "You know where it is?"

"The garage. Right inside the door."

Sam nodded. "Okay, go. I can't keep pulling these stones out of here piecemeal. It'd be a lot easier to break them up." He tossed her the car keys, and she brushed the dirt off them. "I'll just start digging on the surface right around here. I can't go any deeper without the iron."

She waved good-bye and started up the trail to where they had parked the car. Sam, left alone, sat on the stump where Esther had stationed herself, and brushed the dirt from his hands. There had been so little rain that the earth was dry, and he blew his nose to clear the dust from it. He pressed his shoulders back to try and ease the tightness in his chest then stood up again, grabbed his shovel, and went back to the hole he had begun. He looked at it with exhaustion, then stepped a few feet nearer to the massive pine, and started to dig in its shadow.

A few inches down, he heard the subtle scrape of the blade hitting something that he knew was not stone. He tapped tentatively for a moment, then fell to his hands and knees and dug in the dirt like a badger until his fingers contacted something roughly textured but regular in shape.

Sam pulled it from the ground, and groaned as he saw that it was only a small spike, about five inches long and as thick as a finger. The point, though rusted, was still sharp. He wondered if antique spikes were worth anything, and loosely placed it into a knot in the pine so that he could find it later.

He continued to dig shallow holes all around the trunk of the pine tree, scraping away the topsoil and digging down until his shovel hit stone, then moving on. As he dug, he thought he heard the wind gather strength in the treetops, and hoped that it meant rain. It would mean that he would have to come back another day, but he was tired of digging and growing discouraged as well.

But when he paused and looked around him, he saw that the limbs of the trees were not shaking in a breeze, and the leaves did not tremble. He felt no wind at all. So why, he wondered, was he still hearing that soft rustling sound, like pine boughs in a gentle wind?

Then he looked up at the pine tree beneath which he stood, and his breath caught like ice in his throat.

The limbs were moving, but not with the motion of the wind or the swaying of the tree. They were moving independently of one another, like thick, brown serpents or long, dark arms reaching for him, for Sam Hershey, and he could not move, could not run away from them.

The last rational thought he had was that this was not real, this was impossible, this was a dream. But then the pain began, began and would not end, and the pain convinced him of its reality. Pain was real. No matter how much else was nightmare, the pain was real.

And the pain was endless. The pain was black and white and red and cold and hot. The pain was the texture of the pine bark against his flesh, the sharp needles grasping him, the spike . . .

The spike.

The pain was being driven, being made to run, and as he ran, feeling himself grow heavier with every step but somehow growing lighter as well, becoming less every time he made a circle around the tree . . .

Becoming less.

And himself, what he was, flowing away from him, and he lost himself, until something stopped him, pushed him into the tree, and now the pain was the worst of all, the pain growing so big and black and red that the pain was the world, the world where he would live forever after, and he slid down now, slid down the tree, but the tree was no longer rough and brown, no, now the tree was pale and pink and streaked with red, the tree was soft and wet and slippery, and he knew that the pain was the tree, and he was the pain, and he was the tree forever.

Esther returned fifty minutes after she had left. The digging iron was not behind the garage door where she had thought it was, and she had to spend some time looking for it. She finally found it in the rafters of the garage, and had to climb up on a wooden box to reach it. It was heavier than she had remembered, and when it tipped downward, she was unable to hold on to it. The sharp end of the iron struck the garage floor and put a large crack in the cement. Sam would surely be annoyed about that, she thought, and hoped that he would have found something by the time she returned to the grove so that he would be in good spirits when she told him of the mishap.

She was humming when she entered the grove, but stopped when she saw Sam lying on the ground twenty yards away, his back to her. At first she thought the exertion had given him a heart attack, but then she noticed that the trunk of the tree beside which he lay seemed coated with something strange. No, not coated, but *wrapped,* wound around like a thick, wet, grayish-pink ribbon. A ribbon. Attached to Sam. And the other end, was it attached to that nail in the tree, that big nail?

Numb, she walked closer. Even a few feet away, she could not determine what it was that encircled the tree. She had never seen anything like it before. Even when she stepped around Sam's body and saw the red, gaping crater of his abdomen, even when she started to scream, she still did not know what it was. Even when the hikers heard her and found her and got help, when she was taken away in the ambulance, still screaming with no voice left to scream, she still did not know. She had never before seen her husband's, or anyone's, viscera.

> He jested, that he might not weep.
> —Alexander Smith, *Dreamthorp*

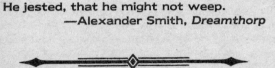

Tom Brewer sat on his front porch and swung back and forth in the old metal glider. His mother was cleaning out the pantry, his father was sitting in the living room reading every word of the latest issue of *History,* and his son was watching, or was pretending to watch, *Star Trek* in his bedroom. The evening was hot and dry, the beer tasted flat, and Tom was bored and edgy. Every time he heard a car, he looked down the street to see if it was Laura Stark's, but it never was. God, he thought, what a workaholic she must be. Even if he did see her car coming, he didn't know what he would do—go down and talk to her? He felt the need to talk to somebody other than his parents, other than his uncommunicative son.

As if in answer to his prayer, he saw Charlie Lewis walking down Emerson, coming the opposite way from his house. Tom waved, and when Charlie reached Tom's stairs, he came up them and sat on the glider. "Things are getting worse," Tom said.

"They are. That's why I'm here."

"Huh?"

"Collecting money for the Save the Old Farts Foundation." His words were as dry as the air.

"What are you talking about?"

"Donations for security cops," Charlie said. "It seems that Pancho and Cisco over in Chalmers can't keep the homicidal maniacs off our backs, so we're taking the law into our own gnarled and wrinkled hands. There's an agency in Harrisburg where we can get guys for fifteen dollars an hour."

"Just at night or around the clock?"

"Well, since Sam Hershey was killed in broad daylight, I hardly think just a midnight patrol would do much good."

"They can't patrol the woods, though," Tom said.

"You think anybody will be in the woods after this?"

"Good point." Tom cleared his throat. "What the hell happened anyway?"

Charlie leaned back and looked up at the porch roof. "Bret Walters told me all about it. I think he wanted to share the horror so that if he spread it around it might not be so strong in himself. It must have been terrible."

Tom glanced at the screen door to make sure no one else was listening. "Go on. The news didn't say much about what happened. They did say 'mutilated,' though."

"That doesn't begin to touch it." Charlie turned and looked at Tom. "Bret said that Sam Hershey's small intestine was wound around that big old pine tree."

"What? You've got to be kidding or Bret was kidding *you.*"

"God's truth. I've never seen Bret pale before, but this did it."

"Jesus, how the hell—"

"You want to hear this?"

"*Yes,* I want to hear it."

"You want to get an old man a drink first? For his heart?"

Tom went into the kitchen and came out with two Jack Daniel's on the rocks. Charlie drank half of his in one swallow. "His navel—and the skin around his navel—had been torn out, and nailed to the tree—"

"Charlie—"

"Nailed to the tree with an old spike. His intestine was wound around it for its whole length. Three times around, Bret said. And that's a thick tree." Charlie's voice was beginning to rasp, and he took another swallow. "And the other end was still attached to Sam Hershey."

Tom feverishly tried to comprehend the physical logistics, as if imagining the logic of the act itself could help him deal with the madness behind its motivation. "But how could anyone . . . *do* that?"

"I don't know. But Sam did."

"*Sam* did? What do you mean?"

"I mean that Sam Hershey walked around that tree himself. *After* he was nailed to it. His footprints were in the blood."

"You can't mean that it was suicide."

"No. Bret said the medical examiner thought that he was *driven* around the tree. His body was bruised and lacerated. And there was blood and bits of . . . of flesh on some of the branches, like someone bent them down and was hitting Sam Hershey with them." Charlie shook his head. "I've never heard of anything so . . . ungodly."

"Sweet Jesus . . ." Tom muttered. "Who else knows about this?"

"Well, Bret told me, with very little urging. Like I said, though, I suspect that he had to tell somebody about it just to help get it out of his system. And I've told you, because I knew you could take it, after what happened with Martha Sipling. But the details are going to be kept secret. It's been reported as murder, sure enough, but unless the *National Enquirer* gets hold of it, that's all most people are going to know."

Tom smiled grimly. "So much for bucolic rusticity."

"Bet your damn life on it," Charlie said. "So, aside from living in a sylvan village where a homicidal maniac who makes Jack the Ripper look like the Tidy-Bowl Man is terrorizing the populace, how's life been treating you?"

Tom couldn't laugh. He shrugged instead. "Going though changes."

"Woman changes?"

"That's part of it." He tried to keep his mind on the conversation but could not drive the image of Sam Hershey out of his mind.

"You seeing my neighbor? I heard you two were spotted sharing an ice cream together."

"We had a talk."

"Better be careful. Here in Dreamthorp, lesser things have led to shotgun weddings. Does this mean it's off between you and your coed cutie?"

Tom was slightly amused, slightly annoyed. "Do you know you can be a pretty nosy old man?"

"One of the perks of the elderly, being nosy. It's in the Constitution." Charlie spun his ice around in his glass, tipped it back, and sucked on a cube. "How's Josh these days?" he asked out of the side of his mouth.

"Josh is . . . Josh. Not much change."

"I'd have thought that your . . . separation from your young female friend would have buoyed him considerably."

"Not especially."

"Give him time, Tom."

"He's a good worker. At the Mobil. Ted told me. He said he's real pleased with Josh."

"He's a nice kid. A little confused now, that's all. He's got to put his life back together. That's a hard job for a young-ster."

"It ain't that easy for us old guys either," Tom said.

Nor was it easy for a woman, particularly when she felt that she had never had her life together to begin with.

Laura arrived home at 8:30, just before dark. Darkness always came earlier under the trees of Dreamthorp, and she had to poke her key at the lock several times before it slipped in. She entered the house, turned on the lights, checked the rooms to make sure that she was alone, poured herself a drink, and began to worry.

She worried about the lunatic who had killed Sam Hershey and, probably, Mrs. Sipling; she worried about the new ac-count the company had landed—a chain of Philadelphia-based auto supply shops; and she worried about herself, the way she thought, the things she did and didn't do. Finally she threw a Lean Cuisine in the microwave and turned on the TV. A Clint Eastwood movie was on, and she ate while she watched the Man with No Name clean up the vermin of Italy's version of the old west. At ten o'clock, when the movie was over, she went upstairs, took a shower, and walked na-ked into her bedroom.

The bedroom shade was up only two inches to let in a little fresh air, but Laura crossed the room in the dark and lowered it. As her fingers fumbled for the light switch, she heard a scuffling sound outside. She froze, then knelt by the window, and pulled back the shade, just far enough to see out.

Someone was there. In what she called her backyard, a piece of earth so steeply pitched that one could not easily stand on it, a dark figure moved against the deeper darkness of the ground. It moved slowly, going up the hill toward the back of her lot, pausing, then moving again, now slipping, catching itself, moving higher up. Now it was almost on the level of her bedroom window, though thirty feet away.

She did not turn on the light. Instead she found the back of her bedroom door, took her bathrobe from the hook, and slipped it on. Then she went into the guest room across the hall and took a .22 semiautomatic target pistol from the case that sat on top of the dresser. She loaded it with a filled clip, and went back into her bedroom, but when she looked out into the darkness she no longer saw the figure.

Laura waited, but nothing moved. She listened, but heard nothing.

Gilbert? Are you still alive?

It was absurd. Of course he wasn't. He was dead, and nothing was going to change that. That there was a madman in Dreamthorp was a given, but there were, regrettably, a multitude of madmen in the world. The beast called Gilbert Rodman had no corner on the market.

Laura looked and waited, but nothing changed. She reached behind the blind, lowered and locked the window, and turned on the light. The telephone sat on the bedside table, her lifeline to the world, and she picked it up and dialed Tom Brewer's number. After the fourth ring, she heard the handset lift and Tom's voice say hello.

"Tom, this is Laura. Laura Stark."

He sounded happy to hear from her. "Yeah, how *are* you?"

"Well, a little spooked just now. There was somebody prowling outside my place."

His voice became edged with steel. "Front or back?"

"Back, but—"

"I'll be right over."

"No, they're gone now, whoever it was. There's no need."

"They may still be around."

"Really, Tom, it's all right. I've got a gun." She chuckled. "Several guns."

"This is nothing to fool with, Laura. There's somebody very nasty on the loose around here."

"I know. But really, I didn't want you to come and rescue me."

"What *do* you want then?" His voice was mild, inquisitive, not at all accusatory.

"I just . . . wanted to talk to you."

They talked. They talked for well over an hour about food and theatre and films and places they had both been; they talked about San Francisco and New Orleans and Manhattan; they talked about Seattle and Baltimore and Philadelphia.

They talked about Chicago.

Unsuspected, this idea of death lurks in
the sweetness of music . . .
—Alexander Smith, *Dreamthorp*

And just as Tom Brewer and Laura Stark were talking about
Chicago, a plumbing supplies salesman pulled to the side of
the Dwight D. Eisenhower Parkway and let Gilbert Rodman
out of his car. Within a few minutes, Gilbert was on West
Van Buren, walking east toward the Loop. He found a cheap
hotel and ate his meals at the counter of a nearby diner. It
took him two days to gather the courage to look up the name
in the phone book.

It was there. Daniel H. Vernon. The address was listed as
well. He put a coin into the slot and dialed. A woman answered.

"Danny there?" Gilbert asked. He made no attempt to
disguise his voice. No one would recognize it.

"Danny's playing tonight." She sounded tired and
grouchy.

"Playing where?"

"The Blue Light, Christ, where he always plays. Who the
hell is this?" Gilbert hung up. He found an address for the
Blue Light, then hailed a cab.

The Blue Light, true to its name, had a blue light hanging
outside the door. It helped disguise some of the dirt on the
sidewalk. The name of the club was also spelled out in blue
neon in the front window, along with Budweiser in red. A
worn-looking card sat on an easel in the window. It read, The
Al Joss Quartet—Appearing Nightly.

It cost Gilbert two dollars to get in, and he sat at the bar and ordered a beer. Only after he drank half of it did he look toward the tiny stage, where the Al Joss Quartet was playing. They were halfway through an up-tempo version of Dexter Gordon's "Bikini," and sounded cool and together. The drummer, a middle-aged black man with several days growth of gray whiskers, was setting a firm, steady rhythm, while the pianist, a white-haired white man, was doing wonders in the upper half of the keyboard. The bass man, black as night, was slapping the strings like a baby's bottom, and the alto sax man, not playing, had his back to the audience. The light hit his hair, a blue-eyed soul "do," and shone on it like a nimbus.

When he finally turned and began to play, the notes starting down as low as dirt and just as rough, Gilbert recognized his father immediately. He hadn't seen him for fifteen years, but there was no mistaking the trademark fright wig of hair, now slathered generously with gray or the bump in the nose from where it had been broken by a Storyville beer bottle when Gilbert was four.

And even if the man had looked totally different, there was no mistaking the sound of his sax. It wailed like a woman, Gilbert thought, like a woman getting what she wanted, what *all* women wanted. It screamed in pain and ecstasy, shouting its fulfillment, its destiny, to the world. Ever since he'd been small, the sound of his daddy's saxophone had always made him feel funny down there. Even now, with nothing there at all, he still had the feeling.

He should have known all along that his daddy could save him.

His mother had told him, years before, that "the bastard" had run off to Chicago, and he could go and damn him anyway. Gilbert decided then that he would go and visit his father when he was older, go and listen to him play his saxophone again, and maybe his father would teach him to play, to make the kind of sounds that drove people crazy, but *wonderful* crazy.

But then he became a motherfucker. He fucked his father's wife, and that was wrong because they told him so. He could prove it was wrong because his mother had died from it, hadn't she? After that, he knew he could not face his father, not ever again, and whenever his wanderings took him through Illinois, he always stayed away from Chicago. He thought about Chicago as the ancient explorers thought about the places on the map that said, Here There Be Dragons.

But things were different now. What had gotten him into trouble in the first place was gone. The Lesser Bitch had taken it, destroyed it forever, so that he could never betray his father with it again. So couldn't he talk to him now? Couldn't everything be forgotten and forgiven, now that he had paid so great a price?

His mouth was dry, so he finished his beer and ordered another while the quartet played ''Lady Be Good.'' They segued into ''Moon Rays,'' and then took a break. When his father and his golden saxophone disappeared behind a curtain at the left of the stage, Gilbert finally looked around the club.

It was racially split between blacks and white, though most people sat with those of their own race. The crowd was quiet and older. Gilbert thought he might be the youngest person there, though he did see one table of yuppies in their late twenties, whose too-studied dress and loud manner suggested to Gilbert that they were slumming or at least not regulars. The crowd seemed to be there for the music, not the drinking, for there was a sense of quiet waiting as they sat and sipped their drinks, most of them beers or tall cocktails.

No one spoke to Gilbert except the bartender and then only to ask him if he was ready for another beer. As he sat, he eavesdropped on the conversations around him and found that they were either about women or music. But it was mostly music, and the music was jazz. He caught the names of Coleman and Coltrane, Gillespie, Miles, and Bird, along with mentions of more recent artists—Weather Report, Oregon, Stanley Jordan—the list of musicians under discussion was encyclopedic. He thought of joining in but felt unaccountably shy, so he drank his beer and waited, like the others.

Five minutes later his father and the bass player came out from backstage and walked up to the bar. His father was wearing a pale blue shirt with a frayed collar and no tie, a blue blazer with shiny elbows, and dark slacks that looked as if they'd been slept in too many nights. There were more lines in his face than there had been before, but Gilbert could not remember his father ever looking young. His hair was even more impressive up close. The only other man Gilbert had ever seen wear his hair like that was Don King, the fight

promoter, and he was black. His father must have had it
permed, and then set it every day. A hell of a lot of work,
Gilbert thought, but the effect was certainly impressive.

The two men stood ten feet away from where Gilbert sat
on his stool. He cleared his throat and said in a voice he
hoped his father would not recognize, "I liked your music a
lot. Can I buy you a drink?"

The bass man smiled broadly with yellow teeth, but his
father, with the old aloofness that had always awed and
frightened Gilbert, only looked at him straight-faced and
nodded. "Usual, Billy," he told the bartender.

"Same here," the bass man said, and walked over to Gilbert. "Like jazz, huh."

"Sure do. You guys play nice. That was a terrific 'Moon
Rays.' "

"Well, at least you know its name," Gilbert's father said,
accepting the CC and water the bartender handed him and
sitting on the stool next to Gilbert. "You know who wrote
it?"

"Horace Silver," Gilbert immediately answered.

"Good for you," his father said dryly in a voice that held
the black accents of the street.

"What's your name, son?" the bass man asked.

He couldn't tell him it was Gilbert. "John Rodman.
Johnny."

"Johnny. I'm Freddy, and this's Danny. You from around
here?"

"No," Gilbert said. "Down South, originally."

"You don't sound like no Southern boy."

"I left pretty young. Guess the dialect didn't have a chance
to rub off on me."

"Whereabouts down South?" Danny said. He didn't look
at Gilbert. He sat with his elbows on the bar, staring at the
array of bottles on the glass shelves.

"Louisiana. New Orleans."

Gilbert held his breath but needn't have worried. There
was not the slightest note of recognition in Danny's soft,
slurring voice. "I worked in Orleans for a while. Years ago.
Great town for jazz."

"Hey . . ." Gilbert said slowly, as if the truth was dawn-
ing. "You're Danny Vernon!"

His father nodded.

"I've got your record—the one you did with Hampton Hawes on Prestige?"

"Holy shit," Danny said. "That's gotta be thirty years ago." The hint of a smile touched his lips.

"It's a classic," Gilbert said. "I wore one copy of it out, had to buy another."

The pianist appeared from behind the curtain and waved to Danny and Freddy, who finished their drinks and stood up. "Okay, kid," Danny said. "It's time for the next set. You bought us a drink, so you got a request?"

Gilbert thought for a moment. "How about 'Groovin' High?' " He remembered his father practicing the Parker riffs over and over again, cursing savagely when the subtle licks defeated him, cheering exultantly when he got through it flawlessly.

Now Danny grinned for the first time. "I love that fucker," he said. "We'll do it good for you, kid." He started toward the stage, then turned back. "You gonna be here after, hang around. We'll have a drink. Talk."

Danny didn't lie. "Groovin' High" was good all right, the best Gilbert had ever heard. Gilbert hung around, and Danny and Freddy joined him afterwards, while the piano man and drummer went home to their wives. They drank a lot and talked more, and when they parted, Gilbert told them that he would come back and hear them play again.

As he lay in his spongy hotel room bed, his head woozy from the beer, Gilbert told himself that the business he had in Pennsylvania could wait for a while. Laura would be there when he was ready for her. After all, he was dead. She wasn't going anywhere. Laura would wait for him. Laura would wait.

July

Usually one has less occupation in summer than in winter, and the surplusage of summer light, a stage too large for the play, wearies, oppresses, sometimes appalls. . . . We see too much of the sky, and the long, lovely, pathetic, lingering evening light, with its suggestions of eternity and death, which one cannot for the soul of one put into words, is somewhat too much for the comfort of a sensitive human mortal. The day dies, and makes no apology for being such an unconscionable time in dying; and all the while it colours our thoughts with its own solemnity. There is no relief from this kind of thing at midsummer.

—Alexander Smith, *Dreamthorp*

"Children are afraid even of those they love best, and are best acquainted with, when disguised in a vizor. . . ."
—Montaigne, quoted in Alexander Smith,
Dreamthorp

The picnic at Dreamthorp that Fourth of July was not the cheeriest the community had ever seen. The recent deaths hung a pall of depression over the picnic grounds. Attendance was limited to Dreamthorp residents and their invited guests, and the crowd numbered less than two hundred. Faces smiled, and laughter was heard, but they were the smiles and laughter of frightened people.

"Look at everyone," Laura said quietly to Tom as she took a hamburger from the grill and slipped it into a bun. "They look like the crew of the *Titanic* waiting for the iceberg."

"They *are* a grim lot, aren't they?" he said, taking the sandwich and putting it on the large plate with the others. He looked around the shady grove at the dozens of picnic tables, like islands in a brown sea, the individual grills beside each. Then he looked at their own table a few yards away, at the faces of his mother and father, vacant and bored, at the stolid and unsmiling face of his son, who was looking at a magazine, aloof from the activities, even from the food on his plate.

"Anyone else want another hamburger?" Laura asked.

Josh did not respond. Ed shook his head and mumbled,

"No thank you." Frances only smiled and began to pick up the paper plates and cups and carry them to the trash can.

"Mom, I'll do that. Sit down," Tom said.

"It's all right; it's no trouble," Frances answered, snatching up soiled paper like a gull swooping down on bread crusts thrown from the backs of boats. "I can clean this all up. Why don't you two go for a walk or something?"

Tom sighed and glanced at Laura, who was looking at his mother benignly, almost patronizingly. "Want to go for a walk?" he asked her.

"Sure. Josh want to join us?"

"Josh?" Tom said. "Want to come down to the lake?"

Josh looked up and actually seemed to think about it but shook his head. "No thanks," he said, and turned back to his magazine. Tom shrugged, and he and Laura began to walk toward the lake, several hundred yards away.

"Almost had him that time," Tom said when they were out of earshot. "I actually thought he was going to go with us."

"He'd have been welcome to," Laura said.

"I think he knew that." They walked for a while. When they reached the path to the lake, Tom said, "I believe he likes you."

"He's pretty quiet about it."

"If he didn't like you, he'd be noisy about it."

"Really?"

"I know from experience." Tom told Laura about Karen then, and of Josh's vocal disapproval of the match. "But now that it's over, he still hasn't eased up."

"May I . . . make an observation?" she said tentatively.

"Sure."

"You may not want to hear it."

"It's all right."

"I haven't known Josh for long. You told me about him, but today's the first day that I've really come in contact with him, so maybe it's out of place for me to say this . . ." She hesitated.

"No, go ahead, please."

"I think . . . that Josh is very disturbed. Much more than he appears to be."

Tom took a deep breath. "What makes you think that?"

"A lot of things. The way he moves. The way he looks at

people when he thinks no one is watching him. When he was reading that magazine . . .''

"Yes?"

"He didn't turn the page. Not once in twenty minutes. I looked over his shoulder. There was a page of text—something about the stock market—and an ad. That was it. He wasn't in that magazine at all. He was somewhere else entirely, thinking about something completely different for all that time. That doesn't seem normal, to be that wrapped up in your own thoughts, even when you're that age."

They were at the lake now, and sat down on the low stone wall that marked the edge of the beach. "I know that he's been upset ever since his mother's death," Tom said. "But I don't know what to do about it. I thought maybe that my folks being here would pick him up—he's always gotten along well with them. But he ignores them just as much as he does me. I thought maybe a job would be good for him, and he's doing well, but it still hasn't brought him out of himself." Tom shook his head. "I don't know, Laura. I really don't know what to do next."

Laura took a deep breath. "Have you thought about psychiatric help for him?"

"I . . . I have. Yes."

"But you haven't done anything about it."

"No. It's always seemed like a last resort."

"It shouldn't. It's just a tool. Something to help."

"My parents will be leaving in a couple of weeks. I'll set up an appointment for then."

"Not before?"

Tom gave a bitter smile. "You don't know my mother very well. I'd never hear the end of it, turning Josh over to the headshrinkers. It's the stigma, you see. God help the family if anyone ever learned that one of us had to seek psychiatric help. Me, she might accept—she's convinced that I'm screwed up past all hope. But Josh? Never."

Laura pushed herself to her feet and dug the toes of her right sneaker into the sand. "Tom, I didn't mean to sound pushy. I hate it when—"

"You don't sound pushy. I've known that he needs help, but I guess I just needed someone else to tell me. Charlie Lewis might have been trying to, but psychiatric help isn't something that his generation might think of right away. I . . . appreciate your candor. Really. Thank you.''

"Just don't let it happen again, right?"

Tom laughed, then sobered. "Maybe I need a little . . . analysis myself, come to think of it.''

"You seem to be pretty well-adjusted—from a layman's point of view, anyway.''

"Nothing fatal, I guess." He stood up next to her, and they started walking down the beach, pausing only to remove their shoes and socks. "But enough about my problems. How's your business going?''

"Busy. Too busy, really. We've got a new account in Philly. Renco Auto Parts?''

"Sure. There's one over in Lebanon. Pretty big chain, isn't it?''

"Twenty-three stores in the state and five in Jersey. We were lucky to get it. But it's kept me busy every damn day. I don't get home until dark, and my weekends are full of it too. I really didn't even have time for the picnic today, but I thought the hell with it. I'll be ready by Monday.''

"What's Monday?" They arrived at the playground, and Tom sat on a swing. Laura took the one next to him and they swung gently, pushing at the bare earth with bare feet.

"We're starting the taping for a commercial. Down in Philly.''

"Starting? How long is it going to take?''

"Three days. I hope no longer, or we'll bust the hell out of the budget. It's that clay animation stuff. I wouldn't have to be there until Wednesday for the edit, but it's the first time we've ever tried anything like this and I want to see how it's done, find out what the limitations are.''

"When are you leaving?''

"Tomorrow afternoon. We start in the studio first thing Monday morning.''

"When are you coming back?''

"Thursday, if everything goes well.''

"How about dinner Thursday then? To celebrate a successful . . . what do you call it, a shoot?''

"Shoot." She nodded. "Sounds great. But can we make it Friday instead? Just in case we go over?''

"Fine. We can have dinner, then go to the show afterwards.''

She cocked an eyebrow at him. "Dutch?"

"If you like, you can pick up the whole tab."

Laura laughed. "It's a deal. I'll call you when I get home."

They walked on to the ruins of the playhouse. The roof had been dismantled and carried away, but the broken posts and splintered benches still lay there, surrounded by a yellow police line. The investigation was not over. There were still too many unanswered questions, unexplained deaths.

"I wish they'd clean it up," Tom said, "and be done with it."

"I know," said Laura. "I do too. But it takes time, I guess. Something that mysterious. It takes time to find out everything." Then she added, "If they ever can."

Dreamthorp's weekend passed in safety and silence. There were no hideous deaths, no reports of strangers lurking in bushes. The security team hired by the residents patrolled the streets faithfully, carrying dimly glowing lanterns after dark so no one would think they were prowlers. Still, everyone was uneasy.

Sunday evening, Tom suggested to his parents that, in light of the danger that had come to Dreamthorp, they might want to cut short their visit and return to the relative safety of Miami. But Frances said they would not even consider leaving now. A few more weeks, and this maniac would be found out sure enough—people like that always make a stupid mistake. Although Tom had the feeling that his father was only too anxious to get back to Florida, Ed said nothing, leaving the decision in Frances's hands, as always.

On Monday Josh worked all day at Ted's Mobil, and when he came home at five o'clock he went upstairs and into his room. When Tom called him for dinner there was no answer, and he found the boy sleeping crosswise on his bed.

"Josh?" Tom said, then shook him gently.

Josh awoke with a start, and Tom saw fear in his eyes, fear that did not disappear when he saw who stood over him.

"What is it?" Tom asked him. "What's wrong, Josh?"

The boy shook his head. "Nothing. Nothing."

"You tired?"

"Yeah."

"Is it your work? Do want to cut back on the hours?"

"No, the work's okay."

Tom sat down on the bed but didn't touch his son. He remembered when Josh had been younger, when he tucked him in at night, resting a hand on his forehead or his shoulder, kissing that impossibly soft cheek. How many years ago had that been? It couldn't have been more than four or five, but now it seemed as though a lifetime separated them. Or a life, he thought sadly.

"What is it then, Josh?" Tom spoke quietly, wanting the boy to hear the compassion, the concern, the love he felt for him.

"Nothing." Josh's voice was distant but not hostile.

"Why are you so tired? You can tell me, really. It doesn't matter what it is, I'll try to help." Drugs? Tom wondered, almost hoping it was, hoping for an external reason for the boy's attitude and lassitude. External things could be dealt with, separated from the person. But how could you separate someone from their own mind? "I know you've been depressed. I have too."

Josh looked at him with a trace of anger.

"I loved her, Josh. She was my life."

The anger faded slowly, and the boy turned his face to the wall.

"I miss her as much as you do. You can believe that or not. But it doesn't make it any less true." Tom sighed. "If there's anything I can do, Josh . . . anything, let me know. You're my son and I love you. Maybe I can help." Very lightly, he let his hand rest on the boy's arm. "Maybe you can help me too."

Josh turned, and Tom saw tears in his eyes. "Dad," he said, "I . . . I want to tell you . . . something that I—"

Suddenly from the bottom of the stairs came Frances's shout. *"Hey,* you two! Come on, hurry up, the meat's going to get dry!"

A cloud passed over the boy's face. Tom had lost him. "We better go down," Josh said.

"Damn the meat," Tom growled. "Never mind her, Josh. What is it?"

"Nothing. It was . . ." The boy shook his head as if shaking away a bad dream. "Nothing . . ."

It *was* something, Tom thought savagely. It was *everything,* and now it had been lost because of some goddam fucking roast beef that she always overcooked anyway. Josh began to get up, and Tom stopped him. "Wait. Wait a minute. There's something I want to tell you. I want us to . . . to go into therapy together."

Josh looked at his father's hand on his arm, then at the man's face. "Therapy?" he said, as if the word were new to him.

"Yes."

"You think I'm crazy?" The fear was back now, the same fear that Tom had seen when the boy woke.

"No, no, of course not, I just think that—"

"I *won't,*" Josh said, pushing away Tom's arm and sitting up on the bed. "I just won't do it."

"Can we at least talk about it?"

"No!" the boy yelled, then leaped off the bed and bolted through the door.

"Josh, wait!" Tom went after him, but Josh ran down the stairs, jumping down the last few steps, and dashed outside, the screen door slamming in his wake.

"Good heavens," said Frances, "where is *he* off to? Doesn't he know it's dinnertime?"

"Sure," Tom said coldly. "He knows. We *all* know. We just don't happen to be hungry right now." He walked to the cellar door and opened it. "I'm going down there to work. I don't want to be disturbed. Not for *anything.*"

He slammed the door behind him, leaving his mother, for once, speechless.

Tom found no solace in his work. The chunk of wood that he had abused several days earlier looked raw and lifeless. He picked away at it nonetheless, trying to clear his mind of everything but the chisel, the mallet, and the wood.

It was futile. He kept thinking of Josh, wondering what his son had been going to tell him, what he had finally decided to share with him before Frances had ruined everything with her cry from below.

A cry from below.

And what, he wondered, could he create to make his own cry heard?

With that thought in mind, he bent over the block again, pleading with sharpened edge and heavy mallet for something to come out of the wood, for something to be born. But as he pummeled and battered and gouged, he realized that nothing would come out of this particular piece of wood. It was wrong somehow. He needed something more.

He needed size.

Yes. That was it. He need bulk and heft and mass. What he wanted, *needed* to say, was something that could not be bound by the size of a bird, even an eagle. It would have to be man-sized. The size of a man. Of a man's cries. Of a man's pain.

Josh leaned against a tree and sobbed. He had run all the way down Emerson until he came to the woods, and then, without hesitation, rushed into them. No one saw him go.

"Mom . . ." he whispered, as if expecting her to be there, to put her arms around him and hold him like she always did when something went wrong.

But she wasn't there, and he turned his back to the smooth-barked oak and slid down it, until he was sitting on the dry ground, his back against the trunk. He had almost weakened, and it made him angry. He had almost surrendered to the man whom nature had made his father, had almost cried in his arms and told him everything, told him what he had done and was going to do again. That would have been a mistake, because he knew his father was lying to him when he said he loved his mother. He didn't love her, he couldn't have, and then done the things he did with those women—first the kid, the one almost as young as him, and now this older one. She was nicer at least, but still it wasn't right.

Josh knew all about how things should be. He had read *Hamlet*. Not the whole thing, just the Classic Comic from a boxful that had been his dad's when he was a kid, but Josh had understood the story all right. Hamlet had loved his father and had gone crazy when he died and his mother got married right away to his uncle. It wasn't so much the uncle part that had made Hamlet mad as it was that his mom couldn't even wait until his father was cold in his grave. In Josh's case, the mother and father roles were reversed, but otherwise it was the same. He hadn't even seen his father cry, not once. Not at the funeral and not later at home, when the slightest thing would bring tears to Josh's eyes.

When people got married, they *stayed* married. That was the way it was supposed to be. Sure there were divorces, a lot of his friends' parents were divorced. But that was because they hadn't loved each other enough to begin with. And his dad wasn't divorced, he was a *widower,* and that meant that he was supposed to *grieve,* and he *hadn't,* and Josh didn't know *why.*

Married people were supposed to love each other, not just forget about the other one when they died, not just go on to other people the way his dad had done.

Married people were supposed to *love* each other, and he wanted to see that.

He thought about Mrs. Goodwin. She was married, and she probably loved her husband. He was sure they made the old mattress jump, like Artie Huber used to say when Artie was still his friend. Made the old mattress jump. Just like Mom and Dad had done when she was still alive. He had heard them sometimes in the night when he got up for a drink of water or to go to the bathroom. At first it frightened him, but when he was old enough to know what they were doing, he had felt okay about it. It meant that they still loved each other, didn't it? And when he knew that those noises his mom made were happy instead of hurting, that was okay too. He wanted his mom to be happy, and he realized that you couldn't marry your mother yourself. It was okay.

But when the mattress started jumping with his dad and that little cunt from the college, well, shit, that was different. Josh kept thinking that they were doing it on the same bed where his dad had done it with his mom, and that seemed so damn wrong, sacrilegious, really. And she was so *loud.* His mom had never been that loud.

The first night after he heard his dad and that Karen together was the night that he dreamed about his mom. He had had wet dreams before, but never about his mother, and he woke in the middle of the night, sticky and tired and immeasurably guilty, for he distinctly remembered that it had been his mother, naked and warm and so soft, to whom he had been doing things, and who had been doing things to him.

Oh Jesus, his *mother.*

It seemed so sick and wrong, but he brought it back to mind—all the details—and after he tossed his soiled pajamas in the hamper and lay in bed once again, he thought about it over and over, and masturbated into a handful of tissue, which he then rolled up and put under his bed. That was the first and last time that he dreamed about his mother.

But he did not forget about her, and projected her onto other women, older women, with whom he came in contact. Such a woman was Mrs. Goodwin. She was in her mid thirties, tall and slim, with a pretty, prim, patrician face set off by ash blonde hair tied at the nape of her neck, where soft tendrils fine as spun gold trailed down over her collar. She got her gas at Ted's Mobil, and was always friendly to Josh, never missing a chance to talk to him when he served her. She drove a little red MG. When Josh asked her about it, she told him it was a 1967 model that her husband had restored. Josh had seen her husband once or twice, a short, balding man who wore suits and ties during the week and muscle shirts on weekends, and drove a gray Audi. He seemed nice too, though he didn't talk to Josh the way his wife did. They lived three blocks away, up on Longfellow, in a heavily wooded lot.

At the thought of Mrs. Goodwin, Josh pushed himself to his feet and began to walk up the side of the hill through the woods. When he reached Longfellow, he came out of the brush and walked down the street. The Goodwin's cottage was the fourth one from the end, and Mr. and Mrs. Goodwin were sitting on their front porch. Mr. Goodwin was smoking a cigarette, and Mrs. Goodwin was drinking something that Josh thought might have been iced tea. She waved to him when she saw him, and her husband raised a hand in greeting.

"Hello, Josh," she called. "Patrolling the streets tonight?"

Josh smiled. "Nah, just a walk." The front, he thought, was no good, so he walked to the end of Longfellow, went up Elm, and went back in the direction he had come on Alcott, past the cottage whose backyard met the rear of the Goodwins' place.

This was better. The trees were thick here, and the cottage on Alcott was empty and for sale. He walked through the brush to its rear and saw the Goodwins' cottage through the trees. Pines predominated, but there were also large oaks, easy to climb. Josh calculated that a person could look into, maybe even reach, the upstairs windows by climbing up that large oak next to the little woodshed.

He licked his lips, then looked around. Dusk was coming

on, and the community was getting darker and darker. His time of day, he thought.

Josh turned and walked down the street, heading for home. He was hungry and tired, and would not come back tonight.

But he would come back later, even though he hated the thought of it, and the guilt weighed down upon him like lead. He had almost told his father about it, caught himself just in time, and that was good. His father would not have understood. No one, Josh thought, would understand. He was not even sure if he did himself.

> A great ... tree ... grows out of tradition and a past order of things, and is pathetic with the suggestions of dead generations.
> —Alexander Smith, *Dreamthorp*

———◆———

"So you think you ought to wait a few weeks to start treatment?" Charlie Lewis asked Tom. It was late afternoon of the following day, and the two of them were picking their way through the tall weeds that surrounded the site of the old sawmill.

"I think so," Tom answered, bending back a branch and holding it until Charlie, following, could grab it for himself. "I've brought up the idea now, so I figure he can use some time to get used to it."

"Maybe," Charlie said, "but if he's really in as much pain as you think, I'd guess the sooner the better."

"Well, I want to wait until my folks leave."

"That's understandable. When will that be, Christmas?" A thin twig swatted Charlie across the forehead, and he cursed. "I *knew* we should've taken that dirt road."

"You're the one who said you wanted a hike, Charlie," Tom said, laughing. "Something about walking being good for the heart?"

"And you listen to a senile old man?"

"I don't even know why we're doing this."

"Morbid curiosity. Pretend we're the Hardy Boys and we're going to find some clues that Inspector Lestrade missed."

"Inspector Lestrade was in the Sherlock Holmes stories."

"Details, details," Charlie muttered.

In another minute Tom and Charlie pushed through a final clutter of brush and found themselves in the clearing. "This is it?" Tom asked.

"Yep. Welcome to the Haunted Forest. And there's the tree, most likely. Only one big enough."

They walked over to the huge white pine, one of the largest Tom had ever seen. He guessed it to be over three feet thick through the center. The bottom five feet of the trunk were considerably darker than the upper portion, and Tom examined it closely. "Somebody threw water on it," he said.

Charlie nodded. "To wash off the . . . whatever, I suppose." He squinted at the bark. "You can still see it, though. Good God, pieces of him."

Tom looked. In the fissures of the rough bark, things moist and organic glimmered in the sunlight that slipped through the treetops. A spot darker than the others, two and a half feet up, caught his attention. "The nail hole," he said, inspecting it. "And blood."

"There's blood all over the ground too," Charlie said. "You can see where they tried to rake it over. Did a lousy job." He shook his head. "Unbelievable. Even when you stand here and look at it, when the evidence is right in front of you, it still seems unbelievable. That anyone would be insane enough to do something like that to someone. Jesus. They can't cut it down too soon to suit me."

"Cut it down?"

"That's what Bret told me. They've got all the evidence they need—took a lot of photographs, I gather. I wouldn't want to see them, either. I pity the jury when they find the guy and the case comes to trail."

"But why are they cutting it down?" Tom asked so intently that Charlie looked at him.

"I don't know, maybe they're superstitious, maybe they don't want to be reminded of it, maybe they simply don't want thrill seekers doing just what we're doing."

Tom looked at the tree again, then took out a pocketknife, opened the blade, and dug into the bark.

"I didn't know you collected souvenirs of evisceration murders," Charlie said.

"Not a souvenir. It just struck me that there might be a hell of a good, big block of wood locked up in this tree."

"That's more than a trifle morbid."

Tom picked away a large chunk of bark and scraped at the wood he had revealed. "It's nice," he said. "And if they're going to take it down anyway . . ."

"My God, mother, the man is serious about this. Tom, come home with me, have a beer, let them chop up and burn this son of a bitch."

"It's just a tree, Charlie. And I've been needing a piece this size. I'm damned if I couldn't get a six-foot-high, two-foot-square block out of it."

Charlie sighed. "Don't tell me about it, tell Bret. He was going to send some boys out the end of the week to drop it. But maybe if you offer to do it and save the taxpayers some money . . ."

"That's not a bad idea. He might go for it."

Bret Walters did go for it, but made Tom promise that he would not use the provenance of the wood as a selling point for whatever he carved from it, and Tom agreed.

The next day he and Charlie went back out to the site, this time on the overgrown dirt road in a pickup truck borrowed from Ted's Mobil. They had two young men with them, a pair of Tom's better sculpture students, to help them saw down the tree with a crosscut saw. It was over fifty feet tall, and when it fell it took several smaller, younger trees with it. Then they sawed it up into eight separate sections, the largest of which was the trunk, which they loaded, grunting and sweating in the dry heat, into the bed of the pickup. The other sections they hauled further into the brush and left there.

The men at Burke's Lumber yard in Lebanon shook their heads in bemusement when Tom drove into their compound with his tree trunk. He stood by as they prepared it to his order, shaving off the bark, then slicing the arcs off on each side until all that remained was a block a little over six feet long and roughly two feet wide. The students and Tom lugged it back into the truck, and they and Charlie drove back to Tom's cottage. They muscled it off the pickup, and, after Tom removed the screws that held his jigsaw to the floor and moved the heavy piece of equipment out of the way, they managed to cajole it through the basement door into the workshop, parking its massive bulk next to the carving bench.

Tom thanked the boys for their help, and gave them each a ten dollar bill. He drove them back to campus, and then returned with Charlie to his workshop, where the block sat waiting.

"Well, there it is, Michelangelo," Charlie said softly. "*David*'s in there just waiting to be born."

"*David* was marble," Tom said. "This is wood."

"Okay, *Pinocchio*'s in there. Happy?"

"Not really." Tom reached out a hand and let his fingers trail down over the rough-grained wood. "I don't know *who's* in there yet."

Charlie shrugged. "Give it time. You'll find out." He watched Tom staring at the wood, then cleared his throat. "Well, I guess I'll leave the two of you alone now that the ice is broken."

Tom turned and faced him. "Thanks for the help, Charlie."

"Sure. Hauling five-hundred-pound blocks of pine is my specialty."

"I'll get you a case of beer, okay?"

"I'd settle for the ten bucks you gave the kids." Then he grinned. "See you," he said, and left Tom alone with the wood.

For a long time he examined it, walking around it, touching it from all sides, gauging the direction of the grain, probing the knots with his fingertips, looking for areas of softness, patches of rot, but finding none. The wood seemed as hard as iron.

It's in there, he thought. It's waiting for me. Up to me now. I have to bring it out.

Then he sat on a stool and looked at it some more. But it was silent. It said nothing. It gave no indication of who it was, who it might have been, or who it might become.

> We are our own despots,—we tremble at
> a neighbor's whisper.
> —Alexander Smith, *Dreamthorp*

On the monitors, the bear reached out and grabbed an automobile muffler as tall as he was. He turned his pale, shining snout to the viewer and grinned a grin that showed at least twenty teeth, then popped the muffler, which suddenly shrank to the size of a football, into a beehive the bear was holding. Then he went skipping down the aisle, and the monitors went black.

"So," said the engineer, punching buttons on the control panel as he spoke, "what do you think?"

Laura Stark sighed and sipped from her Styrofoam cup of coffee. "He's still skipping," she said wearily. "Why is he still skipping?"

"He's not really *skipping* anymore, do you think?" said the bald man next to the engineer. "I mean, I took the skips *out*. You told me to, so I did. What do *you* think, Billy?"

The engineer shrugged. "Hell, I don't know."

"He's *skipping*," Laura said, annoyed.

"*I* think he's *hopping*," the bald man said insistently. "What do *you* think, Billy?"

Laura breathed out with a hiss. "Billy's not your client. Kevin—*I'm* your client. And that goddam bear is *skipping*. When the foot hits the ground twice on each step, that is out and out *skipping*. Now I told you yesterday that the Renco Bear does not skip—that's not my opinion nor my prejudice, that is the opinion and prejudice of the president and owner

176

of Renco. And he happens to be *my* client. I try to do what he wants, and I expect you to do what *I* want, okay?''

''But the skipping is *cute,* it's *bear*like!''

''The Renco Bear is not *supposed* to be cute, he's supposed to be *macho.* He's not a goddam *Care* Bear, Kevin. These are auto parts, okay? *Guys* buy auto parts, and they don't want to identify with a wimpy bear.''

''So what are you saying?'' Kevin asked, his nostrils flaring.

''I'm saying butch him up, and get rid of that goddam *skip!* Just give me what I asked for in the first place. Okay?''

Kevin's jaw trembled, and for a moment Laura was afraid he was going to cry. But he clamped down hard and said through clenched teeth, ''I'm going to have to stay up all night to do it. I certainly didn't figure on this when I gave you the figure.''

''I'm sorry, Kevin,'' she said, ''but your not giving me what I want is costing me a bundle of studio time, so to ask me for overtime to correct your mistakes is more than a little presumptuous.'' She turned to the engineer. ''What do *you* think, Billy?''

Billy stifled a laugh and shook his head. ''Leave me out of it,'' he said. ''I plead ignorance. All I do is push the buttons.''

''All right, fine,'' Kevin said. ''You want it changed, I'll change it. A *macho* walk, right?''

Laura nodded slowly. ''Macho,'' she said, trying not to laugh herself as the little bald man drew himself up to his full five and a half feet and strode from the room. As soon as the soundproof door wheezed shut, both she and Billy exploded in giggles.

''That was great,'' Billy said, wiping his eyes. ''He does that constantly, Laura. If you don't sit on him like you did, he'll make a marine sergeant mince.''

''Do you think he'll be ready by tomorrow?'' Laura asked, suddenly sobered by the thought of Kevin falling behind on purpose or, even worse, turning the Renco Bear into a drag queen out of spite.

''He'll be ready,'' Billy said. ''He's a pain, but once you kick his ass the way you did, he produces. We'll be ready to edit tomorrow, don't worry.''

She shook her head. "It's just that we're going to be two days over schedule."

"You build in a contingency, don't you?" In response to her affirmative nod, he went on. "That's the way. Turn it into the client's problem."

"Oh, he'll pay for it, it's just that it cuts down on our profit."

Billy smiled. "Well, I've got one way you could keep your travel expense at a reasonable level—let me buy you dinner tonight."

"Oh, Billy, no, really . . ."

"Why not? We've been working together for three days now, I think it's time to find out about each other as people, don't you? Just a friendly meal."

She looked at him for a long time and saw neither threat nor menace in him. On the contrary, he had made the three days at least bearable with his willingness to please and his constant good humor. Also, he was not unattractive. From his salt and pepper hair, Laura guessed that he was in his early forties. His features were sharp but handsome, and he was tall and well built. But most importantly he was nice, and after working with Kevin for most of the day, Laura decided that she could use some friendly company instead of returning to the Hyatt and ordering room service so that she would not feel self-conscious eating alone.

They drove to a small restaurant Billy knew of that featured New Orleans cuisine, and, at Billy's urging, they ate blackened redfish, which Laura had never tried before and which she really did not care for but finished anyway. "You liked it, huh?" Billy said, mopping up the last of his sauce with a piece of sourdough bread.

"It's very good," she lied. "Different. Pretty spicy."

"What makes life worth living. So, Laura, you married?"

The question made her uncomfortable. If he had the slightest suspicion that she was married, why, she wondered, had he asked her to dinner? "No. I'm not."

"Ever been?"

"I . . . yes. I was once."

"Me too. Didn't work out. You have any kids?"

"No. Thank goodness."

"Oh, they're not so bad. I've got two. Boys. I get to see them every other weekend, and two weeks in the summer. We generally go fishing up in New York state. They're twelve and thirteen now, so they really get into it.''

They ordered dessert and had sherry afterwards. Billy kept the conversation going, telling Laura more about his children and why his marriage had failed, about his job, about how he hoped to open his own studio in a year or so. When the clerk came, Laura offered to pay her share, but Billy adamantly refused. "I asked you to dinner, remember? My treat.''

It was cool and comfortable out on the street, and Laura, despite her distaste for the redfish, felt full and satisfied as she climbed into Billy's car. She expected him to drive her back to the hotel right away, since it was nearly eleven, and they had an early start in the morning. But he did not start the car. Instead he leaned toward her, put his arm around her shoulder, and drew her toward him with the unmistakable intention of kissing her.

Laura stiffened. Her hands came up to his chest and pushed him back, gently but firmly. His eyes, narrowed to what she felt he assumed were passionate slits, widened in surprise, real or feigned, and then he frowned.

"Aren't we both a little too old for this?" he said.

"For . . . for parking in *cars, yes.*"

"I meant for the games. For the hard-to-get stuff." He smiled and shrugged. "Come on, Laura, I know how you feel. It's how I feel too. We're adults, there's nothing to stop us, no one to betray, no reason to feel guilty later.''

She was astonished, and then angry at herself for being so. She should have known. She really should have known. "It's not that," she said coldly.

"Well, look, if it's your health you're worried about, I'm okay in that department. I mean, I even got checked for AIDS the last time I gave blood, and no go, it was negative, so you can put your mind at ease. And if you're still squeamish, I'm the kind of guy who doesn't mind condoms. In fact, I think they're a pretty good idea, to tell the truth. Anything to make people relax, you know?''

"Billy," Laura said, trying to keep her voice from shaking with the fury she felt, "I think you had just better take me back to the Hyatt while I can still pretend to be able to continue a professional relationship with you for the next day or so—''

"Hey, now look—"

"Because right now I'm really feeling pretty pissed off at you."

"Pissed off?" He sound honestly surprised. *"Why?"*

"Your . . . *assumption* that you could take me to bed, that's why." Her hand was trembling, and she made a fist out of it.

"Well, I'm *sorry,* but hell, this is the twentieth century, you know, and I think I can read people pretty well, and—"

He was babbling now, and she could tell she had him on the defensive. "You didn't read *me* very well," she said.

Billy shut up and looked at her, slowly and appraisingly. "No," he said finally. "No, I didn't." Then he turned away, started the car, pulled it out of the lot, and did a U-turn so that they were heading toward the Hyatt. "Maybe Kevin was right," he mumbled to himself.

"Right about what?" she said.

"Nothing." He shook his head as though he had not intended her to hear, but she was certain he had.

"Tell me."

"It's *nothing.*"

"Well, if it's nothing, it won't matter, will it?" She felt foolish. It was the kind of repartee that eight year olds indulge in, but she wanted to know, to have her suspicions confirmed. And too, she felt that Billy really wanted to tell her something that might hurt her.

"Aw, hell, it's stupid. He was just pissed off himself." He paused for a moment before he went on, needing no further urging. "He said . . . he said he thought you were the type who hit the Venus after work, that's all."

"The Venus?" she repeated. "What the hell's the Venus?"

"Just a bar. Like a club, really." Then he said, with just the slightest note of contempt, "For women."

Laura felt suddenly chilled, and the thought came unbidden of Kitty, naked in her arms. When she spoke, her voice sounded weak, and she had to clear her throat and start again. "So what's wrong with a women's club?"

"These are women who like women." Billy gave a little laugh. "I don't mean to imply anything, okay? Kevin was just bitchy, you know? Fucking nancies get that way sometimes."

They drove the rest of the way in silence, until Billy stopped his car at the main entrance of the Hyatt. "Thank you for the dinner," Laura said coldly, opening her door.

"Hey, I apologize, all right? Really, I'm sorry. I just read it wrong. I feel pretty stupid."

At the pity she heard in his voice, she whirled on him. "Why?" she said. "Because you think you put the moves on a *dyke?*"

He looked at her, breathed deeply, and let the air flow out in a long sigh. "That's your lookout, Laura. None of my business."

"You're right," she said, climbing out of the car. "You're goddam *right* it's not!" She slammed the door and did not look back until she was safely in the lobby. Then she turned. Billy's car was no longer in the driveway. She was alone.

Laura went to the bar, sat at a table, and ordered a gin and tonic, drinking it quickly and angrily when it came. She had another, which she drank more slowly but no less intently. After the second, on top of the drinks and sherry she had with dinner, she found that her thoughts were neither as controlled nor lucid as before, that the memories of Kitty which she had tried to repress were now flickering across the screen of her senses so that she remembered not only the sight of Kitty but also the soft touch of her skin, the sweet scent of her perfume, even the taste of her lips. "Kitty," she murmured. "Aw, Kitty . . ."

Maybe that son of a bitch Billy was right. Maybe that little faggot Kevin was right too. She smiled grimly at *that* thought. Yes, maybe she and Kevin had more in common than she realized. Does it take one, she wondered blearily, to know one? And how much did Kevin know? Was he right? Was she the kind of woman to go to the Venus?

The Venus. Maybe that *was* what she needed, what she wanted. Here was her chance. Alone. Unknown. Alone and unknown, with no one to know.

If she had been sober, she never would have done it. But the drinks had confused her as much as Billy's intimations had upset her and the memories of Kitty had simultaneously aroused and disturbed her. She scribbled her room number and name on the tab, then got up and went to the row of pay phones, where she looked for the Venus in the phone book. It was there. Just the name, the street address, and the num-

ber. She put a quarter in the slot and dialed. A woman's voice
answered and gave Laura the information she needed: no,
there were no membership requirements; yes, people could
come in alone (the woman chuckled at that one); of course
they were open now, and would be until two; thank you, and
we hope to see you here.

Laura thought about going to her room to freshen up, but
decided that if she did, her courage might fail, and she would
not leave it again that night. Instead, she went into the ladies'
room, adjusted her makeup, brushed her hair, gave herself a
quick squirt of Binaca, and went outside to wait for a cab.

> I kept my passion to myself, like a cake,
> and nibbled it in private.
>   —Alexander Smith, *Dreamthorp*

The Venus was on a quiet street with trees imprisoned in black wrought iron cages. It was the third house in a row of old brownstones brightly lit by street lights. The neighborhood was not what Laura had expected. It felt safer than she had thought it would. A hand-carved sign edged in gilt said The Venus. That was all. There were no neon signs, no red lights. Whatever else the place was, it was discreet.

The cab ride had taken twenty minutes, and on the way Laura had sobered up mentally, if not altogether physically. When the cab stopped, she nearly told the driver to take her back to the hotel, but steeled herself, overtipped him, and got out. She stood on the sidewalk for a long time, watching the red taillights disappear down the street. Then she walked up the stone steps, hoping to find truth. She hesitated for a moment, trying to decide if she should knock on the glass-paned door or simply open it and walk in. She chose the latter.

The first thing she saw was an attractive middle-aged woman dressed resplendently in a tuxedo. She was standing behind an ornately carved counter on which a large book lay open. "Good evening," the woman said with a smile. "Your name?"

"Oh," Laura stammered, "I'm . . . not a member, but on the phone they said—"

"Of course," the woman said. "You may purchase a single evening membership for twenty-five dollars."

"Oh . . . all right, fine . . ." Laura took the money from her purse and paid the woman, who smiled and gestured toward a heavily carved oak door at the far end of the entry.

As Laura walked the dozen feet to the door, she looked about her in surprise. The room reminded her of her grandmother's house but better appointed and kept up more beautifully. Elegant red hangings covered the walls, and a crystal chandelier shed a warm yellow light on the brown and green oriental rug that ran the length of the room.

At the door, Laura turned and looked back at the woman, who nodded supportively. "Go ahead," she said. "Have a nice time." Laura took a deep breath and pushed open the door.

The interior of the Venus did not, to Laura's eye, appear decadent at all. In fact it looked Victorian, almost stodgy, like a woman's idea of a snobbish British men's club barroom. The furnishings were comprised of heavy leather pieces arranged in islands about the large room. A bar ran the length of the left side of the room, and only a few women sat there. Most were in the small groups that clustered at the tables. It reminded Laura of the lobby of the Algonquin Hotel, only darker.

All of the women were well dressed, and none, Laura was relieved to see, was wearing motorcycle boots or chains. They seemed to be in their thirties or older, and sat drinking, talking quietly, while baroque music played softly. The low hum of their talk vanished as Laura entered, and the faces turned in her direction, curious and expectant, Laura thought. In that instant she felt distinctly apprehensive, as though she were a rare butterfly that had accidentally flown into a convention of entomologists.

Despite her discomfort, she walked to the bar, sat on one of the high-backed stools near the end, and ordered a gin and tonic from the bartender, a girl in her early twenties, who as a mild concession to sexual fantasy, was dressed in a Victorian maid's costume with a very short skirt that exposed a pair of lacy panties when she bent down to get the bottle of Bombay. The girl smiled at Laura coquettishly as she mixed and served her drink.

Laura swallowed the gin, trying to analyze her emotions.

to decide whether the tension she felt was sexual excitement or simply fear and uncertainty at being in a place so alien, so forbidden. The drinks she had at dinner and the Hyatt did nothing to clarify her analysis, and she closed her eyes, her head down, trying to remember why she was in this place, what she was trying to learn, perhaps whom she was trying to meet.

She was just about to order another drink from the girl, who was standing nearby, smiling familiarly and a bit lasciviously at her, when she felt a hand on her shoulder and turned to see a woman taller than herself, her black hair flecked with strands of gray. She was wearing a black, high-necked dress and a jeweled cross pendant with a central diamond that looked too garish to be synthetic. "I'm Diane," the woman said through white, straight teeth. Her voice was low and husky, and Laura caught the smell of cigarettes and whisky on it. "My friends and I couldn't help but notice that you were alone. We were wondering if you'd like to join us."

Laura forced a smile. "Thank you. That's very nice of you. But I . . ." She had no excuse to offer. Why would a woman come here if not to meet other women? She had to go with them. Inside her mind, she had no other choice.

Diane seemed to know that. "Oh, come on. You don't want to drink alone, there's no fun in that. That's how you become an alcoholic." Her hand, long-fingered and cool, touched Laura's. "Come on. The chairs are very comfortable."

When Laura got to her feet, she realized how badly the drinks were affecting her, but still wanted another. "I . . . I ought to get another gin and tonic."

Diane nodded and looked at the girl behind the bar. "Margo, bring one over." Then she took Laura's upper arm, pressing more firmly than she would have had to, letting her fingers rub the smoothness of Laura's soft, bare skin.

There were three other women sitting in the leather wing chairs around the small table. All of them appeared to be in their late thirties or early forties. Glasses sat on the table in front of them, along with ashtrays that Margo emptied when she brought Laura's drink.

"Your first time here?" asked the woman on Laura's left. She was a few pounds overweight, though not unattractively so, and had a round, pink face that smiled cherubically.

"Yes it is." Laura clutched her drink like a lifeline. On her right, Diane rested her hand possessively on the arm of Laura's chair.

"What's your name, dear?" the woman across from Laura asked. She wore a red dress that displayed her prodigious cleavage to best advantage, but the deep-cut lines of her face told Laura that she was older than her companions.

"Laura."

"Laura," the older woman said. "That's a lovely name. I had a friend named Laura."

The remaining woman, who had not yet spoken, now leaned across the table and looked at Laura. She was beautiful, Laura thought, with large, violet eyes and beautifully tanned skin with not a trace of the leathery surface that so often accompanies it. Her blonde hair fell in waves, softly framing the perfection of her face. The violet eyes caught and held Laura as she was bringing her drink to her lips, and she paused, discomfited and fascinated by the intensity of the woman's gaze.

"Laura . . ." the woman whispered.

She had to swallow hard before she could answer. The room seemed gelid, luminous, dreamlike. "Yes . . . ?" she said, feeling foolish and shy in this woman's presence. There was something imperious about her, something that invited worship.

"I'm Janet," the woman said. She smiled warmly. "Don't be uncomfortable. We won't bite."

At that, they all chuckled, and Laura finally smiled. They started to talk then, and it seemed to Laura no more esoteric than a typical hen party at a country club bar. They discussed their jobs, clothes, television, a number of other subjects, and the only hint of their sexual preference could be found in the disparaging way they referred to their male co-workers or bosses.

Time passed, and Laura slowly found herself gravitating toward Janet and away from Diane, who by now was resting an acquisitive hand on Laura's forearm. When Diane finally left the table for a few minutes to go to the rest room, Janet moved next to Laura and spoke to her softly, while the other women chattered on. "I'd love to go upstairs with you," she said.

"Upstairs?" Laura repeated dumbly.

"Diane is as cold a lover as she looks. But you and I . . . I think it could be very lovely." Janet touched Laura's cheek and smiled softly. "Let's be gone when she comes back."

Janet stood up and took Laura's hand. Laura stood dizzily, and the other women looked at them with a kind of grudging acceptance that told Laura that she was not the first woman to go upstairs with Janet.

The climb up the stairs was something out of a dream. Laura led and Janet followed, her hands on Laura's hips as they ascended. At the top, Janet took the lead once more, and they went down a long hall and into a cavernous and dimly lit room which seemed to Laura's hazy vision to contain nothing but a bed, a giant four-poster that swayed like a ship. She sat down on it at Janet's guidance, and the woman began to caress her bare arms, then move her hands lightly over Laura's breasts. Laura froze, unable to respond, unable to stand or protest the touches that became more intimate.

The beautiful woman with the violet eyes fell to her knees by the side of the bed, and Laura watched as she moved a hand between Laura's bare legs and up the roundness of her thighs, then extend her tongue and lick, very lightly, behind Laura's knee. Laura trembled, not with the warm ecstasy that she had known with Kitty, but with shame and fear.

"No . . ." she whimpered. "No, please . . ."

Now Janet's right hand touched the hem of Laura's panties, and her left hand touched her right breast, circling the nipple through the thin cotton blouse, making it harden involuntarily as the violet-eyed woman's fingers slipped beneath the fabric, touching Laura's sex, exploring the folds, the crevices that refused to moisten, that fear would not allow to be made damp.

Laura sat as still as stone, refusing to fall backward, and when Janet looked up curiously at her, Laura told her to stop, and she did, puzzled, confusion and annoyance on her face. Laura stood up, clutching her purse, which she had grabbed when they had left the table and not released since. She rearranged her clothing, edged her way past Janet, and went downstairs, where she put a twenty dollar bill on the bar, and walked out past the inquisitive eyes of the women at the table, out onto the steps, closing the door behind her, and then down to the street, where she walked two blocks before she had to stop, cling to an iron cage around a tree, and throw up her entire dinner, all the drinks, all the humiliation.

Laura stood panting for another few minutes, her head throbbing, then walked slowly down to the next corner, where the bright lights told her that she had come out of the residential district, away from the brownstones. A cab came by, and she weakly hailed it.

It took her back to the Hyatt, where she went directly to her room, stripped, and took a scalding shower. Afterwards, she vomited again, into the toilet, and fell into bed. She awoke before dawn, felt the peristalsis begin, and managed to reach the plastic wastebasket in time. In the morning, still sick, she washed the wastebasket out in the tub. As the detritus was swept away, she stared into the swirling eye of the water and began to cry, her head resting on the cool, white porcelain. She cried for a long time, then cleaned herself up, got dressed, and went back into the world.

> The worth I credited him with, the cleverness, the goodness, the everything!
> —Alexander Smith, *Dreamthorp*

"Life is good, Freddy," said Danny Vernon, taking another toke. "Music is good, pussy is good, life is good."

"Yeah, well, too much reefer *ain't* good, Danny. Don't be smokin' too much of that shit before we done playin', you hear?"

"Hell, nah, it ain't too much. You want a little more?" Danny held out the joint to Freddy. There was a good inch and a half left to it.

"No. Neither do you."

"Shit, Freddy, you gettin' to be like my old lady. How 'bout you, Johnny?" Danny held out the joint to the boy, who shook his head politely.

"No thanks, Danny. I'll stick to the beer."

God*dam,* but he was a funny kid, Danny thought. Not that there was anything funny about turning down reefer, hell, a lot of folks were against anything that made their bodies goofy these days. It was something about his eyes, the way he looked at Danny sometimes when he didn't think Danny was looking at him. Shit, Johnny seemed nice enough—had come to hear them every night for a week now, knew his jazz like a true disciple, even though he didn't play anything himself. Finally on Wednesday night Danny started to invite him backstage between sets.

Not that it was much of a backstage, just a little area with a john, a few worn-out easy chairs, a couch, and a bunch of pedestal ashtrays. But at least it was someplace where you could smoke reefer or snort a line of coke when a well-heeled jazz buff slipped you a gram or two as payment for a request. Johnny seemed to like it just fine, and acted, Danny told Freddy later, as though he'd been given an audience with the goddam pope or something.

Al Joss, the pianist the group was named after, asked Danny what the hell he meant by bringing somebody backstage, but after Johnny talked to him for awhile, the man was won over, and now spent as much time with him as any of them. Only Sam, the drummer, seemed to have no time for the kid, and when he found him backstage, went out to the bar without a word. "Fuck 'im," Danny told Johnny, when the boy seemed pained by the rebuff. "Nigger hasn't smiled since Bird died. Says he's in a state of 'perpetual mourning,' but I think the cocksucker's just a prick. Ignore 'im."

After the sessions were over, they would sit at the bar and chatter until closing, then go home, although Johnny never said where he lived. But tonight was Friday, and Fridays, dammit, were *special* for Danny Vernon and Freddy Jefferson. Al and Sam still went home on Fridays, just like every other night, but Friday night (or Saturday morning) was *pussy* for Danny and Freddy. They'd been doing it for seven years now, and as Danny pushed back the plastic curtain that separated their little green room from the john and tossed the roach into the toilet bowl, he wondered if maybe they might not have a third party along this Friday night.

He suggested it to Freddy between the numbers of the last set, and the bass man's black face turned into a webwork of quizzical wrinkles. "You think he like dark meat, man?"

Danny shrugged. "If he's ever had it, he can't help but like it, and if he ain't had it, I think we owe it to the boy to increase his education."

Finally the set ended, and Danny and Freddy met Johnny at the bar, where he was waiting for them. Danny liked the way the kid's face lit up when he saw the two jazzmen, and he signaled to the bartender to bring them their usual, but Danny held up a hand.

"Whoa, not tonight, Johnny, my man. Tonight's more special than Michelob, know what I'm sayin'? We goin' someplace *different* tonight, and you're invited to come along with us."

Johnny's face grew puzzled, almost angry, Danny thought, as though he were upset that the traditional drinks and talk would be someplace else. Danny smiled as he thought happily that this could be the start of a whole *new* tradition for Johnny. Shit, maybe a whole new way of life, once he was initiated into the pleasures of Miss Minnie's. Once you split the black oak, oh *my* yes . . .

"Where?" Johnny asked, disappointment in his voice.

"Little place we know," Freddy answered, his grin almost neon in its intensity.

"You'll like it," Danny said. "Swear to God, son."

Something even weirder than usual came over the kid's face then, and Danny wondered what the hell he had said to cause it. The kid was spooky, no shit, but there was something about him Danny couldn't help but like.

No, he thought that maybe *like* wasn't the right word. Something he was *drawn to* was closer, wasn't it? Yeah, it sure was. He hoped to hell he wasn't getting queer in his old age, but then he thought of Peaches lying on her back, her legs spread and her huge titties flopping to either side, dark brown nipples against those white, white sheets, and decided that being queer was the least of his worries.

"Yeah," Johnny said, "but *where?*"

"Min-nie's," Freddy pronounced polysyllabically, and gave an expectant and theatrical shudder.

"What, like a jazz place?"

"*Jazz* is right," laughed Danny. "Jazz all night."

"Yeah?" Johnny smiled weakly. "Sounds good. Is this like a blues place? I mean, like *Memphis* Minnie, you know?"

"This is *Chicago* Minnie," Freddy told the kid, laying a hand on his shoulder. "You gonna find it . . . different."

"But good," Danny added. "Come on. We take Freddy's car."

Freddy's car was a 1968 red Cadillac limo, impeccably appointed and freshly waxed. Freddy drove, Johnny sat in the front seat, and Danny stretched out in the back, smiling in the darkness at the kid's reaction to the car. "Is this like a *limo?*" Johnny asked.

Freddy nodded. "I used to drive this—was a chauffeur when I wasn't playin', you know? The main man died and left it to me in his will, you believe that? I took it glad enough, though I painted her red. Looked like a fuckin' hearse when it was black. They call it a stretch limo, and let me tell you, boy, a lot of women been stretched out in that backseat.''

"That why it smell like fish back here, Freddy?'' Danny said.

"You got it. Don't stick to the seat now.''

"Bullshit. You keep this car cleaner than a rich baby's ass.''

"How, uh . . .'' Johnny cleared his throat. "How many miles to the gallon do you get in something like this?''

"Shit, two, three, I don't know. Never checked. Don't matter, though. All I do's drive around town anyway.''

"So, Johnny,'' Danny asked after a few minutes of silence had passed, "what you think of the Blue Light so far?''

He could see Johnny's head nodding. "Great place. Great music especially. How did you guys ever get together?''

"Why shouldn't we have?'' Danny asked.

"Well, I mean, uh . . . I guess I meant . . .''

"You meant since Al and I are white and Freddy and Sam are black?''

"No, no! No, I didn't mean that.''

"It's okay, kid,'' Danny said. "Jazz is a lot more ready to mix the races than most other things in this fuckin' society. Besides, I'm just a white nigger anyway.'' Freddy chuckled softly, and Danny laughed in response, then went on. "I like black people. I like their music—because jazz *is* their music—the best jazz, anyway. I like the way they walk, and talk, and the way their women can love you. I work with black folk, and I'm married to a black woman.''

"You're married?'' the kid asked.

"That's right. Never know it, would you? Been married four times too. Each bitch was worse than the one before, but I still kept doin' it. I shoulda stuck with the first one, I guess. She was the best of a bad lot.'' Danny didn't know why he was telling the kid all this, but now that he had started, he figured he might as well go ahead. "Funny thing is that she was the only white one too. Though she *looked* dark. She was part Indian—Seminole, not curry-breath Indian, you know? Hell, I could believe it, the way she used to whoop when we were doin' it. Christ, that was back in Orleans, must've been what, twenty-five years ago? She died a long time ago. We never did get a divorce. I think I married Eula before I found out my first wife died, so I guess I must've been a bigamist for a while. Never got arrested anyway, and it's too late now. Statute of limitations long run out.''

"Statute of limitations?'' Freddy said. "I thought that's what you use to figure out if a girl is old enough to fuck or not.''

"Oh, did I forget?'' Danny said to Johnny. "I love nigger *humor* too. Well, kid, I told you all about myself, what about you?''

"What about me?''

"Nothin' personal if you don't want. How about jazz? Why you like jazz so fuckin' much?''

Johnny looked out the window at the lights flashing by. "I don't know. The sound of it, I guess. And the life.''

"The life? What you mean, the life?'' Freddy asked.

"It's like . . . like dying young and beautiful.''

"Well, you with the wrong bunch, Johnny,'' Danny said. "We ain't young and we sure as shit ain't beautiful.''

"Speak for yourself, brother,'' Freddy said, chuckling.

"No, no,'' Johnny said. "I just mean that so many of them—Bird and Coltrane, Bud Powell, Dolphy, Clifford Brown—they died so young. Left so much.''

"We living proof you can grow old in jazz,'' Freddy said. "And what about Ellington and Sidney Bechet and Louis Armstrong? And Dexter Gordon's still around—made a goddam *movie*. Becomes a movie star in his sixties. Man, there's hope for me yet.''

"I meant . . .'' Johnny went on, "I just meant that it seems . . . romantic.''

"Nothin' romantic about dyin' young,'' Danny said. "Or dyin' old.''

They drove several more blocks, and Freddy pulled into an all-night parking lot, handed the attendant three bucks, and locked the doors. "Gotta lock up here. Spics'll rob you blind.''

Danny watched Johnny as they walked up the street. The kid was curious, he could tell, but also jumpy as hell, and Danny patted him on the shoulder. "Relax, son,'' he said. "Everything be cool.''

They stopped in front of a long, rectangular building that looked like an apartment house and went into the lobby. An old black man in a doorman's uniform sat on a folding chair, and smiled at them with yellow teeth as they walked to the elevator. "Howya doin' tonight, Frank?" Freddy said.

"Good, good, now don't you dip it too deep tonight," the doorman said, and cackled like a woman.

"Ain't no such a thing as too deep at Minnie's," Danny answered, and the old man cackled again and slapped his thigh.

"Frank's been here longer than dirt," said Freddy as the elevator doors closed on them. "Long's *I* been coming here anyway."

Johnny cleared his throat. "There's, uh . . . there's no sign out front."

Both older men laughed. "Not the kind of place you advertise," Danny said. "Sort of a word-of-mouth kind of place."

"Yeah, mouth is right," Freddy agreed. "Mouth and a whole lotta other places too."

Danny looked closely at Johnny. "You kiddin', son? You really don't know what this is?"

Johnny nodded. "I think so. A whorehouse."

"Now you talkin'," Freddy said.

Danny waved a hand at Freddy to be quiet. "Just a minute." Then he turned to Johnny. "That bother you, Johnny? You rather not come with us? Because, I mean, we thought you'd enjoy it. But if you ain't, well, you don't have to come along." The elevator stopped, but Danny pushed the button to hold the doors closed. "You know?"

Danny felt uncomfortable as he looked into Johnny's eyes. He couldn't tell if the boy was angry or frightened or upset or feeling some other emotion that he couldn't read.

"I'll come," he said finally, and Danny took his finger off the elevator button.

The doors opened and they stepped out into a utilitarian hall walled with concrete blocks painted yellow. "Down this way," Danny said. "Minnie's got this whole floor. Used to be part of a housing development. Built back in the early sixties. Then it got trashed and regentrified, but Minnie's been here all these years."

Danny tried hard not to grin. He was sure that Johnny was picturing a fat, black madam dressed in feathers and silk—a mixture of Mammy and Belle Watkins in *Gone With the Wind*. So when the door opened and Minnie stood there, tall and svelte and dressed in a white satin gown that hugged every curve and yelled bullshit to her fifty-plus years, he bit back a chuckle and patted Johnny on the shoulder. "Evening, Minnie. We've brought along a friend tonight. His name's Johnny."

"Well, isn't that nice," Minnie said in a husky voice, smiling a smile that once could have had half the men,— white and black—of Chicago down on their knees to lick her toes. "We'll take good care of him." She tilted her head and gazed at Johnny, and Danny wondered what she saw there. "You a little nervous, Johnny?" Johnny shook his head. "Well, good. You don't have to be. My girls are all safe. They get blood tests once a month for AIDS, and nobody does a thing without a condom. I hope that's all right with you?" Johnny nodded again. "The girls have them, so you don't have to run out to the drugstore or anything." She turned to Danny. "Peaches is ready, Danny. And Freddy, Sheila is waiting for you." Then she looked appraisingly at Johnny. "Johnny—I think maybe Cindy would suit you. Very young, very pretty. You'll like her. You two veterans, you know where to go. Johnny, you come with me."

Minnie led the boy away then, and Danny watched him go. There was something about the way his shoulders were set, some indication of tension Danny read in his back, that made him wonder if he had really done the right thing bringing him here. Then he remembered Cindy. Although he had never been with her, he had talked to her a few times. She was a sweet girl, kind and gentle. If anyone could settle Johnny down, it would be Cindy.

Cindy Jackson was tired. She had had four men already that night, beginning at eight o'clock. Two had been regular clients, older men who were undemanding, predictable, and tired easily, the type of man she could ball all night and still have energy enough for tennis the next morning.

But the other two had been young and full of juice, all of which, she truly believed, they had sprayed into their condoms. The first had used two, apparently not getting enough the first time, and wanting anal sex for the encore. She didn't like it that way, but if they used a rubber and paid enough, she allowed it, trying to make her moans of discomfort sound like moans of passion. That was very important, Miss Minnie had always told her. No matter if it hurts so much you scream, darlin', make it a scream of passion, and they'll love you for it. And after all, she'd never been hurt, not really. That type of man didn't come to Minnie's.

There was a quiet knock on the door of her room, and she sat up on the bed, patting her hair into place, and crossed her legs demurely. "Come in," she called.

The door opened, and Minnie stood there, a tall and good-looking white boy behind her. "Cindy, honey, this is Johnny. It's his first time here, so you be real sweet to him, all right?"

"Whatever he wants, Miss Minnie. I'm all his." She smiled at the boy, but felt something very much like fear lance through her when she saw his answering expression. He smiled, but it was an icy smile, edged with cruelty. Miss Minnie did not see it, for when she turned around it lightened like the sun spearing through clouds. She ushered him into the room, then went out, closing the door behind her.

"Hi," she said. "Well, here we are."

His smile vanished now. He nodded.

"Do you, uh . . . want to come over here and sit down with me?"

"I want you to take your clothes off," he said flatly.

She nodded, stood up, and began to undress, stopping with her panties.

"Everything," he said, and she slipped them off as well, then sat down on the bed, leaning back in a practiced, languorous pose.

"You want to come over here with me?" she said. "It's lonely on this big bed all by myself." He walked to the bed and stood beside it, looking down at her, his gaze roaming over her light mocha skin, the large breasts, narrow waist, slim, almost boyish hips. "I can . . . take you in my mouth," she said. "You don't have to wear a condom for that."

He looked down at her, and finally said, "I'll wear a condom. Where is it?"

Cindy reached over to the small nightstand beside the bed and pulled open a drawer. From it she took a small, foil-wrapped object and held it out to the man. "It's sheepskin. They're more expensive, but they feel a lot better. It'll feel like you're not wearing anything at all."

The man weighed the wrapped condom in his hand for a moment, then tore open the package and withdrew it, dropping the foil on the carpet next to the bed. He unfolded it and let it dangle. Then he slipped a finger into the opening, and another, and another, pulling it and stretching it around his hand like a tight mitten. Cindy gasped when he took a knife from his pocket and opened the blade, but he used it only to cut the string at the opening, to widen it so that he could slip his hand further inside. Now he had all four fingers encased, but try as he might, he could not get his thumb in. The tough, resistant membrane would not stretch that far.

At last he gave up his effort, and held up his hand. Through the layer of sheep gut, it looked like the hand of a dead man, pale yellow, glistening with lubricant.

"It's safe now," he said. "Safe sex."

He leaned down and she closed her eyes, remembering that it had never hurt before, not really, and praying that this time would be no different, even as she knew beyond a doubt that it would. This, she feared, would be very, very different indeed.

> The howling of the winter wind outside increases the warm satisfaction of a man in bed, but this satisfaction is succeeded by quite another feeling when the wind grows into a tempest, and threatens to blow the house down.
>
> —Alexander Smith, *Dreamthorp*

Dreamthorp welcomed Laura home with a mother's love. At least it seemed that way to her as she drove into its warm and leafy embrace. It was a haven of normality in a world of chaos, and even the recent deaths could not change that. The killings were an affliction, a cancer that would be discovered and expunged, so that everything would be normal again. The killer would be found, she knew that. Dreamthorp would not allow such things to happen for long.

The last two days of her five-day sojourn in Philadelphia had been the best of the lot. Although she felt like hell Thursday morning, she had taken command nonetheless, and, with her cold fury that allowed for nothing less than perfection, had completely terrified Kevin and even cowed Billy. She had no concern over whether Kevin or Billy thought she was a dyke, for she knew now that she was not, at least not in the casual and carnal sense of the women at the Venus. She considered that she was still capable of a lesbian love—after all, she had experienced one—but she rationalized it by telling herself what she firmly believed to be the truth, that anyone was capable of any act under a certain set of circumstances, and decided that she would no longer worry about herself sexually.

At least she would try not to.

It was noon when she arrived in Dreamthorp. She had the master three-quarter-inch videotape in her briefcase, and she felt she had sweated blood to get it. By Friday afternoon she was satisfied with the final edit, and had driven over to Renco's headquarters to show it to the CEO. When the thirty-second spot was over, he turned to her, gave a tight-lipped smile, and nodded. "Damn nice bear," he said, and she knew she had him.

Now she had a pleasant afternoon of being a porch potato to look forward to, and going to dinner and the theatre with Tom Brewer that evening. As she walked up her cottage steps, her relief at being home again was so great that she nearly cried. What was supposed to have been two days had turned into a budget-busting week. Oh well, she thought, it had happened before and would happen again. They might actually lose a bit of money on this one, but they had a new and satisfied client, so it was worth it.

Laura made a light lunch, then went onto the porch, sat on the swing, and read for an hour, after which she went inside and took a deep and satisfying nap. The phone woke her at four o'clock. It was Tom, who sounded as happy to hear her voice as she was to hear his. He told her that he had tried to call several times beginning Wednesday evening to make sure that they were still on for tonight, and promised to be at her place at six o'clock.

He was punctual, and they had dinner and arrived early at the Hall of Culture. She told him about the nightmares of her week in Philadelphia, leaving out only the dinner with Billy and the subsequent visit to the Venus. He was appropriately amused and sympathetic, and by the time the first act of *Ten Little Indians* began, they had regained the rapport she had felt the last time they were together, and she decided that she liked Tom Brewer immensely.

After the play, they went again to the Ice Cream Shoppe, and then Laura invited Tom back to her cottage for a drink, claiming that it was her turn to provide the hospitality. They mixed the drinks in the kitchen—a gin and tonic for Laura, a scotch on the rocks for Tom—then took them onto the porch, where they sat side by side on the swing and sipped them slowly. Tom told her what little there was to tell about the quiet week in Dreamthorp, and about Josh's reaction to his suggestion that they undergo therapy together. Laura took his hand then and told him that it was easy to understand why the boy would feel that way, but that it must not let Tom change his plans. Josh had to have help, whether he realized it or not, and Tom agreed.

Laura did not take her hand away, and neither did Tom. They sat there silently, looking into the dark street. "I feel like your parents should be inside peeking at us from behind the curtain," Tom finally said, and they both laughed.

"It does have that Victorian feel to it, doesn't it," Laura said more quietly. "The swing, the porch, the summer night . . ."

He squeezed her hand gently, and she returned the pressure, not looking at his face. Then she felt his hand touch her chin, and she turned her head and looked into his soft eyes. He leaned toward her and they kissed, close-mouthed and chastely with warmth, not lust, although she felt a flicker of passion deep within her. But she felt too that Tom's kiss was not offered as a prelude to sex but simply as an expression of warmth, even love, she thought, and, she was surprised to find, she hoped.

They drew away from each other then, and a look passed between them that told Laura that there was no hurry, that they had time, the rest of their lives. He would not push her. There would be no haste, for there was no need of it.

His look was so serene, so filled with patience, that she nearly asked him to take her inside then and there and make love to her. But she did not. Something held her back.

When she was able to speak again, she said, "It's getting late."

"Yeah," he said. "It is." He sighed and smiled. "Maybe I should leave."

She made her face grow serious. "You . . . have quite a long walk ahead of you." They both laughed then. "Do you want another drink?"

"No, not really." He looked at her for a moment, and she could tell he very much liked what he saw. "I should go." He paused. "Shouldn't I?"

"Yes. I guess so. Before my parents chase you home."

They stood up then, and he took her in his arms. She put

her arms around him, loving the girth and the strength that she felt in him, and they kissed again, more deeply this time. Afterward, he touched her hair and whispered good night, then turned and walked away, looking back to wave to her.

Laura slept deeply and well that night. She awoke only once, thinking for an excited and pleasant moment that Tom was lying beside her, and, when she realized she was alone, went back to sleep and dreamed him there.

"But what did he *do* to her?"

"I don't *know,* Danny. Fuckin' Minnie wouldn't tell me."

"Well, did he *hurt* her at all?"

"I don't *think* so. If he had, she woulda yowled."

"Well, what the hell'd he *do,* Freddy?"

"He scared her. That's what Minnie said."

"He scared her with what, though? A fifteen-inch dick? Shit, man, why didn't you make her tell you?"

"Why didn't *you,* you such a tough guy?"

"I was gone, man. You know how 'Becca gets when I come home too late. Sniffin' around me like a bitch in heat, smellin' for other women. And hell, I come out of Peaches' room and the kid is sittin' there in the hall, I figure he's done, pay for him and me and give him a lift back to his hotel. I don't see that little whore Cindy at *all.*"

"That's because she's in there cryin' for a while, Minnie says. Shit, she near to tore my head off, I come outta the room. 'Don't you *never* bring that boy back here again, I ain't havin' none of that sick shit pesterin' my girls' and on and on and I don't know what the hell she talkin' about and she ain't gonna tell me, just that he scared poor little Cindy half outta her wits and he come in there again she have Big Jim drop him offa the fuckin' roof. So I don't argue, I just pay and get the hell outta there before she tell Big Jim to drop *me* offa the roof because the kid come in with me. So let's not take him back there, okay?"

"Yeah. Yeah, sure. I don't think he enjoyed it all that much anyway. He said he did, but I could tell he was lyin'. No. Hell, no. We don't take him back there again."

"I don't want to take him *nowhere* again, Danny. That boy is weird. He can be nice, but I don't trust him. He's just . . . freaky somehow."

"He's okay."

"Shit my ass. He's *weird.*"

"Aw, you're a goddam old woman. So Johnny treats whores a little strange, a *lot* of people treat whores strange. That's why whores charge money, to do things that wives and girlfriends don't like to do. Hazards of the trade, man."

"Well, I just want him out of my face."

"I say he's all right."

"What the fuck? You sweet on him or somethin'?"

"I can beat you, Freddy. I can whip your black ass, and you know I can because I've done it. And I can do it again. Right now, right here in this bar if you say somethin' like that again. Now Johnny's all right, I tell you. Don't you bad-mouth him any more."

"All right. All right, that's the way you feel."

"That's the way I feel. I don't really know why, but it is. That's all there is to it. We don't take him back to Minnie's, but he comes to the Blue Light often as he wants."

"Okay . . . okay. Now don't get pissed off, but why you like this kid so much, Danny?"

"I . . . shit, I don't know."

"Well, shit, I don't know either."

The love of fathers for their sons, Tom Brewer thought, could excuse a great many mistakes and weaknesses. He lay in bed thinking of several things, among them his feelings for Laura Stark and how his son would react to them. That Laura was much closer to his own age was an advantage, as was the fact that she was a resident of Dreamthorp. Familiarity would be easy to come by, with her only two houses away. With such close proximity, it would be, Tom thought, like the widowed master of the house falling for the governess.

And too, Laura seemed to like Josh, from the little he had seen of the two of them together. And even if she didn't, at least she was sympathetic toward his problems, certainly more so than Karen had ever been. There had been an adversarial relationship from the beginning between those two. He berated himself for the hundredth time, wondering why he had ever started the affair, thinking that the sex he had gotten had in no way been worth the problems it had caused Josh. What a selfish son of a bitch he was.

He looked at the clock and saw that it was just after 11:30.

Though he had an early class the next day, he could not sleep. The last three nights had been the same. His head was full of Laura Stark, Laura Stark and whatever the future might hold for the pair of them. He realized that he was taking a good deal for granted on the basis of two dates and as many kisses, but Tom, without a spouse, was a romantic, with the unwanted and anxiety-laden ability to view every woman with whom he came into contact as not so much a bedmate as a possible life mate. And Laura Stark seemed a highly favorable prospect.

He felt like a mooning teenager lying in his bed, wondering if he loved her and how she felt about him, if they could have a honeymoon, and if Josh would mind if they went off by themselves for a few days. He would not, he swore to himself, make the mistake of considering the boy a second class citizen again. He was his dearest blood, his son, and by God he would never again treat him so shabbily.

On the edge of sleep, Tom heard the sound. It was faraway, and sounded like a paper bag popping, but it was loud enough for him to sit up and listen for a repetition that did not come. He heard the creaking of his parents' bed in the room across the hall, but there was nothing more until the siren began fifteen minutes later.

Concerned over the possibility of fire, he leaped from his bed and went to the window. The siren grew louder, and he realized that it was not the fire siren and thanked God for it. But from the flashes of red that ripped through the darkness he also knew that two bubble-topped vehicles, perhaps a police car and an ambulance, were climbing toward the top of the hill. He continued to listen through the screen, and from the sound decided that they must have turned onto Longfellow or Channing.

He sat by the window for a few minutes, torn between wanting to go back to bed and wanting to get dressed to see what had happened. Finally he compromised by going to the bathroom and getting a drink. On the way back to his room, he listened at Josh's door, but heard nothing. Pushing it open a crack, he saw the familiar form under the sheet, but also noticed that the screen was pushed up slightly, and wondered why, since Josh hated bugs in his room.

Silently, he crossed the room and slid the screen back down until it was tight against the frame, then stood beside Josh's bed. In the dim light from the hall, he could see that something was not right, that the form beneath the sheet was not that of his son. Suddenly afraid, he tugged back the sheet and saw blankets and a pillow artlessly rolled to a rough approximation of the human shape. At that moment, his door bell rang.

Fear went deeper into him, like a hook with barbs that twisted into the flesh and would not let go, and he remembered that other night, less than a year before, and felt that if a policeman was somberly standing on his porch, that he would die of sorrow in that instant.

Tom Brewer did not die, though the policeman was there. It was Bret Walters, and the look on his face was so pained that Tom immediately knew what had happened.

"Josh?" Tom said thickly.

Bret licked his lips and nodded.

From upstairs Tom could hear his mother's voice through the loud rushing in his ears. "Tom? Is anything wrong?"

"Go back to bed, Mom. Everything's all right." He could not cope with her reactions to whatever had happened. He had to be alone with it first. He was afraid that he would strike her.

"But I heard those sirens . . ."

"Go back to *bed!*" He heard her gasp, and then the bedroom door slammed shut. "What happened?" he asked Bret.

The chief of police shook his head. "Not sure how it all happened, but . . . your boy . . . Josh . . . he was shot."

"Is he dead?"

Bret Walters hesitated, then nodded. "I'm sorry, Tom."

Tom nodded back. He felt empty, incapable of speech. He walked to the clothes tree, took down his raincoat, and slipped it on over his lightweight pajamas. Then he joined Bret Walters on the porch. He started to walk down the steps, but his legs trembled, and he sat helplessly, shaking his head.

"The bastard . . ." Tom whispered. "The bastard killed my boy . . . that . . . fucking . . . *maniac.*" He grabbed the hem of Bret's khaki jacket. "You've got to stop him, Bret, you've got to find that son of a bitch and *stop* him. . . ."

Bret looked horribly surprised. He sat down next to Tom and put an arm around his shoulder. Tom could tell that the gesture made Bret uncomfortable, but he did it anyway. "No, Tom . . . you got it wrong. We know who killed Josh."

Tom's body stiffened. "Who?"

"Ralph Goodwin."

"Ralph . . . Ralph *Goodwin?*" Ralph Goodwin, his neighbor? Friendly, short, balding Ralph Goodwin with the pretty wife and the red MG? Ralph Goodwin the man who had eviscerated Sam Hershey and mutilated Martha Sipling? And now killed Josh? It wasn't possible. It couldn't be. "Ralph Goodwin? The . . . the killer?"

Bret Walter's face was a study in frustration. He shook his head savagely. "Ralph shot your boy from his bedroom, Tom. Josh was outside his window. Up in a tree. He had a knife, Tom."

"I . . . I don't . . ."

"The state police are here, Tom. They think your boy's been the prowler. Maybe even . . ." Bret paused and released a huge sigh, then spoke very softly, ". . . the killer."

"That's . . ." The words came as if from out of a deep well. "That's a lie."

"Yeah, yeah, I know, Tom. But I mean look at the circumstances—they find him up a tree with a knife, and, goddamit, you know that everybody's edgy as hell with these killings and all—"

"That's a *lie*, Bret!"

"Tom?" someone said. Tom turned and saw Charlie Lewis over on his porch. "What happened?"

Tom couldn't speak. "There's been . . . an accident," Bret said. "Tom's boy's been shot."

"Oh Jesus," Charlie said. He crossed the yard toward the other two men. By the time he reached the porch Tom was on his feet.

"I've got to go up there now. Got to see Josh."

"All right, Tom, sure," Bret said. "But, Tom . . . aw God, Tom, he got hit in the, the head. Aw Jesus, Tom, I'm sorry."

"Okay, okay." Tom began to walk. He couldn't let himself cry now or he would never stop. He had to hold it back, wait until he had seen Josh. Then later, later he could cry, he could let himself go. But not now. Not yet. Control. Now, just keep it under control.

Bret Walters was right. It was very bad. The bullet, fired from a Mauser rifle, had penetrated the top of the skull, and taken away the top left part of the head. The face, however, was untouched, and although the medics had closed the eyes and the mouth, there was no hiding the expression of surprise on Josh's face.

My poor baby. My poor, poor baby.

He touched Josh's cheek with his hand. The skin was still smooth. There were no whiskers, just that fine, downy fuzz.

Oh my baby.

For the first time, he found himself glad that Susan was dead, and, certainly not for the first time nor for the last, found himself wishing that he was dead as well.

When he climbed down out of the ambulance, he looked up at the Goodwins' cottage, and through the window he saw the shiny pate of Ralph Goodwin. He was wearing a bathrobe and standing at the window, and he was crying. His wife, half a head taller than he, had her arm around him, and from the way her shoulders were shaking, Tom could see that she was crying too. They had known Josh. If they had thought he was the killer, would they have been crying, shedding tears over a monster? No, Ralph Goodwin knew what had happened, knew what a terrible and sad mistake he had made.

And Josh had made.

And Tom Brewer had made as well.

Tom looked at Charlie Lewis, and saw tears in his eyes. Everyone seemed to be crying but Tom, and he felt that that was the saddest thing of all.

The man who has a grave or two in his heart, does not need to haunt churchyards.

—Alexander Smith, *Dreamthorp*

Laura called Tom the next evening. She had gotten home late the night before and had heard nothing, having slept through the gunshot and the sirens. She only learned of the shooting when she read about it in the newspaper over dinner in the restaurant she stopped at on her way home. Back at her cottage, she dialed Tom's number.

"Tom, it's Laura," she said when he answered. "I just heard about Josh. Oh Tom . . . Tom, I am so sorry."

"It's all right." His voice was low but sounded under control. "An accident. A mistake." He sounded, she thought, *too* controlled, like a computerized voice.

"Tom, are you all right?"

"I'm fine."

"Can I do anything for you?"

"No."

There was pain there, she heard it. Tremendous, unbearable pain that she could sense beneath the layer of hardened indifference with which he tried to mask it. He was locking it away, locking *himself* away. "Have you talked to anyone about this yet?"

"The police."

"What about your parents?"

She heard him take a deep breath. "My mother is . . . not

capable of talking right now. My father doesn't seem to want to."

"I want to see you, Tom."

"No, Laura."

"I want to talk to you. I'm coming over."

"No." There was silence on his end of the line. Then he said, "I'll come over there."

A few minutes later he came walking up her cottage steps like a dead man. His eyes were dry and hollow, his hair was uncombed, and the skin of his face was pale and pouched. He looked as though he had aged five years, and she knew he had not slept for a long time.

"Hello," he said to her in a lifeless tone.

"Come in," she said, holding the door open as he shuffled through. They went across the hall into the small living room and Tom sat down on the couch, his shoulders slumped, his knotted hands hanging between his knees. She sat in a chair across from him. "How did it happen, Tom?"

"Did you read the papers?"

"I want *you* to tell me. You knew Josh. You know that what the papers said is a lie."

"Oh, they didn't come out and *say* it," Tom said with a bitter smile. "They just implied. I talked to the police again this afternoon around four, and they found out that Josh couldn't have had anything to do with Sam Hershey's death. He was working at Ted's all that afternoon, and Ted swore to it. Besides, how the hell would Josh have had the strength to do . . . what that maniac did? Bastards. Stupid bastards."

"So what did happen?"

He looked up at her, her face twisted. "He was *peeping,* that's what happened. He was peeping in people's windows at night. He had a pair of binoculars on his belt, but the paper didn't say anything about *that,* because that wouldn't have meant that he was the killer. All they talked about was the knife."

"Why did he have a knife?"

"Jesus, I don't know. Maybe he was scared, but not scared enough to stop what he was doing, so he took along what he thought was some protection. Christ, he must've been . . ." Tom shook his head and looked down again.

She finished it for him. "Obsessed. I know."

"I knew he was upset," Tom whispered, "but I didn't know

how much. If I would've seen it earlier, maybe I could've done something before he . . ." He gave his head a quick, savage shake. "I don't blame Ralph Goodwin," he went on in a softer voice. "I mean, you hear something outside your bedroom window, and you know that somebody's been killing people right and left, and you get your gun and you look out and see somebody in a tree, maybe with a gun, maybe Ralph even saw the knife, I don't know, and you're scared and you shoot, because for Christ's sake, he was just a few feet away from the window. . . ." He sighed. "No, I don't blame Ralph. I *hate* him, you know, for killing . . . my boy. But I don't blame him, isn't that weird? I can understand it. I can understand it. But I can't . . . *accept* it."

Tom Brewer's face was red now, and he was hyperventilating. Laura leaned forward in her chair, ready to get to her feet, to grab him, hold him, do whatever she had to.

"I haven't cried yet," he went on. "Isn't that . . . remarkable? That I haven't cried yet? I tell myself later, I'll do it later." The muscles of his face quivered. "But maybe if I wait too much longer, it'll be *too* late, and I won't at all . . . I won't be able to at all . . . like with Susan. . . ."

Suddenly his mouth stretched wide as in a death rictus, and sobs came leaping out of him, tears streamed from his eyes. Laura was beside him in an instant, her arms around him, trying to contain in their circle an infinite amount of grief finally released. It seemed to go on forever, a series of wracking sobs followed by a high, agonized whine; then a long, shuddering intake of breath; the sobs again, the whine, and always the tears, the drenching, cleansing tears. She held him like a child, and he surrendered to her embrace, leaning against her, trusting her with his weakness, as if knowing that only this weakness could restore him to strength.

At last his cries subsided, and he fell back from her embrace, resting his head on the back of the couch. "I . . ." he began to say, but his voice choked. He cleared his throat and went on, his gaze on the ceiling. "I was just going to say that I was sorry. But I'm not. I'm glad." He looked at her, and saw that her own eyes were watery with tears. "Thank you."

She nodded. "We're so close," she said, knowing that he would not understand it. "Oh, we are so close."

He didn't seem to have to understand. He simply took her

hand, wet with his tears, and held it. "I can't go back tonight. Not to that house. My parents . . . and just being in there . . ."

"Stay here."

He looked at her intently. "I don't mean to imply anything, you understand? I'll sleep down here. If I can sleep at all."

"It doesn't matter," she said. "One way or the other it's inevitable. Let me hold you tonight. You need to be held. And so do I. It's been such a long time, a long time since I've cried too."

There were no more words. It did not require the joining of flesh to make them lovers.

In the morning Tom awoke without illusions. Laura Stark was beside him, and he knew it the second his eyes opened. It was not Karen, nor was it dear, lost Susan. It was Laura, who loved him, and whom he loved. Laura, who saw his guilt and was willing to share it, who felt his pain and was willing to share that as well.

He watched her for a long time in the dim morning light that came through the bedroom window. Her face was delicately lined with years and experience and her own pain too, Tom thought. There were also the lines that smiles had made, but they were ghosts in comparison to the furrows between her eyes, those marks of sadness, of concern.

And when he thought of sadness he thought of Josh. Poor, dead Josh lying in the mortician's building in Chalmers, poor Josh, whom he might have saved had he known the depth to which his mother's loss and the perception of his father's infidelity had touched the boy. He got up from the bed and went into the hall, where he sat at the top of the stairs and cried again, this time alone, cried and asked God and Josh to forgive him, but prayed that he could someday forgive himself.

At least there was Dreamthorp. And now there was Laura.

They ate a light breakfast in her small kitchen, and talked little. The funeral was scheduled for the following day, and Laura told Tom that she would like to go. "I can take you," he said.

"Won't your parents be upset by that?" she asked.

"They can't be any more upset. They're drained."

"No, I don't think so," she said. "I'm sure Charlie's going. I'll go with him."

Tom nodded. "All right. It might be best." Then he looked at her curiously, and he thought she flinched a bit at his gaze.

"What is it?" she said.

"Tell me about the friend you lost. When you mentioned it before, I didn't understand. But now I think I might. Tell me."

Laura went to the coffee carafe and poured another cup before she started to speak. Then she told Tom Brewer about Kitty, and about Gilbert Rodman and what he had done, and what she had done to Gilbert Rodman and its aftermath. The only thing she did not talk about was what she and Kitty had felt and done before Rodman came slashing through their tent.

"Gilbert Rodman wasn't his name," Laura said, watching the patterns forming in the thin film of coffee oil that covered the liquid in her cup. "It's as if . . ." She paused and corrected herself. "It *was* as if he didn't need a name. He seemed like something inhuman. Like a force of nature. Oh, not in the bar where we met him, but when I came to and saw him . . ." her voice thickened, ". . . saw him hunched over Kitty. He was like a demon. Coated in blood. Hideous. Barbaric. I've never seen—and had never *imagined*—anything so terrible. And though I know he's dead, I'm still . . . afraid. I still think about him so much. And I think about Kitty. . . ."

Tom reached across the table and rested his hand on hers. "God, Laura, I'm so sorry."

"It's over," she said.

He shook his head. "Nothing's ever over. But you'll learn to live with it. Just like . . . I'll live with Josh."

She smiled bitterly. "It seems like every love . . . every attachment . . . sets you up for sorrow, doesn't it?"

"That's the price, I guess."

"It's high," she said, her eyes fixed on him.

"You're right. But sometimes we have no choice." He took a last gulp of his coffee and set down the cup. "I've got to go. There are so many things to be done."

"Will you be all right?"

"I'll be too busy to think. I pray to God I will, anyway."

"Call me if you need me."

She stood on the porch and watched him walk home. It

was still early, and no one was outside, so no one would know that he had spent the night there. Her practical side was relieved by that knowledge, but that side of her, she found, was shrinking, growing weaker. She had loved sleeping beside Tom Brewer, had loved waking up to his touch, sharing her morning coffee with him, telling him about herself, about what she feared. Perhaps one day, she thought, she could even tell him everything.

Then she remembered his son, and grieved for him, feeling guilty for thinking about her own wishes and needs and fears, while that boy with the sad and tragic and too short life lay dead with nothing to look forward to except his own funeral. Laura felt her throat close then and tears begin to form. Poor Josh, she thought. Poor Tom. Poor everyone.

And Tom, walking home, felt guilty as well. For in spite of sharing Laura's story, in spite of his son's death, in spite of everything with which fate had bludgeoned him, he could not help feeling something small and secret inside him that would help him keep his sanity and the days ahead. At last he had something for which he had been searching, and though it was not his son's love, which now he would never have, or the proven and unselfish love of a woman, which still could lie ahead, it was *something*.

At last he had his subject. At last he knew what he would bring out of the man-sized block of wood in his cellar.

At last he had Gilbert Rodman.

> Who would have thought of encountering
> a funeral in this place?
> —Alexander Smith, *Dreamthorp*

The people at the cemetery breathed the dust of the grave.

It was a hot and dry Friday, and the gusty winds that kicked up when least expected brought no relief. They brought only bits of soil that lodged in the eyes, so that even those not pricked by grief or guilt rubbed tears away.

The funeral message was brief, preached by the minister of the church whose adjoining cemetery held the Brewer plot, a small parcel containing the earthly remains of Tom's paternal grandparents and an uncle who had died, only slightly older than Josh, in Germany during World War II. Susan's body had been interred there, and now Josh's was lying, coffin encased, on a bier next to his mother's grave.

Together again, Tom thought, and wished that he were with them in some better place. He felt miserable at the way the finality of the open grave, despite the minister's apocalyptic words, crushed his hope of eternity, smothered the last surviving vestiges of his childhood indoctrination. He had not been inside a church since Josh had begun to protest against being dragged to Sunday school. Maybe he should start going again, he thought. Even if, as he feared and suspected, the church taught lies, they were deeply felt and comforting ones. God knew he could use a little comfort.

He was sweltering in his suit, over eight years old and out of style but the only dark one he owned. Sweat was gathering in his armpits, and he could feel dampness in the small of his back. Even his feet felt choked. He blinked as another bit of dust blew into his eyes, and scrubbed it away with a knuckle. He found the dust welcoming. It gave him an excuse for his tears, as though, he told himself, he needed any. Men could cry; there was nothing wrong with that. Still, it made him feel weak, and he had to be strong, for his mother at least.

She had been crushed by Josh's death. As "odd," as she put it, as her grandson had become in the past year, she still loved him deeply, with the unquestioning generosity and support that a break in generations allows. When Tom returned to his house on Tuesday night and told his parents about Josh's death, Frances had become hysterical, delaying Ed's response until they had her calmed down and tucked into bed. Ed stayed by her side until she slept, and then had come downstairs to join Tom.

Tom could see that he had been crying. His cheeks were red where he had been rubbing them, and his eyes gleamed wetly. "I'm sorry, Tommy," he said, placing his hand on his son's shoulder. "I don't . . . I can't say . . . I find it *hard* to say what I feel. But I know how I would have felt if this had happened to you when you were young. There's nothing like . . . like your son. Even if you don't always get along. There's still something there that's so big. . . ." He sighed and a sob escaped him. "I love you, Tommy, I really do. I'm proud of you, I've always *been* proud. And Josh was . . . a good boy. He was."

The old man shook his head then and gave Tom's shoulder a final squeeze, then went upstairs to his wife. He didn't speak to Tom again about Josh's death, but now the silences that passed between them were filled with something other than space, and the task of mentally sedating Frances gave them a common goal.

Still, Tom could not help but feel that his father blamed him for Josh's death, even as he realized the feeling was illogical. He blamed himself, and so saw judgment on the faces of everyone else. Now, as he looked at the blinking, tear-stained faces of the people at the funeral, he saw no blame in their eyes. Their tears were for Josh and for Tom's loss. His mother, beside him, clung to his hand with a grip so strong he feared his fingers would break. He was glad for the pain and the distraction it caused him.

Laura sat three rows back, next to Charlie Lewis. She was blinking and sniffing frequently, but met his gaze steadily when he looked at her. Charlie was dry eyed but miserable looking. He had moved into his house when Josh was five, and the man and the boy had taken to each other instantly. It was only since Susan's death that Josh had grown away from Charlie's camaraderie, as he had grown away from so much else.

Tom saw a number of Josh's classmates as well, some of them friends he had stopped seeing, who had now come to say their last good-bye. His teachers were there too, and the principal of the middle school, along with a wide assortment of Tom's neighbors and colleagues from Harris Valley College. There must have been well over a hundred people, and Tom wondered sardonically if they didn't get tired of coming to Brewer funerals.

The drone of words from the minister stopped. Tom looked up and saw that the service was over. There would be, he had decided, no reception at his house, no dishes full of plastic-wrapped cold cuts, no full coffeepots bubbling in the kitchen, no gathering of people not knowing what to say. This was no death of an aged relative, and that ever-so-useful line, "It really was a blessing that he didn't suffer any longer," was totally unsuitable in this situation. No, when the funeral director had brought up the idea, Tom had said that everybody could just go home. And they did.

Tom went home as well. He felt no urge to remain and watch the casket lowered, the grave filled in. He needed no further evidence that Josh was dead.

Back at the house, the only person who came over was Charlie Lewis. Tom was sitting on the porch with his parents when Charlie paid his respects and offered his sympathy in such a courtly manner that Tom had to smile. "I'll be over shortly, Charlie," Tom finally said. "Make sure the beer's cold." Charlie smiled sadly, nodded, and returned to his cottage.

"Tommy," Ed said after a few minutes, "we'll be going back to Florida on Monday. I called and got tickets last night."

"Dad, you don't have to do that. . . ."

"No, it's best. You need time to yourself now." Ed shook his head. "We shouldn't have come to begin with. Bad timing. You still needed to adjust, you didn't need us around. But if there's anything we can do to help, just say so, all right?''

Tom put an arm around his father's shoulder. "Sure, Dad. Thank you."

He had a light lunch with his parents, then went over to Charlie's and had that beer. They talked for a while, mostly about baseball and the weather, nothing at all about Josh. The conversation drifted to Laura Stark, and Charlie intimated none too subtly that Tom could do a lot worse than to get involved with her. Tom smiled in tacit agreement, and went home after another beer.

He called Laura and thanked her for coming to the funeral, and begged off taking her to the show at the playhouse the following night, a request to which she graciously acquiesced. Then he hung up, told his father he would be in his workshop, and went down into the cellar where the block of wood waited for him.

Gilbert Rodman was in there, and as Tom examined the piece of wood he could see him inside, waiting for release. He did not know what Gilbert Rodman looked like, but he knew what he was—a brutal and malignant force, rough-hewn and savage. Tom circled the block warily, as if the creature inside could doff his mantle of wood and spring out at him as ferociously as on the night he had cut his way into Laura's tent.

And slowly, as he scrutinized the block, he became aware that not only was Gilbert Rodman there, but something else as well. This was the tree, he thought, on which Sam Hershey had died in agony. And though he knew that wood was not sentient, Tom felt the presence of that other nameless, faceless killer who had murdered two people and been indirectly responsible for the death of a third, his own son. They were both in there, maybe one and the same, or at least the same mad rage that drove them both.

He touched the wood and could almost imagine that it was warm, that the thing inside was eager to be free.

All right then. He would free it. His craft, his art would free it.

He picked up his tools.

* * *

Tom Brewer spent the rest of Friday and most of Saturday laboring over the block of pine, stopping only to sleep and eat and talk to Bret Walters on the telephone when Bret called to tell him that no charges were going to be brought against Ralph Goodwin, a decision that Tom agreed with. He pitied Ralph, and was not surprised when Bret told him that Ralph and his wife were planning to sell their house and move away from Dreamthorp. Tom's lack of vengefulness surprised him, but still, he wished Ralph Goodwin nothing but peace.

By Sunday morning, Tom had nearly finished the basic form of the sculpture. All the corners were hacked off, the projections removed. What remained was the configuration of a giant in a low crouch. Tom removed the last large chunk and stepped back to observe his work.

It was a good start, he thought. Crude, but a powerful shape. There was potential there for a masterful piece, the best he had ever done.

"You're there, Gilbert," he said with quiet intensity. "I know you're there now. I can *see* you."

Did that man with the idiotic laugh and the blurred utterance ever love?
    —Alexander Smith, *Dreamthorp*

Gilbert Rodman, the real Gilbert Rodman, if such a being existed, was not in Tom Brewer's workshop in Dreamthorp. He was in Chicago, waking up on a sofa in the living room of Danny Vernon's apartment. His mouth tasted like the paper on the bottom of a bird cage. The last thing he remembered before sleep was his father guiding him up a flight of stairs, saying, "Can't go home tonight like you are . . . sleep onna sofa . . . have 'nother drink firs' . . ."

They had both been terribly drunk. There had been a scene with Freddy, who had wanted to go to Minnie's but refused to go with Gilbert. Danny wouldn't go, "Not unless Johnny comes too," and there was a lot of "Well, fuck you," "Oh yeah, fuck *you*," "Well, fuck you and fuck Minnie too, man," and on and on.

Gilbert had no desire to go to Minnie's again. He had almost lost control the first time and didn't want a repeat performance. Besides, he thought, how many times can you go to a whorehouse without dropping your pants? So Danny had told Freddy to go alone then and fuck you one last time, and he and Gilbert had hopped around to the clubs that were still open past two, listened to jazz, and drank more and more. Gilbert had tried to limit himself to beer, but Danny kept plying him with bourbon, and Gilbert kept drinking it, feeling foolish, knowing all the while that he would be sick, and that the only reason he was doing it was to please and impress his father.

Before he even realized it, he was a giggling drunk, barely capable of standing on his own power. That had been when Danny had taken him back to his apartment. Gilbert remembered going up the stairs, but that was all.

Now he was awake, and the smell of fresh coffee was strong and tempting. The room he was in was decorated, if that was the word, in a shabby Danish modern. There were a few pictures on the wall, one a nude of a black woman with a rampant afro, another an oil on velvet painting of a black saxophone player. Gilbert thought it was supposed to be Coleman Hawkins, but wasn't sure.

Then he felt something stir at his feet and started violently. A cat fatter than any he had ever seen uncoiled itself, oblivious to Gilbert's sudden motion, stretched, yawned, and rolled as much as it jumped off the sofa, and lumbered through a doorway into another room.

"Hey, Fats," he heard Danny's voice say. "What you want, huh?" There followed the sound of a chair sliding across linoleum, then footsteps, and Gilbert saw Danny, wearing a pair of bermuda shorts and a t-shirt, standing in the doorway. "Well, you awake, sleeping beauty? 'Bout time. It's almost noon. You think you could keep down some breakfast?"

Gilbert cleared his throat. "Uh, yeah, I guess so. A little."

"Fine." He turned toward someone in the other room. " 'Becca, how about rustlin' us up some eggs. Put a little onion and peppers in 'em."

"We ain't got no eggs," the voice said, and Gilbert was certain that it was the woman he had talked to on the telephone when he dialed his father's number several weeks before.

"What do you mean we ain't got no eggs?"

"We're *out* of eggs. You eat too many eggs anyway. That cholesterol ain't good for you."

"Says who?"

"Says Dr. Art Ulene. All the time."

"Who the hell's Dr. Art Ulene?"

"That doctor on TV—the *Today Show.*"

"Well, fuck Dr. Art Ulene—go down to the store and get some eggs."

"Hell, no. I ain't your goddam servant, and if you want eggs you can get 'em yourself. I ain't gonna help put you in an early grave. It's bad enough you smoke and drink so much and god only knows what else. One of these days you gonna bring home somethin' you catch from messin' around out there and I'm gonna laugh."

"Well, if I bring it home, you'll get it too."

"Maybe I just better cut you off then. Or cut *it* off, I don't know which."

"Shit." Danny looked back at Gilbert. "This's my wife, Johnny. Don't ever get married."

"Says you," came the voice from the kitchen.

"I'm goin' down for some eggs," Danny said, heading for the door. "Be back in fifteen." The door closed behind him.

Gilbert sat up, still dressed, and ran a hand through his hair. He needed to find the bathroom, both to drain away what he had to drink the night before, and to splash cold water in his face and mouth. Then 'Becca walked through the doorway to the kitchen.

Gilbert was surprised by her appearance. He had expected a human equivalent of the cat, fat, slovenly, and much the worse for wear. But 'Becca was a handsome woman who appeared to be in her early forties. She was tall and slender with skin the color of milky cocoa. Her straightened hair fell to her shoulders, and she held a cup of coffee in one long-nailed hand.

"Well well well," she said in a voice much softer than the one that had come stridently from the kitchen. "You're a whole lot cuter than most of the trash Danny brings home. Johnny, is it?"

He nodded. "Yeah. Johnny."

"And you're white. That don't happen often neither." She smiled and breathed deeply, pushing the lapels of the thin robe she wore further apart, so that the inner arcs of her breasts were visible. Gilbert looked down at the floor.

"Do you . . . uh, where's the bathroom?" he asked her.

"Planning to escape? Don't worry, honey, I ain't plannin' on hurtin' you." She sidled over and sat next to him on the couch. He began to get up, but she put a hand on his arm and held on. "What's the matter? You don't like me or some-thin'?" There was a teasing, petulant smile on her face.

"Yeah . . . sure, I like you fine."

"Well, loosen up then. My husband sure does loosen up. And what's sauce for the goose . . ." She set her coffee cup on the floor and leaned back against the sofa cushions. "Now Danny gonna be gone for quite a while after those eggs. How you think we could spend the time? Doin' somethin' con-structive?"

Gilbert felt a rush of nausea sweep over him, and he started to tremble. 'Becca's expression grew serious, and she leaned toward him, oblivious of the way her robe opened, and put an arm around him.

"Whoa, whoa," she said. "Hey, you really *are* sick. Re-lax now, I was just foolin'."

"What the *fuck?*"

Gilbert had not heard the door open. Now, as he looked up, he saw his father standing in the doorway, his hands on his hips, his jaw thrust forward pugnaciously. "What the hell you doin' here?" 'Becca said, pushing herself away from Gilbert and drawing the front of her robe together.

"I come back for my *wallet*. What the hell are *you* doin'?"

"The kid's sick."

"And you sure enough look like you're tryin' to mother him!"

"Hell, Danny, I was just foolin' around, just teasin' him a little . . ."

"Teasin' him? That what you call stickin' your titties in his face? Teasin' him? Get the fuck outa here, Johnny!"

Gilbert looked from the man to the woman and back again. "No," he said softly. Though he was still shaking, he felt strangely in control.

"No? Whaddya mean, no?"

"I mean no. It wasn't all her fault."

"Oh, now you sayin' you had somethin' to do with it? I ask a guy to my home and he starts tryin' to dick my wife? Well, that's just fine, and I'll deal with you later, you moth-erfucker—"

motherfucker

"—but I want to deal with this bitch right now, so you get the hell out of here while you can still walk. . . ."

"No."

Danny's eyes narrowed. "Hey, boy," he said, and went over to a small desk in the corner of the room. He opened a drawer and took a knife from it. When Gilbert saw it, he smiled. It was shiny and curved and long, a knife to gut a deer with. "Now did you hear me or didn't you?" Danny went on, holding up the knife.

Gilbert kept smiling.

"Danny," 'Becca whispered, "don't you be a fool."

"Shut up. Go next door, 'Becca. I'll deal with you later. Right now I'm dealing with this boy."

"I ain't goin' nowhere."

"Go," Gilbert said, his eyes still on the knife, wanting it. "Go on, Mother."

"You watch what you call my wife, you little fucker!"

"You said it yourself. She was mothering me."

"*Move*, 'Becca!" Danny snarled, turning the knife in her direction.

"You put that knife away first," she said.

Danny took a step toward her and flicked it across the front of her robe. It ripped the material and made a narrow gash in her flesh. Gilbert thought it looked as though Danny had drawn a narrow paint brush across her skin. She gave a short, tiny scream, as though she could not believe what her husband had done, and backed away from him.

"Next time, 'Becca," Danny said, "it'll be worse."

"You *bastard!*"

"*Out,* 'Becca!"

Sobbing, she ran to the open door and went through it into the hall. Gilbert heard her bare feet pounding down the stairs. He wondered how much time he had before she came back with someone. Probably not very much, but time enough to tell him.

"It wasn't all her fault," Gilbert said again. "You see, I always thought it was, always blamed her, never you. But now I know better."

"What the hell are you talkin' about?"

"You did the same thing today, didn't you? You went away and left us. You left us both. And the same thing happened all over again, didn't it?"

Danny looked understandably puzzled. "You still drunk or what?"

"No no," Gilbert answered, still smiling. "I'm very sober, believe me. And I can see very, very clearly now. I thought you'd be different, but you're not. You did it again, went away and left me with that Great Bitch. And she wanted it, just like they all want it. Oh, I blame her, but I can't blame *only* her anymore."

"You're nuts, kid," Danny said. He was holding the knife toward Gilbert, and his hand was shaking. "You're either nuts or drunk or stoned. That it? You stoned?" He laughed crazily. "You got some shit you weren't gonna share with your old buddy Danny? That ain't very nice after I shared my place, my *wife*—"

"It's not the first time . . . Father."

"Father? You *must* be stoned. You think I'm a priest?" Danny asked, chuckling.

"Oh no. Priests are good men. They wouldn't go away and leave their wives alone with their sons, if they *had* wives. Or sons."

Danny frowned more deeply, as if trying to resolve a particularly irresoluble paradox or accept an impossible anachronism. "Sons . . ." he whispered, the point of the knife slowly pointing downward as he struggled in thought.

"Sons," Gilbert said, "Father."

At last Danny understood and spoke one word, Gilbert's given Christian name. It was the last thing he ever said. Gilbert was by his side in an instant, taking the knife, whipping it up and across Danny's throat, then leaping back to avoid the rush of blood that spattered the floor. Danny, like a tree falling, followed his blood to the floor. He lay on his side, and was still alive when his son knelt next to him, pulled Danny's right hand from beneath his body, slammed it flat against the floor, and sawed through the four fingertips with the knife.

"No more jazz, old man," Gilbert said as he swept the four bits of flesh and bone away with the knife blade, then took the left hand, slapped it down, and began to hack.

"No . . . more . . . fucking . . . *JAZZ!*"

Danny was dead by the time Gilbert had severed the remaining fingers, and did not see Gilbert cavalierly whisk them across the bloody rug and stick the knife into the floor.

The last thing Gilbert did before he left the apartment was to take the saxophone from its case and toss it on top of his father's body. "And no more requests," Gilbert added as he went out the door. "Not from me."

The hall was empty when he stepped into it, and he saw no one as he made his way down the stairs. He wondered where 'Becca was, then decided that it didn't matter. He couldn't risk waiting for her to come back, because he didn't know who she might have with her.

He took a cab back to his hotel, packed the few things he had, paid his bill for the week, and started to walk toward the Kennedy Expressway to catch a ride south around the lake, and then east. He should not have done it, he thought. He should never have come to Chicago, never have seen that man whom he remembered as being his father.

But perhaps, he thought, it had been for the best. It had written an end to a part of his life that had tormented him for years. But now, no longer bound by illusions of filial love, he was finally free, free to go east, free to find the Bitch. His father's sin had in no way expiated her guilt or the guilt of the Great Bitch herself, for that matter. They were all at fault, and as he paused and jotted down the name of Danny Vernon and the date on the slip of paper he carried in his backpack, he thought that what he would do to Laura would make what he had done to his father look like love.

> The spectre has the most cunning disguises, and often when near us we are unaware of the fact of proximity.
> —Alexander Smith, *Dreamthorp*

Tom Brewer was working in his basement when the noise began. Loud noises were unknown on Dreamthorp Sunday mornings, so the first sound made Tom look up from his bench.

It was a hollow thud, as though a heavy book had fallen on the floor upstairs. Immediately he tried to think of where everyone was. His father was probably seated on the small chair in the entry reading the paper—he had been bothered by a particularly insistent wasp on the porch. His mother was probably having a cup of coffee in the kitchen and staring at the wall, the same thing she had done since hearing of Josh's death. Tom was worried about her, and so, he knew, was his father. She seemed almost catatonic. But when either of them suggested seeing a doctor, she would have none of it. And Josh was probably still sleeping upstairs. . . .

Josh. He remembered. Josh wasn't sleeping upstairs, was he? Josh was sleeping in the cemetery, and Tom was alone now.

There was another noise overhead, and Tom jerked his head up. He thought he heard a cry but was not sure. He listened.

Were those footsteps, he wondered, the sound of feet leaping about, almost dancing but for their irregularity? The sound went on for a few more seconds, and then there was a heavier, more solid thump, the unmistakable sound of a body hitting the floor.

Tom whirled around and headed for the steps, which he took three at a time. When he hit the top, the first thing he saw was his mother standing just inside the entry, holding something in her hand. He was surprised to see that it was the carving of the woodpecker he had made, the one that sat on the entry bookshelves. He saw too that the painted wood was spotted with blood, the beak a solid red. And, finally, he saw his father's feet sticking out from around the corner.

"Dad!" he gasped, pushing his mother out of the way and stepping into the entry. His father was still alive, but when Tom knelt next to him he knew that he would not be alive for long. His face was pierced in a dozen places, and although the wounds were small, as if the skin had elastically closed back up after what had stabbed it had been removed, the amount of blood that had flowed from the neck wounds was frightening. The entry carpet was saturated.

His father's eyes had mercifully, Tom thought, been spared, and they looked at him now, blinking out of pools of blood from the wounds in his face. "Brrr . . ." his father said, his whole body trembling with pain and shock.

"I'll get an ambulance, Dad," Tom babbled, patting the man on the shoulder. "We'll get a doctor right away. . . ." He stood up and began to move toward the phone in the kitchen, and saw, for the first time since he had come upstairs, his mother's face.

The look on it froze him in place. Her eyes were wide and staring, and the front of her yellow blouse was bright with her husband's blood. She still held the carving in her right hand, and blood slowly dripped from its beak onto the floor.

Tom had been so alarmed by his father's condition that he had taken scarcely a moment to consider its source. Now, though he could scarcely admit it to himself, he knew. As he and his father had both feared, his mother had gone mad. He could not leave her here alone for another second with his father. This time she might finish what she had begun.

"Mother," he said, hating the way his voice shook, "give it to me."

She stood there, staring straight ahead, her eyes not seeing him. He reached down and grasped the carving, but she would not relinquish her hold. She said nothing, made no shake of her head or other indication of her tenacity. She only held on with a grip of iron that Tom could not loosen, even when he tried to bend back her fingers one at a time.

At last he took her by the arm and began to guide her into the kitchen. He was rigid with the tension of fear, ready for anything, for her to lift the carving and try to drive it into his own face. He prayed she wouldn't. He didn't want to hurt her.

But before he could get her out of the entry and into the short hall that led to the kitchen, a cry came from his father. *"Nuuuh!"*

Tom stopped and looked down at the man, whose face was a mottled map of red and white. "Burrr . . . burrrd," he said, blood bubbling from his lips. He coughed, and Tom saw with horror a spot on his father's cheek open just wide enough to release a bubble of pink froth that popped instantly, coating the already blood-wet cheek with a new, glistening residue. "Uh . . . *luhn* . . ."

"Bird?" Tom repeated. "Alone?"

"Yuuuh . . ." Ed breathed out, forcing his head into a painful nod.

Tom tried to understand. "It was . . . the *bird?* The bird *alone?*"

"Yuh . . ." He could not have said *yes*. What was left of his mouth was incapable of making sibilants. Suddenly Ed took in a short, quick breath, stiffened, and died. His life left him on his final exhalation, an endless, rattling moan that grew deeper and deeper in tone until Tom's hearing could no longer sense it.

"Dad?" Tom said, knowing that there would be no answer.

"Dad?"

Ignoring his mother, he fell on hands and knees next to his father, feeling for a pulse that would not be there. When he finally looked back up, his mother had not changed position.

"Mom?" he said, straightening and putting an arm around her. "Mom, what happened? What was it? Who did this?" Had she done it? Had his father simply said what he had to try and protect her, knowing that she was mad and was therefore not responsible? Though he hated to imagine it, it was the only answer that made any sense. The pain and ferocity of the attack had probably maddened his father as well, for him to say that it was the bird that had done it, the bird alone, as if a carved bird were capable of murder.

The thought of the bird reminded him that it was still in his mother's hand. And while one side of his mind, itself maddened by what he had just seen, by the loss of his father and his son to death and his mother to insanity, told him that it didn't matter, let her have the bird, his rational side struggled against the grief, against the overwhelming urge to lie down and weep and let the woman, now a stranger, kill him too if that was what she wanted. No, he told himself, he would not do that. He would, as always, weep later.

"Mother," he said sharply.

There was no response. He held her right wrist and shook her left shoulder, but still she did not react. Finally he slapped her lightly on the face. Her head jerked back, and she blinked rapidly. The surprise was great enough to make her loosen her grip, and he wrenched away the carving, only to see her fist tighten again, her face once more become catatonic.

He led her into the living room, got her seated on the sofa, and, still holding the carving, went into the kitchen to call the ambulance. He set it down so that he could dial the phone, but when a voice answered at the emergency number, he was unable to speak, for he had noticed that the carved woodpecker was not the same as it had been before.

The blood had discolored the paint, but there was more to it than that. The wings had been only partially spread, as though the bird were about to take off. But the carving in the table before him was that of a bird whose wings were fully spread and pushed back, as if in the very act of flying, of driving itself through the air.

Or against an obstacle.

"Hello? . . . hello? . . . This is 911 . . ." The voice sounded thin and faraway, and Tom didn't know how many times he heard it before he finally spoke.

He gave his name and address, and told, very briefly, what had occurred. He asked for an ambulance, and also asked that the Chalmers police be called as well.

After he hung up the phone he looked at the bird for a long time. When he picked it up, he did so gingerly, as if expecting it to come to life in his hands. It was the bird he had carved all right, the one Bill Singer had painted. But he hadn't carved it in flight. He *knew* he hadn't. Damn it, he was practically in shock, and felt nearly as insane as his mother truly was, but the one thing he knew, the one thing he was *sure* of, was his work. And this *was* his work, but it was *not* what he had carved.

The bird. Alone.

What if it had, Tom wondered. What if it had come to life and attacked his father, and his mother had grabbed it, grabbed it and held on to it and broken its magic. . . .

Magic?

Jesus, he *was* going crazy, wasn't he? No matter what had happened, no matter if the bird had grown horns and whistled fucking Dixie, there had to be a logical, rational explanation, there *had* to be.

And if the only rational explanation was that his mother had attacked his father, that his father lied to clear her, and that Tom, because of shock, was hallucinating a memory that made his carving something other than it really was—well then, that was what had happened.

It was what *had* to have happened.

He made himself look away from the bird, thinking that he would remember it differently when this was all over, and then made himself go into the living room and join his mother.

She sat on the sofa where he had placed her and had apparently not moved since. Her eyes were wide and staring, and her right fist was clenched without being closed, as though something invisible was held within. "Mom?" he whispered to her, and then said louder, "Mother?" But she did not answer.

As he waited for someone to come, he felt disoriented, strangely apart from what had happened. It was all too absurd, losing so much in so short a time—his wife, his son, his parents—and he thought wildly, *Another funeral, I cannot go to another funeral,* and almost, but not quite, found himself laughing and wondered if he had not lost himself as well.

It was not until the ambulance came, with Bret Walters trailing after, that Tom Brewer even entertained the idea that someone other than his mother might have been responsible for his father's death. It was the first thing that Bret thought of, and Tom felt ashamed that he had not thought of it himself.

"It had to be somebody else," Bret said to him as they watched the ambulance take away his mother. The body of his father would have to remain until the state police came.

"Maybe I should buy one," Tom said softly.

"What? Buy what?" Bret said.

"An ambulance," Tom answered, turning to Bret with an edgy smile. "They keep coming."

Bret looked away for a moment, as if he hadn't wanted to hear the comment. "It had to be somebody else," he said again. "Your mother isn't all that strong. Your father could've fought her off. Besides, why would she do it? It doesn't make sense any way you look at it."

"Nothing does," Tom said, then added, "My father said the bird did it. That doesn't make any sense either. Unless he was trying to protect her."

The state police contingent arrived a few minutes later, and Tom overheard one of the officers grimly tell Bret that this was getting to be a nasty habit. He took Tom back into the kitchen and questioned him, while the other policeman, the medical examiner, and a photographer busied themselves in the entry over Ed's body. The interrogating officer was polite, and apologized for the abruptness of the questioning, but explained that the sooner witnesses were questioned, the more likely they were to remember details.

But there were no details for Tom to remember—only the noises from upstairs and the sight of his mother standing over his father's body, the bloody carving in her hand. The officer went over the same ground several times, but Tom was able to tell him nothing new. Yes, it was possible that someone else could have been in the house, yes, it was possible, anything was possible. Especially, Tom added with no humor in his voice, in Dreamthorp.

When Tom and the officer came out of the kitchen, Tom saw that his father had been taken to the ambulance, which was not leaving, and that a police line had been placed across his front walk. On the other side of it were a number of neighbors, among them Charlie Lewis and Laura. When he saw the look of concern on her face, he tried to smile bravely at her, but his face cracked, and the tears started to come.

If the . . . fetter must be worn, let it be
worn as lightly as possible. It should never
be permitted to canker the limbs.
　　　　　—Alexander Smith, *Dreamthorp*

"I remember reading about Teddy Roosevelt—how he lost
both his wife and his mother on the same day. And I thought,
Jesus, it would take somebody like Teddy Roosevelt to cope
with something like that. You know, somebody with tremendous endurance?"

Tom Brewer stood up from where he was sitting next to
Laura Stark on the swing on his front porch and stepped to
the railing, which he placed his hands upon, and gazed into the darkness like a sea captain, Laura thought. Like the
Flying Dutchman, alone for eternity.

"But then I realized," Tom went on, "that it's just something you have to do. Accept loss. It's there and you live with
it, with all the memories and everything else that goes with
it, because what else can you do except die? Anyone can deal
with anything if they want to. If they have to." He turned
toward her with a tight smile. "Does that sound at all reasonable? Logical?"

She nodded. "Yes. It does."

"Does it sound cold?"

"I don't think so," she answered honestly. "It's a matter
of perspective, I suppose. You have to . . . put up barriers to
pain. People who can't . . ." Laura paused.

"Go crazy. Like my mother. Or kill themselves, maybe."

He sighed. "Adaptation is a blessing. But it makes me feel guiltier than hell."

"There's nothing to feel guilty for."

"I'm afraid there is. It all hinges on Josh's death. Which wouldn't have happened if I'd just been more . . . something, I don't know . . . more aware, more loving. If I had, he might still be alive, my mother might still be . . . *sane,* and my dad would be alive too."

"It still might have been someone else. You know what the police said. About the murder."

"Yeah, I know. Physical evidence. They don't think my mother did it, but they're not sure. Nobody's sure of anything. Dad wasn't either. The bird . . ." He trailed off, shaking his head.

Laura looked away from him out into the darkness into which he was gazing, with no more hope of finding the truth there than he had. They had spoken of these things before in the week they had spent together since the funeral, a small and uneasy affair in which Ed Brewer was placed beneath the earth near his grandson and daughter-in-law. Those who attended were numb with a surfeit of violence. Frances, the widow and partially suspected killer, did not attend. She was herself in attendance in a state mental facility until Tom was able to go through the task of finding her a private one.

The head of the art department at Harris Valley College suggested that another professor should take over Tom's classes for the rest of the summer, and Tom had acquiesced. When he asked Laura if she thought he had made the right decision, she told him he had, though in truth she thought it would have been better for him to continue teaching after a hiatus of a week or two. A long period of mourning could only lead to introspection and brooding.

For that reason she decided to spend as much time with Tom as possible, to be a sounding board, to be his friend, to let him know that there were people who cared. Charlie Lewis spent much of the day with Tom when Laura was at work in Lancaster. She talked to Charlie privately about him, and they decided together that he would be all right, though his disposition was, not unreasonably, morbid at present. But that would change, they thought, with time. Charlie continued to entertain him during the day with jazz and beer, Laura at night with talk, dinner, and movies on her VCR.

On the single night they had slept together, they had done so chastely, and even now had not yet become lovers, although they held hands and he put his arm around her when they sat together on her sofa or on his porch swing. They kissed good night too, warm, loving kisses with only the teasing promise of true lovemaking. Although Laura wanted him as a lover, she felt, strangely, that to take him into her bed now would be to take advantage of his grief, and so far he had made no overtures to her. His mind, she thought, was too full of other things, dark things that would have to be put down before love could become real.

When she asked Tom what else he did during the day besides visit Charlie and listen to jazz, he told her that he was carving. When she asked to see what he was working on, he became reticent and told her that he wasn't ready to have anyone see it.

"The Kurtzes left today," he said suddenly, and she looked up in surprise.

"The Kurtzes?"

"Down on Hawthorne. I saw the moving van when I went to the post office. I asked Mrs. Purviance, and she said they were moving."

"Did they sell their cottage?"

"Mrs. Purviance said no, they didn't want to sell. But they wanted to get out because they were afraid for their little girl. I guess they're figuring on coming back when . . . *if* the person gets caught who . . . did everything."

"That's too bad," Laura said, thinking that the Kurtzes were not the first to go, nor would they be the last. In the past few weeks, and particularly since Sam Hershey's gruesome death, families had been leaving Dreamthorp on a regular basis. Most of them were summer people who simply breathed more easily away from what they now considered to be the murderous air of the town, but there were a few year-rounders like the Kurtzes who had packed their bags to stay with nearby relatives until the reign of terror ended.

And a reign of terror was how more than one national news magazine had described the string of events that this hot, dry summer had brought to the village. The media had swarmed in the day after Ed Brewer's death with their cameras and tape recorders and notepads, only to find the residents united in silence. Few people had any comment to make, and those they did make were noncommittal and scarcely newsworthy. The newest in the line of murders was dutifully reported all the same, duly noted, and consequently forgotten by all those except the suffering residents of Dreamthorp, who awoke every morning wondering if one of their neighbors had died cruelly in the night. More than one became convinced upon awakening that they had heard the sound of sirens pierce through the thick stockade of trees and the thicker blanket of sleep, though the night had been quiet.

All the nights were quiet. A week went by after Ed Brewer's death, a week without incident. Another quiet week followed, and by the first weekend in August, people had begun to think that perhaps the siege had ended, that perhaps the monster who had killed so horribly had died or melted or moved on to some other unfortunate town. People were beginning to smile on the narrow little streets again, to putter about their cottages with a renewed lightness of heart.

August

There they stand, in sun and shower, the broad-armed witnesses of perished centuries; and sore must his need be who commands a woodland massacre.

—Alexander Smith, *Dreamthorp*

It may not be so difficult, may not be so
terrible, as our fears whisper.
—Alexander Smith, *Dreamthorp*

The first Monday in August, Tom and Laura went to the Hall
of Culture to hear the Dreamthorp Playhouse company present a reading of *A Streetcar Named Desire*. That particular
play was not, they both agreed before the actors seated themselves on their stools in front of their individual lecterns, the
ideal vehicle for a dramatic reading, since there was so much
physical action revolving around the character of Stanley Ko-
walski. The resultant reading did nothing to change their
opinion, and by mutual gestures, squeezes of the hands, and
smiles, they tacitly determined not to return for the second
act once the rising lights freed them from their folding-chair
bondage.

However, before the close of the first act, there was an
interruption in the form of a scream that made everyone,
including the actors, pause for a moment and look up like
rabbits getting the scent of a fox. In that second, fear per-
meated the large room like a living thing, and Tom thought
he could smell it, chill and metallic, like cold meat in a
freezer, and the look on all the faces spoke the same thought:
The monster's back.

People continued to listen and heard a sound that was either many voices talking at once or the rush of waters, a
sound unknown in Dreamthorp. Then the actress playing
Blanche began to read her line, tentatively at first, then with
more conviction, and slowly the attention in the room turned

back to the stage and the story of violence and passion told
in voices.

A few minutes more and the act was over. As the house
lights came up over the clatter of chairs sliding back, everyone heard the siren, real this time, not a siren of dreams, but
real, a siren of nightmares. Like some great protozoan, the
audience moved en masse to the doors, down the steps between the massive wooden pillars, onto the carpet of pine
needles, looking with one intelligence toward the Ice Cream
Shoppe a hundred yards away, where an ambulance and a
Chalmers police car were parked, their red lights whirling
like lighthouses seen through blood.

"Come on," Tom said to Laura. He took her hand and led
her down the sylvan path lit by iron-framed lights staked in
the ground. As they drew near the Ice Cream Shoppe, they
could see that the action was centered on the large, outside
deck, which held more than thirty square tables and four
times as many cane-backed chairs, a number of which, Tom
noticed, were lying where they had fallen, perhaps when the
patrons, alarmed by whatever had caused the scream Tom and
Laura had heard, pushed them back and rose quickly. The
yellow bug lights that rimmed the deck cast a sickly glow
upon the pale faces of the onlookers, and among them Tom
saw Charlie Lewis standing next to Sam Coffey.

"Charlie," Tom said as he and Laura came up to the two
older men. "Charlie, what happened?"

Tom didn't think that Charlie heard him at first. He just
kept watching the activity on the deck, where a group of men
were down on their hands and knees. Tom could not make
out what they were doing, for only the upper parts of their
bodies were visible above the heads of the crowd, but it
looked as though they were exerting great, if carefully controlled, force upon something hidden from Tom's view.

"*Charlie,*" Laura said, tugging at the man's arm.

Charlie Lewis turned, his mouth half open, pain in his
face. "Oh. Laura. Tom. Hello."

"Charlie, what is it? What happened?" Laura asked.

"Another . . . accident," Charlie said, his voice hollow.
"The Warfel boy. You know him? Cute little kid. Parents
live on Fuller. The green cottage near the post office." Tom
nodded dumbly, but Charlie took no notice and went on like
a man recounting a bad dream. "Sam and I were sitting a

few tables away from him and his folks—right by the railing there. I was having a butterscotch cashew sundae, and Sam . . . What *were* you having, Sam?"

"A, uh . . . a grape rickey," Sam Coffey said. He too sounded drugged.

"A grape rickey," Charlie repeated. "And Petey—that's the boy's name, isn't it?" he asked Sam Coffey. "Petey?"

"Petey," Sam said, nodding. "That's what she yelled."

"That's right. That's right, she did. So Petey went running inside from the deck for something, a drink of water, maybe, and he came running back out, and . . . and he just went through the floor."

"Through the *floor?*" Tom said.

"Yeah. We couldn't see real well, like I said, we were a few tables away, but we looked when we heard this cracking sound, and we saw the boy—Petey—just disappear, sink down."

"Like he fell," Sam said, "Straight down. Like a trap door opened."

"Which was what happened," Charlie said, his eyes suddenly alight. "I mean, that must have been precisely what *happened*. The floor boards split apart right where he was, and he fell right through."

"We heard the cracking," Sam said.

"And then . . . then they closed back up again," Charlie said, turning his gaze back onto the deck, from where banging sounds were now coming, horribly loud in the night.

"They closed back up?" Laura said. "You mean they trapped him down there?"

"No," Charlie said, and when he turned back toward them Tom saw tears in his eyes. "They . . . they *caught* him. They caught his neck. Jesus, they nearly took his head off . . . and the blood. My God, there's blood everywhere."

"Everywhere," Sam agreed in a whisper.

"Now wait a minute," Tom said. "You mean the boards broke and this boy fell through, and then the boards closed up again . . . while the boy was there in the gap?"

Sam Coffey nodded. "I know it's hard to believe, Tom. But we were there. We saw it or saw it after it happened. There were a lot of other people there too. We all saw it. Don Henderson over there, talking to that cop? He saw it as it happened, he told us about it. He said the boards split and went down, and then after the boy was in the hole, they came back up again. Like a garage door. That's just what he said. Like a garage door.''

''We saw it,'' Charlie added. ''It's the only way it could have . . .'' Suddenly he stopped, and inhaled sharply.

''What is it, Charlie?'' Tom asked.

''I knew there was something,'' Charlie said quietly. ''Something that I couldn't think of, and now I know.'' He turned on them almost savagely. ''The *pillars!*'' he said. ''In the playhouse. It was the same thing, don't you see? The wood did what it wasn't supposed to do—what it *couldn't* do. But still it *did.*''

''Charlie . . .''

''Tom, listen. Sure, it was possible for the boards to break and the kid to fall down through, but it *wasn't* possible for the boards to pop up again and cut through his neck.''

''You don't know that. There could have been stresses, pressure . . .'' Tom trailed off weakly.

''Not that *great.* I'm a goddam structural engineer, Tom— or at least I used to be—and I know what the hell I'm talking about when it comes to stress. What happened now—and what happened at the playhouse—was simply not possible according to the laws of physics.''

''But it happened, Charlie,'' Laura said, ''laws of physics or not.''

''I know,'' Charlie said, less frenziedly now. ''And that's what bothers the hell out of me.''

The death, on the heels of all the rest, brought only more fear to Dreamthorp. Although there were witnesses to claim that what had happened to young Petey Warfel was an accident, the hideousness of the tragedy cast still another layer on the already thick pall that covered the village, and those who were close to leaving were pushed over the edge. Five more families moved out before the next weekend and the two deaths that happened on Saturday.

In the intervening days, Tom Brewer and Laura Stark became lovers. It was a natural consequence of their relationship, occurring almost as an afterthought, but nonetheless momentous for all its unexpectedness.

On Thursday evening, Laura invited Tom to her cottage for dinner. Afterward, they took their coffee out on the porch and listened to the music coming from Charlie Lewis's place. It was bluesy and romantic. Early Coltrane, Tom thought. They talked quietly as they sipped their coffee, and when it was nearly dark Laura asked Tom if he wanted to watch a movie.

"I don't think so," Tom said. "I'd rather do something else."

"What?" she said, looking at him curiously, and knowing.

He set his coffee mug on the floor, leaned over, and kissed her, his mouth partially open. She gave herself to the moment, and tasted the coffee, a touch of mint from the dessert she had made, and something else that was distinctly and pleasantly his. When the kiss was over, he drew away from her and looked at her. "Don't you think it's time that we made love?" he said, no trace of a smile on his face. She wondered if the thought of it made him sad.

"I think I'd like that," she said. It was not entirely the truth. She felt close to him and wanted to be closer, but she was also afraid, afraid that she would not respond the way she wanted to, afraid that the excitement she felt when he kissed her and held her would diminish when it came time for the act itself, unsure if the affection and even love that she thought she felt for him could be translated and extended into the realm of the purely physical.

"You're shaking," he said, a look of concern crossing his face. She clenched her jaw, furious at herself for letting it show. "Don't be afraid," he said, and she marveled like a schoolgirl at how well he seemed to know her, how he could tell what she was thinking, and she knew then that there could never be anything purely physical with Tom, that behind that physical joining would be a psychic joining as well, and she grew so anxious to experience it that she grasped his hand and held it hard.

"I'm not afraid," she told him. "Let's go inside. Take me to bed. I want you to."

They undressed each other tenderly, smiling as each piece of clothing was removed, like explorers coming upon previously undiscovered landscapes in a new world filled with mysterious beauty. Their bodies fit together as if ordained, and when, after long flights of kisses and touches, they joined, it was not as though she had been occupied, but rather as though she had been filled and fulfilled, made complete and whole. She felt healed.

At the end, lying tired and happy in the web of each other's arms, Tom had spoken first. "I love you, Laura," he said. "I do love you." And she fell asleep, hearing those words in her dreams, dreams that she finally experienced and re-membered when she woke up next to him in the morning.

> More than twenty years ago, I saw two
> men executed, and the impression then
> made remains fresh to this day.
> —Alexander Smith, *Dreamthorp*

They were together when the next deaths occurred, and although they did not see the actual event, they saw the aftermath and the victims. It was on Saturday, and the day was hot and humid, the sky a flat, dull blue, filled with moisture that refused to fall as rain. The cloying heat that bathed Dreamthorp seemed to mirror the fears of its inhabitants, clinging to the skin in tight beads that could be brushed away, but only momentarily, returning in an instant, a constant reminder of the tyranny of the skies and the fates.

Tom and Laura watched the finals of the Dreamthorp tennis tournament for most of the morning, and agreed that the fortyish yuppies who participated did surprisingly well on the two clay courts despite the sweltering heat. After a particularly grueling match, Tom and Laura went back to his cottage for lunch.

"I've found a place for my mother," he said as he carried the tuna salad to the table. "It's on the other side of Harrisburg near Camp Hill. Nice. Out in the country, a lot of trees. I think she'll like it." He sat down and sighed. "As much as she can like anything, I suppose."

Tom's mother had been cleared of the death of his father. Forensic evidence had proven that, from the angle of the wounds, the force with which they were driven, and a number of other contradictory details, it was highly unlikely that she could have been responsible. What the authorities had not mentioned was that it was highly unlikely that *anyone* could have been responsible. To say that the medical examiner was perplexed would have been an understatement. In private, he told his associates that he had seen nothing to equal the uniqueness of this attack in thirty years, and it would take him another thirty to figure it out. Detailed reports had been sent to the Federal Bureau of Investigation, and the M.E. was awaiting their response, though he expected no solutions.

The local and state police were as baffled as he was. The whole county was crying out for whoever was responsible for the series of murders, but there was no physical evidence—none at all—to indicate that a person or persons unknown had even been present when most of the deaths occurred. "We're gonna have to wait," the detective in charge of the cases told his men, "until this bastard slips up. He'll make a mistake. They always do." And in the meantime, the police gathered what evidence they could, going from cottage to cottage, asking questions, traipsing the woods, slipping debris into glassine envelopes.

Although Frances Brewer was cleared of the crime, her mind remained muddied. She had not spoken a word since her husband's death, and slept fitfully, awaking with starts and unintelligible screams. Tom had only briefly toyed with the idea of taking care of her himself, realizing that she was in desperate need of the kind of special care he was incapable of giving. Still, his guilt at forsaking her was deep, particularly when added to that which he felt over his son's and father's deaths.

"When is she going in?" Laura asked.

"Next week. It'll be good to get her some decent care. The hospital's all right, but they can't give her the kind of attention she needs."

They ate in silence for a while, then Laura asked, "So what have you been doing this week besides looking for a place for your mother?"

He shrugged. "Not much."

"Carving?"

"Some."

"How are you coming on that large piece?"

"It's coming," he said, and changed the subject to the tennis matches. Tom didn't want to talk about the carving.

especially not to Laura, not yet. In a way he felt guilty about that too, as though he had stolen something from her by using her experience, personal and painful, with Gilbert Rodman as a subject for sculpture. He hadn't decided how and when he would tell her about it, but he thought he would wait until the piece was finished, then talk to her about it and describe it in detail before he let her see it.

And if she didn't want to, if the memories were too strong, too vivid, that would be all right too. Still, knowing Laura the way he did, he knew that she would want to see it, would want to face the symbolic embodiment of her fears. She was a brave woman, braver, he felt, than he was.

After lunch they went back down and watched more tennis, then went over to the gift shop, formerly the chautauqua caretaker's cottage, across the road from the Ice Cream Shoppe. It had recently been painted a pale yellow, except for the white columns that surrounded the broad, shady porch. Some new Christmas tree ornaments had arrived, and Laura chose several, one of which was a small, but beautifully carved *bellschnickle*.

"Bell-*what?*" Tom asked her.

"*Bellschnickle,*" she said. "See? It's a German Santa Claus."

"He looks mean," Tom said, taking and examining the three-inch figure.

"He *was* mean," Laura told him. "You see those sticks he's holding? They were to beat bad children."

"What happened to coal in the stocking?"

"Teutonic temperament, I guess." Laura laughed. "You *better* be good."

Tom looked more closely at the gaunt face, the severely pointed beard. "This is not the man I'd want coming to my house on Christmas Eve."

"Then be a good boy." She smiled at him. "And get good things."

"I've already got one," he told her, taking her hand.

Laura paid for the three ornaments, and was receiving her change from the elderly woman who owned the store, when a tremendous crash of wood shook the small building. Laura's coins went rolling and scattering across the floor, the shelves staggered, pieces of pottery and glassware fell and burst like shells on the hardwood floor.

Jesus, oh Jesus, *now* what? thought Tom as he grabbed Laura's arm and ran toward the door. If the building was collapsing, or if it was an earthquake—unheard of in this area—they were better off outside. The owner looked around in panic, then apparently decided her life was worth more than her wares, and followed Tom to the wooden screen door.

But that door, as Tom quickly learned, refused to open. It was blocked by one of the two columns that had fallen across each other and across two people who were sitting in the cane rockers on the porch, one on either side of the door. Tom had recognized them when he came in as the two violinists in the Dreamthorp String Quartet, a chamber music ensemble that played two concerts a week in the Hall of Culture.

He looked through the screen to see the white columns, each a foot thick, splashed with red. Only the one body was visible. It was that of the first violinist, and lay on its side, arms pressed into its torso so deeply that they seemed to be all one piece. Only the right hand stuck out loosely, in the manner of a flipper. The eyes bulged, and the mouth was a cavern filled with blood which bubbled with the man's labored breathing.

Suddenly Tom heard a ripping sound from above and looked up to see that part of the porch roof directly over the door, now unsupported by the fallen columns, was swaying downward. "Out the back," he said sharply to the two women, and the owner led the way through a storeroom and out through a door on the other side of the building.

"Oh my goodness, oh my goodness," she muttered as she scuttled around the front of the shop, where a crowd had now gathered, some of whom were trying to shift the columns off the man and woman who lay beneath. The would-be rescuers kept looking up, leaping back and away as the roof continued to sag in lurches, then moving in cautiously once again, pulling at the columns that seemed far heavier than they should have been.

At last several men managed to move the columns enough for others to grab the musicians and pull them away from the building, unheedful of the edict about moving accident victims. Had they let them remain where they were, the porch roof might have fallen on them. As it was, it did not, but continued to shift and sway and moan with a voice of wrenched and torn wood for hours before it finally subsided.

By that time, barriers were erected around the entire building, and both of the victims were lying dead in the Lebanon County Hospital morgue. The woman had died instantly, and the man had expired just before the ambulance arrived.

After answering the necessary questions, Tom and Laura went back to her cottage, where they had stiff drinks and sat for a long time with their arms around each other. Charlie Lewis joined them for dinner that night as planned. He had heard the crash that afternoon, had come down from Emerson, and had helped get the people out. Now, over soup, he nodded sagely and determinedly. "One more thing," he said. "One more thing that couldn't have happened."

"The building is old, Charlie," Tom said with some exasperation. "It must have been wood rot or something."

Charlie shook his head sadly. "Wood rot. It amazes me that you won't believe your own eyes. You saw that wood, you helped lift it, you felt how solid and heavy it was. And you saw it afterward. That was strong, seasoned white oak, not a damn thing wrong with it, not a trace of weakness where it split. You know wood, Tom, you could see that."

"But Charlie," Laura said, "how can that be? There must have been a flaw there . . . something that we couldn't see."

The older man raised a finger. "There you are," he said with satisfaction. "Something we couldn't see. Just like all the rest of these deaths."

"Christ," Tom said, "don't go trying to connect this with the other killings! Believe me, nobody would commit murder like that."

"I don't know if it's murder," Charlie said quietly. "But I do know that it's all part and parcel, whether you like it or not. What killed Martha Sipling and Sam Hershey and the Warfel boy and maybe even your father . . . and what knocked down the playhouse and the gift shop . . . it's all part of the same thing. And I'm tired of it."

"You're leaving?" Laura asked.

"No. But I'm going to do something about it."

"Do something?" Tom said. "No offense, Charlie. I know you mean well, but what can you do that the police haven't been able to?"

"Something." He smiled and picked up his soup spoon. "In fact, I've already started."

"What do you mean?" Laura asked.

"You'll see. I'm not quite ready to tell you yet, but you'll know when the time comes."

Tom felt annoyed. "Under the circumstances, I hardly think this is the time for secrecy. After all that's happened, all the . . . deaths, you're playing games?"

"I'm not playing games, Tom, believe me. I'm deadly serious. But I don't want to tell you right now."

"When then?"

"Next Tuesday." Charlie took a swallow of soup. "There'll be someone I want you to meet. You too, Laura. Tuesday evening."

"Who is it?" Tom asked persistently. "An investigator?"

"Of a sort," Charlie said with a weak smile. "Of a sort."

> There are the realms on which the cres-
> cent beams, the monstrous many-headed
> gods of India, the Chinaman's heathen-
> ism, the African's devil-rites. These are, to
> a large extent, principalities and powers
> of darkness with which our religion has
> never been brought into collision, save at
> trivial and far separated points, and in
> these cases the attack has never been
> made in strength.
> —Alexander Smith, *Dreamthorp*

By the following Tuesday a great many changes had occurred
in Dreamthorp. The population had diminished by another
thirty-two percent, the remaining run of the Dreamthorp
Playhouse and the Dreamthorp Music Festival were can-
celled, and all public buildings, including the Hall of Culture
and the Ice Cream Shoppe, were temporarily closed until some
cause could be found to explain the structural failures that
seemed to be plaguing them.

Residents were likewise reluctant to enter other buildings
that had been built in the same decade, such as the general
store and the post office. Indeed, Mrs. Purviance elected to
take what she termed early retirement rather than remain in
the ramshackle but charming building in which she had spent
most of her life.

Engineers were consulted, and they came and saw and
concurred that there was nothing whatsoever wrong with the
wood of the buildings or with their construction. Geologists

brought their instruments and made measurements, only to find that the land upon which Dreamthorp was built was as sound as Gibraltar. No explanation was found or given for the breakage of the pillars of the gift shop or the floor of the Ice Cream Shoppe's deck, just as no explanation had been found or given for the collapse of the playhouse. There were only theories, most of them absurd and unvoiced.

In the back of her mind, Laura Stark had her own absurd theory that consisted of Gilbert Rodman still being alive and somehow responsible for all that had happened in Dreamthorp. She knew that he was *not* alive, and that even if he were there was no way he could have been responsible for the bizarre and seemingly inexplicable occurrences that tormented the town.

Still, Gilbert Rodman had seemed to her such a *force,* such an unrelieved concentration of evil, that in the nights she did not sleep with Tom, she could imagine, just before she dropped off to sleep, that his contagion was spreading, like ink on a tissue, across the country, coming to rest there, next to her, in the darkness of Dreamthorp.

It certainly was an absurd notion, she told herself when the sun was shining once again, when she was in her office surrounded by her friends and associates, when she was with Tom, talking quietly, holding him, making love, and loving him. But she learned that the absurdity of that notion seemed easy to accept next to the theories of Grover Kraybill.

Kraybill was sitting on the front porch with Charlie Lewis when Laura and Tom arrived at Charlie's cottage on Tuesday night. He was wearing a long-sleeved tan shirt that looked too warm for the weather, a loose-fitting pair of gray pants, and leather work boots, and was smoking a dark-burled pipe with a stem of transparent blue plastic. His clean-shaven face was mapped with wrinkles, and a shock of hair, blindingly white, crowned his head. He stared at Tom and Laura from behind wire frame bifocals, and Laura thought that although the man must have been in his seventies, his eyes were even older.

"Laura, Tom, this is Grover Kraybill," Charlie said. "Laura Stark and Tom Brewer."

Grover Kraybill took his pipe from his mouth and nodded. "Glad to meet you," he said in a tenor voice as worn as his face. The voice was strongly laced with the flat "Dutch" accent, the remnant of the Pennsylvania German dialect so prevalent in the farming communities of south-central Pennsylvania. "Mr. Lewis told me a lot about you."

Tom and Laura sat across from the two older men. "Well, he's told us absolutely nothing about you," Tom said with a smile.

"Mr. Kraybill is . . ." Charlie hesitated. "Well, he's sort of an occult investigator."

"Call me what I am, Mr. Lewis," Kraybill said. "A powwow man. I ain't ashamed of it."

"A *powwow* man?" Laura asked, trying to keep any mockery out of her tone. She could see Tom's spine stiffen, his face grow stern.

"That's right, Miss Stark," Kraybill said.

"A witch doctor," Tom said, frowning. "You brought in a witch doctor, Charlie?"

Charlie sighed. "You see why I didn't want to tell you about this before. I didn't need the grief. Look, Tom, Mr. Kraybill is no witch doctor. Powwow is—"

"Of all people, Charlie, you're the one I'd least expect to fall for something like this."

"Tom, I haven't fallen for *anything*—"

"How much is he charging for his services, Charlie?"

"I'm not charging a penny," Kraybill said calmly. "I don't need Mr. Lewis's money and I don't need yours. I get enough social security from the government, and barter my services for food mostly. I never charge anyone nothing. They give me what they think my service is worth. And in a case like this, I don't want no money for it. There's something bad here needs to be got rid of. If I can help, that's payment enough."

The man was so self-controlled that Laura believed him instantly, although she had doubts about his effectiveness against whatever it was that was besetting Dreamthorp.

"All right," Tom said, holding up his hands placatingly. "If I've misread your intentions, I'm sorry. It's just that I put very little faith in the kind of thing you . . . represent. You're talking magic here, right?"

Kraybill puffed on his pipe and nodded. "It's possible."

"And that's where you and I differ," Tom said. "I don't think it *is* possible."

"Mr. Brewer," Kraybill said softly, taking out his pipe

and setting it on the side table, "if you had seen what I have seen, and lived through what I have lived through, you might not be so doubtful. Powwow has been passed down through my family for almost two hundred years now. My mother's mother was a Hohman."

"I don't get the point," Tom said.

"Hohman," Charlie said. "John George Hohman wrote the first powwow book."

"I thought all that stuff was down South."

Charlie shook his head. "I've told you to pay more attention to local history. Hohman lived near Reading, right here in Pennsylvania. *Powwows, or The Long-Lost Friend,* his book, was published there in 1820. I have a copy—out of historical interest, of course," Charlie clarified.

"And he taught one of his sons, and that son taught one of his, and so on down the years," Kraybill said, "until it reached my grandma, then my mother, and finally me."

"That's all well and good, but what does a Pennsylvania Dutch folk art have to do with what's been going on here in Dreamthorp? And more to the point, what can you do to stop it?"

"Well, for one thing, I think I know what's been causing it," Kraybill said. He stated it with no apparent satisfaction, but merely as a fact.

"You do, huh?" Tom was becoming sarcastic, and it made Laura uncomfortable.

"Tom," she said quietly, "we can at least listen."

Tom gave a small snort of exasperation. "Okay, fine, I'll listen. So what *has* been causing all our problems, Mr. Kraybill?"

Kraybill breathed deeply and put his head back so that he was staring at the narrow, flat boards of the porch ceiling. "I believe that it's a spirit," he said.

Tom shook his head in disbelief. "Somehow I expected you to say something like that. So what are you going to do, channel an Indian spirit guide to tell it to go away and stop bothering us?" He turned to Charlie and laughed bitterly. "This guy doesn't belong here, Charlie, he belongs on Phil Donahue."

"I saw those fellas on Phil Donahue," Kraybill said. He did not seem agitated or at all defensive. "They were frauds."

"Oh, you could tell?" Tom said, baiting him. "Like knows like?"

"Truth knows lies, Mr. Brewer. When a man starts charging two hundred dollars an hour, you can be pretty sure that his main concern isn't with the spiritual."

"And yours is."

"Yes, it is." Kraybill picked up his pipe and looked at it. "Mr. Lewis tells me you're a woodcarver."

"That's right."

"What you think about wood?"

"What do I *think* about it? What do you mean?"

"Why do you use wood and not something else?"

"Well . . . wood is different."

"Because it was alive once?"

Laura saw Tom look narrowly at Kraybill. "Yes, that's right. It has a pattern to it."

"Like a life has a pattern. A pattern you can see. Like a living thing. Which, of course, it is."

"Look," Tom said, "why all this talk about wood?"

"Because that's where the spirit lives. What the spirit possesses."

Tom looked at Kraybill dumbly for a moment. "Wood? You're talking about a wood spirit? Like a nature spirit of some kind?"

Kraybill puffed his pipe into smoky life. "I sure am. It's plain to see."

"Maybe you'd like to clarify for those of us a little less knowledgeable about the—what shall I call them, the black arts?—than yourself."

"I'd be happy to, Mr. Brewer. But the black arts aren't anything I practice. Powwow is good magic, healing magic, nothing more. It's achieved through prayer mostly."

"All right, I'm sorry," Tom said, and Laura thought that he really was. "It's just that I really don't believe in . . ." He paused.

"In any religion at all?" Kraybill finished for him. "I can understand that, especially after what Mr. Lewis here tells me you've been through in the past year or so. It's hard to hold on to faith when it seems that God has no mercy. But he does, Mr. Brewer. He truly does, whether he's a god of the Christians or the Hindus or the Buddhists or the American Indians."

Tom finally smiled. "Forgive me, but I'm a little surprised to hear that you're so . . . polytheistic."

"Oh no, I believe in one God all right, but he's the God of everybody. Powwow has prayers from many different faiths. After all, the very name 'powwow' comes from the Indians. The healing powers of the shamans were a lot like Hohman's remedies and spells."

Kraybill sucked on his pipe, but Laura saw no smoke come from the creased corners of his mouth. He held up the pipe and gestured to the porch railing. "May I?" he asked Charlie.

"Use the ash can there," Charlie said, pointing to a little fire bucket filled with sand that stood against the porch wall. "It's so dry up here we have to be careful of sparks."

Kraybill knocked out his pipe, then removed a pouch of Union Leader from his voluminous shirt pocket, packed tobacco into the pipe bowl, and ignited it. Blue smoke once more filled the hot, dry air. "Anyways," he said, leaning back, "listen to my reasons and see if they make sense to you. Treat them like you'd treat evidence if you heard it in a courtroom and you were on the jury. Then judge."

Tom nodded. "Seems fair enough. But I'm a tough juror."

"I'm sure you are, and even though Miss Stark isn't saying much, I can see she doesn't believe too."

At first, Laura felt embarrassed, but a second later realized that anyone would feel doubtful about the theory Kraybill had proposed. "It's rather hard to believe," she said by way of explanation.

"Let me try and convince you," Kraybill said. "Now the deaths, even though they may not appear to at first glance, show a pattern. Let's take them one by one. First of all was the playhouse falling down. Then the Thatcher man."

"Thatcher?" Laura asked.

"The old fellow down on Fuller Street who fell down his stairs," Charlie explained.

"But that was an accident, wasn't it?" Tom said. "A loose board."

"Then Mrs. Sipling," Kraybill went on. "Then Mr. Hershey. Then . . . I'm sorry, Mr. Brewer, your son. And your father. Following that, the little boy in the Ice Cream Shoppe, and the two people on the porch."

"We know all that," Tom said.

"Sure you do," Kraybill replied patiently, "but you don't know who's responsible."

"And you do?"

The old man nodded. "The wood. The spirit in the wood."

"Oh Christ," Tom said, laughing.

"The playhouse was first," Kraybill continued imperturbably. "The pillars were all wooden, they all split without anything being wrong with them. Mr. Lewis told me how it happened. Then, less than a week later, Mr. Thatcher falls to his death because of a loose wooden board on his steps. Mrs. Sipling's crushed by the lid of a wooden chest. Mr. Hershey is found beaten by branches, dead on a tree."

Kraybill sighed and spoke in a softer tone. "Next is your son. But we don't need an explanation, because we know how he was killed. But then comes the death of your father, once again from wood—the wooden carving. A few weeks later the boy falls through the wooden floorboards and is killed by their sharp, broken edges in a way nobody can explain. And finally, last weekend, the two fiddlers are crushed by wooden columns that have no business falling." Kraybill shook his head. "These aren't cases of murder, they're cases of magic. Or murder *by* magic, maybe."

"Wait a minute," Tom said, and Laura was surprised to hear the wonder in his voice, as though he refused to let himself believe it but did just the same. "You're talking about . . . sentient *wood?*"

"Maybe," Kraybill said. "But not sentient in and of itself. Occupied by something."

"Possession," Laura said.

Kraybill nodded. "Sure. Wood doesn't jump up and do murder on its own."

"Wood doesn't jump up and do murder, period," Laura said. She didn't know why she suddenly felt so angry, but suspected that it might have something to do with the look on Tom's face, a look of acceptance and a trace of what might be wild joy, something that frightened her, that she had not seen on his features before.

"Wood is a living thing, Miss Stark. Mr. Brewer knows that. He also knows the kind of power that can be in it, if I'm not mistaken."

Laura looked at Tom for support, but he only nodded. "Yeah," he said softly. "It's . . . that's true."

"Well, you'll all forgive me," Laura said, "if I say that this all sounds like bullshit to me. Sure, wood's a living thing, but when a tree's cut down and made into something, it's dead. And it doesn't come to life again."

Tom looked at her sharply, as if she'd just given him irrefutable proof of the nonexistence of Santa Claus. He started to say something, but Kraybill cut in. "I know it sounds hard to believe, Miss Stark. But tell me, do you believe that people have souls?"

Her upbringing had been firmly religious, and, in spite of the harsh realities of her life, she did believe that much. "Yes," she told Kraybill reluctantly.

"If a man, then why not an animal? If an animal, why not all living things? The ancients believed that trees were living and knowing creatures. They believed trees had souls and could feel pain. Many even worshipped trees. *The Golden Bough* tells of lots of things like that. And something else too." Kraybill closed his eyes, took his pipe from his mouth, and quoted from memory: " 'How serious that worship was in former times may be gathered from the ferocious penalty appointed by the old German laws for such as dared to peel the bark of a standing tree. The culprit's navel was to be cut out and nailed to the part of the tree which he had peeled, and he was to be driven round and round the tree till all his guts were wound about its trunk.' "

Kraybill opened his eyes and replaced the pipe in the corner of his mouth.

"Good Christ," Tom whispered.

Kraybill nodded. "The same thing that happened to Mr. Hershey."

Laura's cheeks felt flushed. "All that proves is that whoever killed Sam Hershey had read *The Golden Bough*."

"It might also prove," Kraybill said, "that *what*ever killed Mr. Hershey was *living The Golden Bough*."

"It's preposterous."

"Miss Stark, there's more than one possibility. There are also stories of the souls of men inhabiting trees. This could be something like that. Or maybe a natural spirit. There's also the chance this wood, for some reason we can't guess, might be open to some *other* force."

"Like what?" Laura asked.

Kraybill shrugged. "Who can say?"

"You know, Mr. Kraybill," Laura said, "you really do sound like one of these channelers—full of theories with nothing to base them on but folklore and superstitions."

"You're wrong, Miss Stark. These channel people believe in friendly spirits that can give cheap—or not so cheap—advice. But I deal with the truth. There's nothing friendly about whatever's come into the wood of Dreamthorp. Only evil is here—something with a terrible purpose." For a moment, Kraybill sucked at the sweetness of his pipe, then went on. "It may be the same kind of thing that was in a house up in Potter County a few years ago. A spiritual malignancy, you'd call it. The house burned down along with whatever evil possessed it. At least they *think* it did. And I say that because you can never be sure of those things. They're like cancers. You cut it out and you think it's gone, but maybe something's survived and keeps growing until it's stronger than it ever was before."

Kraybill's eyes got a faraway look, and Laura thought for a moment that she could see faces in the pipe smoke. "Life is a constant war against evil," Kraybill said softly, "and you never win, not completely. It's just a series of small victories, keeping it at bay." Then he smiled. "But it's all we can do. And it's enough."

Laura cleared her throat. "And what *do* you plan to do?"

"Talk to people. Learn as much about Dreamthorp and its history as Mr. Lewis can tell me. Find out what power has come here, and then work to banish it."

"How?" Tom asked.

"Prayer, spells. Good things. Powwow is strong. And so is good."

"Mr. Kraybill lives over near Campbelltown," Charlie told Tom and Laura, "but he'll be staying here with me for a few days. Or however long it takes." Charlie shrugged. "I just wanted the two of you to meet him. To find out what I had in mind."

Tom nodded. There was an expression on his face that Laura could not read.

"When Sam Hershey died," Charlie went on, almost as if trying to justify it to himself, "I knew that there had to be more to this than just a series of accidents and some maniac hitting the town at the same time. I love Dreamthorp. You both know that, and you know how much. And I think you feel the same way. So I'm willing to try anything, no matter how farfetched it might seem.'' He cleared his throat, and Laura thought he seemed embarrassed. ''Thanks to both of you for coming over. Mr. Kraybill and I will be going around talking to people tomorrow. If you'd like to come along, you're welcome.''

''I'm sorry, Charlie,'' Laura said, ''but I've got to be in the office.'' She glanced at Tom, who was still wearing that unreadable expression.

''Maybe, Charlie,'' he said, ''I don't know. I'll think about it.''

They said good night, and Tom walked Laura to her door. ''You want to come in?'' she asked him, but he shook his head.

''No thanks. I'm sorry, I'm just a little confused tonight.''

She knew she shouldn't ask it but couldn't help herself. ''Did you buy any of that?''

''I don't know,'' he answered quickly enough. ''I really don't. God knows it sounds almost logical.''

''That's just because there's no other solution right now.''

''You don't think it's possible?''

''I didn't say that. I just think that it's highly unlikely. I'd be willing to believe in the most preposterous natural theory before I'd believe in the *super*natural.''

Tom nodded—grudgingly, Laura thought. ''You're right, I guess.'' But the far-off look in his eyes told her that he really didn't believe it.

When Tom got back to his cottage, he sat down at the kitchen table and made the following list on a yellow legal pad:

    June 14 Playhouse deaths—pillars
    June 18 Thatcher—step
    June 21 Sipling—chest
    June 28 Hershey—tree
    July 19 Brewer—carving
    Aug. 3 Warfel—floorboards
    Aug. 8 Gianini & Forbes—columns

Tom looked at the list for a long time, trying to find something in it, some pattern other than what Kraybill had suggested. But there was none. The dates showed no pattern, nor did the choice of victims. The only constant was the mode of death: in every case it had come from wood.

He stood up, went into the hall, and opened the door to his cellar workshop. Just as his hand touched the light switch, a sound came from below but stopped immediately. He listened for a moment, sweat suddenly clammy on his face, but there was nothing further. A mouse, he thought, or a chipmunk. That was all it was, all that it could be. He forced a chuckle and went down the stairs.

The block was there where he had left it, but it was a simple block no longer. His skill had made it take on the rudiments of a man, and he nearly shuddered at the results of his work. It was huge and megalithic and frightening, a figure from a nightmare. And so it was, he thought. From Laura's nightmare.

It was still tough and crude, and he had much more to do before he could call it complete, but so far it was the finest work, the truest thing he had ever done. In a way he felt guilty over how easy its creation had been. It had not seemed that he was chipping a thing into being as much as merely freeing something held captive within the tree.

After his first day or two of work on it, the shape had nearly dictated itself to him. It was as if it had tried to hide at first, but after more and more of it was exposed it had finally said, *All right then. You want to see me? You shall.* After that, all he had to do was to carve away the extraneous chunks of wood and let the details of the figure appear.

It was a fancy, Tom knew. He supposed that because of his own insecurity, he was telling himself that he was not capable of work this good, and rationalized it by imagining that the wood was doing the work, not himself. Grover Kraybill's wild theory fit his fictitious scenario perfectly, and although he knew all these things, he could not help but look upon his nearly completed carving with a newfound respect.

He touched the wood, roughened by chisel blows, tracing the grain with his fingers that bore two decades worth of scars, scars that had grown over themselves so many times that now, when the chisels slipped and dug into flesh, the wounds no longer bled, but only widened for a moment and closed again, as though he had cut into a resilient clay. He touched the wood, feeling the brawny arms of the figure, its solid, massive chest, and at last the face, only roughly carved as yet. But the features were there: jutting jaw, prominent nose like the beak of a bird of prey, and the hollows from which the eyes would stare out at a fleshy and vulnerable world.

"Hello, Gilbert," he whispered to it, not knowing who it was, only certain that it was *not* Gilbert Rodman, but someone or something far older and certainly far more dangerous.

Tom looked at his wristwatch and saw that it was almost ten o'clock. There was time, he thought. He was not tired. He picked up a mallet and a skew chisel and began to work. Wood can live, he thought, I've spent my life trying to prove it.

> Surely of all superstitions that is the most
> imposing which makes the other world in-
> terested in the events which befall our
> mortal lot.
>
> —Alexander Smith, *Dreamthorp*

The next morning Grover Kraybill was sitting outside on Charlie Lewis's porch when Charlie woke up and came downstairs. "It's only seven," Charlie told the man. "How long have you been up?"

"A little before six," Kraybill said.

"You were up late too. I saw the light under your door when I got up to take a . . . to use the bathroom."

"You don't have to be delicate around me, Mr. Lewis," Kraybill said with a grin. "I've heard .. and *said* worse words than piss."

Charlie chuckled. "I was afraid you'd be offended. . . ."

"Being so religious and all? Well, God doesn't mind good, practical words. He doesn't like his name taken in vain, though, and that I won't do and don't like to hear." Kraybill set down his coffee cup. "I *was* up late last night, you're right. Praying till after midnight. It never hurts to pray, and always helps, I've found. Evil doesn't like prayer, and what you've got here in Dreamthorp is evil, I'm sure of that."

Charlie nodded, wondering if Kraybill had made a large pot of coffee, thinking that the only thing he would pray for right now was a cup of the stuff, black and hot as sin, and Kraybill, as though reading his mind, nodded toward the cot-

tage door. "I made eight cups. I like a lot of coffee in th
morning. Hope you don't mind."

"Mind? I'm delighted. Be right back."

When Charlie returned, wondering how Kraybill made hi
coffee taste so much better than *he* ever did, he found th
powwow man in the living room looking over the rows c
records. "You like jazz," Kraybill observed.

"Devil's music," Charlie said dryly. "You know the ori
gin of the name?"

"Something to do with rutting, wasn't it?"

"It was indeed."

Kraybill shrugged. "It's all right. Music is music. Goo
for the soul. Like tobacco, even though it's bad for the body."
And with that comment, he lit his pipe and kept it going
even while they had breakfast.

"Tell me about this Hershey man," Kraybill asked as the
cleaned up the breakfast dishes. "He died very queer."

"Queer's not the half of it," Charlie said.

"What was he doing in that grove anyway?" Kraybi
asked, handing another dish to Charlie to put away.

"Digging for relics, I guess. He found a quartz carvin
there before."

"A quartz carving? What was it of?"

"Well, I saw it, but it didn't look like much of anything
A human figure, I think. He and his wife sold it to a museum
and the curator told them the same thing I was able to fin
out—that it was Indian and was supposed to be a funera
carving of some sort."

Kraybill raised his white eyebrows. "A funeral carving
Buried with the dead?"

"It may be. I suppose he was digging for more artifacts."

"Where is this grove at?"

Charlie looked at Kraybill sharply. "You think that's it?"

"I don't think anything yet."

"No no," Charlie said, a devilish grin starting to form o
his face. "You really do. An Indian graveyard? An India
curse? Are you serious?"

"You were ready to believe what I said last night."

"Yeah, but there's a difference when you go from the gen
eral to the specific. I mean, an Indian *graveyard?* It jus
sounds too pulpy to be real."

"Old magics are strong, Mr. Lewis. Remember, they were born of wide belief."

"So were the Greek gods, but that doesn't mean they were real." Charlie held up his hands as if to ward off the argument he expected from Kraybill. "Okay, look, I'm sorry, but I've been a beetle-browed agnostic for so long that I just can't change in a few days, no matter what I might see to the contrary. This sculpture theory is . . . a possibility, I admit it. Anything is possible. There. I'm willing to admit that much, okay? So if you think you want to follow it up, fine. I won't scoff; I won't even giggle, you have my word."

"Well, that's fine," Kraybill said with a small smile. "But I have no 'sculpture theory,' as you say. I'd only like to see this grove where Mr. Hershey died."

"I thought you wanted to talk to some of the people in town today," Charlie said.

"The grove first," Kraybill said, refueling his pipe. "Besides, I could use a little walk to get rid of some of that good breakfast."

Charlie nodded. "Let me get out of this bathrobe."

"Just tell me how to get there."

Charlie looked at him. "You don't want to go alone?"

"No harm will come to me."

"That's what Sam Hershey thought."

"You've been to the place since, haven't you?"

"Sure, but not alone. Tell you the truth, I'd feel damn funny going there alone."

"I won't be alone, Mr. Lewis. I'll be safe."

"What do you mean, you won't be alone? You got a mouse in your pocket?"

Kraybill barked a high, phlegmy laugh. "No, no mouse. Something better." He popped his pipe into his mouth, reached behind him, and drew from his hip pocket a small book. It was impossible to say what color the leather that bound it had originally been, but years and use had burnished it to a dull green the shade of copper that has lain in the ground for a long time. He handed it to Charlie, who, upon opening it, was surprised to find how short it was. The paper of the pages had swollen over the years, making the volume of less than a hundred pages appear much thicker.

There was no printing left on the leather spine, so Charlie turned to the title page, where he saw a small, round picture of an owl sitting on the back of a chair, reading a massive book. *"Powwows, or The Long-Lost Friend,"* he read aloud. "I should have known."

"You said you have a copy."

Charlie nodded. "Not this old, though."

"This is the first edition. It was John George Hohman's own copy. The first off the press. It passed from generation to generation, and finally from my mother to me, along with the learning."

"More than is in the book, then."

"Much more. But what's in the book is sufficient unto the day." Kraybill took the book and turned it to the last page. "Look."

A typographic hand pointed to the words, worn to near invisibility on the oily page:

Whoever carries this book with him, is safe from all his enemies, visible or invisible; and whoever has this book with him cannot die without the holy corpse of Jesus Christ, nor drown in any water, nor burn up in any fire, nor can any unjust sentence be passed upon him. So help me.

This was followed by three crosses: a large one in the middle and two smaller crosses on either side.

"The Father, the Son, and the Holy Ghost," Kraybill said.

"It seems to me," Chrlies said, "that this isn't so much a warrant of safe passage as it is the comfort that if you *do* die you'll go to Heaven."

"It's interpreted a number of ways, but I've never come to harm yet."

"You've never tried ghostbusting in Dreamthorp yet," Charlie said, handing Kraybill the book. "I admire your faith, but I've got doubts about your wisdom. Wait until I grab a shower and change my clothes, huh?"

"No, I'm sorry, Mr. Lewis, I don't want you to come. I intend to pray, and I'd rather not have anyone there."

"Secret prayers, huh?"

Kraybill nodded. "Secret prayers."

"I think you're very foolish. And I don't have to tell you where the grove is."

"If you don't, someone else will. Besides, why on earth did you ask me to come here and help if you didn't expect me to do some fighting? There's no way to be safe in the face of something like this. I've got to take risks to confront this evil and pray to God to cast it out. There's no other way.''

Charlie Lewis eyed Kraybill for a long time. ''You really know what you're doing?'' he finally said.

''I know what I'm doing.'' The powwow man patted the book lovingly and slipped it back into his pocket. ''And I'm not going alone.''

''All right then. I'll tell you how to get there. But watch that damn pipe when you go. With everything else that's been happening here, we sure as hell don't need a fire.''

The morning was good, Grover Kraybill thought, just like all things that came from God were good. The sun shone brightly down through the open patches of trees, and even though the air was hot and dry, gray-white clouds were visible high overhead with their promise of rain, rain that would ease this dusty earth and bring new greenness to the yellowing leaves. God would provide.

And God would reveal the truth, a truth which Grover Kraybill already suspected. It was the Indian grave. Something had been disturbed there. Spirits had been freed. And those spirits had somehow linked themselves with or become a wood spirit, had entered the wood of the town, and done terrible things. But God would set it right. God, and the prayers of Grover Kraybill, and the power of powwow.

It was only natural, he thought, that the power should put down the power of these dead, tormented spirits. Had not powwow itself been named after American Indian magic and medicine? There was an affinity there, and Kraybill would use the Indian prayers his mother had taught him, along with the Christian ones, to give these souls peace and to bring peace to this lovely community again.

An open area appeared ahead, and in another dozen paces Grover Kraybill stepped into the grove. He stopped at the perimeter and looked about him.

It seemed a quiet place. Low brush, browned by the heat, covered the ground, and a few bushes, their sere leaves trembling in the slight breeze, pushed out of the scorched dirt. A large, freshly cut stump sat near the edge of the woods, and it was this stump, Kraybill immediately deduced, that was all that was left of the tree on which Sam Hershey had died. He walked over to it, ignoring the small cloud of gnats that circled his head, and saw evidence of shallow digging. A few feet away, nearly covered by brush and filled in by a tire track, he discovered the remains of a deeper hole, which, by the relative settling of the dirt, he decided had been dug before the first ones he had seen.

He pushed his hand down into the dirt, and found it loose to a depth of eight inches, where it became packed once again. He would pray, he thought, then perhaps come back with a spade and see what lay beneath. He felt sure it would be bones, though in what condition they might be after so many centuries was questionable.

Kraybill pushed himself to his feet and walked back to the stump. There he put his pipe in his hip pocket, knelt, lay his hands on the exposed, blond wood, and said a silent prayer in an Indian tongue. Aside from his own emotions, he felt nothing and heard only the electric buzz of the swarm of gnats. Indeed, he had never been physically aware of spiritual presences, had never experienced chills in places reputed to be evil, had never even seen any physical evidence of a ghost or spirit.

Nonetheless, his powwow worked. Many people who came to him for help had been cured of their afflictions after he had blown fire or stopped their blood. Those who bore spells due to witchcraft were the easy cases. All he would do was say a prayer against witchcraft when he powwowed over them, and the spell would come into him instead, after which he would cleanse himself of it by meditation. That was what he planned to do now.

The spell would be strong, he was sure of it, but he did not feel afraid. When it entered him, he would bind it and hold it and take it away, and pray over it and meditate upon it, and soon it would be purged, and his powers would be replenished.

His eyes closed, he prayed more rapidly within his mind, a litany of Christian and Indian and Buddhist and Hindu prayers and chants, creating a phantasmagoria of pleading worship. And for the first time, with a dull shock, he realized that there was an actual physical manifestation. His feet were tingling. The thought intruded upon his prayers that his feet were simply asleep, that his kneeling attitude had cramped his aging muscles. Trying to keep the prayers rolling through his head, he flexed his ankles, wiggled his toes, only to find that the discomfort he felt in his legs had now moved to his hands, as if, instead of binding the power that occupied this place, he was himself bound.

He pressed his eyes together more securely and concentrated harder on his prayers, but his meditations were interrupted again, not by a tingling, but by a real, physical pain that bit into his limbs, a pain that made him gasp even as he opened his eyes and saw thick cords the color of earth grasp his praying hands even more tightly.

They were roots, pushing themselves from the earth like headless and wrinkled snakes. Kraybill gasped and tried to separate his hands, but they were bound together as firmly as if they had been handcuffed. Then, suddenly, the roots holding his hands yanked him forward as those encircling his ankles jerked back, and he fell on his face, his head striking the rough, flat, exposed xylem of the tree stump. His nose broke with the sound of a dry branch snapping, and he moaned from the pain of it.

Kraybill tried to move, tried to roll off the stump, but the intractable roots held him there, helpless, his head on the flat stump as if on a druid's altar. He spat blood from his mouth and began to pray from Hohman's book, his voice pinched and nasal.

"I, Kraybill, conjure thee, sword or knife, as well as all other weapons, by that spear—"

He broke off with a scream as the roots tightened, stretching his body so that he heard the vertebrae pop.

". . . by that . . . spear which pierced Jesus' side, and opened it to the gushing out of blood and . . . and water . . ."

He was, he realized with a rush of panic, losing his concentration, indeed could scarcely remember what came next, as fire seemed to run down the length of his spine.

"God help me . . ." he muttered, trying to remember the spell he had read and recited thousands of times during his long life. ". . . the gushing out of blood and water . . . that he . . . that he keep me from injury as . . . as one of the servants of God."

He heard the cracking sound then, and knew, from the lack of new pain, that it was not his body breaking.

"In the name of the Father . . ."

With an effort, he twisted his head to the side and saw the tree a few yards from the edge of the clearing, a tall oak heavy with leaves, strong and ancient as a monument, its bole thick as a column in the temple of some forgotten, bloodthirsty god.

". . . and the Son . . ."

He saw its leaves tremble in a wind that left the trees around it undisturbed and heard the cracking grow louder, as though it was being wrenched from the earth by a mighty, unseen hand.

And then, just for a moment, Kraybill thought that he was moving, that his God had set him free of the roots and the earth, and that he was being lifted up, up toward the sky, over the tops of the trees . . .

". . . and the Holy Ghost!" he shouted in praise, before he realized that it was not he who was rising but the tree that was descending, falling toward him where he lay bound, a sacrifice to this other god of blood and terror, this false god that today, at least, had won.

In the infinity in which the tree fell, Kraybill felt no regret, only a mixture of sadness that he would not be present for the victory, and joy that in another moment he would be within the arms of his own God, the kind God, the God he had served so long and so truly.

The tree came down, and the thoughts died with the brain of Grover Kraybill. The skull was crushed like an egg, and, like an egg, the semiliquid parts of the head burst from the sides of the tree in a viscous sheet, dispersing in syrupy drops that hung from the blades of dry grass for a long time. Insects gathered instantly, the ants converging on the fluids that coated the surrounding area, the blowflies buzzing around the body itself, seeking entrance to the exposed tissues, a haven in which to lay their own eggs. And the tiny gnats swarmed.

> . . . Murders done on unfrequented roads,
> crimes that seem to have no motive, and
> all the dreary mysteries of the world of
> will. To his chamber of horrors Madame
> Tussaud's is nothing.
>
> —Alexander Smith, *Dreamthorp*

And the gnats swarmed on a rural road near Columbus, Ohio, where the man who called himself Gilbert Rodman straightened up from leaning over a corpse he had just created. When he slid the knife into the man, a marketing manager for a farm supply company, he had whispered, "Laura."

He had whispered her name and thought of her, just as he had with the others between Chicago and here, dreaming what it would be like when he was finally next to her. He wanted, he decided, to sleep with Laura after he did it, to sleep for a long time, and wake up with her beside him, and, in the thin light of morning, do it all over again, even though she would no longer be able to feel it. It would not matter, for he would *see* it. He hoped that he would be able to stay with her for a very long time, the way he had with the turquoise lady. He smiled at the memory and wondered if anyone had found her. If not, she would be quite a sight by now.

He took the wallet of Richard Marczak, wiped the blood off the leather, and removed the cash and credit cards. Then he dragged the body into the ditch, placed it within a storm culvert, wiped his hands on the grass, got back into the car, and began to drive east toward Route 161.

He thought he would be safe as far as Zanesville, where

269

he would leave the car and start again on foot. He might have been able to go further, but he wanted to take no chances. If Richard Marczak was expected in the next town, his disappearance might be noted and a search made for his car. Odds were that it wouldn't happen, but Gilbert refused to play the odds. He wanted Laura too badly to take any chances.

Of course he had killed, but he knew how to do that. Killing wasn't taking a chance. Killing was living, and you had to live. You had to keep your hand in. You had to stay in training for the main event. You had to keep your skills honed. For Laura.

The pressure in his bladder grew greater as he neared New Albany, and he stopped on the shoulder of the road, opened the door on the passenger side, sat down, and urinated onto the gravel. He had grown used to touching himself now. It no longer made him shudder, although he had by no means accepted it. But, strangely enough, in a way he treasured it, for it made him think of Laura, made him think of what he must do, held his purpose before him unforgettably.

He slid back into the passenger seat and remembered the paper. Taking it from his shirt pocket, he found the stub of a pencil in the glove compartment and jotted down Robert Marczak's name and the date.

Gilbert pulled out onto the road again and headed east. It looked like it was going to be a beautiful day. He opened the small box that held Richard Marczak's tape cassettes and found a few easy listening, some country/western, and the Beatles' *Let It Be*. He put in the Beatles tape and cranked up the volume, glad that there wasn't any jazz.

For some reason, Gilbert just didn't like jazz anymore.

And thee, too, with fragrant trencher in hand, over which blue tongues of flame are playing, do I know—most ancient apparition of them all. I remember thy reigning night.

—Alexander Smith, *Dreamthorp*

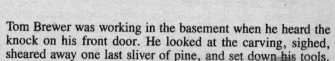

Tom Brewer was working in the basement when he heard the knock on his front door. He looked at the carving, sighed, sheared away one last sliver of pine, and set down his tools.

When he went to his door, he found Charlie Lewis standing on the porch looking down Emerson toward the woods to the north. Tom called his name, and Charlie started slightly.

"Tom," he said, "are you busy?"

"Why? What's wrong?"

"Kraybill went out in the woods over an hour ago and he hasn't come back yet."

"The woods? Where?"

"The grove. The grove where Sam Hershey died."

"You let him go alone?"

"He insisted. Said he'd be safe. But now I'm nervous about him, and *I* damn well don't want to go alone. Can you come along?"

"Sure." Tom dug his keys from his hip pocket, locked his door, and trotted down the steps with Charlie. "Jesus, that was stupid of him to go alone."

"That's what I told him," Charlie said, "but I suppose a warm, personal relationship with the Lord gives one the right to be stupid. At any rate, he seemed confident enough, with his little powwow book stuck in his pocket.''

"You believe what he was saying last night?'' Tom asked.

"Thomas, at this point I don't know *what* to believe. Frankly, his theory makes as much or more sense than anything else I've heard in the past few weeks. You know the old Sherlock Holmes quote—when everything else is ruled out, whatever's left, no matter how goddamned horse's ass it seems, has got to be right.''

"I don't think Doyle said 'horse's ass.' ''

"Well, hell, I got the spirit of the thing anyway.''

At the end of Emerson, they turned left and walked up Pine Road past Thoreau until they reached the path that led to the site of the old sawmill. Tom sucked in his cheeks as they walked, trying to create moisture in his mouth. Its dryness, he knew, was due not only to the arid heat of the morning but also to the thought of what they might find when they reached the old grove.

What his imagination had suggested came in a dull second to what they actually found. When Tom saw the body lying across the open space, its head seemingly turned into part of the tree that had fallen on it, he put a hand on Charlie's shoulder. "Stay here, Charlie,'' he said. "Let me go look.''

"No,'' Charlie said. "I'm . . . all right. Come on.''

Grover Kraybill's body was visible through the light cloud of insects that surrounded it. He was lying on his stomach, what was left of his head on the stump beneath the fallen tree. His arms, unbound, lay limply at his sides, and the toes of his feet pointed outward. The blue-stemmed pipe jutted from one hip pocket, the powwow book from the other. The book's worn, leather cover was splashed with blood that had dried to the color of old rust.

"Sweet Jesus,'' Charlie whispered, then turned around, rested his hands on his knees, and vomited onto the ground. Tom's throat leapt in sympathetic peristalsis, but he swallowed hard and looked away.

"We'd better go back,'' he said when the sound of Charlie's retching had stopped. "Get the police. Again.''

Charlie spat several times, then took a handkerchief from his hip pocket and wiped his nose. "What . . .'' He paused and cleared his throat. "What the hell did it?''

"A tree fell,'' Tom said.

Charlie snorted, and looked down at the body. "Some goddamned coincidence. You think . . ." He paused for a moment. "Look at his hands . . . the wrists."

Tom did and saw red marks there. "Rope burns?"

"Something held him down," Charlie said, then whipped up his head and looked around the clearing, staring into where the trees grew thick. "Something . . ."

Trying not to look at the upper part of the body or at the fluids drying on the grass, Tom knelt by Kraybill's legs. "There's dirt here. Around his pants legs. And what . . ." He narrowed his eyes and looked closely at the earth. "The ground's been disturbed here. There are holes, almost like a cane or a stick was poking in . . ."

He examined the small indentations which the dirt had partially filled again. Because of the dryness of the soil, he could see miniature jigsaw puzzle slabs of caked earth that reminded him of photographs he had seen of parched plains crossed with a spiderweb of cracks. But the corners of the tiny slabs were pointing upward toward the centers of the holes, and as he realized what that signified, he drew his hand back and jumped to his feet as though a snake had just leapt from one of the holes.

"What's wrong?" Charlie asked, ready to flee at a moment's notice.

"Holy shit," Tom whispered. "Roots."

"*What?*"

"The *roots*. Son of a *bitch*, I don't believe this. Look, Charlie—don't get near it but just look. Those holes there, see them? They weren't made by a stick. They came up from *beneath*. *Roots* held him down. They held him down so that goddamned tree could fall on his head."

Charlie looked, then stepped back cautiously. "Let's get out of here. Let's go get the police."

Tom had no better suggestion, so they dogtrotted back up the path to Tom's cottage and called Bret Walters in Chalmers. He wasn't happy to get the call.

"Aw, hell," he moaned into the phone. "All right, Tom, I'll be out just as soon as I call the staters." Tom heard him sigh deeply. "Aw, *hell.*"

Tom and Charlie walked back to the clearing but stopped on its perimeter, neither one anxious to get too near the body or what might still be lurking beside or beneath it.

"He was right," Tom said quietly as they stood together, waiting for the police to arrive.

"He?"

"Kraybill. About it being the wood. The trees, God knows what else."

"Tom . . ." Charlie shook his head. "I just . . . I'm sorry, I thought I could believe it, that's why I contacted Kraybill in the first place. But *Jesus,* moving trees, it sounds like something in *The Wizard of Oz*—we steal their apples and they get pissed off."

Tom looked sharply at Charlie. "Why did Kraybill come here?"

"I . . . I asked him to."

"I don't mean Dreamthorp, I mean *here,* the grove. What did he think he was going to find?"

Charlie sighed, as though to show that it was all too absurd to take seriously, but the gesture was unconvincing. "I told him about the carving—the piece of quartz Sam Hershey found. It put a burr up his . . ." Charlie stopped, glanced at the corpse across the clearing, and began again. "It seemed to strike a chord. I kidded him about Indian curses, but the next thing I knew he was on his way here, and then he didn't come back."

Charlie shrugged and looked across the clearing again. When he looked back, Tom saw tears in his eyes, a thing that surprised him even more than Grover Kraybill's inexplicable death.

"I'm scared, Tom. I am goddamned scared, because I don't know what this is all about. If I did, even if it were something insane, something that everyone else said was impossible, it still wouldn't be as bad. But I just don't know. My logic and common sense won't let me believe in what seems to be the truth." He brushed away his tears with a sleeve. "All my life I've lived by logic. By mathematics and calculations and physics. The closest I've ever come to emotion alone has been jazz, but I've always been partial to it for its *structures,* for God's sake, for the beautiful way in which even the freest improvisations are constructed. And now I find something happening that completely refutes my life. My *life,* goddamit." He shook his head savagely.

"Charlie . . ." Tom began but didn't know what more to say.

"I've just got to get away for a while. For a few days. Away from Dreamthorp to someplace where I can just relax and stop being afraid—because I am—and think things through." He looked up at Tom and smiled. "Then I'll come back. I'll always come back to Dreamthorp. The goddamned place owns me, Tom."

Tom smiled and nodded. "I know. Go ahead, get away. We'll talk when you come back. But come back soon. Honest to God, I don't know how much more time this town has."

The police arrived then, and the ceremonies that now seemed to be an everyday part of life in Dreamthorp began— the picture taking, the declaration of death, the searches, the interviews of witnesses, in this case Tom and a thoroughly subdued Charlie Lewis, who went back to his cabin to pack after the questions were asked.

"What do they think, Bret?" Tom asked Walters after the state police and detectives had investigated the scene for an hour.

"Looks like an accident," Walters said.

"An accident," Tom said flatly.

"Yeah," Walters said, not looking at Tom. "That tree was pretty well rotted at the base. Ready to fall."

"Did they see the marks on Kraybill's wrists? The marks on his pants?"

"Yeah, yeah."

"And?"

"And what?"

"Don't get pissy, Bret. *And* wouldn't that seem to indicate that he was tied up?"

"Maybe, maybe not. He went through a lot of brush to get here, coming along that path. Might've got the dirt on his pants if he fell or something. Maybe he scratched his wrists on the path or fooling around with the rough wood on that stump."

"That's a crock."

"Well, what the fuck have *you* got?" Bret spat at him. "Somebody tied him down and pushed a tree over on him, then cut him loose? That'd really make a helluva lot of sense, wouldn't it?"

Tom could feel the blood rushing to his face. "So it's an accident then?"

"Yeah, that's what it looks like."

"Boy, we sure as hell have a *lot* of accidents around here, don't we, Bret? And the nice things about accidents is that you don't have to solve them."

"What are you getting at, Tom?"

"You figure out what accident killed my father, Bret?"

"Okay, Tom—"

"I never thought I'd see you go belly-up, Bret. What's happening? A little too much pressure?"

Bret Walters jammed his hands into his uniform pants pockets and turned away, back toward the place where several policemen were rolling the fallen tree off Grover Kraybill's head. Tom watched for a moment more, a dozen insults coming to mind, but he bit them back and walked down the path toward Pine Road.

Charlie Lewis's car was gone by the time Tom got back to his cottage, but Laura's Cressida was sitting in front of her place.

"Hi," she said when she saw him through the screen door.

"How long have you been here?" he asked, trying to smile.

"Couple of hours. I had some work I could do at home, so I came back. Why? What's wrong? You look funny."

He came inside and they sat in the living room, where he told her about what had happened to Grover Kraybill. Her face grew pale, even though he left out the details. "That poor man," she said when he had finished.

"The police say it's an accident."

"And you don't think it is?"

"I don't think it is."

She pressed her lips together as though she were reluctant to say it. "I don't think it is either."

Despite the official verdict of accidental death that appeared in the newspapers and on the television news that night, more people left Dreamthorp. There were only thirty cottages occupied on the following weekend, and although the post office, general store, and Ted's Mobil remained open, the other few business establishments had closed their doors, apparently due to lack of business but in truth because their proprietors had temporarily left town.

Tom Brewer had received a phone call from Charlie Lewis on Wednesday night, the same day Grover Kraybill died.

Charlie told Tom he was staying at the Americana Host Farm in Lancaster, and gave him a number where he could be reached in case of an emergency. "Like what?" Tom had asked.

"A string of murders, the explosion of the town, my house falling down, a hangnail, things like that."

"You sound chipper again."

"Amazing what a change of scene from the morgue will do for a person."

Now it was Sunday morning, hours before dawn, and Tom lay in his bed next to Laura. He had been awakened out of a light sleep to a sound he thought was Josh's footsteps in the hall, a gentle sound that he recalled from years before when Josh was little, the scuffling of a small boy's feet as he made his early morning way to the bathroom.

But he remembered that Josh was not little anymore, and then he remembered that Josh was not even there anymore, and realized that the sound had been that of his own eyelashes fluttering open against the stiff pillowcase.

He rolled over and lay on his back for a moment, listening to Laura's soft breathing. The clock radio's numerals read 4:48, and although he closed his eyes and tried to reenter sleep, he could not. So he slipped out of the bed, pulled on a pair of jeans, and went downstairs. He thought about making coffee, but decided not to since the noise of the grinder might wake Laura. Instead, he went down into his workshop.

Laura Stark awoke at 7:30, and did not move. Her face was at the edge of the bed, and she looked at the graphics on the wall a few feet away. She did not want to turn to Tom yet, and hold him and maybe make love to him. Not yet. She wanted to be alone with her thoughts for a while and concentrated her gaze upon the largest lithograph, a burst of pale blue against an irregular background of black, bordered on the right by an upright rectangle of gray. 4/5 Miller '73, read the limitation at the bottom, and she wondered for a moment where the other four numbers of the edition were, and decided that it really didn't matter.

What mattered was Tom. Finally, after thirty-four years of living, she had found someone who loved her the way she had always wanted to be loved, generously and without expectations. In bed and out of it, he was solicitous toward her, making sure that her needs were met before his own. It was not a sexist, demeaning attitude on his part, in the tradition of a superior doling out favors to a menial, but a humane, caring response to a person he loved. It was good, she thought, to be loved at last.

With that thought in mind, she closed her eyes and rolled over toward where she expected him to be, but her questing arm found only the empty bedclothes. Not even his warmth remained in them. "Tom?" she called tentatively, but no one answered. She listened a bit longer to see if she could hear the shower running or the coffeemaker bubbling downstairs. But no normal morning sound came to her, nor did any scent of coffee or bacon frying.

She threw back the sheet and climbed off the high bed, tossed the hand towel she'd been lying on into the wicker hamper, and covered her nudity with a short cotton robe she now kept in Tom's closet. She was on the stairs before she began to hear the sounds from the basement, a soft yet insistent noise of something being . . . brushed, was it? But when she arrived on the first floor and realized that the sound was coming from the open cellar door, she knew it had to be Tom sanding wood.

Laura did not go down the stairs immediately. She had not been in Tom's workshop for several weeks, not because he had expressly asked her not to, but because of his implication that he did not want her to see the work he had in progress.

"It's something kind of different for me," he had told her when she had remarked, not at all disparagingly, upon the amount of time he had been spending in his workshop. "I'm a little self-conscious about it now. Really rather not have anyone see it until it's finished." He had chuckled. "And maybe not even then, depending on how it comes out. I may just wind up with some interesting firewood."

But although she did not descend the stairs, she stood at the top of them in the doorway, listening to him work, wanting to be with him. After a few minutes the sound of sanding stopped, and there was only silence. Then she heard him call her name.

"Laura? Are you up there?" His voice sounded tired and gentle.

"Yes, Tom." She felt like a child caught listening outside her parents' bedroom door.

"Come down," he said. "Come on down. I'm finished. The carving is done."

She swallowed hard and began to walk down the steps, hoping that she would like what he had done, that she could honestly tell him it was his best piece of work that she had seen. She hoped it would be, because she knew she could not lie to him.

"Just remember," he said to her, and now his tone held a note of joy, "I told you it was different."

It was different, all right. When she saw it her breath locked in her throat, her eyes widened, and she felt obscenely naked under the light robe. She also felt terrified.

A dim light, though more haunting, would have been kinder than the stark white, fluorescent lights of the basement, for it would have been far less revealing. As it was, she could see every detail of the figure that faced her, slightly smaller than life-size.

The shoulders were as humped as those of an ape, the legs were splayed outward at the knee, and the arms were slightly lifted from the body so that the hands were at the level of the groin. It struck Laura as a frighteningly ambivalent gesture. The hands, with fingers like knotted branches, seemed to be in the act of reaching threateningly forward while they also seemed about to grasp the figure's own undelineated genitals, little more than a shadowy but massive bolus of wood.

Perhaps, she thought with a new rush of terror, the gesture was ambivalent because the creature intended to do both.

"Gilbert."

She heard the word in her mind, but did not realize she had spoken it until Tom came to her side, a look of deep concern on his face, and put a protective arm around her. "I'm sorry," he said, "God, Laura, I'm sorry, I had no idea you would see it as that."

"But it *is* that, isn't it?" she said weakly.

"Your story gave me the inspiration, yes. But it isn't meant to be . . . to be him specifically. I mean, the face isn't his. I never *saw* his face. . . ."

Laura looked at the ridges of wood that formed lips and cheeks, nose and hollows of the eyes. "It doesn't need a face," she said. "That's how strong it is."

"You . . . you think it's good?"

"I think it's the most . . . extraordinary piece of work I've ever seen. I've never been as . . ." She searched for the word. "As *moved* . . . or as *terrified* in my life. No!"—she corrected herself immediately—"Once before. You know. Once before. But not before that. Or since. Until now."

"Then you like it?"

She shook her head in confusion. "You can't . . . *like* something like that. But you can admire it . . . be stunned by its power. I don't like it, no. I hate it, Tom. I hate it because of how it makes me feel. But the fact that you have done that to me means that you've created something that no one else can."

When she looked up into his face, she was unable to read his expression. Either there was nothing at all there, or a great many things, all working together. She thought it was the latter.

"I'm sorry, Laura," he said finally. "I didn't mean to . . . to use your experience. It was just that hearing about it, along with everything that's happened to me lately and everything in Dreamthorp . . . it was as though it was something inside me, or inside the wood, that needed to come out. Something I had to do." Tom shook his head. "To get out all the rage, maybe, I don't know. But it was there and it was real." He nodded toward the carving. "You can see that it was real. Maybe it still is, but it isn't in me anymore, if it ever was."

"No," Laura agreed. "It's there now." She squeezed his arm. "What are you going to do with it?"

"I almost feel like I should destroy it."

"No, Tom, you don't feel that. And you can't *do* that. It's too good, too important. You have to show it. But before you do, just promise me one thing."

"What?"

Laura licked her lips and glanced at the carving. "Don't keep it out. Not where I can see it. Cover it when I'm here. I see too many bad memories in it."

"All right." Tom nodded. "I promise you'll never have to see it here again."

Later that morning, on the short walk back to her cottage, Laura thought about what Tom had said about using her experience as a basis for the work. She knew that such things were necessary to produce art, but she couldn't decide if she preferred to have him be guilty and apologetic, as he had been, or for him to have been completely dispassionate about it. If he had acted that way, she thought she might have felt less betrayed.

He *had* betrayed her, he thought, as he stood in the cellar, examining the carving from a dozen different angles, and then finding a dozen more. He should not have done it. It was not fair to subject her to those memories all over again.

Still, he had had no choice, not really. It all seemed predestined somehow—meeting and loving Laura, the tree, her story—all those things had come together to create . . .

No. That was bullshit. That was rationalization of the most feeble and self-deceptive kind. He had chosen to do what he had done. It had been up to him all the time. He only hoped that she understood enough so that she could forgive him. But she was a wise lady, and he loved her, and he had seen forgiveness in her already, even as she trembled because of what he had done.

And Jesus, what he had done was impressive. It was powerful and strong and transcendent. It held him as though under a spell, and he had to look away from it for a long time before he was able to go outside and get a small tarpaulin out of the woodshed, bring it back down to the workshop, cover up the carving, and move it into the corner. Even after he did, its presence remained overwhelming, the disguised bulk of it possessing the realm of the cellar like a genius loci.

Tom went upstairs, showered, and dressed. He was to pick up Laura at twelve-thirty and it was now only eleven. For a few minutes, he sat down with the newspaper, but found nothing to hold his interest. At last he got up and with all the hesitance, guilt, and excitement of a man in the grip of a loved and hated secret vice, went down into the cellar, removed the tarpaulin, and watched his creation for signs of life until he heard the knock on his cottage door and went up to Laura, whom he loved but had for a time forgotten.

Unseen by us, the ore has been dug, and
smelted in secret furnaces. . . .
　　　　　　—Alexander Smith, *Dreamthorp*

Charlie Lewis returned to Dreamthorp two days later, on
Tuesday morning. Tom Brewer was sitting on his porch whit-
tling a ball in a box when Charlie came up to his cottage.

"You're back," Tom said, smiling. "Get your head
cleared?"

Charlie nodded. "I got it cleared all right. So cleared that
I'm almost sorry I did. But I know what I think now." He
took a wicker chair next to Tom and looked out at the trees
as he talked. "I'm scared, Tom. I told you that already. The
only reason I don't get out of this place and *stay* out is because I love it so goddam much. I mean, *look* at the damn
place . . . Dreamthorp. . . ."

He gestured expansively with his right arm to indicate the
legions of tall pines and oaks, the crushed carpet of needles,
and the little houses, close as brothers, white and green and
brown and dusty red, embellished with lattice and delicate
trim, row on sloping row.

"There's no place like it. And I'm not going to be chased
away from it because of something I can't even see. I won't."
He turned to Tom and looked at him squarely. "Kraybill was
right. I've thought about it over and over in the days I've
been away, and there's no getting around it. He was right.
It's something supernatural. Something that police and investigations can't fight."

Tom sighed. "Charlie, that's just . . . not logical."

"No, Tom, it's logical. But it's got its *own* logic, you see? No matter how strong it is or *what* it is, it can be dealt with." He looked out at the trees again. "Kraybill was overconfident. He didn't know how damn strong this thing was. I should say *is*. So I followed his lead. I didn't just sit around the cocktail lounge for five days. I went in to the college in Lancaster—Franklin and Marshall—and went through *The Golden Bough*. Now Frazer doesn't *believe* in magic, but he shows it evolved *logically*. And he gives enough examples of it that it's almost impossible to read the damn thing and not come away with the idea that maybe, from time to time and for reasons nobody knows, the damn stuff *works.*"

Charlie sat back and spoke more quietly. "And I think I know how.

"I *even* think that I may know what to do about it. But I need your help. I don't want to go alone."

"Go . . . to the clearing, you mean. The old grove," Tom said.

"You know," Charlie answered. "You know that's where it all is, don't you?"

"I've suspected."

"And you're starting to believe it too, aren't you?"

Tom's mouth twisted. "Don't tell my friends, all right? They'll put me in the loony bin with you." Then he remembered his mother, and wanted not to have spoken those words.

Charlie seemed to understand, and laid a hand on Tom's shoulder. "Will you come with me?"

"Come and do what?"

"Come and dig. Right where Sam Hershey was digging. Where he found that quartz carving."

"How do you know that whatever did in Hershey and Kraybill won't do us?"

"We can watch out for each other."

"Oh, goodie. That should be sufficient. And I suppose our strength is as the strength of ten—"

"Because our hearts are pure. You bet." Charlie smiled.

"I'm serious, Charlie. Isn't it pretty stupid to mess around there if you think it's dangerous?"

"Kraybill and Hershey were alone when . . . when things happened. We won't be. Besides, I've decided that I'm going to die in this damn town anyway, so—"

"So you don't mind if you take a friend along. Thanks a lot."

"I need you, Tom." There was no humor on Charlie's face now, only a pleading that Tom could not ignore.

"All right, Charlie," he said. "But at the first sign of anything strange happening—a storm, the leaves blowing on the trees, anything—we leave. Right away. That's the only way I go."

"Son of a bitch," Charlie breathed. "You *do* believe it, don't you?"

Tom didn't answer. He only got up and went behind the cottage to the woodshed from which he took a shovel and a digging iron. Then, together, he and Charlie Lewis walked down Emerson, up Pine, and into the forest.

When they arrived at the clearing, the sun was nearly overhead, its harsh light leaching what little life remained in the yellow grass and dry brush. The stump upon which Grover Kraybill had died bore wide patches of a chestnut brown color, and when he saw it, Tom shook his head. "Never get that out," he said. "Even if we had a rain that lasted days. It gets in that porous wood, it's there forever. Poor bastard." He turned to Charlie. "Where do we dig?"

"Over there," Charlie said, pointing to a spot a few yards north of the stump. His face was pale, and Tom was sure he was remembering the day last week when they had found Kraybill. Tom didn't look too closely at the grass. There had been no rain to wash any debris away, and he was afraid of what else he might see beside the blood on the stump.

They dug nervously, looking around constantly for any evidence of motion. But there was none except for their own constant digging, and in less than twenty minutes Tom's shovel scraped on something that was too smooth to be rock.

"What is it?" Charlie asked. Tom could see that his knuckles were white around the digging iron.

"I don't know . . . just a minute . . ." Tom knelt by the side of the foot-deep hole and began to remove the earth with his hands. After several handfuls, just as he was reaching back in, something pushed itself from the soil only an inch from his dirt-caked fingertips, and he jumped back with a gasp.

"What is it!" Charlie cried, but Tom only chuckled self-consciously.

"A worm," he said, watching the creature pivot its cylindrical head, trying to sense what had violated its dark home. Tom picked it up gently and set it in the grass several feet away. "Just a fucking worm." He once more began to remove the dirt.

At last his fingers touched something cool and smooth, and wandered over it until he felt a rough edge. Then he dug in with both hands, and brought up to the sunlight a skull, its jawbone missing. "Holy shit," he whispered to Charlie, who nodded thoughtfully.

"Yes indeed," said Charlie. "Holy shit is just about right. And so was Kraybill. Can you keep digging?"

It took two hours until they were sure they had found all the bones. There were eight complete skulls, and many more fragments, as well as a large number of other bones in various stages of decay. Many crumbled into a gray powder when Tom tried to extricate them from the mass in which they were entangled.

He and Charlie said little during the disinterment. Tom would hold up a splintered femur or a skull with a shattered crown, and Charlie would nod at the evidence of violent death. But at last the butchered pile was complete, and the two living men stood together, looking at it.

"You want me to tell you?" Charlie asked. "Or do you know?"

"Tell me anyway."

"All right. These are Indians, God only knows what tribe. They were murdered or maybe they were killed in battle, I guess we'll never know. But they died violently, and whoever killed them buried them here."

"How do you know that?" Tom asked. "How do you know they weren't buried by their families?"

"I don't know much about local Indians, but I do know from talking to Pete Zerphey that they didn't go in for mass burials. Everyone had his own grave. So my guess is that they were dumped here, and the quartz carving that Sam Hershey found was intended to keep their spirits quiet. Only Sam Hershey found it."

"And took it away," Tom finished.

"Yes. He took it away. And freed their spirits. And I would guess, from the way that they died, that their spirits would have been righteously pissed off."

Tom nodded. "Extremely." He choked back a laugh.

Charlie's eyes widened. "You find this amusing?"

"Well. Maybe a little. See, the weird fucking thing is that I think I believe it. Maybe I'm laughing at that. Or maybe I'm laughing because I'm a little nervous about what comes next. Like, if their spirits *were* freed, why did they go into *wood?*"

"Because the trees grew over them," Charlie said softly. "Because their spirits were trapped and had nowhere else to go. So when the trees grew, the spirits mingled with the roots, maybe over this whole grove, or what's left of it, and went up into the trees themselves."

"And became part of the trees."

"Yes."

"And when the trees were cut down for lumber, the spirits stayed in the wood. . . ."

"Yes."

"So everything that was made with wood from this grove . . ." Tom thought it out painfully.

"Shelters these spirits, who are hungry for revenge."

"But, Charlie, if the wood was cut down and taken away and made into things—furniture like Martha Sipling's blanket box, and, and . . ." He tried to think of what else. Charlie told him.

"And the playhouse pillars and floorboards for the Ice Cream Shoppe and gift shop columns and the steps that old Thatcher fell down, and . . ." Charlie paused.

"And my carvings," Tom said.

"And your carvings."

"But what *took* so long?" Tom said, almost desperately. "Those things were taken away from this grove, away from the quartz totem, or whatever the hell it was. Why didn't they . . . *do* something right away. If they were free?"

"Maybe the fact that the totem was still over the bones was enough, I don't know. But once it was removed, the spirits were freed, no matter where they were or what they had become."

"I think," Tom said slowly, "that you're trying to create too complete a theory."

"As far as I'm concerned, there can't be too complete a theory. Like I said, this *has* an internal logic."

"Okay, okay, sure, if you accept its existence, maybe it

does. But make sure that you're not seeing things that aren't there just because they fit your theory.''

"Tom," Charlie said patiently, "if you . . . if *anyone* can come up with something that makes more sense . . . even if you make it out of whole cloth . . . I'll grab it and be delighted. But, Tom''—he whispered the final three words— "there *isn't* anything.''

Tom stood there for a long time, thinking about the wood, about the deaths, about Grover Kraybill and what he had believed, about his father's final words. He thought too about the carving he had made, about the lambent life he had seen in it. Then he looked down at the pile of bones, at the skulls leering up at him with their shattered, gray-yellow grins, and he knew that what Charlie said was true. He also knew that he was denying it because it went against everything he had ever learned or believed. But dammit, dammit, oh goddamit, it had to be true.

"What do we do then?" he said.

"You believe me?"

"Yes.''

"Well, thank God for that. Now, as for what to do . . . you're with me? You don't want to leave? Just pack up and move away?''

"Charlie, I've lost an awful lot in the past year, what most people take a lifetime to lose. I'm damned if I'm going to lose Dreamthorp as well. It's all I've got left. And there's something . . . someone else.''

"Laura.''

"Yes. I love her, and this is her home too, just like it is mine.'' He reached out, grasped his friend's hand, and held on tight. "I'm in it.''

"And thank God for that too,'' Charlie said, smiling. "But what about Laura? You think she'll believe it?''

Tom wasn't sure and didn't want to answer for her. He had been with Laura long enough to know that she was her own person. Too, he had felt her doubts, far stronger than his own, when they had met Grover Kraybill. "I don't know. She lives very much in the real world.''

"We all do. But when something from the shadow world comes into our real world, we've got to do something about it.''

"And what *do* we do?''

Charlie looked around nervously. "We get out of here, for one thing. It feels too goddam naked, too exposed. I feel like we're talking military secrets in the enemy's camp."

Tom nodded at the bones. "What do we do about those?"

"Let's cover them up. We can find them when we need to."

"And why do we *want* to find them again?"

"I'll tell you once we're out of here." Charlie forced a grin, then knelt by the hole and took out a small handful of objects that might have been beads.

"What are those for?" Tom asked.

"We may need them later. You'll see." Charlie straightened and pointed at the hole. "So dig, boy, dig."

"Dig we must," Tom said, kneeling and putting the bones back into the hole.

"Once a bopster, always a bopster."

Laura saw Tom and Charlie come walking down Emerson at six o'clock, and she waved to them from her porch. She thought they looked uneasy as they joined her, and the two gin and tonics she gave them quelled that uneasiness only a little.

"What is it?" she asked Tom, and he told her then, too carefully and logically, she felt, as though he were talking to a child, what they had found and what they believed. At one point he asked her for a pencil and paper and wrote down a list of the occurrences, the dates, and the mode of death, which he handed back to her. When he finished talking, both men looked at Laura, waiting.

"I don't know," she finally said. "I don't think I can accept that."

"It's the only thing that makes sense," Tom said.

"The only thing we *know* of that does," Laura replied. "But maybe we don't know everything."

"What bothers you about it?" Tom asked. "The supernatural? The magic?"

She nodded. "I guess the magic. Amulets, evil spirits, wood demons, whatever you want to call them. It just seems like it's all out of an old book. It's not that I disbelieve it—I guess I'm just"—she smiled—"an agnostic about it."

"But if there's no harm done," Charlie said, "will you help us when you can?"

Laura shrugged. "Yes, all right, I suppose so, if I can."

"But your heart's not in it," Tom said with a little smile. Laura was glad to see the smile, glad that he was not hurt by her disbelief.

"No. Not really. But like I said, I'll do what I can to help. I'm not leaving either." She looked out at the darkening trees. "I let fear—and the memory of fear—chase me out of one place. It won't chase me out of Dreamthorp." She turned toward Charlie. "So you found this grave. What's next?"

"Well," Charlie said, almost as if he were embarrassed, "I think that tomorrow you and I, Tom, ought to go to the State Museum in Harrisburg."

"To try and get the carving?" Tom asked.

"Yeah."

"They'll never let us have it."

"They'll have to. We'll tell them the story."

Tom winced. "Oh no, Charlie . . ."

"We *have* to. In confidence. One person. And go from there."

"They may think you're crazy. Or call the police," Laura said.

"We have to take the chance. The only way to end this is to lay those things the way somebody did before. It was that carving that held them down, nothing else. And the day the Hersheys found it was the day the playhouse fell down, the day this whole thing started. So maybe if it's replaced, put back over the bones where it was, it might all stop. I'm not sure, I ain't gonna put any money on it, but it's the first order of business all the same. And the only way to do it is to get that figure back."

They talked for a while longer, and then Laura made club sandwiches and they talked some more. She contributed little to the conversation, but glanced from time to time at the piece of paper on which Tom had written the details of the deaths.

Charlie went back to his cottage at ten o'clock, and Tom and Laura sat on the couch together, their arms around each other, and went to bed shortly thereafter. At no time did Tom reproach her for not sharing his belief in the supernatural origins of whatever was stalking Dreamthorp, and she was grateful to him, as she was grateful to him so much of the time. After they made love, she lay awake for a while, hoping that she was not *too* grateful to this man for loving her, and decided that there was far more to their relationship than gratitude on her part and desire on his.

She awoke in the middle of the night, aware of Tom trembling beside her. She reached out to him, touched his face, and found it wet with tears. "What is it?" she asked.

"I was dreaming. . . ." he said. "I dreamt about Susan. And Josh. I dreamt about them dying."

"Tom," she said, holding him.

"I can't forget it. I just can't seem to forget it."

"You won't forget it. And you don't want to. Remember them. Not their dying, but remember *them.*"

"I'm . . . I'm sorry."

"Don't be sorry. Go to sleep now. There. I have you. Now go to sleep."

She held him like a mother holding a little boy, and after he had gone back to sleep she was still awake, looking into the night, thinking how much of little boys remained in men, thinking of Tom and Charlie and what they would do tomorrow.

They both seemed so sincere, so eager to engage this demon or troll or bogeyman in which they believed. Like little boys, she thought, with their romance and their foolishness and their irrationality.

They really were, weren't they? No matter how old they got. Maybe that was why so many of them were selfish.

And why a few of them, she thought, remembering a red and thunderous night, a very frightening few, were crazy.

Everything is sweetened by risk.
　　　—Alexander Smith, *Dreamthorp*

"Miss Peters died two weeks ago," said the officious man, whose dress belied his manner. He was wearing a plaid shirt, unbuttoned at the neck, and a loosely knotted knit tie. Tom couldn't see what his pants were like behind the desk, but he guessed khakis or neatly pressed, very dark blue Levi's.

"She was the one who made the purchase," the man, whose name was Dr. Spencer, went on. He shook his head sadly. "She had a stroke in her apartment, where she lived alone. Unfortunately. If someone had been there to call an ambulance or give her CPR, she might have lived. As it was . . ." He shrugged. "But what's your interest in the piece?"

Charlie Brewer cleared his throat. "It was found by a friend of ours. A very good friend named Sam Hershey. Sam loved metal detecting, Mr. Spencer, but he . . . well, he wasn't very good at it. Never found much of anything except for that Indian carving." Charlie chuckled. "Funny thing is, he didn't *need* a metal detector to find it. Wouldn't have picked it up, you know?"

Spencer smiled and nodded. He seemed, Tom thought, friendly enough, if a bit pompous.

"So, anyway, after he died—I guess you read about it in the papers?—his daughter, who's a friend of ours too, a school teacher, she said as how she sure wished her father hadn't sold that piece to the museum, where it'll probably sit in some storage room for the next hundred years, because if he'd kept it in the family, well, it would be in a place of honor for all the grandchildren to see and remember their grandpa, and of course she could take it to school when she was teaching about Indians, and there could be some *use* made of it, you know?'' Charlie paused, breathless. Tom wondered if Charlie seemed as transparent a liar to Spencer as he did to him.

''So what exactly are you getting at, Mr. Lewis?''

''Well,'' Charlie said, ''we'd like to buy the carving back again. For Sam's daughter.''

Spencer raised his eyebrows. ''I see.''

''We'd be willing to pay more than the museum paid originally, of course,'' Charlie said. ''I mean, you probably had paperwork expenses, things like that. And of course you're entitled to a profit.''

''Why didn't Mr. Hershey's daughter come herself to ask about repurchasing it?'' Spencer asked.

''We wanted to surprise her,'' Tom said, trying to smile as sincerely as he knew how. It felt terribly awkward on his face, as though he was wearing a false moustache on which the adhesive was drying up.

''I'm sorry,'' Spencer said, giving no indication of whether he believed them or not, ''but the museum really can't sell items to individuals.''

''But it's not *selling,* is it?'' Charlie said. ''It's more like repurchasing. Or in this case, you could just pretend that it was on loan to the museum, and now the owner wants it back.''

''I'm sorry,'' Spencer said again, ''but we can't really pretend, as you put it, any such thing. The item *is* in storage, in fact, but may be put on display someday. If Mr. Hershey's daughter wants to come here and bring her family or her class, for that matter, we'll be happy to bring out the piece for them to see—it's just in that room behind us—*if* she calls ahead of time.''

Tom looked at Charlie out of the corner of his eye and found that Charlie was looking at him in precisely the same way.

''There's no way to buy it then?'' Tom asked.

''No, I'm afraid not.''

''Not at any price?'' Charlie asked.

''Cost really has nothing to do with it,'' Spencer said.

''It might,'' Charlie said quietly. ''We'd be willing to spend a lot. A *lot*. Ten times what the museum paid for it. More. Whatever it takes.''

Uh-oh, Tom thought. That put Spencer on his guard. He was looking at Charlie narrowly now, and his good humor had all but vanished. ''I said that cost has nothing to do with it.''

''Not even if we could make it worth your own while too?''

Oh shit, that had done it. Tom watched as Spencer's cheeks reddened and his jaw set. He had never seen a more adamantine countenance. It was as though Spencer's face had suddenly been carved in red sandstone. ''I think you *gentlemen*''—he growled the word—''have taken enough of my time. Can you find your own way out, or shall I call security to help you?''

''Mr. Spencer,'' Tom said, leaning forward in his chair, ''I'm sorry. We didn't mean to offend you. Charlie was . . . he was lying, because we didn't want to tell you the truth. We were . . . *are* afraid that you won't believe us.''

Spencer's mouth wrinkled in something that might have been a smile or a sneer. ''Try me.''

''Okay. This is going to sound crazy, but we're convinced that it's true.'' Then Tom told Spencer about how the deaths in Dreamthorp related to the finding of the quartz carving. He told him about the modes of death, some of which had not been reported in the media, about what Grover Kraybill had thought and how he had died, and about the theory they had evolved. ''So,'' he finished, ''we think that if we replace the carving over the graves, the deaths will stop. It's that simple.'' Tom sighed deeply. ''And that crazy.''

Spencer's face had not lost its cynical smile throughout Tom's telling of the tale. ''That's a very interesting story.''

Charlie reached into his pocket and removed a small plastic bag, whose contents he poured onto Spencer's desk. ''These are some beads we found in the grave. I don't know if they'll help you believe us or not.''

Spencer eyed the beads suspiciously, then pushed them about gingerly with an index finger. He picked up several of them, examining them, Tom thought, like a jeweler with a loupe. Finally he pushed them together in a neat pile and slid them across the desk to Charlie. ''Mr. Lewis, Mr. Brewer, you are entertaining liars, but you are liars.''

''What do you—'' Charlie began, but Spencer went on.

"You didn't find those beads near Dreamthorp. That's impossible. Those are Alligewi in origin. Very rare too. But the Alligewi's farthest eastern settlement is two hundred miles west of here. So you see, you couldn't have found them near here." Spencer leaned his swivel chair back, put his hands behind his head, and looked at the ceiling. "Now if you want to know what *I* think, I think you're working for some private collector who's trying anything he can think of to get his hands on what is really a very scarce Lenape artifact. Those beads are simply a prop. They look old, they *are* old, and maybe your boss . . . your *client,* should I say? . . . thought that I could be fooled with them. But if so, he underestimated me."

With a bang that made both Tom and Charlie jump, Spencer brought his seat down and slammed his arms on the top of his desk. "Your story is nothing but a tremendous crock of manure. The door's that way, and I suggest you use it. Now."

Tom and Charlie stood up, nodded to Spencer, and walked to the door, where Tom turned back for a moment. "It's the truth, Mr. Spencer. I'm sorry we lied to you at first, but the rest *was* the truth."

Spencer looked at them coldly. "Good-*bye,* gentlemen."

In the elevator, Tom and Charlie stared at the floor until Charlie finally looked up at Tom. "Smooth talker," he said.

"Me?" Tom said unbelievingly. "What about you and that story about the daughter? Jesus, I had no idea you were going to say that!"

"Neither did I, right up to the point where I started it. I guess I just didn't think he'd go for the truth."

"You were right," Tom said as the elevator doors opened on the ground floor. "Boy, were you right." They stepped out. "So what do we do now?"

"We go to the archives," Charlie said. "I want to find out more about the Alligewi, whoever they were."

Together, Tom and Charlie went through several books before they found one that mentioned the tribe. It was Shephard's *History of Pennsylvania,* and Charlie read the section softly to Tom.

" 'The Lenape spies brought back word that the country east of the Mississippi was tenanted by a powerful nation of tall and savage natives, some of whom were purported to be of gigantic stature. These warriors were called Alligewi, and the Lenape requested permission to cross their river and seek another country to the eastward. But whilst the Lenape were crossing, the Alligewi, alarmed at their great number, fell upon those who had reached the eastern shore and destroyed them, and threatened a like fate to any who dared attempt the stream. The Lenape then fell in with the Mengwe, and waged a terrible war of many years duration upon the Alligewi that ended with the total destruction of the Alligewi nation, though stories were told of a small group of Alligewi who survived by fleeing down the Namaesi Sipu (the Mississippi), and who interbred with the native tribes of the southeast, such as the Creek and the Seminole, who still reside in the area.' ''

"Okay," Tom said when Charlie was done. "So what does that tell us?"

"It tells us who these spirits are," Charlie answered. "Savage, the man said. And easily riled, since they attacked the Lenape for no good reason." Charlie closed the heavy book. "Spencer was wrong. The Alligewi *were* in Dreamthorp. I'm guessing . . . just guessing that there were a bunch of warriors the Lenape chased east and finally caught up with where Dreamthorp is now. They killed them, buried them in that grove, and put that totem over them to make their spirits behave."

Tom frowned. " 'The best laid plans . . .' Well, at least now we know what we're fighting. What next?"

"We get the carving."

"And how do we do that? Our friend Spencer isn't going to hand it over."

Charlie's eyes danced. "He doesn't have to. You're going to steal it."

"Bullshit."

"There's no other way we can get it, is there? You want to go to the authorities and explain this whole thing to them? See how fast they'll help us out?"

"It's not going to be any help at all if I get caught."

"Tom, you won't get caught."

"How can you be so sure?"

"Trust me, will you?"

"I trusted you to talk Spencer into selling us the carving, and look how effective you were."

"It's not nice to use irony on your elders."

But ultimately Tom trusted Charlie enough to listen to him tell how he could steal the carving.

The next day, a Thursday, they spent most of the day in the museum, going from room to room, checking on the comings and goings of the museum guards and the areas of the building in which Tom might be able to remain unseen until closing time. They finally decided upon a replica dry goods store that stood, with a number of other dimly lit establishments known as the Village Square, on the first floor of the vast building. That afternoon, on the way back to Dreamthorp, they stopped at a cycle shop in Cleona and bought an inexpensive helmet and a small biker's backpack.

That evening over dinner, Tom told Laura that they had been unsuccessful in retrieving the carving. "So what now?" she asked him.

"We're going to take it anyway."

"Steal it?"

He nodded. "Charlie and I have it worked out. I'm going to spend the night in the place. I'll have a backpack on, and I'll be carrying a helmet. I'll have food and whatever else I'll need, I'll hole up behind one of the exhibits, grab the thing at night, and leave the next morning."

She shook her head. "Tom, this is going . . . too far. If you get caught, you'll go to jail, it's no joke."

"And it's no joke that if I don't do it, these killings might keep happening until everybody dumb enough to stay in this town is dead."

"That's still just a theory."

"And the only one we've got." He took her hand. "Laura, I've got to do this."

"I love you. I just don't want anything to happen to you. I don't want you in jail. They're bound to have an alarm system."

"They do. A Pyrothonics X63. I don't know what it does, but with that name I wouldn't be surprised if it fired heat-seeking missiles."

"Tom . . ."

"It's not like I'm breaking in. I'll already *be* there. And I won't get caught, I promise. All right?"

She squeezed his hand hard. "If you really think you have to."

Tom smiled. "Hey, a man's gotta do—"

"What a man's gotta do, I know." She smiled back. "That's what the Duke said before the Indians shot him."

At the mention of Indians, their smiles faded. They sighed, and finished their dinner in silence.

Tom and Charlie didn't go to the museum until mid afternoon, and were surprised and dismayed to find several groups touring the facility. "Friday must be bus day or something," Charlie said despondently.

"Good timing, mastermind."

"Well, how the hell was I supposed to know? It doesn't matter anyway. They'll clear out. The place is dark, you can see if anybody's coming, and once you're behind that counter, nobody will know you're there."

"What if there's an electric eye? Or guard dogs? Or heat-sensing devices—that X63 thing?"

"This is a state-funded museum, pal, not *Star Trek*. And you think they'd leave guard dogs where they could gnaw on all these expensive antiques? Hey, do you have to go to the bathroom? You're going to be hiding back there a long time, and you really shouldn't use them once the place is closed. The less you have to move around the better."

Tom went one last time, and rejoined Charlie in the Village Square. "Four-thirty," Tom said. "Closing's in a half hour. And there's nobody around."

Charlie nodded and stuck out his hand. Tom shook it. "Go for it," Charlie said.

Tom climbed over the wooden barrier onto the porch, and stepped inside the small building. He paused for a moment, his heart thudding, expecting to hear alarm bells go off at any second. But nothing happened, and he moved quickly behind the counter. He was relieved to see that there was nothing already behind it, and that it was open underneath, so that he could lie in its shelter. The only way anyone could see him would be for them to come the whole way around the counter, and the odds against anyone doing that were long. He hoped.

"Okay?" he heard Charlie whisper.

"Okay," he replied, and listened to Charlie's footsteps moving away across the wooden plank floor. He was alone now, and he felt scared and excited all at once. It made him feel like a kid again, playing hide and seek, crouching in the dark summer night, listening for the soft footfalls of the person who was seeking, but hearing only his own heartbeat, his own quick breaths, so loud he thought the whole world had to hear them.

The excitement was strangely sexual as well. He had had his first waking erection playing hide and seek, and he realized he had one now. For a moment he wished Laura were with him, and that they were both naked under the counter, making hot, quick love, stifling their moans of pleasure, feeling their silent climaxes only in the other's trembling.

Okay, he thought, enough of that. Keep your mind on business. Be quiet. Just remember to be quiet.

He sweated each time he heard footsteps, and before too long a group stopped right in front of his building, and a guide began to talk about it for what seemed an interminable amount of time. As the lecture went on, Tom realized with a shock that he recognized the voice and in another second he knew that it was Spencer.

He listened, hardly daring to breathe, as Spencer described what commerce was like in the nineteenth century, the types of dry goods sold, the prices paid, and a number of dry details. Just as Tom thought there was no more to say, he heard Spencer speak words that cramped his gut and brought his heart rate to a rapid tattoo.

"And now, so that you can get a better idea of what these old general stores were really like, I'll open this gate, and you may step inside for a moment. Please be careful not to touch any of the items on display, as they are all authentic and some are very delicate."

Oh Jesus, Tom thought, I've had it, I am fucking dead. There was, he felt, no alternative to discovery. A dozen scenarios raced thought his mind as he heard a latch click open, and by the time the first footsteps hit the porch, he thought the best one would be to simply wait until they filed in, then stand up and try to join them, stick to the rear of the group until they hit a place where he could slip away, and hope to God that no one was boorish enough to say something like, "Hey, what were you doing behind that counter?"

Now the footsteps were crashing dangerously near him, and he tensed, preparing to slip around the side of the counter and straighten up, praying that he would not do so directly in front of Spencer's beady eyes.

But just as Tom was about to move, he heard Spencer say,

in the tone of a maiden aunt who observes her rambunctious nephews preparing to gambol in her glassware, "All right, that's far enough, I think you can see everything from here."

Atta*boy*, Spencer, Tom thought wildly. Keep 'em back. Don't let 'em touch those cracker boxes.

Then, just as Tom was feeling as if he could finally take a very quiet, very shallow breath, a child's head came around the side of the counter, and the child's eyes looked directly at him. Tom froze.

"Is any of this stuff still good to eat?" another child's voice asked.

"Oh no," Spencer said. "All of these boxes are empty. There's no food in them"

The boy continued to watch Tom. There was no expression on his face at all.

"Where'd they keep the ice cream?" another voice said.

"Well, they didn't sell packaged ice cream. They had to make it at home. You see, back then there were no freezers. . . ."

Spencer rambled on, and Tom and the little boy kept looking at each other. It was a standoff, Tom thought, in more ways than one. The kid saw him, but it could have been worse. Tom could have stood up and attempted to surreptitiously mingle with a bunch of four-foot-high children.

"Well, it's almost closing time, so let's all go back out to the lobby now," said Spencer wearily.

The little boy kept looking at Tom. Finally his mouth opened. "There's a man back there," he said.

Tom scarcely had time to shudder before he heard another adult's voice. "Come on, Bobby."

Bobby took one last look, then turned and walked out of Tom's line of vision. "There's a man back there," Bobby said again, in the same flat tone.

"Yes, all right, come on," said the blessedly unbelieving parent or teacher or chaperon, and the voices and the footsteps slowly faded away, leaving Tom in safe, lovely silence.

"Thank you, God," he whispered so that only he and God could hear, and then he relaxed, let himself slump down onto the wooden floor, his hands beneath his head, and began to wait.

Tom did not stir from his shelter until after midnight. By then he had become familiar with the schedule of the guard, at least for the area in which he hid. He had heard someone walking by, keys jingling, at 6:20, 8:24, and 10:27. He waited for the guard's return, and was not disappointed, for at 12:22 he heard the familiar footsteps.

Just before they faded away, he crawled out from under the counter, stretched his legs, and went in the direction he thought the guard had taken. It would be better, he and Charlie had figured, to stay near the guard. That way he would know where the man was at all times, and the guard would not be able to take Tom by surprise.

Tom drifted silently in his Reeboks across the smooth floors and followed the guard toward the lobby, where Tom waited until the gray-clad man climbed up the escalator steps to the second and then the third floor. When Tom heard him walk into the exhibit area on his right, he ran up the stairs himself, three at a time, dashed around the huge curving mezzanine that surrounded the gigantic sculpture of William Penn, and leapt up the steps to the third floor. At the top he listened for the guard's progress through the Hall of Geology, then stepped inside the doorway and stood behind a giant globe, where he waited until he heard the guard come out the other side and descend the escalator stairs again.

On his way back down, Tom thought. He wasn't, thank God, checking the offices on the fourth floor where they had talked to Spencer and where the carving was stored. He found the nearest stairway, but hesitated before pushing it open, wondering if an alarm would sound. Then he decided it probably wouldn't, that if power to the escalators and elevators was shut off, any alarms on the stairs would probably be disconnected for the guards. God, but there were a lot of things he hadn't thought about. And Charlie hadn't either. When and if Tom got out of here, he intended to roast the older man thoroughly for it.

It turned out to be easier than he had thought. Unlike the exhibit areas, the offices were dark but unlocked, and Tom used the flashlight he had brought in his backpack to find Spencer's desk. The room behind it, however, where Spencer had indicated that the carving was kept, was locked, as was the desk, and there was no way of forcing it. But Tom had worked around offices, so he slipped on his Playtex gloves and found a thin, silver key under the carpet remnant on which Spencer kept his typewriter. The key unlocked the desk, and in the center drawer Tom found a ring of larger keys, one of which fit the storage room lock. He entered the room, closed the door behind him, shone the flashlight around to make sure there were no windows, and flicked on the light.

Wooden shelves lined the room, making it feel smaller than it really was. The shelves were quite worn, and Tom suspected that they had been moved here from some older building. Tables ran the twenty-foot length of the room as well, and on them were a variety of objects—a multitude of arrowheads and axe heads, dusty beads of all shapes and sizes, a scattering of what looked like very old human bones, and a number of crude carvings. Tom saw the quartz almost immediately.

It must be his imagination, he thought, but the white quartz seemed luminously bright, and when he picked it up he could have sworn that it shivered like something living in his grasp, as if it knew it had a purpose to fulfill and that he was the instrument of its rescue.

Attached to it with a piece of string was a tag that read, "Lenape/S. Hershey—6/24." Tom put the carving in his backpack, moved to the door, turned off the light, and went back into the office. He locked the storage room, replaced the keys in Spencer's desk, locked it, and slipped the desk key back into its hiding place. Then, listening for the footsteps of the dutifully constant guard, he made his way back down to the exhibit area, down the escalator stairs, and into the prototypical turn of the century town, where he crawled into his under-the-counter sanctuary with a great deal of relief.

He did not dare sleep for fear of snoring while the guard passed by, so he put the knapsack under his head and let the hard, irregular carving prod his skull as he considered how he and Charlie—and Laura, if she were willing—would replace it in the grave from which it had been taken.

Despite such morbid thoughts and the physical discomfort his knotty, quartz pillow caused him, Tom fell asleep, and awoke to the sound of footsteps and strange voices. He almost cried out when he opened his eyes and saw the panel of rough wood above him. For a split second he thought that he was dead and in his coffin before he realized where he really was. Then he breathed a sigh of relief and stretched his limbs. He looked at his watch and saw that it was just after opening time, nine o'clock. Charlie was due to arrive between nine-thirty and ten.

Just after ten o'clock, Tom heard Charlie's voice. "Allie-allie in free, campers," it said.

Tom wasted no time. He rolled out from under the counter, grabbed the backpack, and jumped to his feet. His legs, cramped from their long rest, nearly buckled under him, but he stayed on his feet, came out on the porch, climbed over the rail, and stood next to Charlie Lewis. His smile told Charlie all he needed to know.

"You got it," Charlie said.

"I got it."

"Excellent. Then may I suggest, Raffles, that we get the hell out of here before the swag is missed?"

Tom was apprehensive as he crossed the lobby and rode down the escalator, but no one approached them, no burly guard yelled, "Hey! What you got in that knapsack?" and in a few minutes they were out on the street walking toward Charlie's car. "And now?" Tom asked as they drove toward Dreamthorp.

"And now we bury it. The thing you risked life, limb, and liberty for, we're going to stick in the ground."

"Did you call Laura?"

"Yeah. She's going to meet us."

Despite the hot summer air blowing in through the car windows, a chill ran through Tom. "Jesus, Charlie, not at the grove?"

"Of course not, you think we're stupid? At her cottage." Charlie frowned. "She doesn't seem too enthralled by all this."

"Doesn't believe it, you mean?" Charlie nodded. "Laura's a very practical lady. And there are easier things to believe."

"Not about all this, my boy," Charlie said.

As she waited, Laura thought about magic. If what Charlie
and Tom believed was true, then magic existed. Old magic.
The magic of shamans and medicine men and painted prim-
itives dancing beneath trees, worshipping strange gods.

She couldn't believe it. She had tried, had endeavored with
all her might to enter into their fantasy, to believe that all
these deaths were caused by old magic, by disturbed spirits,
by wood haunted by long-dead Indians, still vengeful, still
violent.

But it seemed too absurd, like an old movie on *Night Owl
Theatre* with Christopher Lee, and she wondered how many
of those Tom and Charlie had seen in their lives. Maybe it
was easy for them to believe such things with the evidence
they had.

But Laura was different from them. Laura had gazed upon
the face of true evil in a lantern-lit tent on a summer night,
and she would know forever after that what she had then seen
was the true magic, the new magic, the twentieth century
magic of madness and hate that no incantation could drive
away. No mystic words or charms or gestures could defeat
the magic of nameless Gilbert Rodman and his faceless kind.
Only force, heavy and terrible, could destroy that heavy and

303

terrible magic. No weaving of spells, as delicate as a tapestry, would do. Instead of a tapestry, this new magic called for a plastic bag, thick as lead, tied over the face of this new evil to suffocate it in the breath of its own depravity. Instead of a quartz amulet, it called for a bullet in the head, a knife under the heart, a shotgun blast to the face. Only such things could wipe away its smug, confident leer, its expression of power, supreme and lofty, knowing and unknown.

Laura's hands drifted over her collection of firearms, picking them up one by one, feeling the superb balance, the craftsmanship visible in the fit of the housing, the silken polish of the wood, beautifully grained and finished. She hefted a twelve-gauge Purdy that had been her father's, held the butt to her shoulder, aimed across the room at the opposite wall, felt the warmth of the wood against her cheek, caught the scent, light and spectral and momentary, of her father, then the odor of burnt gunpowder, power released.

She brought the shotgun down and touched the stock where her cheek had rested. It was still warm from her skin, beaded like dew with her sweat. She brushed away the light dampness, but the warmth remained, and the walnut wood seemed alive and stirring, like a pool into which her fingers might gladly plunge.

Wood.

This was wood too, wasn't it? Just like deadly pillars, fatal trunks, treacherous planks and boards. But this wood could protect her. This wood and this metal, for in it was power, power to kill the new magic, the modern magic that still haunted her, despite love and what she knew to be truth.

She heard a car pull up outside and looked out the window, the shotgun still in her hand. It was Charlie's car, and Charlie and Tom were climbing out of it. Tom was carrying a backpack and biker's helmet, but whether he had the figure or not she neither knew nor cared. All she cared about was that he was safe and had not been caught.

She put the shotgun back in the gun case, closed the glass door, and went out onto the porch. She met Tom on the steps, and held him without saying a word. When they finally separated, he smiled and told her that he had gotten the carving.

"All right," she said, "all right. But come in and have some lunch. You must be starving."

He shook his head. "I'm okay. The main thing I want to

do now is to get that carving buried. If Spencer at the museum notices that it's missing and puts two and two together, I don't want it found in my knapsack."

"Besides," Charlie said, "the faster we get it back where it belongs, the faster this place gets back to normal." Although she was not aware of it, Laura must have expressed her disbelief in some small way, for Charlie added dryly, "Believe it or not."

"I'm sorry, Charlie," she said. "I don't mean to throw a damper on your . . . burglary."

"Don't use that word," he said. "You want to send your boyfriend to Sing Sing for the rest of his natural life?" The teasing tone vanished from his voice as suddenly as it had come, and she could tell that he felt self-conscious about what he and Tom had done and were still planning to do. "So. Do you want to come with us?"

"Do you want me to?"

"The more the merrier," Charlie said, "and I don't mean that facetiously. I really think that the more people who are there when we . . . re-inter this thing, the better."

"The more people?" Laura asked. "Or the more believers?"

Charlie was silent for amoment. "I don't know that it makes any difference."

"I'd like to have you come, Laura," Tom said flatly.

"All right then. I will." She smiled more airily than she felt. "Does this make me an accomplice?"

Charlie nodded. "But don't worry. They have coed cells in Sing Sing now."

Tom got a small shovel from his woodshed, and the three of them went to the site of the former sawmill, where Tom dug a small hole directly above where he had reburied the bones of the Indians. Charlie took the quartz carving from the backpack, knelt, and placed it into the grave. Then Tom shoveled the dirt back over it, patted it down, and strewed dead leaves and grass over the bare earth. They stood there silently for a while, until Charlie cleared his throat.

"I, uh, thought it might be a good thing to use one of Grover Kraybill's . . . spells." He said the word as if he was embarrassed to. "So I brought a copy of his *Powwow* book along. Not his, the police kept that. Just a copy." Charlie opened the thin, paperbound book. "I didn't know which one

to use, but I found a few that seem . . . relevant. This first
one is to keep people from doing you an injury.'' He cleared
his throat again, and Laura looked down at the ground.
'' 'Dullix, ix, ux. Yea, you can't come over Pontio; Pontio
is above Pilato. In the name of the Father, and the Son, and
the Holy Ghost.' Uh, I don't know what that one really
means. The others make a little more sense.''

Laura looked at Tom and saw that he was having trouble
keeping a smile off his face.

"This one," Charlie went on, "is to fasten or spellbind
anything, it says, so I guess that would include spirits." He
paused, then said, offended, "Tom, are you amused?"

"No, Charlie."

"Well, look, I feel like enough of an asshole doing this,
okay? So can we get serious?"

"I'm sorry, Charlie. I'm just . . . uncomfortable, I guess.
Nervous, you know?"

Charlie gave him another disdainful look, then turned back
to the book. " 'Christ's cross and Christ's crown, Christ Jesus' colored blood, be thou every hour good. God, the Father, is before us; God, the Son, is beside us; God, the Holy
Ghost, is behind us. Whoever now is stronger than these
three persons may come, by day or night, to attack us.' We're
supposed to say the Lord's Prayer now. Three times. 'Our
Father—' ''

The three of them prayed together, going through the prayer
three times. At the end, Charlie opened the book again.
"Okay, this last one is a charm to gain advantage of a man
of superior strength, which isn't quite what we've got here,
but I figure it can't hurt." He cleared his throat again and
began:

'' 'I, Charles Lewis, breathe upon thee. Three drops of
blood I take from thee: the first out of thy heart, the other
out of thy liver, and the third out of thy vital powers; and in
this I deprive thee of thy strength and manliness. Hbbi Massa
danti Lantien. I. I. I.' ''

Tom snorted a laugh that he instantly tried to disguise as
a cough.

"You've got something to say, Tom?" Charlie asked angrily.

"What, uh, does that mean, Charlie?"

"Hell, I don't know, I didn't write it, okay?"

"Right. Sorry. Go ahead."

"I'm *finished*."

"Oh." Tom nodded. "So, uh, that's it?"

"That's it. I hope you were amused."

"Charlie," Tom said, grinning, "I'm sorry, I really am. You know that I believe in what we're doing, but it's just that, once we were really doing it, it . . . I guess it seemed . . ."

"Silly," Laura said. "It seemed silly. And you both felt self-conscious about it."

"God's own truth," Charlie said, no less annoyed. "But I don't care whether it seems like a goddam laugh riot or not, it was what needed to be done, and we did it."

"And now we wait," Laura said softly. "Wait and see if you're right."

"And you don't think we are," Tom said.

"I don't pretend to know. But if it's what you think it is, I don't believe that anything so strong can be laid to rest so easily."

She watched the two men as they looked uncomfortably at each other, then down at the ground where they had buried the quartz carving. They said nothing on their way back to the cottages. Laura went first down the path, and they followed with heads bowed, like reprimanded children following their mother.

The police did not come to Tom Brewer's cottage to inquire about the carving until Tuesday afternoon. Spencer, the curator, had discovered that the artifact was missing that morning, had reported its loss to the police, and had given them the names of the two suspicious and duplicitous men who had tried to acquire the piece the previous week.

Stu Bottomly knocked on the door and introduced Tom to a Lieutenant Hidley, a tall, prematurely white-haired man who was a detective on the Harrisburg police force. Tom denied that he was anywhere near the museum since the day he and Charlie had visited Spencer, and told Hidley that he had no knowledge of where the carving was. He even invited him inside to look for it, but Hidley declined to do so. When he asked Tom if he could account for his whereabouts during the past few days, Tom said that he'd been spending time working alone, with Charlie, or with Laura Stark, and he certainly didn't have an ironclad alibi for every hour of the previous week. "I didn't think I'd need one," he told Hidley with a smile.

Hidley thanked Tom, and he and Stu Bottomly went next door to Charlie's house, where Charlie would, as Tom well knew, give them the same story he had. Later, over beers, Charlie told Tom that he had suggested to Hidley that Spencer take another look in the storeroom.

"I told him that fella struck me as not being able to locate his posterior with both hands. Stu laughed, but Hidley didn't. Some people have no sense of humor."

They didn't hear from Hidley again.

The rest of the week was very quiet. It was quiet because there were very few people left in Dreamthorp, and it was quiet because none of those particular people happened to be killed.

Charlie and Tom talked about it frequently, and grimly teased each other about keeping the deathwatch. But as every day passed without incident, they began to feel less foolish about what they had done. On Friday afternoon they were sitting together on Charlie's porch drinking beers and listening to the sounds of John Coltrane's "Giant Steps" coming from inside, when Charlie told Tom that he had been down to the site of the old sawmill.

"Alone?" Tom asked him, with only a trace of alarm.

"Yeah. Maybe it was foolish, but I felt like I just wanted to go down there and . . . and *feel*. See if what we did had any effect."

"And did it?"

"I think it did. I'm alive to tell the tale, aren't I? And I didn't *feel* a damn thing. Not to say that I would have in any case, since I probably don't have a psychic bone in my body."

"I don't think psychic powers exist in your bones, Charlie, but I know what you mean." Tom smiled. "I went over there myself."

Charlie raised an eyebrow. "And?"

"And the same as you. I sit here untouched, and I didn't feel or see or hear anything out of the ordinary either."

"You think we done busted dem ghosts?"

"I'm not breathing easy yet. And I wouldn't suggest a wholesale migration back to Dreamthorp either. But I do have my fingers crossed."

On Sunday, Laura took Tom to her rod and gun club, and they shot at targets on the outdoor range. It was a hot day and dry, as though it had always been dry, and there were no other shooters on the range. They fired competition .22s and a .38 special, with Laura outscoring Tom in every round, although not by much.

"You're good," she told him. "I thought you said you haven't shot in years."

"I haven't," he said, smiling at her compliment. "I used to go out with my Uncle Jack sometimes and plunk at tin cans."

"I didn't know you had an uncle."

"I don't anymore. He died of lung cancer when I was in school. Heavy smoker." Tom looked to the right of the range at the long, low brick building nearly hidden in the trees. "Your dad founded this place?"

"He helped. Was the first president. He loved the outdoors."

"He hunted a lot?"

"He did, yes, but still he was a very . . . a *gentle* man, you know? Like that Robert DeNiro movie—he never fired unless he was sure he could kill in one shot. He hated to see animals suffer. After my mother died, he stopped hunting altogether. Just shot skeet and target. He still went fishing, though."

Tom sat next to her on the bench rest and put an arm around her. "You loved him very much, didn't you?"

"Yes. I did. He taught me an awful lot." She leaned against him, and he loved feeling the firm weight of her, the tightness of her muscles, the softness of her breasts against his chest. She was as tall as he was, but it didn't matter. They fit each other perfectly. He didn't have to bend to kiss her cheek—it was right there on the level of his lips—and he thought that the petite woman/tall man syndrome that had flourished over the years left a lot to be desired in the face of the real equality that he shared with Laura.

Her size made her no less a woman. She had proven that both in and out of bed. Her orgasms had been stronger and more intense than Susan's or Karen's, as if she had been celibate for many years and was now discovering sex for the first time, although he knew that was impossible. She had been married, after all, and surely she must have had lovers before him. Still, at times she reminded him of a young girl in the first stages of love for whom every word, act, and touch was a further step into a new, strange, and wonderful land. She was a woman, mature and wise, and he knew that she loved him and knew that he loved her.

"I love you, Laura," he whispered into her ear, and she turned toward him and kissed him. "I think . . ." he went on slowly, meticulously, "I think that we should get married."

Her eyes glittered suddenly like a frightened doe's, as if she had been hoping to hear such words but, now that they were spoken, was afraid of them. "Oh, Tom," she said softly, and he could not tell what the words meant—agreement and submission, or sad denial.

"There's nothing to stop us." He smiled and turned her face toward his. "We've been spending so much time together that we might as well be married. And I want to, Laura. I want to spend the rest of my life with you. I think we'd be happy together. I know we would. So. Will you? Marry me?"

As he looked into her face, he saw now that it *was* sadness, and he felt a coldness deep inside him and tried to prepare for refusal, though he did not know how he could bear it. "Tom," she said, drawing away from him, "I can't say yes or no. It . . . it isn't that simple."

"Why not?"

"I've got to tell you something first. . . ."

"No you don't."

"What?" She looked puzzled.

"You don't have to tell me anything you don't want to. I don't want to pry into your past. What happened before doesn't matter." He said it partly because it was true and partly because he did not want to know, did not want to hear any stories of past indiscretions to bother his dreams.

"But I *want* to tell you this. You have to know. It's something you have to know about me. Something that I didn't know about myself until . . . until recently."

She looked at him with desperate, pleading eyes, and he was suddenly afraid to hear what she had to say. "All right," he said, regardless of his fear, "if you want to tell me, I'll listen."

Then she told him, slowly but relentlessly, what she had

felt for Kitty Soames, what she thought Kitty had felt for her, and what they had done together on the night that Gilbert Rodman had slashed his way into her life. "I loved her, Tom," she said. "I don't know what would have happened between us after that night, if we would have stayed together, I just don't know. But I believe that I loved her then as much as I had ever loved anyone before. Certainly more than I'd loved my husband.

"But not as much as I love you now."

He took her hand, kissed it, and held it against his cheek. "I think I understand," he said. "I really think I do. The . . . biology of it is just secondary. You needed someone, that was all. And Kitty was there for you."

"And can you forget about it? Can you forgive it?"

"I can't forget about it, no, because it's helped to make you who you are, so that's all right. As for forgiving it, I would if there were anything to forgive."

"You say that now. But I want you to take time and think about it."

"It won't make any difference if I think about it or not. I'll still love you."

"You say that, Tom, but there have to be some doubts now. Some questions. Will I do it again? Will I slip?"

"You wanted love, Laura. I'll give you all you need."

"It's not that easy. You can't just say it and have it be so." She shook her head, stood up, and started to pack the pistols back into their padded cases. "Think about it for a day or two. Let it work on your mind. And if you still want me to, then I'll marry you, Tom." She looked at him, and he saw tears in her eyes. "I do love you, Tom. More than ever. More than anyone or anything."

She picked up the cased guns and hurried toward the car. He followed, no longer knowing what to say or do. Although he had said what he felt he had to, he also felt horribly confused, and he knew that she was right. He had to think about what she had told him for a time, even though he felt that it would make no difference, that he would continue to love her and want her to share his life.

But the image of the two women together intruded upon his thoughts, not with the simple and adolescent jealousy of a lover's past love but with the gnawing insistence that the memory of pornography exerts upon the penitent, seeking to subsume the sins of the flesh in contemplations of sanctity.

Why had she told him? she wondered. And above all why had she *not* told him of what she had done in Philadelphia, of the revulsion she had felt, of the violent fear of those women that had made her physically ill?

Because, she decided, she wanted no alibi. She had not wanted to say, Oh yes, I was bad, but I'm all right now, I'm normal now—heterosexual all the way. Because she wasn't, and she knew it. She had within her the capacity for love outside of biological preferences, she saw that now. The loathing she had felt toward those sad, desperate women was the same loathing she would have felt for sad and desperate men who were willing to give up their humanity and identity for a quick and loveless moment of animal passion.

But she knew something else about herself as well. She was capable of giving love and receiving love exclusively. If she married Tom—and she wanted to—there was as little danger of her having an affair with a woman as there was of her having one with another man. It would not be difficult for her either, because one person loving her was all she needed, everything she wanted. She was sure of herself, and Tom's love had made her even more sure.

So it was up to him. She had had to tell him. There had been no choice in the matter. She had known that he would talk about marriage someday, and had decided that when that day came she would tell him everything, and now she had. Now it was his choice. She had told him what she was, but, more importantly, he knew *who* she was.

September

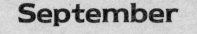

"Every day travels toward death; the last only arrives at it."

—Montaigne, quoted in Alexander Smith,
Dreamthorp

Nor does he work in black and white
alone.

—Alexander Smith, *Dreamthorp*

"But *where* are you, my sweet Laura," whispered Gilbert
Rodman.

The strip of highway on which he stood seemed to contain
a new mall every few hundred feet. It was not how he had
pictured Lancaster, Pennsylvania, when he had taken the time
to picture it at all. In Gilbert's mind the place was Pennsylvania Dutch country, filled with solemn-faced Amishmen
wearing black hats and driving horses and buggies. But now
he was faced with Hardee's and Brewer's Outlet and Radio
Shack and *Chi-Chi's*, for crissake, as if an Amishman would
eat at Chi-Chi's! Oh well, he thought, maybe I came in the
wrong way.

It had been the most direct way. He'd gotten off the Pennsylvania Turnpike at Harrisburg, then hitched his way down
Route 283 until he started seeing exit signs for Lancaster.
His driver, a trucker with A. Duie Pyle (with whom he made
manure jokes about the company's name), told him that
Prince Street would take him right downtown after a two mile
walk, if he couldn't get a hitch from there.

As it turned out, he couldn't. Gilbert was not looking his
best. The jaunt across Indiana, Ohio, and Pennsylvania had
not been an easy one. He had not wanted to kill and had not
done so. But since killing his victims was the only way that
Gilbert felt secure enough to rob them, he had stolen nothing
and had eaten little on the way, conserving his money, and

slept either while he was riding or by the side of the road, far enough off the shoulder so that he would not be spotted by the police.

But here he was at last—the Holy City to which his pilgrimage had finally brought him—Lancaster. The dwelling of the one he had thought of as the Lesser Bitch but who now had assumed all the qualities of the Great Bitch herself, so that in Gilbert's mind she had begun to exist as simply the Bitch.

The Bitch and be damned.

Gilbert had no plans beyond Laura Stark's death. It was the only thing he had lived for, and now, for the first time, he looked beyond it.

What would he do when she was gone? What would he live for? If they caught him or if he died with her, that would be all right. But now on this late summer evening, walking along the highway, cars darting past, their radios blaring, Gilbert felt for the first time that there was life after death, for what he had suffered at Laura's hands was death, sure enough. But he had overcome it. Death was swallowed up in victory, or at least would be once he got his hands on her and into her.

And then? He had learned that there was more to killing than the physical, and he supposed there always had been. But he had never noticed it before, because the physical response had always been so overwhelming, so deliriously delicious.

Things were different now. Now, when he killed, he felt the power of his mind, not his cock, and that power seemed so great in comparison that he was grateful to Laura for opening the door, letting him see the light. Now when he killed, he could feel the power inside him, feel it surging out of him, across the sky, into the universe, as bright as lightning, loud as thunder. He could feel the great, hot length of it as it crossed the miles, even spanned the years.

Oh yes, Master of Space and Time, that was him all right. And he had arrived. He was there.

Hello, Laura.

But where the hell was she? Lancaster, even though a small city, was big enough that he couldn't go door to door asking for her. He stopped at a phone booth and looked in the directory. God, he thought happily, you're on my side after all. There it was as big as life—STARK LAURA 1367 Barevl Pk.

The number followed, but he didn't need the number. He wasn't going to call her to let her know he was coming. No, it would be much nicer, and a lot more fun, to surprise her.

Boo, Laura.

Gilbert made his way to downtown Lancaster and bought a map of the city at a small newsstand that seemed to specialize in lottery tickets. He sat outside on the wheelchair ramp, and in the fading light of dusk found that Bareville Pike was back in the direction he had come. The fact did not make him angry, for he wanted it to be fully dark by the time he went to the place Laura lived. To help kill the time, he went into a little diner next to the newsstand and had a sandwich, soup, and coffee.

While he ate, he took out his list, the list he had kept for Laura, and amused himself by thinking back to each one of them, finding new memories, recalling screams for mercy, the sound of flesh parting, moans, whimpers, screams. He did not realize that he was chuckling until the man sitting two stools away from him mumbled something to himself and shook his head.

Gilbert looked at the man, a short, wizened black man with gray-white hair, and grinned. The man didn't grin back but kept mumbling to himself, and Gilbert thought that maybe something was wrong with the old man's mind. Jesus, what a shame, Gilbert thought. It must be awful to be crazy.

When he went back outside, it was fully dark, the street illuminated only by the hot, bright lamps and the headlights of passing cars. Gilbert started walking toward the perimeter of the city again, and in forty-five minutes reached the apartment complex that was 1367 Bareville Pike.

There were three red brick buildings arranged around a central court. They were each two stories, and white pillars fronted them. From the layout, Gilbert assumed that there were eight apartments in each building. As he walked closer, he could see that the ground floor apartments had their own individual entrances, while those on the second floor were accessible by a common stairs in the building's center.

He took the building on the left first. Two of the ground floor apartments had Big Wheels and bicycles in front of them, so he dismissed them immediately. He walked up to the mailboxes that hung outside the others, and read the names. Neither was Laura's.

Then he went inside the door to the stairway and read the names on the four mailboxes, but Laura's was not among them. He did the same with the other buildings, but Laura's name was not there.

"Where are you, Laura?" he asked the night as he stepped out of the last stairway. A noise made him jerk his head around, and he saw a dog, no longer young enough to be called a puppy but not yet fully grown. It was of no identifiable breed. Its hair was a long tangle of brown and white, its ears were as floppy as a spaniel's, its eyes sparkled with the excitement of youth, and its tail wagged fiercely at Gilbert.

Gilbert looked around but saw no one. He and the dog stood alone in a pool of darkness. "Hello, boy," he said gently, not wanting to scare the dog away. "How are ya, huh?"

He knelt and held out a hand. The dog came closer, sniffing at Gilbert as though he were an old friend.

"Attaboy. C'mon . . ."

The dog advanced, and Gilbert reached out and grabbed its collar, drawing it to him. He waited for a moment, but the dog kept wagging its tail, panting, looking at Gilbert with friendly, trusting eyes.

Gilbert held the collar with one hand, patted the dog's head with the other, and then put his face against the dog's furry head. It felt soft and warm, and Gilbert released the collar, put his arms around the young dog, and wept.

When he was finished, he wiped his eyes on his sleeve, and scratched the dog between its ears. "I wish I had something for you, fella. A treat or something."

He stood up, leaned over to pat the dog again, then walked away. He would go back downtown and find a cheap hotel where he could finally get a good night's sleep in a bed that didn't have dirt under it.

He awoke the next morning in his bed in the James Street Hotel, a little hole in the wall that had taken cash in advance and no questions asked when he signed the register John Smith. After checking out, he went to a phone booth, called directory assistance, and asked for the number of Laura Stark.

"I'm sorry, sir," the operator's voice droned. "There is no listing for a Laura Stark in the Lancaster exchange."

So what did she do? Change it to unlisted? Had he simply gotten an old phone directory the evening before? He checked the directory in the booth, found Laura's number again at the Bareville Pike address, and dialed it. It rang one time, and he heard a recorded message that stated that the number he had dialed was no longer in service. Ignoring the admonition to recheck the number or dial again, he hung up the phone and kicked the door, causing the booth to shudder.

He thought savagely for a moment, and then remembered. The girl he had loved before Laura woke up . . . Kitty Soames, that was it. It was a long shot, but it might work. Of course, the risk was that the Soames survivors might decide there was something fishy going on and call Laura. So he had to be sincere.

He could do that, he thought. He was very good at being sincere.

There was only one Soames listed in the Lancaster exchange—SOAMES JOHN J. Gilbert looked at the wristwatch he had taken from Robert Marczak several hundred miles and what seemed like a hundred years ago, and saw that it was 9:47. That was good. It meant that Soames, John J., would probably be at work in his office somewhere and Mrs. Soames, John J., would be home alone. Women were far less suspicious about some things.

She answered on the third ring. Just her hello told Gilbert that she was a rich bitch country club twat who could count the last time she'd been laid in decades.

"Hello, Mrs. Soames?" Gilbert said, shyly and a bit tentatively.

"Yes?"

"Are you the Mrs. Soames who was, uh, Kitty's mother?"

A pause there. He had hit the right one. "Yes." Very quietly she said it.

"Mrs. Soames, my name is Bob Andrews." Bob. There was something bluff and honest about *Bob*. And Andrews had WASP written all over it. Just like Archie. Red hair, freckles, bow tie, wouldn't hurt a fly. "I'm a friend of Laura Stark's, but I've been out of the country on government business for a while." The government—that was a good touch. The woman *had* to be Republican. "Laura wrote to me shortly after that . . . terrible thing that happened to your daughter. But I wasn't able to communicate with her after that, and I've come back to the area to visit my folks and thought I'd try to see her, but I find she's moved, and gee, I really don't know how to get in touch with her. You were the only other person I thought might know where she would be."

The woman didn't say anything. Oh shit, Gilbert thought. What is it? Did I say something wrong? Was the *gee* just a little too fucking sweet to be believed?

Then he heard her voice but was unable to understand what she had said. "I'm sorry, Mrs. Soames, but I think we have a bad connection. Could you repeat that?"

"Laura moved away from Lancaster." The voice was louder now, but it shook, as if unpleasant memories were being unearthed.

"Oh, I see," Gilbert said with sympathy. He had no idea why he should sound sympathetic, but the woman's tone of voice seemed to call for it. "Do you have her current address? Or her phone number?"

"I don't have her number, no, but she moved to Dreamthorp."

"Dreamthorp, oh sure," Gilbert said, although he had no idea whatsoever of where or what Dreamthorp was. "Well, I'll find her somehow. Thank you very much, Mrs. Soames. And I'm terribly sorry about your daughter."

"Thank you," Mrs. Soames said.

"Good-bye."

"Good-bye."

Gilbert hung up the phone, then looked in the phone book, but found that the Dreamthorp listings were not in the Lancaster directory. He called information and asked for Laura's number in Dreamthorp but received a message that informed him that the number was unlisted.

"Bitch," he muttered, at both the computerized voice and at Laura herself. Then he got out his map of Lancaster, and on the back found a larger scale map of the surrounding area. There in the northwest corner he found a little village named Dreamthorp.

"Nice," he muttered to himself. Dreamthorp. It sounded

quiet and peaceful. He smiled, thinking that quiet, peaceful Dreamthorp would have a big surprise coming when they found his dear, sweet Laura. Nothing like *that* had ever happened in Dreamthorp before. He was sure of it.

The evening came at last which had been
looked forward to for a couple of months
or more.

          —Alexander Smith, *Dreamthorp*

Although Gilbert Rodman was wrong in one respect, he was
right in another. Unknown to him, terrible things had happened in Dreamthorp, but the village was indeed quiet and
peaceful, due in large part to the small percentage of the
population that still remained in their cottages. The woods
were silent too. No drops of rainfall pattered upon the leaves,
and fewer insects sang day or night. The area directly around
the town looked like a blighted heath, its yellow leaves and
dry branches like something out of Poe's literary landscapes.
Even the pines seemed crisp and brittle.

Rain had fallen in surrounding areas. The usual summer
storms had raged and tossed rainwater in bucketfuls upon the
earth, everywhere except upon the arid soil and withered
leaves of Dreamthorp, as though the town were granted—or
cursed even more, some said—with a special dispensation of
dryness.

The passing of Labor Day had given the few tenacious
summer people the reason to leave, and of those who lived
there year-round, less than a half dozen households remained, the older ones with nowhere else to go or with the
desire to go nowhere else. The ineffectual security men were
gone too, the victims of indifference and increased financial
burdens on those who remained. Charlie Lewis had dismissed them just before Labor Day, and they left gladly, hav-

'ing in all those weeks never accosted a single suspicious
character.

None to accost, Tom Brewer thought, looking out at the
trees that used to be green. How do you catch spirits? Lure
them into a sack and throw them into the river? He remembered hearing a story like that when he was a kid. But it
hadn't worked, had it? Hadn't they turned themselves into
wind and blown through the weave of the cloth? Something
like that.

He looked at the kitchen clock and saw that it would be
another two hours before Laura came home from work. He
was looking forward to the start of the fall semester next
Tuesday. He had spent too much time idle, too much time
thinking and brooding. The carving of Rodman was completed, but he had been unable to begin work on anything
else. It was as though he had accomplished in wood what he
had been striving all his life to do, and now that it was finished, he felt lost.

Tom finished the milk he had been drinking and put the
glass into the sink. Then he picked up the bill from the home
in which his mother was now living and looked it over again.
It was high, but fortunately his parents had always been in-
veterate savers. The size of their bank accounts had amazed
him. Had this been what they had been saving all their lives
for, he wondered sadly. To preserve the survivor of the pair
in what was really little more than an elegant madhouse? Was
such the end of life and love? For they had loved each other,
Tom well knew. They were always happiest when they were
alone with each other.

He thought of Laura then, and of how happy he was with
her. He had not seen her since the previous Sunday when he
had taken her home from the rod and gun club. He had come
into her living room and watched as she put the weapons
away, all except the .38, which she pushed deep down behind
a sofa cushion.

"You always do that?" he had asked her.

"Since the killings started. Now it's habit."

He couldn't blame her, a woman living alone. But he hoped
she wouldn't be living alone much longer. He had acceded
to her request not to see her for a few days, to take time to
think about what she had told him. He had done so and found

that she was right, that it was not as easy to dismiss as he had hoped it would be.

But it was not easy to dismiss any thoughts that came between him and the woman he loved. For years after he had married Susan he had been bothered by the fact that she had had lovers before him. It was not sexist as much as it was selfish. He had irrationally wanted *all* her love, even that which she had given before he knew her. It was absurd and adolescent, to be sure, but it was nonetheless real.

He had dealt with it, however, and with the years, as he became convinced beyond the slightest doubt of his wife's love for him, it had dissipated, and he was sure his discomfort over Laura's admission would do the same. Besides, what did it matter? He was older now, and could understand. She had needed love and had taken it when it was offered. That was no sin, nothing to even be ashamed of. Her life had made her what she was, so he should be thankful for it.

But try as he might, he could not be thankful for Gilbert Rodman and what Gilbert Rodman had done.

He went down into the cellar then to look at what he had done with Laura's fear, to examine his artistic embodiment of it. It was he, he thought, who should be asking for forgiveness. Had he used her? he wondered, then decided, hoped, that you could never use someone you loved.

The carving stood in the corner where he had left it, and he yanked off the tarpaulin, bringing it from darkness to light.

It had not changed. It was as he had carved it, filled with bundled strength, huge with repressed hate. Jesus, but it was ugly and beautiful at once. It frightened him as he looked at it, and he considered again whether it had been he who created it, or if it had been there all the time and he had simply freed it.

Tom raised his hand to touch the wood, but paused, and found that he did not want to. Instead, he suddenly wanted to be with someone, someone alive and friendly, someone whose eyes were not shadowy wells of darkness.

He picked up the tarpaulin and drew his arms back to throw the heavy cloth over the figure, but found that he could not. It was as though the carving itself was telling him to leave it uncovered, let it breathe.

Let it live.

Tom shivered, dropped the cloth, and let it lie where it had fallen. With an effort, he turned his back on the thing and ascended the stairs, turning out the light and securing the door firmly behind him. If it had had a lock he would have locked it.

It was with mingled dismay and delight that he considered the effect the carving had upon him. This was nothing but wood, something he had made with his own hands and his own imagination, and if it was capable of frightening its creator, how much greater would be the effect on a gallery full of patrons? "It's just a carving," he whispered to himself in the same way that, years ago, he whispered "it's just a story" to Josh when the little boy had trouble going to sleep after watching a scary television show. "Just a carving."

And although he knew it was, he decided to go over and visit Charlie Lewis just the same.

Charlie was sitting on his porch reading a copy of *Smithsonian*, listening to jazz, as always. "Don't tell me," Tom said. "Bird?"

"You're pretty good, kid. Who's on trumpet?"

Tom listened for a moment. "Miles?"

"I take it back, you're not that good. Dizzy. Massey Hall. Come set a spell." Tom slipped thankfully into a wicker chair. "You look peaked," Charlie said.

"You look a bit jittery yourself. Do you always jiggle magazines when you read them?"

Charlie looked down at his left leg, the one the magazine was resting on. It was shaking as if with St. Vitus's Dance. Charlie slapped his hand on it and it stopped. He removed the hand and the trembling started again, while Charlie did a slow burn. Tom laughed. "I suppose I am feeling a mite apprehensive," Charlie said, tossing the magazine aside and crossing his legs. "The longer we wait the more nervous I get. Sort of like the girl who did it for the first time, waiting to see if she's pregnant."

"No deaths," Tom said. "And it's been nearly two weeks."

"I know. But there were gaps before, longer than that. Back in August before the Warfel boy died, that was more than two weeks . . ."

"Since my father was killed."

Charlie nodded. "Maybe we did it."

"Maybe we did."

"Think we could make it rain?"

"It'll rain. Eventually."

Charlie looked upward through the trees. "Weatherman's been calling for it. A big storm, possibility of small stream flooding, all that good stuff. And it looks mighty gray up there. Maybe the gods will smile."

"Maybe they will."

"You know," Charlie said, "I can't help but think that would mean something, that if it rained, if the sky just opened up and dropped buckets on us, that it would be nature's way of saying, 'Hey guys, you done good. No more deaths. Injuns in de cold, cold ground.' " He chuckled deep in his throat. "But if it does or it doesn't, I'm staying."

"And waiting."

Charlie nodded. "And waiting. I hope I have to wait forever."

"Seems quiet."

"You realize that if this were a Tarzan movie I would grunt and say, 'Too quiet.' Only Dreamthorp can't be too quiet." Suddenly Charlie paused. "You hear that?"

"Thunder?"

"I think so."

"Or a car," Tom said as he saw Laura's Toyota pull around the corner at the end of Emerson.

"Damn. Go get your woman, son."

Tom stood and stretched. "I want to go for a little walk after dinner, check things out. I'm kind of concerned now about burglaries, what with so many people away. You want to come?"

"No, I'll just have my shabby TV dinner and watch the news. Besides"—he winked—"it looks like rain."

"God willing. I'll see you later, Charlie." Tom walked down the steps toward Laura's car. She was still sitting inside, watching him. He smiled, went to the passenger side, and got in next to her.

"Hey, lady," he said, "wanta take a guy out to dinner?"

She looked at him. "What does that mean?"

"It means I love you. It means I want you to marry me. It means that if Charlie Lewis weren't sitting up on his porch right now watching every move we make I'd grab you and smother you with kisses to make you see how much I mean it."

She began to nod her head very slowly, and her mouth twisted in a wry smile that held more humor than irony.

"My Laura-proscribed time of contemplation is over," Tom went on, smiling himself now. "I thought about what you told me to think about, and it doesn't matter. Nothing matters but us." He took her hand. "You're the person I want to spend the rest of my life with, Laura. Okay?"

"The hell with Charlie," she said, and embraced him.

They kissed for a long time, and, when they broke for air, they both looked up at Charlie's porch and waved. Charlie shook his head disapprovingly, and they heard his "tsk tsk tsk" through the open car window. "Kids today, it's shameful." Still shaking his head like an offended grandfather, he got up and went into his cottage.

Laura and Tom laughed for a long time, then looked at each other as the laughter died away. "I knew you'd say that," Laura said. "Even if you're not telling the truth, I knew you'd say it."

"It is the truth," Tom said. "The truth is that I love you. When I thought about it, it bothered me, sure. But it would have bothered me if it had been another man. And if I've got to balance that little, gnawing annoyance against my loving you, then loving you wins hands down." He touched her hair and smiled. "I love you more than I love my ego. More than I love Dreamthorp, or my work, or anything I can name. I need to be with you. More than anything, I need that."

"I never . . ." Laura said, then paused. "I never knew a really good man except for my father. A man that I could really trust. With everything. But I know another one now. If you said it didn't concern you, then I'd know you were lying. But because it did, and you could accept it anyway . . . I know I've got a good man now."

"And I've got a good woman."

Her smile came back. "That sounds like a song cue."

"All this mushy stuff sounds like song cues. That's the risk you take." He kissed her again. "You want to go out to dinner? Celebrate our engagement?"

"Yes," she said, touching his lips with her index finger. "But first I want to go inside and make love."

"That would be a much more interesting way to celebrate."

"And less fattening," she said.

She gave herself to him more freely now, Tom thought. Before, even though she had been passionate, he had always had the feeling that she was holding a part of herself back, but no longer. He felt changed somehow too, less rigid, as though they were flowing together into one body. It was intense and warm and filled with love, and by the time they had made love, taken a short, afterglow nap, and gotten dressed, it was nearly eight o'clock.

They drove in Tom's car to the Chalmers Inn, a refurbished farmhouse that served great beef and as decent seafood as could be procured inland. When their cocktails were served, they lifted their glasses and clicked them together.

"To a long and happy life with you," Tom said.

"And to Dreamthorp," Laura added.

> Every window in the little village has its
> light, and to the traveler coming on, en-
> veloped in his breath, the whole place
> shines like a congregation of glow-worms
> ... To revisit that city is like walking
> away back into my yesterdays.
> —Alexander Smith, *Dreamthorp*

God, this place seemed familiar.

As Gilbert Rodman walked through the streets of Dreamthorp, he could have sworn that he had been there before. It
was not the cottages that gave him the sense of déjà vu as
much as it was the land itself, the towering trees, the topog-
raphy of the hillside, the way the little stream near the road
wound its way through the brush.

It was as if he remembered the stream being larger somehow, and when he stepped off the road to examine it more
closely, he could see by the light of the half moon that it had
been much higher not too long before. Place needed rain,
Gilbert thought. He would give it rain. Red rain.

Gilbert smiled as he saw Laura's cottage ahead. He had
hitchhiked out to Dreamthorp, scrutinized the roads into the
tiny community, and discovered that only two, Pine Road and
Elm Road, provided legitimate entrances to the small square
of cottages that comprised the village. There had been an
abandoned Mobil station between the two roads, and he had
waited there since three o'clock, sitting on the bench at the
side of the station, or standing in the phone booth, pretending
to use the phone when infrequent cars passed.

The town seemed deserted, Gilbert thought. Only one car turned into the town in all the time he was waiting, and that was a late model Buick driven by a man in his seventies. Only one car, that is, until Laura drove in at six o'clock.

She still had the Toyota. He remembered it outside the tent. And he remembered her, too. She didn't see him standing there watching her. She didn't see him follow the car, running alongside Pine Road, staying in the shelter of the trees, following her for the five short blocks it took to reach Emerson. He stopped at the end of the street and watched as the man came down to meet her and climbed into the car with her. He watched as they went into the cottage together, watched as they came out two hours later (and what the fuck were they *doing* for those two hours?—wasn't she a dyke?), watched as they drove away together.

Gilbert went up to Thoreau then, and saw no cars parked in front of any of the cottages. What the hell was wrong with this place? Black plague? He was curious, but thankful, and made his way in the darkness down over the hillside to the back door of what he assumed was Laura's place.

The lock was easy to jimmy, and he entered quietly, just in case she had a roommate. He found himself in a small kitchen and noticed a light coming from beneath the door. He slowly pushed it open, and saw that Laura had left on a small desk lamp in the living room. There were no windows at the back of the room, but there was one along the side, and through it Gilbert could see light glowing from the windows of the cottage next door. On his hands and knees, he crawled over to the window and, with infinite patience, slowly turned the stick to close the Levelor blinds.

At last he stood up, and, confident that he was unseen, walked around the room. It was Laura's, all right. He could tell by the cutesy-poo decor, all the goddam trendy colors, everything in its proper place, positioned just so to impress all her bull dyke friends, or her faggots, since she had left with a guy. Gilbert wondered how that pale blue (she probably called it turquoise) and that soft orange (apricot, if you please) would look when her blood was splashed all over it. Jesus, he could hardly wait. Just so she didn't bring back the faggot with her.

But what the hell, if she did, she did. He could slice the guy first, real fast, just like he'd done Hod before he'd begun

to work on Cherry. Maybe he would just bleed the guy, keep
him alive so he could watch.

No. No. He wanted to be *alone* with Laura. No one watching this time. This time would be very, very special.

Very sincere.

He took the piece of paper from his pocket and looked at
it. All those dates. All those people, lovers, friends, carefully
listed so that Laura would know that he had been practicing,
keeping his hand in. Staying ready. For her.

Now, where could he put it? On the desk, he decided. She
would be sure to see it there when she went to turn off the
light before she went to bed. It might take a while, but
he didn't care. The anticipation was delicious, and he didn't
want to rush it. He put the list on the desk top and noticed,
as he did so, another piece of paper next to the brass lamp.
A spear of incongruity went through him as he glanced at it
and saw that it too was a list of dates with names next to
each. He looked at it more carefully, and then at his own,
pencil-scrawled list, and shook his head.

"Jesus," he said. "Ain't *that* a gas?"

Then he shook his head at the wonder of coincidence, and
looked around the living room, trying to decide where to
hide. There were not many options, for the room was small.
There was a couch, a few chairs, a wall full of stereo and
video equipment, bookcases that housed an assortment of
books, records, and videocassettes, a couch against the other
wall, and a gun cabinet.

The gun cabinet made Gilbert uneasy, even though he saw
no handguns, only rifles and shotguns. He wondered if she still
had the revolver she had shot him with. Wouldn't that be poetic
justice, though, for him to finish her with it. . . .

But then he decided not to, even if he could have found it.
Guns were not Gilbert's style. Guns had always frightened him,
with their fire and their noise. The knife was so much more
subtle, more sincere. You had to come in contact with your
victim with a knife. You had to touch. And you could do so
many things with a knife that you couldn't do with a gun.

He shook his head as he looked into the cabinet and then
tried the door. It was locked, and that was good. That meant
that she couldn't go dashing to it to pull out a gun and try to
hurt him again.

At last he decided to lie behind the couch. There was only

a foot of space between it and the wall, but it was wide enough if he lay on his side. He didn't want to go back there right away, though. His muscles were likely to cramp if he stayed there too long, and he wanted to be as supple as a tiger when Laura came home. So he looked through the things on her shelves for a while, paying special attention to the records. Just out of curiosity, he perused her small jazz collection. It didn't take long. There were a few Miles Davis albums. Coltrane's *A Love Supreme* (did she ever listen to it, he wondered), Wynton Marsalis's *Hothouse Flowers,* several by Pat Metheny, and a bunch of those fucking Windham Hill aural wallpaper things. Probably used them, Gilbert thought, to ease her weary mind. Potato music. Aside from the Davis and Coltrane, none of the old classics.

What the fuck did he care anyway? Jazz. Old man's music. His old man . . .

His fingertips riffled along the edges of the albums, into rock now—Beatles, Springsteen, U2, Joplin, the Doors, the Police, a helluva lot of it, almost a yard's worth. . . .

A Yard . . .

Yardbird . . . Bird . . . oh, yeah, he could hear it now—Charlie Parker, the *Summit Meeting at Birdland* album. His old man had had it. "Groovin' High," that was the song. Listen to that fucking alto, will you. Shitty sound, those radio transcriptions, but still there was that alto riding out over everything, the way his father had played it, just like Bird. . . .

He blew out hard, shook it off, tried not to hear the music coming from the next cottage. Fuck it, forget it, here was classical, look at the classical. Gilbert didn't know classical very well, but Laura had a *lot* of classical—a foot of Haydn, almost as much Beethoven, Mozart, Tchaikovsky, and a bunch Gilbert had never heard of, like Bruch, Albinoni, Reicha, Stamitz, who the hell *were* these guys? No operas, though, he had to give her that. All that goddam whooping and screeching, like they were getting carved in front of the microphone or something. But shows, she had a lot of shows, like *Cats,* he'd heard of that one, and *La Cage aux Folles,* that was the one about the faggots, and *Sweeney Todd,* oh *yeah,* he'd actually *seen* that one when he was moving through L.A. The ad had a guy with a razor and blood all around, and he had wondered what the hell and had gone that night and gotten in.

It had been pretty much like a goddam opera, and there were some dull parts where the women were singing, but the parts where this barber was cutting people's throats was terrific. There was a lot about baking the dead people into pies, which was pretty silly but kind of funny. But the good part, the *really* good part, was when he sang a song to his razors, about what he was going to do with them, about *who* he was going to do. Gilbert liked that. Gilbert liked that very much.

He would have liked to have listened to it now, but he couldn't take the chance of the neighbors hearing music when nobody was home or, even worse, of Laura hearing it when she returned. Maybe afterward he could play it very low. He could play it for Laura, even if she could no longer hear it.

That sweet alto of Bird's had stopped playing in the cottage next to Laura's, and it was so quiet that Gilbert could hear the beating of his own heart. It was fast and excited, and he told himself to try and relax, to wait, just wait, and she would come.

Now he heard a soft drum beat from the cottage next door, and in another four bars a piano began to play "Round Midnight." Gilbert listened. It sounded familiar, so very familiar that he could not identify it. But after another sixteen bars, the alto sax began to play, and then Gilbert knew what it was.

It was not a record. He knew that sound too well. It sounded too real, too . . . alive.

His father.

Yes. It was his father and Hampton Hawes on piano, there in Dreamthorp, playing right there in the cottage next door. But he had *killed* his father, hadn't he? Then how could he be playing?

All right then. All right. If he killed him once, he could kill him again.

The music was too loud for Charlie Lewis to hear the screen door opening. He was standing facing the big Pioneer speaker that pumped out the left channel, the one on which Danny Vernon's alto was wailing. Charlie had read about Vernon's death in the newspaper a few weeks before, and had finally gotten around to hauling out the Hampton Hawes Prestige set, the only recording he knew of that Vernon had made. The man hadn't really been in the top rank, but he blew some licks hot enough to get Charlie off his feet and standing by the speaker for one of his rare appearances on air sax. The blinds were all down, and, what the hell, nobody was around to see anyway, so Charlie hunched his shoulders, wiggled his fingers chest and stomach high, and made the proper surrogate motions for the departed saxophonist, whose sounds were now all of him that lived.

"You *stay* dead this time," someone said, and the knife went between Charlie's ribs so smoothly that he was almost surprised to find himself on the floor. He looked up and saw a young man standing over him, holding the knife that had, Charlie thought with surprising logic, just traveled in and out of his back.

Then logic vanished as the pain hit him, and he gave a soundless scream of agony, then looked at the young man again. "I killed you too fast the first time," the man said. "You didn't suffer enough, because if you would have you wouldn't've come back for more. Now you just lie there and play if you want to. You play your swan song. But you don't go *any*where."

The young man knelt next to Charlie, pushed him over on his side, and made two swift cuts behind Charlie's knees. The pain burned through him again, and he nearly fainted. Then the man stood up, walked over to the telephone on the side table, ripped the cord out of the connector, and tossed the instrument into the corner.

Charlie blinked the pain away and looked at the face of the young man, a dark and angular face with the hatchet-sharp features of an Indian.

An Indian . . .

"You . . . you're the one," Charlie said, his soul filled to bursting with horror and understanding. "It's you all along. . . ." He stopped talking when he tasted the froth of blood on his lips.

The man knelt, his face inches away, his eyes burning into Charlie's. "Don't you look at me like that! It wasn't my fault, goddamit, it was *yours*. Damn you, don't *look* at me like that!"

Charlie tried to look away, but it was too late. The knife brought him greater pain than he had thought possible, and then all was darkness.

> People talk of the age of the world! So far
> as I am concerned, it began with my con-
> sciousness, and will end with my decease.
> —Alexander Smith, *Dreamthorp*

Tom and Laura arrived back in Dreamthorp just after eleven
o'clock. They had had a long and leisurely dinner, and several drinks afterward. As they drove up Elm Road, Tom
turned to her. "Should such a lovely evening end so soon?"

"Is that your subtle way of saying 'Your place or mine?' "

"It is."

"Then your place. Drop me off at mine first, though. I
want to pick up a few things."

He grinned. "Aren't my t-shirts good enough for you?"

"Hey, we're engaged now. I'd like to get my flimsiest neg-
ligee tonight."

"Why? You won't be wearing it for long."

"Ho ho," Laura said dryly. "You devil you. All right
then, how about my toothbrush?"

Tom stopped the car in front of Laura's cottage. "Far be
it from me to halt the course of dental hygiene." He leaned
over and kissed her warmly. "Don't be too long, huh?"

"Don't rush the ladies, young man. I want tonight to be
special."

"It already has been. Want me to come in with you?"

"No, I'll come over when I'm ready." She tapped the end
of his nose with her index finger. "Don't be so impatient."

"I love you, Laura."

"I know. I love you too." She kissed him again, and fished

the keys from her purse before she got out of the car. "I'll be over as soon as I can."

She went up the walk of her cottage as Tom drove the twenty yards to his parking place. On the porch, she paused and watched him get out of his car. He looked over, waved, and then gave a hurry-up gesture before he went into his house. God, she thought, how I love him. She could not remember ever having been so happy. And, best of all, it was happiness without guilt.

They had decided to get married as soon as they could get the license. It would be a small, civil ceremony, after which they would take a brief honeymoon if Tom could get another leave of absence from the college. She had not wanted him to, and had told him that they could take a honeymoon next summer, that they had the rest of their lives to take a honeymoon and that just living in Dreamthorp together, a peaceful Dreamthorp, cleansed of the horrors that had tormented it, would be honeymoon enough. But he was insistent and had told her that Dr. Martin was not only compassionate but sympathetic as well, and he was sure she would approve another week—without pay, of course, but that hardly mattered.

They had decided that, as soon as the property values went back up, Laura would sell her cottage and move in with Tom. He had intimated that the unused bedroom would make a good office for her. Although his words were casual, she knew that it was Josh's bedroom he was speaking of, and she saw the fleeting pain in his eyes. There would be difficult moments, of that she had no doubt, but she would help him as he had helped her. Though she could never make him forget—and she had no intention of trying—she could at least ease his pain. And she was not so old that she could not have a child of her own. Of *their* own.

She smiled as she put the key in the lock and turned it. Her little house, in which she had lived so short a time, would soon be hers no longer. But the alternative was so lovely, so much to be desired, that she would feel no reluctance to leave it. Her things would come with her, and would be Tom's things too. She would be his, as much as she wanted to be, and he would be hers.

Then, suddenly, her mood changed. She was aware of something wrong as soon as she stepped into the hall. Poised there, like a wild animal scenting the air for danger, her first thought was to run, to turn and leap down the stairs, and dash down the street to the safety of Tom's house and his arms.

But then civilized rationality took control, and she told herself that nothing was wrong, that it was simply part of the human condition, a feeling that to be happy tempts the fates to bring down unhappiness. It made sense for her to be uneasy, now that she was so close to a life of which she had always dreamed, with the type of partner she had always wanted.

Still, she thought there was something odd about the air in the house, the slightest trace of sweat and . . . freshly cut wood? Was that it?

She made herself laugh aloud. God, Laura, she told herself, just *stop* it. Everything is all right, and in another ten minutes you'll be with Tom, so go upstairs and get your little toothbrush.

She gave a large and purgative shudder, like a dog shaking off water, closed the door behind her, and started down the hall toward the stairs. As she passed the door to her living room, however, she glanced in and noticed that something was different. It was as if the room and its furnishings were slightly awry. Most people would have not have felt it, and it took her a moment to realize what had been changed. Even then she was not sure.

The records, she thought, had been moved ever so slightly on their shelves. Some stuck out more than others. Had she done it herself? She didn't think so. And there, on the desk. Everything had been neatly in its place when she had turned on the lamp as she left, except for the paper that Tom had given her. And now . . . now there seemed to be *two* sheets of paper.

Laura stepped into the room, walked to the desk, and looked at the second piece of paper. It had been folded many times and was wrinkled and stained. The writing, done in pencil, was a list of dates, and she felt an unnerving sense of déjà vu as she read them. There were names next to each date, names she did not recognize, but the dates . . .

She looked at the sheet again, then back at the paper on which Tom had written the dates of the killings, along with the victims' names—the four dates in June, the single death in July of Tom's father, and, finally, the three closely grouped dates in August, the last being the death of Grover Kraybill.

The dates were identical on each sheet of paper.

Laura looked from one to the other, over and over again, but the dates did not change. The dirty, wrinkled paper did not disappear.

"My shopping list," said a quiet voice behind her.

She whirled around and saw, standing behind the sofa as if risen from his coffin, Gilbert Rodman, a long, thick knife glinting in his hand. He was wearing only a pair of yellowed underpants.

"Presents for you, Laura. So you'd know I wasn't just marking time."

Her mind surged, like a machine running too hot. It could not be, yet it was. He was here, standing in front of her, naked, ugly, obscene.

"Forgive my appearance, Laura, but I only have one set of clothes, and if I get . . . anything on them, well . . ."

He shrugged and stepped around the side of the couch so that he was between her and the door to the hall.

"And every one, Laura, every single one of them that I carved, I thought of you. I sent my love, Laura. They were my valentines to you. Did you get the message, Laura?" His face changed, and he snarled at her, his lower jaw jutting out so that she was barely able to understand the words. *"Did* you?"

It was remarkable, Laura thought, how sane she felt. She was face to face with a madman in a situation that should drive *her* mad as well, but she felt in control—of herself at least. Survival was what was important now, not the impossible, nightmarish fact of Gilbert Rodman being there alive, of his list of killings, of what he had just told her. She could deal with that, try and make what little sense there was to make of it, later. But first she had to make sure that there would *be* a later.

"I'm going to make love to you now, Laura, the way we should have done it back there in Wyoming. Not with my cock, no, because you took care of that, didn't you? Oh no, gonna make love to you with this beautiful knife, and it'll take a long time, believe me. Your boyfriend'll come, sure, and when he does I'll kill him before he even knows what's happening."

The gun cabinet was locked, and even if she could have opened it, none of the weapons were loaded. Her only chance was the .38 in the sofa, but he was standing right beside it. . . .

"Did you get my message, Laura? The one I left when I killed the kid and made you all think I was dead? That was crap, you know. Except for the part about the fire cock." He held up the knife and turned it in the light. "This is my cock now, Laura, and believe me, it'll feel like fire."

She had to get to the couch, get her hand under the cushions, a second to grab the gun, another fraction of a second to aim . . .

"What's the matter?" he said, sounding disappointed. "Aren't you going to scream? Beg? Going to try to talk me out of it? Reason with me?"

She shook her head. "Would it do any good?"

"No. None at all. I *want* you to struggle."

"What if I cooperate? Will you kill me fast?"

"No, of course not. I'm going to kill you so slow you won't believe it." He came toward her and she edged away, toward the gun cabinet. "That won't do any good," he said. "I already checked. It's locked."

Gilbert grinned, then said something that made Laura's heart pound even faster. "Why don't you just sit down on the couch and take off your clothes? You can pretend I'm one of your lady friends watching."

She swallowed heavily. There was no point in trying to hide her excitement from him, for everything could be interpreted as fear. Breathing shallowly, she moved toward the blessed couch, her hands in front of her, ready to ward off any preliminary blow he might strike.

"That's right. Just sit down now, that's a girl. . . ."

She slowly sat as he came around the front of the couch and stood looking at her. He was across the width of the living room, a good ten feet away. There would be time, Laura thought. He wouldn't come to her immediately. He liked watching her fear too much to do that. But how to get her hands down near the cushions was the question. She was sitting in the center of the couch, her hands still raised. The gun behind the cushion to her left. But at the first sign of anything suspicious he could be on her in an instant.

"Now let me see it," he whispered.

That was the way. She brought her hands to her blouse, unbuttoned the first two buttons, then pulled it over the top of her head. A thrill of fear went through her as the fabric blindfolded her for a moment, tangling her arms, and then it was free, over her wrists, in her hands. She wore no bra, and she shivered as she watched him staring at her breasts.

It was time. She turned to her left to put the blouse on the couch beside her, dropped it, and plunged her hands behind the cushion.

The gun was gone.

"I hid it," Gilbert said. His smile was insufferable. "I don't like guns."

Rage swept over her as he walked nearer, and she realized how vulnerable he looked, how absurd, with those pathetic stained underpants covering what? A shredded remnant of what he had had, what *she* had done to him.

And what she could do again. What she had no choice but to do.

Laura was large and well-muscled, and although Gilbert Rodman was half a head taller and fifty pounds heavier, she was faster and more supple, which Gilbert quickly learned as he swung a fist at her with the intention of stunning her as he had nearly a year earlier.

But Laura was ready this time, and dodged the blow, returning one of her own that caught him low in the stomach, knocking the breath from him, rocking him back, putting him off balance.

She took the advantage and kicked out, catching Gilbert on the right knee so that he fell heavily, the knife still clutched in his hand. In a second she was on him, her hands grasping his right wrist, squeezing with all her might, trying to make him drop the knife. He hit her on the side of the head with his left fist, but the fall had weakened him, and although pain exploded in her head, she managed to hold on with one hand while she grasped his left wrist with the other.

Nearly naked, they grappled like wrestlers, Laura on top, Gilbert Rodman beneath. But slowly his weight and strength began to tell, and now they were on their sides, their hands struggling for the knife high in the air, their other hand holding their opponent's against the floor. Now Gilbert began to come down inexorably on top of her, though she put all her force against him.

And then the boards beneath them buckled as though an earthquake had struck Dreamthorp, and both fighters lost their grips in surprise.

It was Laura who recovered first.

Over the crack of breaking boards, she wrenched her right hand from beneath her, seized Gilbert's knife hand, and with both arms pushed upwards, so that the blade tore into Gilbert's stomach with the sound of wet leather ripping away.

He made a small, bubbling noise in his throat, and she rolled away from him, scuttling across the suddenly motionless floor until she lay against the bookshelves. Only then did she look back at Gilbert Rodman.

He lay on his back, his arms at his side, the knife like a miniature tombstone set on the pale plain of his stomach. He was not dead. It was not, she realized, a necessarily fatal wound, and there was surprisingly little bleeding. But his hands and feet were trembling, shaking so fast that Laura saw them as only a blur. It was not at all like the death rattle of which she had heard, but rather as though some power had inhabited Gilbert Rodman's body, as if it was being shaken by an unseen force. She crept closer, terrified and unbearably curious at the same time, and when she saw his face, drawn and gaunt and white, yet filled with energy, even with his eyes closed, the image that came to her mind was that of an Indian shaman going into a trance. . . .

The same kind of trance, she thought, that doctors had called a coma. The same kind of trance that had impossibly left Gilbert Rodman free to walk away after his muscles had lain dormant for nine months. The same kind of trance that, on the day he awoke, had produced the power to rip the pillars of the Dreamthorp Playhouse. . . .

The wood. She looked up in panic. The wood had started to move again. The floorboards lurched under her, twisting the carpet like the ocean. The lintels of the doorway were bending like hot steel. Outside, from a house far away, she heard someone scream.

''No,'' she said, pushing herself to her feet. ''No, not *this* time!''

She staggered to the gun cabinet and kicked in the glass door, then reached through and grabbed the .12 gauge double-barreled shotgun that had been her father's. From a shelf she grabbed a box of shells, broke the gun, jammed two shells into the chambers, and snapped it shut.

The floor billowed again, and from everywhere Laura heard the wood snapping, groaning, breaking, and beneath it all, like a throbbing accompaniment, the sound of many voices speaking in tongues Laura had never heard before. She stumbled the few feet to where Gilbert Rodman lay shaking like a saint in the midst of a miracle, and pointed the muzzle of the shotgun down at his head.

"Die, you *mother*fucker!" she howled in fury, and in the split second before she pulled both triggers, Gilbert Rodman's eyes snapped open just long enough for her to see them glaring at her with an unfathomable hate before the wads disintegrated them forever.

The face disappeared, and the head turned to a mass of bloody strands of muscle, gray globules of brain. Laura dropped the shotgun and stood looking down at the ruined head, as if looking long enough would convince her that Gilbert Rodman, and what Gilbert Rodman had become, was really dead. Then, just as she heard footsteps pounding up her porch stairs, she realized that the wood of her little house had stopped moving. Only the twin blast of the shotgun shells exploding echoed in her ears.

"Laura!"

She felt Tom's arms grab her from behind, and only then did she look up. The shock in his eyes told her that the shooting had spattered her skin with Gilbert's blood. "Laura," he said again, and looked at what lay on the floor.

She spoke, but no words came. She tried again, and succeeded in saying, "Gilbert Rodman . . ."

> The distance to which your gun, whether
> rifled or smooth-bored, will carry its shot,
> depends upon the force of its charge.
> —Alexander Smith, *Dreamthorp*

Tom jerked back to Laura. "Rodman?" She nodded dully, and made a weak gesture to the corpse's hips. Tom understood, knelt, pulled back the waistband, and then looked away. "My God, it is," he said. He stood up and put his arms around her. "Oh Jesus, my poor Laura," he whispered into her hair. "Are you all right?"

"He didn't hurt me. He wanted to, he tried, but he didn't."

"Thank God. Thank God for that." Then he remembered what had driven him to her side. "The wood," he said. "The wood in my cottage started moving, breaking, I didn't know what the hell was going on, I thought it was starting all over again, so I came to get you, take you out of here, and I saw *all* the houses, then I heard your shotgun, and . . . Laura, what was it? What's happened?"

The look of strength in her face calmed him, and she put her hands on his shoulders and nodded firmly. "It's all right," she said. "I know now." She walked away from him to the couch, picked up her blouse, and wearily pulled it over her head, ignoring the blood that dappled its front from the contact with her body. Then she took the two lists from the desk.

"It was Gilbert," she said.

"I . . . I know."

"No. I mean it was Gilbert all along." Laura walked back

to Tom, shaking her head. "In the hall," she said. "I don't want to see him."

They walked over the uneven carpet out into the hall, where broken ends of wood stuck up from the floor at sharp angles, and Laura handed Tom the two lists. "Look at these. One is the list you made, the other is a list that Gilbert kept of the people he killed as he came across the country. They match, Tom. The dates are the same. When he killed someone, someone here in Dreamthorp died too. Died because of the wood. I don't know how, but it was him."

Tom looked from one list to the other, frowned, looked again, glanced at Laura, then looked away. "We ought to . . . call the police." He picked up the telephone in the hall and listened for a moment. "It's dead. Now what the hell . . . ?"

"You don't believe me," she said. She sounded almost satisfied, as if she hadn't expected him to.

"But, Laura," he said, replacing the receiver, "how could he do it when he wasn't *here?* When he was thousands of miles away?"

She looked toward the doorway to the living room and shivered. "He said something about thinking of me when he killed them. He called it sending his love, but I know that he sent his hate instead. I don't know how . . . telekinesis, poltergeists . . ."

"The . . . the *carving.* The quartz carving . . . after we buried it the killings stopped."

"It's buried *now,* Tom. But you saw the wood move, you saw it *yourself.* The carving did no good at all."

Tom ran both hands through the hair at his temples and joined his fingers together behind his head, trying to physically hold in his old beliefs. "I can't . . . believe this. I can't believe that one man could have done all this."

Laura spoke through gritted teeth. "Who can believe the power of hate?"

"Laura . . ."

"You were ready to believe in an old Indian legend. But this is a *modern* legend, Tom. This is *real.* If you want to keep calling it magic, and I guess that's the only thing we *can* call it, then it's a *new* magic. And the old rules don't work for it."

He was starting to seriously consider the possibility. "So what do you do then?"

"You make up new rules," she told him.

He walked to the screen door and looked out. "Where is everybody?" he asked. "They had to hear the shots, and if the other houses were doing what ours were . . ."

"There are only four other houses with people in them," she reminded him.

"Where's Charlie, then?" He looked back at her. "God, I wonder if he's okay."

"Let's see," Laura said, and together they went out into the night. "I bet Gilbert cut the phone lines," she said as they walked up the steps to Charlie's porch. "With so few people here, no one might notice for a long time."

"The phone company will notice. They'll have someone out soon." Tom knocked on the door, but there was no answer, no sound at all except for a steady *tick . . . tick . . . tick* over and over again. "Charlie?" Tom called.

"Let's go in."

They found him lying halfway up the staircase. The steps were as bent and twisted as in a funhouse, and the knurled balusters had split in two, skewering Charlie in half a dozen places. He lay with his face away from them. "Aw . . ." Tom said. "Aw, Charlie . . ."

Amazingly, the figure on the stairs moved. The head turned in their direction just enough for Tom and Laura to see the pools of blood that Charlie's eyes had become. His voice rasped. "Better late . . . than never . . ."

Tom gave half a sob, half a laugh, and sat on the steps next to his friend. "We'll get help, Charlie. You'll be okay."

"Bullshit," Charlie said, and Tom knew that every word must be causing excruciating pain. "I've bled . . . to death already. I'm just . . . too mean to die yet . . . or too dumb."

"Charlie . . ."

"We . . . were wrong . . . was a guy . . . real live guy. Stabbed me. He . . . did it all. . . ."

"We know, Charlie," Tom said, tears rolling down his face. "But he's dead. He's dead now. It's over."

"Dead, huh?" Charlie coughed blood. "Lil' bastard. You have no idea . . . how much . . . that cheers me up. . . ."

Charlie gave a final sigh, and his breath whistled away.

"Good-bye, Charlie," Laura said, and touched the man's hand.

Tom wiped his eyes, then looked at Laura. "Maybe you're right, Laura. Charlie seemed to think so." He looked back at Charlie's blind face. "Maybe we were both as full of bullshit as he thought we were sometimes. But if you are right, I just hope to hell that whatever that man unleashed, or whatever he was, is as dead as he looks."

Laura frowned. Death destroys, she thought. But sometimes don't we speak of death as . . .

. . . *freeing?*

It was as though a tornado had struck the house. The lintels and sideposts of the doorways trembled, then fell crashing to the floor, which buckled in an even more savage manner than Laura's floor had done. The banister rail bent and split, hurling the shrapnel of the remaining balusters into the living room, while the stairs ripped themselves upward one by one like giant piano keys, sending Laura and Tom toppling down them.

"Laura!" Tom cried, grasping her arm and trying to keep his balance on the twisting surface of pine boards. "The door!"

They strove to reach it, while the ceiling and walls shuddered around them and the floor bucked beneath. The door's glass pane had shattered, but its ornately carved wood moved only in sympathy to the wood of its frame, and Laura remembered that Charlie had told her it had been carved in Germany.

Tom grabbed the knob and yanked, but one of the floorboards was jammed against the bottom. Laura stamped on it with all her weight, and it sank below the level of the floor. She wrenched out her heel from the hole she had made and grabbed the edge of the door with Tom. Together they forced it open and dashed out onto the porch.

Dreamthorp had gone mad. Every cottage the length of Emerson Street was tensing, flexing, rearing its boards like the talons of giant beasts. Wooden sidings rattled, the boards breaking free, one by one, of the nails that had held them captive nearly a hundred years. Cornices ripped loose and plunged through the treetops like javelins, coming to rest in the soft loam beneath the dry surface of pine needles.

"Come on!" Tom yelled over the dry roar of splintering wood. "Out into the street!"

They leaped off the porch to avoid the steps, landed and rolled on the soft ground. "Stay beneath the trees!" Laura shouted as they got to their feet, for she had noticed that the living trees were not moving and would provide shelter from the projectiles the cottages were making of their own substance. Using the pines as protection, they scurried toward Elm Road.

Laura gasped as she saw the oculus window of the Shaeffer's cottage on Channing just below burst outward, its cross frame whirling toward them in a dark blur. She threw herself to the earth, pulling Tom with her, and one sharp end of the frame bit into the trunk of the tree a foot above her head. Once again they pushed themselves to their feet and ran.

"Your car," Tom said as they passed her cottage, which was pulsing like a giant heart, pieces leaping off with every beat. "Do you have your keys?"

"They're in the cottage . . . I'll look, though." She yanked open the car door, but the keys were not in the ignition. What was there, however, sitting in the concavity of the console, was a box of the small wooden matches with which Trudy Doyle lit her cigarettes. Laura grabbed them and slammed the car door shut.

They kept running, and the houses kept throbbing, spewing random pieces at a terrifying pace. As they passed Alice Penworth's cottage, the entire front door facing flew outward twenty yards and struck Tom in the ankle. He moaned and went down. Laura knelt to help him up, when she saw that the casing, only a few feet away, was moving, shifting sinuously toward them.

She grasped Tom under his arm and helped him to his feet, hearing but not allowing herself to respond to his groan of agony. "Come *on*," she said. "Come on!"

They staggered away from the still-vibrating piece of wood, which had moved scarcely an inch since it had landed. Vibration, Laura thought. Once it's away from the house, it can move only by some inner vibration. "Shit, *that's* good to know," she whispered mockingly to herself.

"What?" Tom asked through clenched teeth.

"Nothing," Laura said. "We're almost there. . . ."

In another minute they had reached Elm Road, which was

twice as wide as Emerson, and they ran and hobbled down
its center. On either side the houses of Dreamthorp shrieked
and split and hurled their pieces at them, as if furious that
Tom and Laura had come this far on their path of escape.
Whole walls broke apart, sending the sharp missiles of their
boards toward the two fleeing people, as Gilbert had sent his
hate.

But as Tom and Laura neared the main road, the activity
of the houses diminished, then ceased altogether, and Laura
realized that these were the cottages that had been built in
the forties and fifties, when the timbering in the grove had
long since ceased.

"We made it," she panted, as exhausted from holding up
Tom as from her own exertions. "Oh, Tom, we made
it. . . ."

"Ted's . . ." Tom said. "Let's go to Ted's. Phone booth
there . . . on a different line from the town."

It was another hundred yards to Ted's Mobil, but they
reached the gas station unmolested. Ted's was silent and still,
and the white light over the phone booth gleamed like a bea-
con of safety. Tom leaned against the glass, while Laura
stepped inside and took the receiver from the hook. She nearly
laughed when she heard the clear hum of the dial tone, and
had just raised her finger to push *O* when she stopped, and
looked into the darkness across the road in the direction of
the cottages, looked and saw a figure moving slowly, painfully, away from the malevolent houses of Dreamthorp and
toward Tom and her.

"Tom?" she said. "There's someone over there . . . oh
God, someone else got out. . . ." She hung up the receiver,
stepped out of the booth, and stood beside Tom, ready to
help the survivor but somehow frightened of what she could
not see.

She was right to be frightened. Out of the darkness, into
the pale pool of light cast by the telephone booth light, staggered a thing of nightmare.

"Gilbert . . ." she whispered.

It was not Gilbert, yet it was, for it was everything that
she and Tom Brewer, who created it, had ever imagined Gilbert Rodman to be.

It was huge and hulking, and the hollow pits of its carved
eyes were black with hatred. Its arms came up with a grind-

ing of the wood from which it was made, and reached toward Laura with blocklike, stubby fingers on hands of strong pine.

Suddenly something came between it and Laura, and she heard the sharp sound of iron on wood. It was Tom, swinging a metal rod several feet long at the creature he had made. He did not knock it down or even make it stagger, but it hesitated, as though its dull intellect was trying to make sense out of this annoyance that had come between it and what it wished to destroy. Tom, the wound in his leg forgotten, beat at the thing like a woodsman swinging an axe.

Laura looked around desperately, saw the pile of iron rods from which Tom had taken his weapon, and ran to it to get one of her own. The thing's head ground toward her, and its massive body turned on its ungainly legs, while Tom continued to batter away at it. All he had succeeded in doing, Laura saw as she turned back, her own rod lifted in defense, was to break off one of the monster's fingers. But it needed no fingers, she thought. It could club them both to death with its bulky arms.

And then she remembered the matches in the pocket of her skirt.

"Tom!" she cried. "Keep at him! Give me time!"

Tom swung with what seemed renewed strength, drawing the thing's dim attention back to him long enough for Laura to step up to the gas pump, insert the rod in the lock, and pull on it with all her might until she heard the snap of broken metal and the ring of the lock striking the cement. She tossed down the rod, jerked the nozzle out of the boot, and flipped the reset lever, feeling relief flood through her as she heard the inner mechanisms hum. Pulling the hose as far as it would go, she shouted to the thing.

"*Here!* I'm *here,* you bastard!"

The thing lurched, and its arm smashed out with a speed Laura had not thought possible, dashing the metal rod from Tom's hand. It came toward her then, step by ponderous step.

When it was only a yard away, she pulled the trigger, and gasoline began to splash out of the spout. She splashed it over the living carving, and thought hysterically that it was like watering flowers, wasn't it? Flowers and Trees. And she remembered the walking trees in that old Disney *Silly Symphony,* and began to giggle, backing away slowly, splashing more and more gasoline on the thing that was stalking her.

The Rodman carving glimmered wetly now, and she re-leased the trigger, tossed the nozzle as far as she could. The thing's arms were waving rapidly, reaching for her, but its legs were slow. Nevertheless, she realized that it was not as stupid as she had thought, and was backing her up against the garage building. Tom had picked up his rod and was smashing it against the creature's back and legs, but it paid him no mind.

Now. She had to do it now, even if she burned too.

Laura dug the box of matches from her pocket and opened it, spilling half of them in the process. Taking one, she held her breath and rubbed the head against the rough striker.

She did not have to throw it. The fumes in the air ignited instantly, and the force of the explosion threw her back against the wall of the garage, stunning her. When she opened her eyes a moment later, she realized that her hair was on fire, and she pulled the back of her blouse up over her head, patting it quickly.

Then she remembered, and saw in front of her a tall, living torch.

The thing's arms, twin ribbons of flame, waved madly in the air, and the heavy legs, also on fire, stumbled backward toward the street. Little pools of flame burned blue on the ground around Laura, but she had thrown the nozzle far enough away so that the tank would not explode.

Now Tom was beside her on his hands and knees, his face reddened from the singeing blast of fire. "Are you okay?" he asked her.

She nodded, and they painfully got to their feet. By now the fiery monster was whirling in ungainly circles, the roar of the fire augmented by a faraway, roaring voice, the kind of sound that might have come from a thick, solid, wooden throat. The thing was across the road now, on the carpet of pine needles that led, unbroken, to the houses of Dream-thorp. It stopped its clumsy dance, raised what remained of its burning arms, gave one final, inarticulate roar, and top-pled over like a falling tree, its impact splashing flames in a nimbus all around it.

Laura and Tom watched as the fingers of fire rapidly spread across the surface of dry needles, reaching the first of the trees, climbing up them with the speed of frightened squir-rels.

"We've got to call, get help," Laura said, limping to the phone booth.

"Laura . . ." She felt Tom's hand on her shoulder. "No."

"But, Tom . . ."

"It's the wood, Laura. It's all the wood. All rotten. All filled with hate. Let the fire have it."

"But, Tom," she said. "Dreamthorp . . ."

"Dreamthorp isn't here anymore. It can be anywhere we want it to be," he said softly, "but not here." He turned and looked at the fire eating the dry trees, the flames leaping from limb to limb, drawing ever closer to the little houses, those houses twitching and reeling with their own vicious life. "Not here. Let it go. Let it all go."

He knelt and picked up the iron rod. "Step away, Laura," he said, and she did as he asked. Then he swung the rod at the pay phone over and over again, until the machine lay in pieces on the metal floor.

"Gilbert," he said. "Gilbert did that too."

They sat and watched the town burn, knowing that someone would soon come, but not soon enough to save Dreamthorp.

A short time later the first of the Chalmers fire trucks arrived and screamed up Elm Road as far as it could go without being roasted. Others from nearby communities followed, and before too long a Chalmers police car pulled up in front of Ted's Mobil. Bret Walters climbed out and looked at Tom and Laura as if he could not believe what he was seeing.

"What the hell happened here, Tom?" he asked.

But it was Laura who answered. "There was a man, sheriff. A man who came here today. His name was Gilbert Rodman."

"He started the fire," Tom said. "He was responsible for everything, Bret. Everything."

"Well . . . well, where the hell *is* he?"

"He's dead now," Laura said. "He's dead."

Bret Walters looked from one to the other but saw nothing that made any sense to him. "But what the hell *happened?*"

Laura looked across the road and up the hill to where the firemen watched Dreamthorp burning. "I'm not sure," she said, "but I think the old magic met the new."

> Dreamthorp is as silent as a picture, the
> voices of the children are mute. . . .
> —Alexander Smith, *Dreamthorp*

Bret Walters drove Tom and Laura to the Lebanon County
Hospital, where their wounds were dressed and they were
placed in a semiprivate room for the night. Bret said he would
come by to take their statements in the morning.

After Bret and the nurse had gone, Tom and Laura got into
one bed together and, careful of their hurts, lay with their
arms around each other, quietly talking, then falling silent,
then talking again as the thoughts came to them, as the ideas
coalesced, as they tried to make out of it what sense they
could.

"Wood lived," Tom said. "And if it lived, it might have
had life remaining in it. Like ghosts of men. And if Gilbert's
hate for you was so strong, and if he had some power that
we can't even conceive of . . ."

"I think he did," Laura said. "In his coma . . . or whatever he was in . . . he might have found it then."

"And that hate came ahead of him, maybe without his
even knowing it, toward you, and took the form of the
wood."

"I don't know." Laura shook her head and held Tom more
tightly. "Maybe the Indians did have something to do with
it. Otherwise why was it just the wood from where they were
buried? I meant it when I told Bret that the new magic met
the old. I think Gilbert was the catalyst. He had Indian blood
in him. He told me as much when I . . . first met him." She

shifted in the bed and adjusted the dressing an intern had put on her reddened forehead. "You remember what Charlie said about the Alligewi? About their dying out but that maybe some of them intermarried with tribes that survived?"

"Yes. I remember."

"What if Gilbert was the last of them? A descendant? And if it wasn't taking away the carving, but the power of his hate that brought the wood to life? The wood where the spirits of his ancestors still lived?"

"A distant relation," Tom said softly. "He did do things at a distance, didn't he?"

She sighed. "And all that wood is burning now."

"Yes . . ."

"But when I thought I killed him . . . all I did was free him. So will this end it? Can we be sure it's dead?"

He didn't answer. "We'll never go back there," he finally said.

"There's nothing to go back to. Besides, I have what I need."

She rested her cheek against his, and after a time they both fell asleep.

Season's End

The dead keep their secrets, and in a little while we
shall be as wise as they—and as taciturn.
                              —Alexander Smith, *Dreamthorp*

It rained the following afternoon, a drenching storm that seemed to hold all the moisture that had been previously denied to Dreamthorp, and the fire burned itself out at last. Its destruction had been complete. Not a cottage was left standing. All had burned to their foundations.

The rain and the hoses of the firemen washed many of the ashes down to the creek, where they were swept away by the now quickly running stream. Several miles away, the stream joined the Susquehanna River, which flowed southeast to the Chesapeake Bay.

Several days later, a large sunfish on the intracoastal waterway near Dares Beach, Maryland, swam through an area that had always been part of its feeding grounds. The water passed across its gills, and less than a minute later the fish was floating, dead, on the surface of the bay.

A family on an anchored pleasure craft saw the fish and brought it aboard in a net. They were unable to determine what had killed it, though they were only mildly curious. The fate of a single fish held little interest for them, and they threw it into a garbage pail.

After a short while, they went for a swim.

Avon Books presents your worst nightmares—

...haunted houses

ADDISON HOUSE   75587-4/$4.50 US/$5.95 Can
Clare McNally

THE ARCHITECTURE OF FEAR
                       70553-2/$3.95 US/$4.95 Can
edited by Kathryn Cramer & Peter D. Pautz

...unspeakable evil

HAUNTING WOMEN   89881-0/$3.95 US/$4.95 Can
edited by Alan Ryan

TROPICAL CHILLS   75500-9/$3.95 US/$4.95 Can
edited by Tim Sullivan

...blood lust

THE HUNGER   70441-2/$4.50 US/$5.95 Can
THE WOLFEN   70440-4/$4.50 US/$5.95 Can
Whitley Strieber